Stars in the Darkness

A Prophecy of Shadows

Book One

F. Barton Davis

Magi Media

For my two amazing daughters, Jacquelyn and Kenya, you are my twin stars that light my path even in the darkest times. And for my brothers and sisters, Joye, Randy, Lenora, Dionne, and Scott, thanks for your unbelievable support. I love you all dearly.

INTRODUCTION

"The darkness never tires; it never wavers; it never sleeps, but hope is a shield that will not fail." – The Herald Siru Khan from *The Book of Triumph*, 4139 B.C.

The Darkness—
Amesemi

Semi beams proudly as she sits back and admires her newly arrived dessert. She did it. She's actually here, no easy thing. And all it took was evading her family, overriding security, hacking Avalon's "un-hackable" computers, and wiping away any evidence of her trip. Oh, and that includes expertly popping in and out of the Gray Zone across five states to make sure she wasn't followed. And she's sure she wasn't—well, pretty sure anyway. Sneaking back home should be a breeze after all that. She's awesome, and she definitely deserves a treat. As she eats a forkful of pie, it's so amazing that she closes her eyes and starts humming. Amesemi considers herself a dessert connoisseur, having devoured pies and pastries in over forty countries, but she's never tasted anything quite like this. With her eyes closed, she feels like she's floating.

She opens them and covertly scans the diner once again. Semi feels the nervous energy flowing through her like a young gazelle all alone at a watering hole. Yes, all alone. It's what she wanted, or so she thought, but now that she's here, well, the enormity of her risk is starting to get to her. Her head tells her to relax, she's safe. No one knows where she is. They may not even be aware that she's gone. It's hard for her to believe that she might actually be getting away with her little adventure because at her core, where her instinct is undeniable, she knows better. Just the thought of getting caught makes her shiver. If that happens, she knows the consequences will be severe.

Semi, girl, you need to calm down, and you know just the thing to get you there.

She reaches into her purse and pulls out a notebook and a fancy flowery pen, her whole face blossoming with joy as she opens it up.

This is her happy place.

"Dear journal, it's been a while. Where do I begin? In my short life, I've been to seven of the nine worlds, learned twenty-seven languages, fourteen dialects, and survived a face-to-face encounter with a trogar, but I have rarely felt as out of place as I do right now."

Amesemi sighs and rolls her eyes as she glances around the entire room—a room full of slow-talking, suspiciously friendly, church-loving, gun-toting, college football fanatics. This place is different. In the Deep South, she's not a fish out of water. She's more like a human stranded on Mars, surrounded by extraterrestrial landscape and unbreathable air. This may be the most alien environment she's visited since that time she got lost in Shambhala, but it's not dull. Their accents are lovely, and while the warm smiles and greetings she gets from these total strangers appear to be insincere, they're far more inviting than what she finds in her hometown of Washington, D.C. And don't even get her started on New York. The trogar that tried to eat her was nicer than her average encounter on the New York subway.

Stop staring, Semi.

But she can't help it; she's capturing it all for her journal. There's a peculiar rhythm to this hole-in-the-wall diner smack dab in the middle of No-where, Georgia. No one rushes, not really. Not the stay-home moms, not the businessman guy on break, not the employees—no one. They savor each moment at their own pace, their own flow, making this diner strangely inviting. And whatever spices and seasonings they put in their pastries are overwhelmingly wonderful. Semi thinks the people, coupled with how amazing everything tastes and smells, make this hidden treasure a unique experience in the nine worlds—or at least in the seven she's visited.

She's jotting all this down into her journal before she forgets. Journaling is her thing, and this small-town adventure certainly deserves a paragraph or two. Wow, if her sisters could see her now.

No. If they find out she's sneaked out here to Penfield, aka Nowhere, Ga, they'll kill her—that is, if her dad and aunt don't kill her first.

Well, everyone has to die of something.

She's risked coming here for a special reason—for history—but no one in this time-stuck miniature town has any idea that it's about to be the epicenter of a potentially world-changing event. And if Semi's people do their job right, no one will ever know.

Yeah, she isn't supposed to be here. Not the way they see it anyway. Semi's supposed to be the only one in her family stuck at home, doing the work that no one else wants to do. She's turning eighteen in two weeks. Despite what her family thinks, she's grown. She's a woman, and Semi is fully ready to be involved in the family business. Her dad couldn't have seriously expected her to sit this out to keep an eye on someone who is already safe, hidden away inside the most secure place in the nine worlds, right? Tricia will be fine. Semi is just going to hang out, keep out of harm's way, be a bystander, witness this historic event, and maybe order another slice of pie.

This is the best pie ever

Yes, she's made the right decision. Taken the risk for the right reason. She *is* supposed to be here. Anyway, she'll be back before anyone knows she's gone. What could go wrong?

They expect the event to happen between 8 and 9 p.m. It's noon. There should be at least a couple more hours before Penfield becomes infested with shadow dancers. Cool, that gives Semi a little more time to kick back, write in her journal, and get another slice or two of that pie. Yeah, she's definitely off her training diet today. She always says, "If you're going to have a cheat day, go all in."

Carrie-Ann, her waitress, jars her out of her introspection. Carrie's a cute, twentyish, happily plump woman with stringy brown hair, a bubbly personality, and the warmest smile.

"So, ma'am, may I help you with anything else? Do you want something else to drink or another slice of pie?"

"Oh, man, that pie was so good. What was it called again?"

"Key-lime, honey, key-lime pie."

"Yes, key-lime, that was so great."

"It's one of the favorites. Although our pumpkin pie might be our most popular, especially this time of year."

"Pumpkin pie, that sounds interesting. I've never had that before."

"You're not from around here, are you, sweetie?" Carrie-Ann asks, giggling.

Semi smiles sheepishly. "No, I'm from up north."

"How long you here for?

"Just for today."

She leans in as if she's telling a secret, placing her hands on her hips. "Well, you only live once, sweetie. Why don't you get both?"

Semi widens her eyes as she answers. "Oh, both sounds fantastic, and ... and can I get a coffee, a cappuccino with almond milk?"

Carrie-Ann looks perplexed as if Semi is speaking some exotic, foreign tongue. "Almond milk? I'm pretty sure we don't carry that. We don't do those fancy coffees."

"OK, what do you recommend?"

"Have you ever had sweet tea?"

"No, what is that?"

Carrie-Ann's already effervescent smile broadens, and her eyes filled with longing joy as if she is reminiscing about her first love.

"Oh, hon," she says, "you are going to love it. We make the best in the state. I'll bring you out a glass with your pie."

Carrie–Ann walks off, looking very pleased with herself. She returns in a couple of minutes and brings Semi's two slices and her sweet tea.

This smells so good.

Semi takes a moment to savor the fresh-baked aroma, then she takes her braids and ties them in a ponytail so that her long hair won't get in the way. She takes a bite of the pumpkin pie and—*oh, that's really good* —then she takes a swig of the sweet tea to wash it down. Her eyes pop open and her taste buds start doing the happy dance.

Oh my, this is incredible! I can't believe I've lived my whole life without this nectar from heaven. OK, it's more like diabetes in a glass, but if loving sweet tea is wrong ... man.

"How's the pie and the sweet tea?" Carrie-Ann asks as she passes by.

Semi tries to reply, but her mouth is stuffed, so she settles for nodding her head approvingly, her enormous grin bearing evidence of the pie's delicate flakey crust.

Carrie-Ann laughs. "I told you so. Let me know if you need anything else."

Semi nods her head affirmatively and goes back to eating her little slices of heaven—one bite of pumpkin, one sip of tea, one bite of key lime, one sip of tea, one bite of pumpkin ...

She takes a fresh look around the diner. Not the diner per se. Aesthetically, it isn't much, merely an anachronism, really. It's the people who interest her. As the afternoon passes, a few more trickle in, ordinary people living ordinary lives.

Behind her, at the very rear, is a white-haired man with round silver spectacles who has been seated since before she'd arrived. He's been reading a paper—Semi didn't know papers were still a thing—and working on the same cup of coffee. In fact, he looks like he's been sitting in the same spot since the place opened, probably back in the forties or fifties.

Diagonally from him is a family, a couple and their baby girl. The dad gets up to get some napkins to clean up a mess that his little girl has made. Semi tries not to, but she finds herself staring at the mom as she dotes on her daughter, humming a children's song. The connection between them seems to be very strong. Semi wonders if her own mom ever felt that way about her. She never knew her. Amesemi's aunt and sisters helped raise her, especially her aunt. They would say that Semi has had many moms. But still, when she sees this mother's eyes, loving this child with every ember of her soul, Semi wonders, and although she has absolutely nothing to base it on, her mind's eye sees her holding the hand of a woman whose face she cannot make out—it's not her aunt or one of her sisters but an elegant woman whose voice is soft like her hand, who seems to be instructing her in the ways of childhood, of life, of living. She talks about the worlds—both their glories and their dangers. But the woman is a mist, a rainbow that fades in the light of the sun.

A few kids, her age or maybe a little older, have just come in and Semi is taken from her reverie. They're probably from a local university.

It's the beginning of Thanksgiving break, and they have bulldogs and UGA all over their clothing, whatever that stands for. While a few of them talk among themselves, one of them breaks off and grabs a table with his girlfriend. They gaze dreamily into each other's eyes, their faces almost breaking from the size of their mammoth smiles. Semi loves the way he looks at her. She isn't trying to read their minds, but it's hard not to. Those two are so in love. Semi's heart drops as he leans over to kiss his girlfriend and ...

"Those two are so cute, aren't they?" says Carrie-Ann.

Semi didn't see her standing there or realize that her gawking was so obvious.

"Yeah, I guess."

"So, you have somebody back home, sweetie?"

"No, not right now."

"Well, a cute girl like you, I'm sure you got the pick of the litter. Take your time, honey. Wait for a good one," she says as she pats Semi on the shoulder as if offering her condolences. "Can I help you with anything else?"

"No, I'm fine. Thanks."

But is she, though? Everyone here is so normal. She's realizing that normal is underrated and so foreign to her own life. Semi's life has always been about purpose, about mission, about destiny. She is surrounded by love from her family and friends but nothing like what that young couple seems to have. That girl chose him; he chose her out of everyone else on the planet. Semi wonders how that feels and wonders if anyone will ever feel that way about her.

She generally doesn't think about it much. She's usually too busy training. She's never been to school, never been to a dance, and never been to a diner with kids her age. Semi has never been in love or even been in like. She's never been kissed, and if she is honest, she isn't really sure if she is someone who is even kissable. Growing up in her family ... well, it's hard not to be a little insecure—OK, maybe a lot insecure. Of course, they tell her that she's beautiful. That's their job. But not only is her family one of heroes, they're all Barac Navaar, blessed with other-worldly pulchritude that defies anything any human could hope to obtain. The women have flawless hair, exquisite bodies, and faces that appear as if they were photo-shopped. For the most part, the men have the features of male models and the bodies of Greek gods. And then there's Semi.

Amesemi is human. Awesome as she is, her DNA is human through and through. It's hard not to feel like the ugly duckling. Is she pretty for a human? Of course, she is—maybe. Everyone says she has beautiful dark skin, like her aunt, full lips, and big brown eyes. But they're really big—maybe too big. Sometimes, she feels like a walking emoji. The women in her family are full of curves, and men stumble over themselves simply to sneak a peek. Contrary to popular belief, Semi's figure isn't quite nonexistent, but it's more athletic than voluptuous. All she knows is that she's never caught anyone sneaking a peek. Semi's been told that she's quirky, has weird interests, and laughs at strange things. And she is constantly walking around writing in a journal in a digital age. She doesn't know how to act in social situations, and she's spent almost her entire life around people much, much older than her. And if she's honest, truly honest, all of this terrifies her. Her family is worried about keeping her safe, preserving her for her "destiny." Semi isn't afraid of dying early. What scares her is losing herself before she discovers who she is meant to be.

That boy at the table in front of her genuinely loves that girl. Just a cursory glimpse of his thoughts, and Semi can see it clearly. He isn't some stupid guy, like so many, driven by his hormones. His eyes aren't focused on her chest, and his mind isn't obsessed with getting in her pants. He's looking at her; he sees her, gazing right into her soul, and he is in love with every quirky imperfect part of her. That kind of love is so rare and so special. Amesemi's certain that this boy loves his girlfriend now, with her beauty in full bloom, and he'll love her when she is pale and sick with the flu; he'll love her when she gains forty pounds carrying their baby, and he'll love her even when she is old and wrinkled, walking with a cane. He will see her, and he will love her. Semi wonders how it feels to be looked at like that.

So, this is what scares her. If she ever achieves this great and awesome destiny she's heard so much about, everything will be different—her looks, her life—everything. Heads will definitely turn then. Everybody will want to be her or want to be with her. They'll want what she can do for them, and they'll see her as a weapon or a trophy or both. They'll see her power; they'll see her beauty; they'll see her curves, but they won't see her. They won't love *her*. When she achieves that destiny, Semi will have missed her chance ever to experience what this couple has, to have someone love her.

Stop being stupid. I'm thinking like some silly teenage girl, a civilian. This isn't like me. I've got a life, I've got a purpose, and I don't need anyone or anything to validate it.

She shakes herself out of it. There's business coming up and she needs to be alert, not whining, fantasizing, and drooping about the place.

She chalks it up to too much sugar and too much idle time. It's time to get her tail up, get out of this diner, and get back to the reason she came here in the first place. But first, she needs to finish the last of her pie and maybe get just one more sweet tea. That stuff is too good.

While Semi is greedily devouring the last couple of bites, three more kids about her age come in, a girl and two guys. It's obvious to Semi that they're not from around here. They stand out enough that she does a cursory scan of their thoughts just to make sure they're not undercover threats. The girl is cute, mixed, and bilingual, probably a boniqua. She's a little under Semi's height, five feet four, more or less, with light brown skin, thick, long, dark hair pulled back in a ponytail, and pretty brown eyes that sparkle with kindness and curiosity. She's wearing jeans, an oversized sweatshirt with Auburn on it, and a baseball cap with the same logo. The nerdy-looking guy next to her is about two inches taller, short for a guy, and merely a shade or two from being vampire pale. He's scrawny, with floppy cinnamon-brown hair, skinny jeans, a hoodie with Alabama on it, and a mind that is both highly intelligent and disgustingly dirty. Even not trying to read his thoughts, all of his teenage man hormones are oozing out. If he even looks in her direction, Semi is going to have to punch him, just on principle and for the honor of all of womankind.

The last one of the friend group saunters in just as Semi is taking a gulp of her second helping of sweet tea, and she comes embarrassingly close to spitting it out. He is ... he is gorgeous. Can a man be gorgeous? She doesn't know, but this one is. He's tall, six feet two or six feet three, with short hair, smooth, dark skin, dashingly handsome features, broad shoulders, and an athletic build. He's wearing a too-tight NYC fire department t-shirt under a denim jacket, and perfect-fitting blue jeans. Maybe it's her imagination, but she swears he's moving in slow motion, and he seems to be slowing down. As he enters the doorway, he puts a Yankees baseball cap on his head—courtesy of Semi's time in New York, it is one of the few sports logos she recognizes. As he adjusts his cap, he hesitates just a little as if he's posing for the paparazzi. OK, that's an entrance. And while she's on the topic of being kissable, this guy definitely qualifies—not that she cares or anything.

She puts her head down to stop herself from gawking. *Semi, what are you doing? Come on, girl, snap out of it. I'm not some stupid teenager. I'm not some civilian high schooler hoping some guy will come in and ask me to the prom. Get a grip, girl. I'm a warrior, a hero-in-waiting. I'm a force, a woman of purpose and drive, strong and independent. I don't believe in love at first sight; I'm not shallow enough to be smitten by some teenage dreamboat, and I'm not the kind of princess who is looking for Prince Charming to come scoop her up and rescue her. When he comes, if he comes, I'll rescue him.*

Still, if Prince Charming does exist, Semi thinks he'd look a lot like this guy.

Snap out of it, Semi. OK, I'm OK. I'm just going to keep my head down, finish up, and get out of here, no distractions. Sounds like a plan. But first, I'm just going to take one more peek.

She looks up as he's sharing a joke with one of his friends. He chuckles a bit and flashes his smile—oh, that smile. It's magical. Semi hopes he never shines it at her. If he were to flash it at her, she feels she might lose her religion, chuck her destiny, and run away with him.

What am I saying? What am I doing? It's the sugar, way too much sugar — no more sweet tea for me. I've got to get out of here before I make a total fool of myself.

She signals Carrie-Ann for her check, and as she does, she sees Prince Dreamboat say something to his friends out of the corner of her eye. Semi's curious, so even though she knows she shouldn't, she decides to deep scan his mind and find out what they're saying. There're strict rules about reading the thoughts of civilians, and she's breaking two or three of them, but she's just going to sneak a peek and—nothing. She read nothing. How's that possible? This is so weird. He's human, normal. He doesn't have powers; he isn't blocking her, so what is this? Semi focuses and tries again when she notices him walking toward her table.

He's not coming toward me, is he? Ignore him. Ignore him, and he'll walk right past. Chill out Semi, just chill.

She looks down, pretending that she doesn't see him. He stops at her table, and Semi feels a drumline performing where her heart is supposed to be. She's trained for so many things, but she hasn't trained for this.

His voice is silky smooth, melodic even, as he asks, "Excuse me, is anyone sitting here?"

Tell him yes. Tell him I'm waiting for my husband, my husband, and my two kids—make that five kids. Tell him something.

"No," she answers, trying to be nonchalant.

Maybe, he just wants to borrow my chair. There are four or five empty tables, but sure, maybe that's it.

"Do you mind if I sit down?" he asks.

OK, what do I do now? Whatever I do, I'm not going to look into his eyes. He has such beautiful eyes. My sisters told me about guys like him. He's a player. If you look into their eyes, that's how they get you. Whatever I do, don't look up; just don't look up.

"Sure, help yourself," she answers, and as she does, she makes the mistake of glancing up.

Their eyes meet, and it feels as if the world pauses. He stares right through her. It is magical. It isn't logical; it makes no sense, but everything in her life has suddenly changed. He looks at her, and he sees her. He sees her. Semi is so done.

Moments ago, a nervous fire had been moving through her. Her muscles stiffened, her heart palpitated, and her stomach had responded to his approach like Cirque du Soleil was performing in it. But as she stares into his eyes, her palpitations cease, and the sensation of cool water flows through her. It extinguishes her inferno of anxiety, evicts the tenants in her gut, and fills every part of her with a preternatural serenity. And instead of freezing or feeling awkward, she experiences warmth throughout her body and a weird calmness.

He seems to feel it too. Their conversation is effortless, first small talk, and then, within minutes, both of them open up as if talking to a long-lost friend. What's come over her? A few seconds ago, her heart was stuttering with panic, but now, it's galloping with joy, and her smile is so wide she might be in danger of straining a muscle. He's a stranger, this boy across from her, but somehow, he doesn't feel like one. Somehow, he feels like home, as if they were separated at birth and just now found their missing part. OK, that's weird, creepy even. That would make them related. It's more like they were formed at the same time from the same celestial dust, creating one complete tapestry that was somehow torn and now, at this moment, is knitting itself back together. Destiny is the word that skitters through her mind and emblazons itself on her heart, a different kind of destiny than she ever imagined.

His name is David Alexander Stone, but his friends call him D-Stone or Stone. Fifteen minutes in, Semi decides to start calling him Charming. In playful retaliation, he calls her Princess, not realizing that she actually is one, and he treats her like she's a star, the most beautiful, most wonderful woman in the world, and he has the honor to sit in her presence and bathe in her light. Semi has never experienced anything like being with him. He can't seem to take his eyes off hers, and she doesn't want him to, and he doesn't get tired of listening to her, in all her quirky glory. They both feel compelled to open up, no façade, no masks.

They go from topic to topic. An hour passes in a blur. The waitress comes by several times, but they are so engrossed that they barely notice, except for that one time David caught Carrie-Ann giving Semi a thumbs-up sign. He seems to have no idea what that was about, but that's OK. Semi understands and gives a subtle nod back, barely missing a beat as she and David seamlessly continue to zoom through topics, scarcely pausing to breathe.

Eventually, the subject switches to their families and Semi starts it off, sharing about the pressure she feels. David hangs on every word. Her family is great, but it seems like everyone is so perfect, and she will never be able to measure up. She's never told anyone this, but Semi lives in fear every day, terrified that she's going to fail and that she's not the person that everyone thinks she is and believes she can be. As she continues to share, Semi's lips start trembling, and a lone tear trickles down her cheek.

"I'm sorry," she apologizes. "I don't know what's going on with me. I'm not normally a crier. You must think I'm some silly girl."

Instinctively, David grabs hold of her hand and looks straight into her eyes reassuringly.

Her heart flutters at first contact, and she feels a kiss of electricity from his touch that tingles her fingers and travels up her spine. But before her body can manifest her surprise, the magic of his brown eyes settles her, and her hand relaxes around his as if it's always been there, easy, comfortable, natural, magnetically attached to his strong but tender grasp. It could stay there forever.

"No, not at all," he answers. "You have nothing to be embarrassed about. Funny thing is for most of my life, I've felt the same way."

"Really?"

He opens up to her, really opens up, about the pressure of being a PK—aka a preacher's kid, his family, his childhood, why he had played football, and even about Monday. Monday is David's birthday, which just so happens to be the first anniversary of his dad's death, the birthday present that keeps on giving. Suddenly, he's the one misty-eyed. He looks embarrassed, and she sees him try to hold in his emotion, but his eyes keep leaking, just a little. Semi doesn't have to read his mind to tell that the mention of his father causes too many feelings to well up. He's drowning in them. Semi squeezes his hand tightly, and when David looks up, he catches her tearing up along with him. Crying in public ... this is very un-Semi-like, but she doesn't care. She looks straight into his eyes attempting to give him strength.

David wipes the moisture from the corner of his eye, swallows hard, and continues. "I get family pressure. I do. My dad was great, a fire-fighter, a beloved pastor, a great husband, father, everything, a regular superhero. I'm not him; I'm never going to be him. I took him for granted, and I let the fear of not measuring up get in my head. Semi, don't get sucked into that trap. I wasted a lot of time being afraid of nothing. I left a lot of things unspoken between us, being an idiot, listening to the wrong voices."

"I'm sure he knows, David."

"Yeah, probably," he responds as he squints to try to stop yet another tear. "I plan on telling my dad anyway when I see him again."

Semi smiles a big smile and squeezes tightly, whispering, "Salioth Algo Daymon."

"What language is that?"

"Oh, it's an obscure expression. It's a promise, a vow shared between two people. Essentially, it means that nothing will keep us apart; I will see you again in this world or the next."

"Very cool."

"Thanks for sharing that, David. You don't know how much that helped me." She stands up. "I've got to run to the ladies' room. All this sweet tea has gotten to me. I'll be right back."

———

He watches in amazement, lingering on her as she walks away. This is unreal; the hairs on his arms are standing at attention, indescribable joy is bubbling up from deep inside, and he feels like he's glowing. Meeting Semi is the most wonderful, most surprising, most perilous thing to ever happen to him. Something about her compels him to do more than just open up to her. He basically took his heart out of his chest and put it in her hands. He's never been this vulnerable with anyone other than Edie, and Edie's family. He's laid bare before Semi, a girl he just met, and somehow, he's more than OK with that. She's put a spell on him, but that's not the scary part. The scary part is he absolutely doesn't want this to end and can't imagine life without it. His dad would always tell the story of how he and Mom met. He would say that when he met her, it was like there was a neon sign overhead saying, "She's the one, dummy, don't mess it up." Well, David's just seen his neon sign in the most unlikely place, and messing it up is definitely not on his agenda.

As Semi heads for the restroom, Edie and B.J. approach. Edie's all smiles, but B.J. has angry eyes, his face all scrunched up and a little red.

"What's up, dude?" B.J. asks, gesturing animatedly, his screechy voice rising an octave to match his emotional temperature. "It's been over an hour. What's the deal?"

Edie smiles and signals for B.J. to shush.

"Isn't it obvious?" she says.

"I think I've just met her, guys. I met the one."

"She's in there?" Edie asks, pointing to the ladies' room. "Suddenly, I need to go too."

David's distracted, listening to B.J.'s nonsense, so it takes him a couple of seconds to realize why Edie's going to the ladies' room. He gets up to stop her, but she's already stepping through the door. This is not good.

"Dude," says B.J., continuing his rant. "I've never seen you like this. You've lost all your cool. Where's your New York swag? I thought I was watching an old episode of Oprah. Is that some new technique, being super sensitive?"

"No strategy, bro, she's the one."

"Really?" he answers, raising an eyebrow. "Some girl you met an hour or so ago in some old diner, she's the one? She's OK, cute in a Disney princess kind of way, but, in your D-Rock days, you used to go out with much hotter girls on an off night. Dude, if you want my advice..."

David puts his finger to his lips, and when B.J. stops flapping his gums, he responds.

"She's the one. She's the one, bro, but do me one favor."

"Anything."

"Don't ever bring up D-Rock again," he says firmly. "D-Rock is dead. He's dead, and nobody misses him but you. D-Rock isn't home anymore. It's just David, bro, just me."

There's an awkward silence.

Finally, he responds, saying, "I guess that's good enough for me." He smiles broadly. "D-Stone it is."

They give each other a pound and grab seats while David begins to talk about Semi, his heart feeling lighter and his smile growing wider and wider as he does. As they wait for the girls to come out, David finds himself gushing, like a proud parent at a reunion, sharing how she's from D.C. but has traveled all over, how she speaks multiple languages, how they've both lost a parent, and all the other things that make her so special. Maybe he's being annoying as he keeps going on and on, but David can't stop himself, and he feels like he'll burst if he tries.

After too much time in the ladies' room, Semi and Edie come out together, arm in arm, as if they're old friends. Edie gives David a wink and a thumbs-up sign. Evidently, Semi has the Eden Grace seal of approval. Semi sits down, but much to David's chagrin, Edie sits next to her. This has just switched to family time. Now, playing the role of David's mom: Eden Grace Garcia. Accordingly, B.J. stays and sits next to David.

What are they doing? Space, guys, space! I want to scream!

But it goes better than expected. The four of them click. Semi is even more amazing in groups. In perfect "mom" fashion, Edie shares one embarrassing story about David after another, but seeing Semi laugh softens the blow. After a while, he doesn't care at all. He's glad that someone else is talking because it allows him to gaze at Semi. He loves her smile, the way she plays with her hair when she's introspective, the way her eyes sparkle, when she giggles, when she's thoughtful, when she simply breathes. From the time that Amesemi first smiled at him, he was done. If this is what it feels like to actually fall in love, he's all in. David has known Semi for a little more than two hours, and he can't think of anywhere he wouldn't go or anything he wouldn't risk for her. How crazy is that?

Suddenly, Semi falls back in her chair, grabbing her head and grimacing. As she quickly stands up, she has the panicked expression of a mom that just lost her child in a mall, saying, "She's here. How can she be here? Tricia can't be here."

"Is everything OK?" David asks.

"No," I'm so sorry, David. There's a family emergency. I've got to run." She puts thirty dollars on the table and hurries for the door, looking over her shoulder at David as she gets there, saying, "I'll call you the minute things calm down. I promise."

Crestfallen, stunned, confused, David feels like a deflated balloon. He waves back with his mouth wide open, shaking his head, and as he looks down, he realizes that Semi left her journal. This is just the excuse David needs to go after her. He grabs it and sprints for the door, calling her name as he makes it to the street, but she's nowhere to be found.

David stands there for a minute, texting Semi. Edie and B.J. are rushing over to join him. And ...

Where is she? David was only seconds behind her, but somehow Semi's gone, completely vanished. They're in a small town, and none of the vehicles parked in front of the diner have moved. No traffic has driven by. She's definitely traveling on foot, but looking in every direction, there's no one around, not one soul. This doesn't make any sense, but beyond the strangeness of it, David feels something else. He's afraid for Semi. That may not be a logical response to what just happened, but he is filled with dread. The eerie stillness screams at him. There's an ominous presence in the air, a bad feeling in his gut telling him that she's in some kind of trouble, and an unexplainable rush of déjà vu. She didn't just run off on him, she's not ignoring his texts, and she's not a ninja who can magically disappear. He knows it deep down. There's more to it, he's sure of it, and if his crazy déjà vu is to be believed, somehow, someway, he's lived this moment before, and it left a bitter taste.

"Oh well," says B.J. at his snarky best. "If something seems too good to be true, it probably is. No worries, dude; you can do better."

Low blow, a very low blow, and David's not in the mood. He bristles, cracks his knuckles, narrows his eyes, and rises to his full height as he takes a step toward B.J., but before he can speak or act, Edie quickly steps between them.

"Shut up, B.J.," she says. She turns to David, putting her hand on his shoulder. "It's going to be OK, mano. I'm sure Semi had a perfectly good reason for running off. You'll probably hear back from her later this afternoon. You'll see."

David steps away from B.J. He can't even look at him after his comment, but B.J. says dumb things. That's his superpower. David just needs to blow that off and focus on tracking down Semi. His friends don't understand the seriousness of the situation, and he doesn't have the energy to explain it or the words for that matter. David just knows what he knows, and he's positive this is not about him or his feelings. It's about Semi and her safety, maybe even her survival. And as irrational as it seems, his instincts tell him that he may be running out of time to find her.

As he paces nervously, he calls her, and when it goes straight to voicemail, he texts her a fourth time. He feels movement on his skin—a chill that tingles the top of his head, pushes down along his spine, and moves throughout his entire body like electric spiders crawling through him, multiplying with every heartbeat. A minor jolt becomes a surge that becomes a shockwave of tremors throughout his musculature, followed by clammy hands, a thumping heart, and a pit in his stomach that feels as though concrete is being poured into it, getting heavier and heavier, leaving him breathless and rigid. His senses make a quick shift from intuitive fear to panicky alarm. Something's coming over him, but he has no idea what it is.

He hears it before he sees it, and the sound forces him to look up. As he does, he sees unusual black clouds. No, it's not clouds at all but hissing, dark creatures, comprised of billowing smoke and bat-like wings. It appears to be tens of thousands of them shrieking and circling above him, blotting out the sky, creating a twister descending from the heavens, their red eyes honing in on their target.

Am I the only one seeing this?

As David taps Edie and points upward, the winged ones swoop down, forming a terrifying, black fog as they do, one that seems to be moving with intentionality.

The world seems to slow down, everything pulsating in with a sluggish motion.

This can't be real. It can't be.

David sees his own words as though written on the sky. The horde seems to answer, not in words, but with an energy that is transmitted without sound. But he feels their answer. He feels it in his bones.

Foolish so foolish— We are very real. We are here. We have always been.

The multitude emanates a singular voice, carried on the shiftless air, its breath intensely cold, like a freezing blast of nitrogen spray. The darkness is real. It weaves toward David, whispering as it draws near, moving like a predator, skulking, determined, merciless. It surrounds him, enveloping him in icy tendrils.

David's heart races. His muscles strain fighting against an impenetrable force. He screams, burning his throat as he tries to break loose, but he cannot hear his own voice. As he fights in vain to free himself, his eyes try to penetrate the blackness as he searches for his friends, but there's no sign. David desperately hopes that they escaped somehow, but he fears that they may be already lost.

Is this what happened to Semi?

Tendrils continue to pin his arms. He struggles to breathe as they begin to compress his lungs. The black cloud wraps around his throat.

"Semi," he mumbles as his consciousness wanes as if the very act of speaking her name can conjure her out of the air, his last hope hanging on some miracle founded in love. He stumbles and falls to the ground like a broken hero who has received his final arrow.

Panic and fear have already been squeezed out of him. His mind wanders somewhere between life and death as images and voices from his past bombard him, flashing indiscriminately in snippets, an old flickering movie reel from bygone times.

Dad would always say, "Life can change in a moment for good or ill."

Fragments from the last few hours race through David's mind. Three hours ago, David met Amesemi, the girl of his dreams, in a hole-in-the-wall diner in a sleepy little town. Three minutes ago, their perfect afternoon was rudely interrupted when Semi clutched her head in pain and abruptly departed. Three seconds ago, he was suddenly cut out of life as he knew it. And by something he neither recognized nor understood. A supernatural phenomenon that is targeting only him.

His father's words are ringing true. Out of nowhere, he's about to die, and there's nothing he can do about it.

He tries to cry out, but he can't. He no longer has the strength to even moan. His enemy engulfs him and there is nothing left but darkness.

The creatures are clawing at his flesh and burrow inside, filling every crevice, consuming all they touch. Strength, light, hope—they swallow it all. But not love, not yet.

"Semi," he whispers, summoning one last breath. "Where are you?"

But there is no answer, no noise, except the sound of flapping wings and the echo of despair.

"The darkness always finds you," it hisses, "and the darkness always wins."

THE LOST DAY—DAVID

Arms flailing, David cries out, "Semi, Semi, where are you?"

He sits up suddenly, with his eyes wide open, the whole world spinning, and his heart pounding furiously. David slumps back down. He takes a deep breath, sucking in air between clenched teeth. He sat up a little too fast and complicated matters by opening his eyes directly into the sun, never a good move. The sunlight hurts, causing him to squint and making it impossible to focus. He covers his eyes and takes another deep breath, waiting for the dizziness to pass. As he steadies himself, he finds he's sprawled out on his truck's front seat. He feels the steady vibration of its engine and is suddenly aware of the funky taste of sleep breath. With his left hand he reaches into the door pocket on the driver's side for the Tic Tacs he keeps there religiously, popping a few into his mouth, sucking on them pensively as he tries to get his bearings.

How'd I get in my truck, and how long has it been running?

His eyes move to the time on its dashboard. That can't be the right time. Something about it doesn't seem right. A whole lot doesn't seem right at the moment.

He feels for something that's digging into the small of his back. It's a book; he's been lying on Semi's journal. Semi, the journal, he remembers now; he remembers it all.

It must have been some crazy dream—a nightmare—otherwise I'd be dead. Whew. But it was all so real—the darkness, the tendrils ...

At least he knows meeting Semi was real. He has her journal.

David's tempted to open it hoping to find something that would lead him to finding Semi. He begins to ruffle the pages, but he stops himself. As much as he'd like to sneak a peek, the idea of looking through her private thoughts just feels fifty shades of wrong. He sees his backpack tucked under the front passenger's seat, grabs it, and carefully places Semi's journal inside. He'll keep it safe until he can return it to her.

David feels sharp pains just from this limited activity. He rolls up his sleeve and notices he has bruises all over his right arm, and he feels like he just finished playing QB in a big game without the benefit of an offensive line. He's sore everywhere. It hurts just to sit up straight—aches on top of aches. He has no idea what could have caused any of this, but none of that matters right now. He can sort it out later. The only relevant questions are where is Semi and where are his friends? His body tenses up, fueled by adrenaline and a sense of dread. He springs up again and desperately looks around for Edie and B.J.

David exhales as he discovers them laid out on the back seat, asleep. Yes, breathing and asleep. He hesitates for a second, tempted to let them lie there, but goes ahead and shakes them before he gets out to take a look around. While they stir, David looks at the dashboard clock again to double-check, turns off the engine, grabs his phone to see if Semi called, and steps out. What he sees brings up even more unsettling questions as he stands there surveying his surroundings. He could tell they were parked on the far end of a massive parking lot, but now he sees that it belongs to ...

B.J. sits up. "When did we drive all the way out here to a Walmart? And what are we doing sleeping in the truck?"

"I'm not sure," David answers, massaging his forehead and putting on his quarterback face, cool and calm under pressure. Of course, it's a mask, one of many, but everyone feels more secure when he's wearing it, including him. "The last thing I remember is standing out in front of

Ed's Diner, looking for Semi. It was about 2:30 p.m. when I first texted Semi after I started looking for her. Before you ask, I know because I noticed the time on my phone when I took it out to reach her. All I know is that it's 3:35 p.m. now. I have no memory of anything that happened over the last hour. What about you guys?"

As Edie and B.J. express similar confusion, David shakes his head. "We lost an hour. That's crazy! Do you guys remember seeing anything weird once we got outside?"

"Other than this? Nah," B.J. replies. "What could be weirder than this?"

"Me either," says Edie. "Why? Like what?"

"Nothing. I just had a really strange dream."

They hear the repeated beeps of numerous messages appearing on their phones as if their service had been off, and it is suddenly updating. Their attention diverted, all three reach for their devices.

Why is Edie staring so hard at her phone? This can't be good.

Edie walks over and taps David on the shoulder, speaking in a voice laced with confusion. She uses her quiet voice, the one she reserves for when she is experiencing hurt or fear too great to measure.

"I...It's crazier than you think, David. Check your phone. If what I'm seeing is accurate, we haven't been out for an hour. It's not Saturday anymore. It's Sunday. We've lost a whole day!"

"What?" He quickly pulls up his phone's calendar and sees a day's worth of missed calls pop up on his screen. "A day? That can't be right. B.J, are you getting the same thing?"

But it is accurate. David sees it with his own eyes. He's still doubtful. Can Verizon make a mistake? Could it be a system failure? He runs across the parking lot to a guy who's walking and texting. He asks what day of the week it is. He doesn't trust the phone. The guy confirms the day and date, and that realization causes David's heart to drop. A deathly silence falls on them. B.J.'s eyes bug out and he starts hyperventilating, and Edie loses all her color and seems like she wants to vomit, but no one says a word.

This is the time when David is supposed to be the strong calm one and take control of the situation, but that's not happening, not now. So much for his QB face. David tries to put it on again, but right now, his mask just doesn't seem to fit. Maybe that's because he can't feel his face. In fact, he can't feel anything at the moment; physically, emotionally, intellectually he's completely numb. He can't seem to reason it out. The whole world seems to be collapsing around him, and every bit of strength has been drained out of him. It's all he can do to force himself not to shake, not to cry, not to scream, no matter how much all three things are going on inside him. If he acknowledges those emotions, if he acknowledges this phenomenon as real, he fears he won't make it. It's best to be numb. So, David has no answers, no soothing words at the moment for him or anyone else. He's just fighting really hard to stand up straight and not melt into a pile of petrified goo.

They stand together quivering in stunned silence, the type where you hear every breath, quake with every heartbeat, and track each bead of sweat as it rolls down your face. The temperature has dropped significantly. Gone is the Indian summer from yesterday. Now, David sees the air escape his lungs, and it feels like, with each gasp, something precious is being taken from him. Hope, courage, sanity, stripped away one breath at a time. And he remembers his dream.

This is all so impossible, and David's head is spinning as he tries to reason through it and come up with a logical explanation. Because right now, they're lead characters in one of those awful, old direct-to-DVD sci-fi movies, featuring a mixture of has-been stars and bad actors in their first professional roles. The scripts in those films are always an afterthought, even worse than the cheap special effects. There are always plot holes so big Godzilla could stumble through them, nothing makes sense, and the endings are entirely unsatisfying. That's what this feels like right now. He doesn't know what's real. Right now, he's hoping none of it is. He calls his mobile phone provider. No, there is no glitch in the system. Yes, your display is reading the correct date, day, and time. David is finding it difficult to breathe. His chest feels heavy. Again, he remembers his dream. Although he is still having a difficult time wrapping his head around this alternative, he senses that they are wandering very deep into crazy land. People just don't lose a day. And the air continues to get colder by the minute.

B.J. points at David's t-shirt and breaks the silence, mouthing words before he can quite get them out. This can't be good either.

"What's that?" he asks, pointing at David's chest, with a hand shaking so badly he resembles an addict in need of a fix.

David looks down, and there's dried blood on his shirt in the shape of a woman's hand. He touches it, traces it, and his heart begins to thump uncontrollably.

"I know whose blood it is." He's barely able to whisper out the words. "Don't ask me how. I just know—it's Semi's."

Edie and B.J. start freaking out. B.J. is screaming frantically. He's gone berserker, shaking and spitting his words, his speech somewhat incoherent. The veins in his neck look like they're about to pop. Edie is pacing back and forth, mumbling the same phrase over and over, her go-to move when she's well beyond her limit. This is Defcon 1. She skips over what would normally be her shouting stage and goes straight to it. But David can't hear either of them, not really. He doesn't care about the lost day, not anymore, how they got out here, none of it, only the handprint on his chest. He closes his eyes and slowly traces it again, remembering her, sensing her, and somehow, he knows that Semi is alive. Now, nothing else matters but finding her.

Yes, something is very wrong. He has no clue what happened to them. He can't begin to fathom what might be going on. He doesn't know anything. But David knows that Semi is real. He knows how he feels about her, and he's going to let that feeling push all the fear, all the questions, all the anxiety aside because they can't take him where he needs to go. All he knows, all he cares to know, is she's in trouble and that she needs him. He will find Semi whatever it takes.

David paces back and forth, walks a little bit from the others, clenches his fists, and makes a vow.

"Salioth Algo Daymon," he whispers. "Nothing will keep us apart."

B.J. and Edie stumble around for a few more minutes and David finds himself doing the same. They're like zombies, making disjointed noises, garbled and rambling, currently lacking the ability to express the insane range of emotions they're experiencing.

Fear, the many different shades of it, tops David's list.

For starters, he fears that the world has gone crazy, or maybe the world is fine, but they're the ones who've lost it. In David's case, after everything that's happened this last year, should that be surprising? But even that is dwarfed by the Death Star of them all, the mother of all fears. What if he can't find Semi, and how is he going to live with himself if he fails?

Finally, Edie is the one who breaks the silence. "Our parents, our families, we've been missing for a day. They must be worried sick."

With that, they start dialing numbers, and David realizes that there's something scarier than all of this—calling his mom. He calls his Uncle Frank first. This weekend, David came to Georgia to swing by the old youth camp he used to attend in Penfield and visit his Uncle Frank in Watkinsville. The three of them were supposed to spend the night at his uncle's, so calling him is a good way to set his uncle's mind at ease and to gauge the temperature of David's mom, who has no doubt been calling Uncle Frank all day. Uncle Frank is pretty easygoing, but the talk is eye-opening. Things are worse than David imagined. Mom is the next call.

She sounds so relieved to hear his voice. His mom's not a crier, but he swears her voice cracks for a second, maybe less. And then the questions start, and it's ten minutes into the call before David can get in more than three words at a time.

"Mom, I understand," he says finally, "but we're OK, really. Nobody was hurt by the storm. I can't get into the details right now, but we got a little turned around. Yes. Yes ma'am, I understand, but according to Uncle Frank, both cell phones and landlines were out all-around Penfield for more than a day. Yes, I know, Mom. I do, but we're OK. Yes, ma'am. We'll spend tonight at Uncle Frank's and head back home tomorrow. We'll be back in Birmingham by five...long before five. Yes ma'am. I'll call as soon as I get there. I love you too."

David hangs up and slowly exhales before glancing over at Edie, who has also just finished her call.

"That bad, huh?" she asks.

"You know my mom. Third-degree all the way; West Indian love at its finest."

"Hey, Mama Stone is no joke. I'm sure she called the police, the fire department, the Marines, and the Impossible Missions Force looking for you. Well, maybe looking for me. I think she likes me more than she likes you. I'm her favorite, followed by Eli and Ellen. Those younger siblings of yours are really something. It must be great to be a twin. You, lil' bro, are a distant fourth at best, barely beating out my brother Justin."

Typical Edie—she's one of the few people in David's life who has always been underwhelmed by him. That's what happens when you've known someone since you both were in diapers. She's rarely impressed and never intimidated. Their families have been close since before they were born. Three weeks older, Edie has essentially been David's "big" sister. She's a five feet four-inch fireball, barely over a hundred pounds, and he's a six feet two-inch ex-football star, and he would bet that, in her soul, she still believes she can pin David to the ground and make him tap out like she did when they were three. And he's not sure he'd bet against her.

"Ha, ha," he replies, dismissing Edie's shade. "How's Aunt June handling it?

"Oh, I didn't speak to my mom," Edie laughs. "You know how she gets. I talked to Dad. He had his share of questions, but he tried to keep it cool. He switched to Spanish a few times, though, so I know he was pretty worried."

"Yeah, that sounds like Uncle Manny. What about you, B.J.? Were you able to catch up to your mom or your uncle?"

B.J. looks pale, paler than usual. He has the glazed eyes that all three of them had a few minutes earlier, but his case is far more severe.

"Nah," he answers. "It'll be a few days before any of them notice that I'm gone." He pauses, shakes his head, and his eyes go from glazed over to full-scale crazy. "No, I just got off the phone with my cousin Trip. They're claiming that it was a freak EF-4 tornado in this area, and get this, somehow it only struck the camp, the same camp we were headed to. It leveled it. Dude, it gets nuttier. It didn't show up on Doppler radar, and there was no coverage of the tornado before or during its occurrence, only after. There's absolutely no footage of it, which is totally impossible in modern times. You telling me that no television crew or millennial or Gen Z with a smart phone happened to get even a little footage? No Doppler, no footage, but somehow there seems to be no shortage of eerily similar eyewitness accounts. And don't get me started with how a tornado could possibly throw us into your truck and drive us out here. And that takes me back to Trip. You know Trip is a dark web genius, right? He says there's some weird chatter, some top-secret cover-up type stuff, and we may not be the only people complaining about lost time. Guys, we're in trouble, so much trouble. We're smack in the middle of something big."

Part Kevin Hart and part Fox Mulder, with a liberal sprinkling of an anxious grandma thrown into the mix, B.J. has been David's best friend since David moved to Birmingham from the Bronx years ago. If he's not laughing, he's worrying.

David walks over and puts his hand on B.J.'s shoulder. "Take a breath, buddy. It's going to be OK. We'll figure it out."

B.J. brushes him off. "OK, how? And please, don't give me any of your famous Stone family pep talks right now, D-Stone. I'm not in the mood. We lost a day, a freaking day. What's going on is real, and we've got to find some real answers."

David shrugs, gives him a side-eye, and takes a step backward as he debates whether he should back off or say something else to lower his temperature.

"So, what are you thinking?"

"I don't know," he answers. "Time travel, dimensional portals, aliens, Big Foot, an alternate reality, it could be anything. Whatever it is, we're in the middle of a massive government coverup, right in the middle of it, and that never ends well. Hey, don't laugh, man. That's the truth, and we are in desperate need of some real science-based answers."

It's not like BJ to be like this. Even with his conspiracies-around-every-corner outlook, this is extreme. B.J. sounds crazy but, in all fairness, everything about their lost day does, so David can't completely rule out the possibility of a coverup. He can't rule out anything.

Edie crosses her arms and is ready to give B.J. some of that Bronx attitude that they all love so much. Half Afro-Puerto Rican, or as her dad would say Nuyorican, and half good ole girl, Edie can be Southern sweet, but boy, she can dial up the attitude when she's inclined. And she can dial it up in two languages.

David can tell that she's ready to go at B.J. for the disrespect, but he puts his arm around her and walks her away from their friend.

"Now's not the time, Edie. Give him some space. He's going to have to find his own way to process this. We all do."

"You're right. You're right, mano. Well, we need to put on happy faces and head over to your uncle's, anyway. If we don't report in soon, Momma Stone is likely to parachute in and look for us herself. So, what's going to be our story when we get there? We're going to have to tell him something, and the truth just makes us sound like we are very high on something very illegal."

"Oh, you'll come up with something. You always do."

She gasps with false indignation. "Why me?"

"Sis, how long have we known each other? We've gotten in trouble together, lots of trouble, in New York, Birmingham, and everywhere in-between. And when we do, you fabricate the story, and I tell it. It's worked this long. Why change now?"

"Whatever," she says with a classic eye roll. "Fine. I'll give you the script. You say the lines. Just don't blow it, mano, and please don't let B.J. say a word."

"C'mon B.J., it's time to go," David calls out. "My uncle's expecting us. Oh, and one word of warning, Mr. Alabama fan and little Miss Auburn, my uncle is the world's biggest Georgia Bulldog fanatic. One 'roll tide' or 'war eagle' and he's likely to shoot you and bury you out back. His house is a no SEC trash talk zone. Is that clear?"

As they nod their heads affirmatively, David pulls off and heads to Watkinsville. After greetings, a soul food dinner, sharing Edie's expertly crafted version of events, several games of UNO, and a go hard or go home game of Spades, David yawns and starts rubbing his eyes.

Edie grabs him before he heads upstairs with everyone else.

"That went surprisingly well," he says, playfully. "I think it was twenty percent script and eighty percent delivery. What about you?"

"You were impressive, lil' bro. You fake it well, you always have, but you don't fool me." She closes the distance between them, turning serious. "B.J. and I spazzed-out pretty badly today, but not you. You seemed relatively cool and focused. How are you doing David, really?"

"I'm holding it together," he answers, averting his eyes.

She cocks her head to the side and crosses her arms sternly. "Now, we both know that's not true, so let's try this again. How are you?"

When he responds with a blank expression, she continues. "David

Alexander Stone, let's do this the hard way. Yes or no, isn't tomorrow your birthday?"

"Yes."

"Isn't it the first anniversary of Papa Stone's death?"

"Yes."

"And before B.J. and I hijacked it and tagged along, didn't you plan this as a solo trip to visit the camp, Ed's diner, and some of the most emotional places from your childhood?"

David's top lip quivers, and his eyes moisten as he once more tries to avert hers.

"And I haven't even gotten to all the creepy stuff that's happened in the last twenty-four hours," she persists. "So, tell me, honestly. How are you?"

"You know how I'm doing, Edie," he answers, his voice cracking as a lone tear trickles down his cheek. "I'm barely holding it together."

She hugs him and squeezes him with a love death grip, and David sheds a couple of more tears on his sister's shoulder. After some time, she whispers in his ear.

"David, I know you feel the need to be strong for everybody, your mom, the twins, B.J., Semi, the whole wide world, but you don't need to be strong with me. You know that, don't you? I've got you."

"Yeah, I know."

"And Semi, the bloody handprint. What the frak is that all about?"

"I can't explain it. I know we just met, but I love her, Edie. I've got to find her."

"I know, mano. We'll find her together. You're not going anywhere without me."

After a little chitchat lightens things up, David grins, knowingly. "Well, now that we're sharing the unvarnished truth, is my mom planning a 5:00 p.m. surprise party for me tomorrow? Because it sure seems that way."

"What do you want me to say, David?" says Edie, laughing. "It's Momma Stone. She loves you."

"Yeah, loves me to death."

'Look, I've got it all figured out," says Edie. "Drop me off early to get my car, so I can go help her set up, then you go to my house and change your clothes. At five sharp, you and B.J. roll in, and you act surprised."

"I'm going to hate it."

"Well, just for tomorrow, you have my permission to fake it."

"I hate you, Edie," he says, grinning as he heads upstairs.

"I love you too, lil' bro. Goodnight."

Noon the next day as they load up the truck, David looks over at BJ. He seems his usual jovial self.

"How are you so energetic?" asks David. "You were up all-night pacing. Are you OK?"

"I stayed up and worked some things out. I've never been better," he answers.

Edie stares. "You mean the stuff from yesterday?"

"Don't want to talk about it; don't need to talk about it. It's behind me, guys. I've never been better."

David isn't buying it, and Edie looks skeptical, but happy B.J. is better than frantic B.J. any day of the week.

As they hop on I-20, Edie rolls to her side. "David, I'm going to take a nap. Wake me up if you get tired and I'll take over."

"Cool."

"D-Stone, I can drive," says B.J.

David's reply is short and sweet. "No."

"I got my license. I can drive."

"Kid, you got it on the seventh try. You're not driving, Betsy. In fact, when you sleep at night, I don't want you to even dream of driving her."

"OK, OK." B.J. peeks at Edie. "Man, she can sleep anywhere. OK, I've got a serious question."

"Shoot," David replies.

"Who wins a fight between the Hulk and Superman?"

"Only because Superman can fly, I go with Superman. Thor and Superman is a push, depending on how the writer handles the magic thing, and Goku would smoke Superman."

"Smoke Superman? You sure about that?"

"I know you're a Superman stan, B.J., but yes, Goku would destroy him."

They go on like this for a while, passing the time, with one pop culture debate after another. David laughs as BJ switches from comics to anime, to movies, to T.V. It's a game they've played as long as they've known each other. It's silly, especially in light of all that's happened, yet it's comforting to do something that feels normal, even if normal is an illusion.

David becomes lost in thought. He remembers the darkness, the icy relentless cold, the whispered threat. He still almost feels the pressure on his chest, his throat, the pain in his lungs. Maybe it was a dream, but Semi vanishing, their lost day ... that was no dream. David can't help but feel that the truth behind all this is not some random storm that even NASA didn't detect. His gut is telling him that this—whatever *this* is— is going to create seismic change. Dad was right. Life can swerve in a moment. His just did. What seems bad right now might end up being for the good, but he feels it coming, something big. He thinks maybe it's best that they hold on to their illusions as long as possible because when they discover the truth of the lost day, there might be no going back. And the bloody handprint ... that's the part that scares him the most.

INTO THE WOODS — DAVID

He's having the dream again, just like the night before and the night before that. Every time he's fallen asleep over the last two weeks, David's mind has journeyed to this amazing world, and tonight it's even more exciting, mind-bending, and horrifying than all the other times it's drawn him in. This fantasy world is always captivating, constantly changing, and its revelations deepening, but none of its riveting complexity matters at this moment. Now, it's time for the main event.

An army is gathering, speaking an ancient, singsong language, and in its midst, she emerges, his favorite part of every dream. Her entrance silences the monsters, gods, and goddesses of this mindscape. Such is the power of her regal bearing that even the greatest of kings bow down before her. Her armor morphs into a form-fitting golden dress. It seems to float on her figure rather than being worn by her. At moments her skin and hair shimmer with otherworldly iridescence, and though there is no breeze about, her gown wavers and ripples. She walks forward and stares ahead, looking straight at David, only at him.

The first few times she appeared in one of his visions, he didn't recognize her, but he does now. It's undeniable. She is Amesemi; he feels it; he feels her. It's Semi, but not just her; somehow, in this place, she shares this body with another, something out worldly, and this union transforms her.

Divine Semi's appearance is very different from the Semi he met in the diner. He stands before her avatar, and the perfection of this new physical form mirrors the beauty of Semi's soul. Her features have traces of Amesemi, but her already beautiful face has been transformed and taken beyond the limits of nature. It is as if an artist has taken the best parts of every imaginable beauty and created an angelic ideal, then formed a body from the clay of the smoldering heart of Africa, the great continent, every detail sculpted with grace and elegance, perfect in all forms. She is a creature with allure dialed up to eleven, a living, breathing embodiment of human fantasy, straight out of a Frank Cho comic. Her appearance is breathtaking, but Dream Semi is more than a pretty face, much more.

Beneath it all, her Egyptian headdress, her golden dress, her braided hair, even her celestial form, she is Semi. And her eyes radiate the same presence, intelligence, warmth, and conviction he glimpsed when he first met her. Whether as a real-world teenager or a goddess in a vision, she is mesmerizing, like pure spirit, and just like when they first met, David cannot look away.

She is standing in an ancient palace, with soldiers, gods, and monsters surrounding her, but he doesn't care about any of them. He only sees her. This world fast-forwards, her surroundings melting away, and he sees Dream Semi in different ensembles from different times. She is in Rome during the first century, in China during the third, in Paris during the 1400s, and in 1930s New York. The times change, as does her attire, but she remains the same, always stunning, always perfect, his Nubian goddess. He sees himself with her, not merely as an observer; he's holding her face to face. David's a little older, dressed in formal attire. Her hair is straight, long, and flowing, and she's wearing a beautiful white gown. They are taking a romantic walk, obviously in love. He holds her hand and caresses her cheek.

She whispers in his ear, her voice like a divine melody. "We are destiny, my love, stars in the darkness intertwined by fate."

David nods in agreement, smiles, and leans forward for a passionate kiss ...

"David. It's time to get up."

Oh, Mom, not now. Please, not now.

David hears his mom's screeching voice ripping him from his paradise.

"Your alarm clock's been ringing for the last ten minutes. You'll be late for school. Remember, my car's in the shop. You have to drop me off first. Get up."

"OK, Mom. You can stop screaming now. I'm up."

He rolls over on his side and forces himself to sit up. Just once, he wants to make it through to the kiss.

David mumbles out loud to no one. "Man, these days, I can't even get the girl of my dreams *in* my dreams. Hey world, my name is David Alexander Stone, and my life sucks."

Nearly four weeks have passed since their lost day, four weeks of exhausting every known resource to locate Semi, and his vow to find her has been reduced to empty words. All he has to show for it are the texts and voicemails he's sent to her phone, these cinematic dreams, and Semi's crazy journal. Oh, and the guilt he experiences from not being able to do something, anything, to locate her. Let's not forget that.

It's hard for him to get out of bed most days, to go to school, help with the wonder twins— rinse, wash, and repeat. The nightmare of the lost day is very much active in the back of his mind, but she's at the forefront, always, and he's spent every free moment exhausting every way to find her. But there's nothing to show for it. Trying his best, it's meaningless, so empty. He's failing her every day—major shocker, David failing someone. Why'd he ever believe it would be different with her? No, he can't think that way, can't give in to those negative thoughts, not like before, how he spiraled after Dad died. He's not that guy anymore, and he's got to hold out hope. Finding Semi is the only reason he's even able to get up, to power through, and he has to keep trying, no matter what.

The dreams gave him some hope, at least at first. They started two weeks ago. He wakes up the morning after, remembering every detail, and as insane as his sleep time visions are, since Penfield, they may make more sense to David than his reality. Nothing seems right or real anymore, not since that lost day. Disney said, "A dream is a wish your heart makes." What do his say about his heart, his life? For two weeks, each time he enters this fantasy world, it takes him a little further, like advancing to different levels of a video game. Maybe these dreams aren't truly dreams, and the answers to whatever is going on are somewhere in these images. And maybe the moon is a giant marshmallow filled with aliens who sing camp songs and eat s'mores all day. He's reaching; he's got nothing, and he knows it.

As he springs out of bed, he winces from a sudden sharp ringing in his ears. He tries to shake it off and rushes to take his shower, but as he reaches the bathroom door, he doubles over. The piercing pain from the ringing becomes intense. He grabs his head and stands up straight, stumbling drunkenly back toward his bedroom, and it eases up a little. He moves a little toward his bed and it increases slightly; a step toward his dresser—where Semi's journal sits like a beacon, it diminishes. He senses that the journal is the cause. It's behaving like a supernatural game of Marco Polo, drawing him to it. And with that realization, the ringing disappears. Is this the break he's been looking for? If there is any truth, any message being imparted by Semi through his dreams, maybe she's now found another way to communicate with him.

Four weeks ago, out of respect for Semi's privacy, he didn't touch the journal at first, treating it like a sacred book. But after a week of dead ends, he cracked it open, searching for clues, and was stunned by what he saw. The whole book is written in a mysterious language that resembles some sort of hieroglyphics. David was so determined to make some sense of it that he even concocted a story about how he got the journal and took it to a friend of his mom's at UAB, a professor in ancient Egyptian studies. But that was a dead end as well, like everything else, at least until now.

It's calling him. He can feel it clearly, now, and its pull is undeniable.

He reaches for the journal and is startled when he receives a jolt of electricity. He recoils quickly. He sucks on his fingertips to ease the tingling and shakes his hand, and after a moment, reaches out for it again, slowly, gingerly. He feels it radiate warmth and it glows slightly when he touches it. With all that's been happening, this doesn't scare him. He's holding a glowing book and somehow it feels comforting.

He swears the book feels alive. It generates a wave of energy, a pulsating rhythm that resembles that of a heartbeat. Maybe he really has lost it. He opens it up, and for the first time, he can read it. He knows what it is. It's the written form of the singsong language from his dreams. Certain pages open before him as if they have a mind of their own. Eyes filled with wonder, he reads through several before he starts to feel his comprehension fading. Whatever residual knowledge he kept from tonight's vision is wearing off. David hurriedly jots down most of what he's able to translate before it fades, puts that paper inside the journal, and throws it into his backpack. He'll see if he can make sense of it later. His mom is starting to yell again. It's getting late, so he's got to get moving.

He drops Mom off at UAB, and the twins off at the front door of their school, AAFA, scrambles to find a parking space, and then he and his backpack make a dead sprint to reach homeroom before the bell rings, putting his 4.3 speed to use. Today's the last day of school before winter break, and he's so thrilled that he's fidgety, barely able to sit through classes. He can use the rest and is looking forward to spending time with his family over the next few weeks, but what really has him excited is what he learned from Semi's glowing journal.

While David's been pretending to listen to his teachers, he's been doing some research on his translations, and he thinks he has something, a genuine lead. He's going to be hanging out with B.J. and Edie at the mall after school, and he can't wait to discuss what he found. Staring at the clock, he impatiently counts down the minutes to the end of the day and makes double-time to his locker as soon as the bell rings.

B.J.'s locker is next to David's. He shows up a few seconds after David gets there. You can't miss him, and you hear him long before you see him. He's the loudest kid in the hallway, and that's saying a lot. He stands behind David with that perpetual smirk they all love so much.

"What's up, D-Stone?"

They pound fists. "Hey, B.J."

"So, what did you think about it?" he asks.

"About that Latin quiz? Could have been worse, I think I did OK."

"No, dummy, not the quiz, that old, Pamela Andrews movie on SYFY last night. It was great, wasn't it?"

David can't do this anymore. This is ridiculous. He moves closer to B.J. so that only he can hear him.

"Huh? Kid, our lives are a sci-fi movie. I can't believe this is the conversation we're having. You've been avoiding talking about what happened since we got back. What's going on, B.J.? You mean you really want to talk about some C-minus movie starring a D-level actress addicted to silicone rather than address the giant, pink, men-in-black-dressed elephant in our lives? Really? Don't you want to know what's going on?"

"I know what happened," he says, leaning forward and whispering in David's ear. "I've known since I left your uncle's."

"Huh? What do you mean?"

B.J. places his finger to his lips.

"We can't talk about it here," he says with a deadly serious tone. "They might be listening."

"They?"

"Yes," he whispers, "they. Be cool. Act natural until we get to the food court. It should be safe to talk there."

David gathers himself by his locker, shaking his head over the bombshell B.J. just dropped and watches B.J. walk off toward the exit, being loud and crazy again. Eventually, David starts to make his way toward the exit as well and bumps into Edie on the way out. One look at her and he knows what she's thinking. With her cute round face and long brown hair, she's far prettier than she realizes, and her huge brown eyes broadcast every emotion in a way that cannot possibly be misunderstood. It makes her a lousy liar but an excellent sister. Besides, lying is not really her thing; she's a straight shooter, often painfully so.

"Hey, are you OK?" she asks.

"I'm just trying to get my head around my talk with B.J."

Her eyes get a little bigger and she cocks her head to the side. "Is he still in denial?"

"No," David replies. "We're definitely past that stage. I think it's safe to say that Conspiracy Guy is alive and well. It should be an interesting time at the mall."

"So, no offense, what exactly are we discussing? Are there new leads? Did B.J.'s weird cousin Trip find anything? "

"No, he says it's like someone erased Amesemi Nicole Brooks from the web. And she has an active cell phone, but he can't trace it, can't find out any information about the account, and it doesn't even seem to use any known carrier."

"OK, so did that Indiana Jones wannabe at UAB crack the code of Semi's journal?"

"No, not really. She says that the writing's not Egyptian or Sumerian, although it shares some characteristics. But to her eyes, it appears much more complex. She wanted to keep it to study, but I wouldn't part with it. I know it's silly, but it's my only connection to Semi, my single link, it and the dreams. She was forced to settle for a few screen shots with her smart phone. "

She scrunches her face and leans in a little closer. "You've been calling Semi's number again, haven't you?"

"Yes."

"Sending texts too?"

"Yeah."

"Once a week?"

"More."

"Once a day?"

David and his lost puppy dog face stay silent.

"It's more, isn't it? Oh, poor baby. You've got it bad, lil' bro. I wish I could help, but I don't know what else we can do."

David grins. "I do. We have a new lead."

"No fair, mano. You literally buried the lead. What is it?"

"Oh, ye of little faith. You have to wait until the mall, but it's good —weird, but good."

"Well, these days, weird is what we do best. I'll see you there."

She starts to walk away, shaking her head, then she turns around.

"Oh, David, I almost forgot. Can you bring Justin with you? He's going to spend the night with Eli. I would drop him off, but I've got to drop some meds by my aunt's house on the way to the mall. You may have to wait a few minutes. He needs to meet with his English teacher about something."

"No problem. I'll squeeze him in. I'll see you at the Galleria."

Her little brother, Justin, is two months younger than the twins.

He's a good kid but a genuine charmer, the kind of charm that can get him in real trouble as he gets older. He's a five feet five-inch ball of energy and Eli's best, sometimes only, friend.

As he steps outside, David bumps into Eli and Ellen hanging out front with Ellen's friends. Good, at least David doesn't have to wait for them today. As a reward for waiting for Justin and now, B.J., who is also riding with him, he gets the "honor" of watching Ellen and Eli interact with her seventh-grade posse. In minimal doses, he finds it both painfully annoying and mildly compelling, in a bad reality TV, guilty pleasure sort of way. But at this point, he's way over his limit.

Oh man, this is mind-numbing. Were we ever this young? I'm getting dumber just listening to their conversations.

He rubs his temples and walks off to look for B.J. and Justin so that he can be put out of his misery. Before David can get too far, B.J. shows up, and he looks a little off.

"You OK, man?" David asks. "You just disappeared."

"I don't know," he replies, inhaling deeply and averting his eyes. "I just saw something...something strange. I'll tell you when we get to the mall."

Finally, Justin shows up, apologizing for the delay. David stuffs the three kids in the back seat, and the five of them head out. The "Three Amigos" in the back are in their own world, so they don't notice that B.J. is white-knuckling his backpack and not saying a word. A speechless B.J. is rarer than a total eclipse. Something is very wrong.

There's not much time until their rendezvous with Edie. David despises being late for anything, for any reason, but he thinks he can pull this off. He arrives home and rushes to heat up yesterday's leftovers for dinner. He'd promised his mom he'd feed the three gremlins before he left. It's no big deal. He intentionally made enough dinner last night to last at least two days. This will only take a minute.

It's gone, all of it.

It was Eli, must have been. All arms and legs, that boy is a black hole. His skinny behind probably got up in the middle of the night and cleaned out the fridge. Great, just great. David was counting on the left-overs to help him have a quick turnaround.

"I don't have time for this," he grumbles. He looks around. "OK, so what can I make quickly? I'd ask B.J. to help, but the kid has absolutely no cooking skills." David continues to think out loud. "He's so dazed and confused right now—totally out of it. I don't know what happened at the school, but whatever it was has really gotten to him. I've rarely known him to have such a hard time shaking something off."

Alright, it's lemonade out of lemons time. While David's busy throwing together plan B, he shoots Edie a text and lets her know that they're running late. "No worries," she texts back. She's going shopping for some silver earrings to reward herself for being on time— typical Edie. Cool. He just needs to let her know when they get to the mall, and they'll meet up at the food court. After cooking up a fast and furious David special, he and B.J. hop in the truck to head out, but just as he's about to pull out of the driveway, David's phone rings. It's Edie.

"Hey, David," she says. "I think we should switch up the plans. Maybe we can meet at the Chicken King, across the street from the mall instead."

"Why the change?"

"I spotted Cliff Wiggins and some of the lineman from Paris Park High prowling the mall. They're in a foul mood, and you guys have history."

"Edie, I quit the team as a junior, months after leading lowly Paris Park to its only state championship. There's bad blood between Cliff and me, me and the whole team, me and just about everyone from Paris Park High, including the grand-moms and the cafeteria ladies. It's no big deal; I can handle it. Besides, Cliff knows what happened the last time we tangled."

"See, that's why I'm worried," she replies.

"What does that mean?"

"I mean, there are five of them, David, and you can 'handle it.' See, that's what's wrong right there, mano. Most of us would be trying to avoid the five oversized Cro-Magnons who are looking to hurt us, but not you, not David Alexander Stone. You've got that firefighter gene in you, always rushing into the fire, and when you get those crazy fire-fighter eyes, you'll take on the whole Marine Corps if you think you're in the right. Lil' bro, you call it fearless, but Mama Stone and I call it stupid. Walk away, bruh."

"OK, you wanna go there? Maybe you forgot that most of the fights that I've ever gotten into were protecting you after you lost your temper and ran your mouth at some guy. I've got receipts, Edie. We can go there if you want to."

There's a moment of silence.

Finally, Edie replies, "That's not the point, David. Look, can't we ... never mind. I think Cliff and his goons left. I'll see you at the food court. We cool, mano?"

"Yeah, sis, we're good. We'll be at the mall in a minute."

And just like that, she hangs up. David shakes his head and continues on to South Hoover Galleria, texting her as they pull into the parking lot, then the two of them hop out of the truck and head for the food court.

"What up, guys?" she hollers as Edie sees them heading down the escalator.

"What up?" B.J. hollers back.

She has her shopping bag in tow and shows off her shiny new earrings as she greets them. They grab some food and find a table, and once they get seated, David doesn't waste any time. He jumps right in.

"OK, B.J., I've got stuff to share, and I'm sure Edie has some too, but let's start with what you told me. Have you really figured all this out?"

B.J. looks around nervously as if impersonating a squirrel looking out for a hawk. Yes, Conspiracy Guy is alive and well.

"Yeah," he answers, hesitating a little before completing his thought. "Give it a minute."

"What?" David asks.

"Trust me," he says as he channels his inner C-list spy and subtly nods toward the people at the table next to them.

As they stand up to leave, he says, "OK, we can talk for real now. Sorry for the stall. I thought they might have been one of them. I couldn't have them listening to our conversation."

"Who?" Edie asks.

"The men in black," B.J. says, shrugging matter-of-factly.

"What are you talking about?" Edie asks, with more than a hint of frustration.

"I know what's going on," he says, with a solemn face. "David, your girl Semi is an alien. I don't know if she's a brain-sucking alien or an E.T. type. She could be a green or a gray, but she's an alien. That probably wasn't even her actual face. She's either a shapeshifter or maybe one of those that uses a human host. I'm not sure yet, but the reason we lost twenty-five hours was that we were abducted. It is so obvious. Once I calmed down and could actually think, it was so clear. I mean, her creepy journal, the fact that she jumped up grabbing her head right before it all happened, the localized nature of the damage in Penfield. It all adds up. There was a UFO, we and some townsfolk got abducted, and the government came in and covered it up afterward. Our memories were wiped after the abduction, either by the aliens or by the men in black. I'm not sure yet."

Edie and David look at each other. David suppresses the laughter that's bubbling up inside him, but she busts out laughing.

She crosses her arms and gives him a side-eye. "Really, B.J., this was your big reveal? Aliens?"

"Why is this so farfetched? You believe in some invisible, all-powerful being, but you can't accept this? Look, this isn't about faith. I'm just looking at the facts."

Edie's teeth clench, her eyes turn into slits, and David swears he sees her temple pulsating, but before she can go off on B.J. for his 'invisible being' jab, David puts his hand on her shoulder to calm her down.

"OK," David says, cutting in. "If this is what you believe, why sit on it for four weeks, and why tell us now?"

"I wanted it to be over," he answers. "Based on what I've read about abductions and government agencies, I knew someone would be keeping tabs on us, seeing if the mind wipe worked. I thought if we acted normal and didn't mention anything about aliens or UFOs, they'd leave us alone, and we could go on with our lives. Your theories were so off base, I figured they'd help our cause, but I thought I needed to keep my mouth shut about what I knew. I figured they'd move on, but now, I'm not so sure."

David isn't ready to totally buy into this, but he sincerely wants to hear him out. Based on her body language, Edie's not buying it at all, and her dismissive stare has made it obvious that she stopped seriously listening after he mentioned the "men in black." David gets it. He's seen the movies, and somehow, he doesn't believe that Will Smith and Tommy Lee Jones are behind all this. And don't get him started on the reboot.

David leans forward. "So, what's changed?"

"I...I don't think they're done with us," B.J. replies. "The aliens, I don't think they're done." He pauses, wringing his hands, then continues. "Lately, I...I've been seeing things, weird things. At first, I thought it was memory residue from the event, like David's dreams, but now, I think someone or something is following me."

OK, now, he has their full attention.

"What have you seen?" Edie asks.

The color leaves B.J.'s face, and his eyes well up as he both wrestles with the insanity of it all and searches for the right words to express the impossible.

"It's hard to explain," he mutters. "Not human, they're like shadows in the shape of men...with red eyes and deep gravelly voices that whisper in some otherworldly language. Sometimes, I hear them and don't see them. Sometimes, I see them following out of the corner of my eye, and then they disappear. Before today, I had never had a clean look, but I got one today. After school, I saw one at AAFA and I tried to follow it, but it vanished. When I got where he—it—had been standing, I felt chills all over. But it wasn't like the chills you get when you're watching a horror movie or you see someone that looks exactly like someone you used to know. I was cold, dude, really cold. I couldn't stop shaking."

Merely sharing about the event has B.J. shaking all over again. His hands and legs are trembling, and there's a slight twitch in his lips, all seeming to increase with each detail he shares. David puts his hand on B.J.'s shoulder to comfort him.

"Breathe," he instructs gently. "Just breathe." As B.J. starts to calm, David asks, "How long?"

"I started hearing voices about two weeks ago," he answers. "I thought...hoped...I was imagining them. The shadows started appearing four or five days ago."

"I've been seeing stuff, too," Edie confesses, her eyes filled with wonder. "It's been about two weeks, now. Lights...not lights exactly... more like beings of light, with voices like music. I feel warm when they're around and peaceful. At first, I would see them in the mornings when I wake up. I always feel like I've been dreaming. Now, I see them floating around me at least a few times a day. Just randomly. Like...like angels."

"Angels?" B.J. asks, squinting disdainfully.

"Yes, angels."

"Look, guys," David interrupts. "Whether you believe we're living out an episode of Supernatural or Star Trek, we're all experiencing stuff, and I don't think any of it is just residual memory from the event, especially not my dreams. I'm sure that my dreams are trying to give me a message. And that woman I told you about, the one I keep seeing, she's Semi or some kind of dream avatar of her. She's not alone. Semi and this presence that is with her, they're calling to me. Semi needs our help."

"And you know this how?" B.J. asks, rolling his eyes.

"I just know."

"Like you know that it was Semi's bloody handprint?" B.J. presses.

"Yes."

He puts his hand on his forehead and shakes his head. "You can't know that, David. Wow, this is what I'm talking about. It's all feelings and faith with you two. If you just take a step back and look at it, the truth should be obvious. Nothing about this, especially you and Semi, makes any sense. You're in love, obsessed with some girl after just one meeting, really? That doesn't strike you as odd? That alien's messed with your head, dude. Why can't you simply look at the facts, take the evidence for what it is?"

"What evidence, B.J.?" David fires back, his calm demeanor starting to show cracks as his irritation bleeds through. "You don't have any facts, just your feelings and hunches, informed by sci-fi movies we've all seen and books written by a bunch of pseudo-scientists. And that's cool. We're all just trying to figure this out and give our thoughts, but just because you think differently doesn't make you the smartest guy in the room, and it doesn't make you right. And what I feel for Semi..." He pauses for a second, composing himself, and continues. "Look, let me show you the one piece of evidence we do have."

David pulls out Semi's journal and puts it on the table, removing the sheet of paper tucked inside it.

"Semi's journal," Edie gasps.

She's seen it before, but it never ceases to freak her out.

"Look, here," David says, opening up to the first translated page. "I woke up this morning from my dream, and there was a glow around this book, and I was able to read this language."

"You were?" B.J. and Edie exclaim simultaneously, the duo far more excited about the news of his ability than they are alarmed by the fact that the journal was glowing, proof that their tolerance for weirdness has grown to disturbing levels.

"Yeah," he replies. "It didn't last long, but I was able to translate most of three pages and several partial sentences and phrases from the first part of a fourth before the knowledge faded." Seeing as how both of them are now spellbound, he opens up his scribbled notes and continues. "OK, the first couple of sentences, she's looking out of the window of a place. I think it's a building that she calls Avalon, commenting about how beautiful the view is. Several times I saw the term Barac Navaar in reference to her family and friends. I'm not sure if it's an ethnic group or a nationality, but it's important, very important to her. Further down, she talks about her training with her aunt, Iset, and her sisters Bast and Athena. She vents about how tough they are on her and how sore she is from the workout the day before."

"What kind of training?" asks B.J.

"Hold that thought," David replies. "Here, Semi talks about how much pressure she feels not to fail, something she mentioned to me at the diner as well. Although at the time, I thought it was more typical teen stuff she was referring to. Anyway, in the journal, Semi says she has to do her part in serving in the Nistarim and prepare to one day join with Sothis and become a bright light in the eternal war. She's supposed to become a soldier, a hero, like the rest of her family. She says that on mornings like this one, she doubts that she'll ever be up to it. There's more general stuff, and then I couldn't translate anymore."

"Wow!" B.J. exclaims.

"That's some freaky stuff," says Edie, in a voice that sounds like the love child of excitement and extreme trepidation.

"Yeah," David agrees, "especially the part about Semi getting ready to be a soldier in this Nistarim thing, actually fighting in some kind of secret war. I did some research, and all the names are from mythology. Semi's name, Amesemi, was the name of a Nubian goddess, and Iset is an ancient pronunciation of the name of the Egyptian goddess, Isis. Bast was also an Egyptian goddess, and Athena, of course, was the Greek goddess of war. Sothis is the Greek pronunciation of the Egyptian goddess Sopdet, who was Sirius's personification, the brightest star in the night sky. In mythology, she's linked with Iset. But the one I found most interesting was the term Nistarim. It's a Hebrew term from Jewish folktales, and it's spooky. Let me just read exactly what I found online. It says:

'The Lamed-Vav Tzaddikim are also called the Nistarim, the concealed ones. In Jewish folk tales, they emerge from their deliberate concealment in times of distress. By their mystic powers, they succeed in averting the threatened disasters of people persecuted by the enemies that surround them. They return to their anonymity as soon as their task is accomplished, concealing themselves once again.'

"The concealed ones—now, tell me that isn't creepy. OK, I've been trying to piece it together, and what I've got so far is ..."

"It's aliens, obviously," B.J. interrupts. "This proves it. No offense, but there are a lot of reputable scholars who theorize that aliens founded the pyramids and the ancient Egyptian and Sumerian civilizations. They believe that the gods and goddesses of myth, including the myths that form the basis of the Judeo-Christian faith and the myths about angels and demons, are all based on ancient man's attempts to make sense of an advanced race and their superior technology. This all totally fits. Maybe there are two sects, one group trying to hurt humankind and the other trying to help. That must be the war she's talking about. I bet ..."

"Slow down, Sherlock," David replies. "We both saw that program too. Look, we can come up with theories all day. All this proves for sure is that something or someone is reaching out to me, to all of us. B.J., those shadowy things you saw...I saw that the day of the alleged super storm, red eyes and everything. Actually, I'm not exactly sure what I saw, but I distinctly remember the darkness. I couldn't breathe. I thought I was dying—dead. Then I—we—woke up in the truck. And the lights or light beings you saw Edie, I've seen them too in my dre ... no visions. They're definitely visions.

"This ability I received to translate this language came from some-where, and it came to me for a reason. I think that's true for all of us. There is purpose guiding all that we've been seeing. The only way we are ever going to get some answers is to trace all this to its source."

Edie leans in, looking David straight in the eye. "And that doesn't scare you?"

"No, Edie, it doesn't. What scares me is not knowing. What terrifies me is never seeing Semi again."

B.J. and Edie are now staring blankly; five beats pass before either of them speaks. B.J. is now rocking back and forth. His arms are folded in front of him and he's clutching his chest. Edie gives her head a shake.

"OK, lil' bro, so do you have a plan?"

"My gut says to go to Penfield. Go to the camp. It's not scientific. It's just a feeling in my bones, but I know we'll find our answers there. We're out of school for the next couple of weeks, and my family is going to Atlanta for a few days. It's only an hour and a half from the camp. I'm thinking of sneaking away for a little while and..."

"No," B.J. interrupts emphatically. "Definitely not."

"What?" says Edie, waving her hands and scowling, her frustration on the verge of becoming the full-blown wrath of Edie. "Will you stop interrupting? You haven't even heard him out."

"I don't need to, Edie," he answers. "This is obviously a don't go in the woods moment."

"A what?" David asks.

"You know, like in horror movies. There's always a group of teens, and one of them hears a noise in the woods. One idiot always says, 'Hey, let's go check it out,' and of course, being a horror movie—and everyone is stupid in horror movies—they agree. The audience is screaming, 'Don't go in the woods,' but of course, they can't hear us, they go in, and bad stuff happens."

"Your point?"

"My point," B.J. continues, "is that this is our get out of the woods moment. Look, I've got my theories, but I'm all talk. Whatever is going on scares me to death. We should be trying to figure out how to run as far away from it as possible, not toward it. This is not the time to be a hero. Whoever Semi is, whatever she is, she's trouble. All of this is trouble."

David crosses his arms confidently and cocks his head to the side. He leans forward and gestures forcefully as he speaks. "Run away? How would you go about doing that? Can we tell someone and get help? No, we'd be putting them in danger, not to mention we'd all be locked up in the funny house. So, we can run, run where? What direction is away? These shadows and lights are following us, remember? Like it or not, the way out is through."

All three of them are silent, letting the truth of his words sink in. They know he's right. Maybe they're scared that he's not *more* scared, but David's clearly right. They're going to have to swallow the red pill and jump into the rabbit hole, like it or not. This time, B.J. is the one to break the silence.

"Well," he chuckles, "if we are going to go into the woods, I've got to warn you. You know the black guy is the guy who always dies first."

"Really," David says, shaking his head, "you're going there?"

"Hey, don't get upset with me," he answers. "You've seen the same movies I've seen. The black guy barely makes it past the opening credits. Now, me, the nerdy comic relief, I make it at least to the closing act."

"Yeah, well, if that's the case," Edie adds, "the beautiful, fearless female lead normally makes it to the end. Sorry about that, guys, no hard feelings."

They all laugh, and as they continue to crack jokes, David feels the obvious tension over their situation deescalate.

"Well, to quote a great man," David answers, smiling cockily, "'never tell me the odds.'"

"Ah, the words of Hans Solo, Wisdom for all occasions." B.J. is now forcing a smile, but his eyes belie his true feelings. He's afraid.

Turning serious, Edie says, "David, if you let me know when you're planning to go to Penfield, I can probably get away and meet you there. B.J., if you want to come too, I..."

She's interrupted by a scrawny kid in a Paris Park High t-shirt, tapping on David's shoulder. He looks to be an undersized freshman, with strawberry blonde hair, freckles, and a pitiful lost puppy expression.

"Excuse me," he says, in the most country accent possible. "I'm sorry to interrupt, but are you David Stone? The one they call D-Rock?"

David is genuinely surprised. It's been a while since he was recognized in public and even longer since it was a good thing.

"Yes."

"It's great to meet you, sir," the kid replies. "My name is Jacob Simms. I'm a freshman at Paris Park. My uncle Henry says nothing but good things about you. Says that not only were you the best player he's ever coached but the best person too."

"That's awfully nice of him. Hold up—Simms? Your uncle is Coach Simms. He was our offensive coordinator, the best coach I ever had. How's he doing? I bet all this losing must be hard on him."

"Well, he ain't at Paris Park no more," he answers. "He and Coach Patton had a fallin' out over how Coach Patton treated you when you stopped playing, so my uncle left. It worked out, though. South Hoover High picked him up. They were so impressed with the work he did wit' you."

"Wow, that's a step up. South Hoover is the best team in the state, a perennial powerhouse. I'm happy for him."

"I don't mean to impose," says Jacob. "But do you guys mind if I sit here wit' you for a bit? I was supposed to meet a date, but he's not here. I feel like an idiot sitting here by myself."

"No problem," Edie and David say in unison.

They exchange introductions and chitchat for a minute. Jacob can't help but pepper David with questions. His playing career isn't his favorite topic, but for the kid's sake, he's trying to be patient.

"I'm sorry for all these questions," Jacob says for the umpteenth time. "It's just that I've heard so much about you. My uncle says that you wuz the best Alabama prospect since Bo Jackson and rated the top quarterback in your recruiting class. Is it really true that you wuz faster than Deion Sanders and that you could fling a ball through the uprights from eighty yards from your knees?"

"I was fast, and I could throw it pretty far," David chuckles, "but I think news of my 'greatness' has been a little bit exaggerated."

"Yeah, I second that," a voice, Cliff Wiggins' voice, says. "You were definitely overrated."

David was so preoccupied with his diminutive fanboy that he didn't notice Cliff and his goons come into the food court. It turns out that they decided not to leave the mall after all. Well, David's not worried. He's got this. He's eager to prove that he can be calm, cool, and mature. No firefighter eyes today.

"How are you doing, Cliff?" David asks without looking up.

Cliff is a 6′ 3″, broad-shouldered, cocky brunette, with a square jaw and insincere eyes. He stands over them, trying too hard to look intimidating, drawing fake courage from the four, very wide linemen, ranging from 6′ 3″ to 6″5″, creating a wall behind him. He edges a little closer to them, standing to David's right, between him and Jacob, doing his best to try to instigate David into making the first move.

"Hard to believe the 'legendary' D-Rock ran off and ditched us for the Alabama Academy of Fine Arts. So, Stone, how are you enjoying your school of freaks and fairies?"

"It's cool."

"And how's your dad?" Cliff quips, eliciting chuckles from his four backup singers.

"I don't know, Cliff," he replies with a smirk, "How're your ribs?"

Cliff mumbles an inaudible response, obviously irritated. You see, Cliff should have read the rule that says never to trade wisecracks with someone from the Bronx, although David's sure that Edie would probably counter that he should have read the rule above it. Never tick off someone who has a group of Neanderthals as his bodyguards. Well, David doesn't scare easily, and he is genuinely determined not to be sucked into Cliff's game.

It's not lost on him that Jacob's right leg is shaking nonstop during all of this, and poor B.J. seems to have shrunken to half his size and lost what little color he had in his face. There's no reason for them to be nervous. Cliff's been a bully for as long as David's known him, and David's been handling him since middle school. When Cliff's not hopped up on liquid courage, he's full of hot air.

Seeing that David's not rattled, Cliff's attention turns to Jacob.

"Hey, Simms, I barely noticed you there," he says. "Haven't seen you much since you quit the team, something you and your new buddy have in common. That's cool."

"Hey, Cliff," he answers, shrinking into his chair.

Something about Jacob seems to give Cliff a new idea about how to antagonize David.

"Hey, Stone," he says with a mischievous grin. "I didn't know you and Simms knew each other. You know he's queer, right? Isn't that right, Simms?" he asks, rubbing Jacob's head. "You know, I heard you left your D-Rock ways behind, Stone. Word on the street is that you've become some kind of soft, uptight, promise ring toting choirboy. Your type doesn't associate with queers and such. You're not thinking about switching teams, are you?"

"Well, here's the thing about all that, Cliff," David answers, putting his hand on Jacob's shoulder. "If done correctly, you love everyone—even you."

"OK," Cliff replies, and as he does, he grabs the hamburger off of Jacob's tray. "Man, that looks good. Thanks, Jacob." He picks up the tray and passes it to his friends, saying, "You guys want some fries. They look very tasty."

Oh no, she's got that look. Edie has had more than enough. She's halfway to her feet to give Cliff a piece of her mind when, thankfully, B.J. pulls on her pants, trying to hold her down. OK, she got the hint; that was a close call. The last problem David needs is for her to escalate this by getting in Cliff's face. She lowers her steely gaze, digs her nails into the table, and forces herself to stay seated. Good.

It's fine. David's not flustered; nothing is going to move him today. He can tell from their faces that Edie and B.J. are confused about whether this is the new and improved Zen David or if he's being sociopath cool. Should they be impressed or terrified? Well, they're worrying over nothing. He's got this.

Hey, Jacob," David asks, "do you like Rudy Ray's?" When Jacob nods his head affirmatively, David continues, "Cool. There's one in the front of the mall. Why don't we go there, my treat?"

"Thanks, David," Jacob says.

"Well, it's been fun, Cliff, but we have to go," David says as he rises out of his seat.

He's more than a little pleased with himself. He glances over and sees that Edie's impressed; stunned but impressed. She has her, "Who is this guy, and what has he done with my brother?" face. David gets it. Sometimes he even surprises himself. Incredible self-control, no fire-fighter eyes, he's become Dr. King 2.0, man of peace. They stand up and start to leave when David gets a glimpse of Cliff's eyes and realizes that he's not about to let this go. This isn't over.

"Cool." Smugness is radiating from Cliff like cheap cologne. "See you around." The next few seconds play out in slow motion. David can see what's about to happen. Cliff does his best *Glee* imitation and throws the soda all over Jacob. "Don't forget your drink, Simms." The jerk and his friends are laughing, and something happens. David knows it's not good, but he can't help himself.

David pivots toward them, all five players, clenching his massive fists as he pulls Jacob behind him. All the cool is out of him now, as is his ability to do simple math. This is insane; even he knows this isn't going to end well.

And just like Edie said he would, David rushes into the fire. His mind goes completely blank, and he just springs forward. Time freezes, and his head starts throbbing, followed by queasiness and a sudden burst of energy. Every muscle, every fiber, is electric, a quickening throughout every cell. The whole world begins to move forward at a crawl, but not him; this time, he's moving lightning fast. And there is an awakening of his senses and perhaps the birth of new ones. He can see everything, the stuff in front of him, the stuff behind him, multiple angles at the same time. He can even feel what others are feeling. It's crazy. Even while David is fighting five goons, he's aware of all that is going on with his friends, like he's starring in a movie, watching the movie, and watching a separate movie about Edie and B.J. at the same time.

He witnesses B.J. frozen in terror, Jacob crouching behind him, and in typical fearless female-lead fashion, Edie grabbing a chair to help him out. He sees her attention suddenly drawn to B.J.'s yelling and pointing at something next to her on the table. The bag that her new earrings are in is glowing, and her silver earrings, now engulfed in yellow fire, are slowly levitating out of it. Edie barely raises an eyebrow. She ignores her flying accessories and stands her ground, chair in hand, ready to help her big little brother.

But before anyone can react, David engages Cliff and his friends. Block, kick, punch, elbow, flip, another kick, David maneuvers so swiftly that he's become like a comic book blur. He's moving fast, too fast for anyone's eyes to follow, and the fight, if you want to call it that, is over in seconds. David is standing in the middle of the food court, and Cliff and his boy band are sprawled out on the floor around him, bruised and moaning.

David feels light, weightless even. He looks around, and he's floating above them all like an invisible specter. Well, he is, and he's not. He looks down and sees himself, his friends, the whole food court, but he's floating outside of his body at the same time. Bystanders panic, scrambling in a delayed response. The fight started and finished before they could react, but they're reacting now, reacting like a bomb just went off in their midst and pointing at him as if he's the bomber. David's alarmed, way past alarmed, but his heart doesn't race, he doesn't clench up, and there's no other physiological response because he can't feel his ghost body at all. Instead, he's still somewhat connected to the sensations of his physical form and maybe several others. He doesn't know what he's feeling or why. And he has absolutely no idea what just happened.

Down below, he's expressionless, frozen in place, mesmerized by his hands that are burning with golden flame, just like Edie's gravity-defying earrings. His three friends are staring. They appear to be in shock.

That's why people are scattering.

Suddenly, the earrings stop floating, fall onto the table, and stop burning. Edie picks them up, and she's surprised that they're cool to the touch, almost soothing. He shouldn't know that, but it feels to David like he's touching the earrings along with her—so weird.

He looks back at his body, and he's standing there, glassy-eyed, as if in a trance.

Why can't I move? How can I be in two places at the same time? Edie, B.J., can you see me?

The flames fade and David staggers forward, reaching in the air as if he's trying to clutch an imaginary object. Edie runs over to him and grabs David by the arm, but his eyes are completely glazed over. He doesn't seem to see her or anyone else. He just keeps reaching for the invisible objects around him.

"David, bro, we've got to go," Edie urges. "Security is coming. Let's go."

She can't budge him. Suddenly, he turns and looks straight at her. His brown eyes are flecked with fiery gold. With great effort, he finally opens his mouth to speak.

"They are among us."

David watches this from above and is as confused as Edie. But there's no time to analyze. His physical body collapses onto the floor, right in front of her. There is no movement; he doesn't even seem to be breathing. David looks down on it all in disbelief.

Get up! Why am I not getting up?

Once more, the world seems to slow down, David's eyes lingering on every image. Edie is staring helplessly at her brother, B.J. is screaming, and David's silent terror grows exponentially with each passing second. His ethereal hands begin to tingle, and he glances at them. His ghost form is dissipating. Everything is becoming blurry, color changing to black and white and then shades of gray. Like it or not, he's in the woods now, definitely deep into the woods.

CENTRAL PARK—DAVID

"We are the Barac Navaar," she whispers. "And you are home."

David's in the dream again, a variation of the one he's seen for weeks, and this is the way it typically begins. Is he asleep? No, this can't be right. He was in the mall, wasn't he? Something seems off, different. He begins to panic, but David hears her voice again. Like a lullaby moving through him, it keeps him grounded. It is always his constant compass amid the radically changing encounters with the strange new universe of his dreamscape. She is his anchor, his lifeline, calling to him, embracing his soul, refusing to let him go until her journey with him is complete. He likes to pretend that she needs him, but in his heart, he knows that he receives more than he could hope to give. Everything changes, but she is always here, his siren, his passion, his protector, and try as he might, he simply cannot walk away from his muse.

At the moment, shadows are dancing in the corners of his mind, alive in the misty haven for undiscovered thoughts, their red eyes piercing holes in the fabric of his awareness, moving closer, threatening to consume him. Then, light appears again, and the darkness dissipates, not slowly but retreating with a snap into an unknown fissure his mind is unable to penetrate. Beautiful luminescence shines, radiant like a thousand brilliant crystals in the throne room of God, and all is good, all is peace. Then, in the midst of this tranquility, a Dark Star rises, its obsidian splendor engulfing the sun-like brilliance. The Dark Star grows, but as suddenly as it appears, it falls, fracturing the earth, shaking the land, and throwing up billows of red smoke. Through the crimson mist arrives a man, but not just any man. He is one David's seen in these visions many times before. He is a man on fire, burning with golden flames and brandishing a scorching katana. He is magnificent and fearsome, moving toward David with determination and purpose, and David cannot sense if he is friend or foe.

Before David is forced to find out, a wall of light forms, quivering between them. As he admires it, the air before him splits as if an ethereal blade has sliced it open, and from this new rift, a door to the lost world emerges. Like so many nights before, David turns to walk away, knowing that no good can come from going further, but he hears her call to him softly. "You are meant for so much more. Come and see your destiny." He is compelled to obey. He steps through, and once more, an alien world opens before him.

He travels through the mysterious world, entering a palace, magnificent and seemingly ancient, with markings and architecture that seem dynastic Egyptian. But there are anachronisms, too many things that do not belong in Egyptian times. He can see that some structures appear much older and others much more advanced. But all of it is a wonder to behold. He surveys the palace and his surroundings. There are beasts, humanoid hybrids, and technology that appear to have been ripped out of a book of fantasy. In his world, they would never exist without the help of a green screen and a sound stage. But it all feels real, so real, and it feels right, like he's experiencing a moment of history rather than a vision from a distant world or a creation of his overactive imagination. It all fits.

He's seen this structure before in earlier journeys, but it has never been quite like this. War has broken out, and its unique madness has consumed the palace. There are people— soldiers, both men and women, scurrying along, preparing for battle. They put on sparse pieces of armor that expand once placed on their bodies until they are entirely covered in "living" metal. Once on, the armor glows, bathing these soldiers in a field of energy. They carry swords and spears made entirely of silver. The warriors glimmer, but their weapons become living fire, golden, azure, and crimson. A few possess what can best be described as a type of futuristic gun.

How can there be space-age guns in ancient Egypt?

But they're here, and it seems right. The combatants look less like men and women and more like the gods and goddesses of myth, come alive from Homer's pages—too muscular, too powerful, too beautiful, too horrifying to be human. Everything is moving fast, too fast for the human eye to follow, but David follows.

Her voice has opened his eyes. He sees everything with a sort of hyper-vision.

He's overwhelmed by the noises caused by the troop movement. Over the clanging of metal, the soldiers shout commands and encouragement in a strange, singsong tongue. It is a language that has probably been extinct for thousands of years, but he understands it, and he knows, if pressed, he can speak it.

Though the palace has been consumed by war, amidst the frenzy, in the center of the main room, she emerges, Amesemi, the living voice. Like so many times before, all movement stops, and silence overtakes the madness; an unspoken obedience; reverence for the creature who has taken center stage and...Something's wrong.

"Wake up!" She yells, turning suddenly and staring straight at him, the power of her voice shaking the earth, the palace, and everyone in it.

The images around her freeze for a second and then begin to shake, some slowly dissipating. The ones that remain turn blood red and then explode into crimson fire.

"David, wake up!" she screams again.

Everything disappears, no Semi, no light, no voice, then there is the sound of rushing wind and a barrage of psychedelic colors. David closes his eyes tightly, resisting the dizzying onslaught. After several seconds, his ears hear evidence of familiar surroundings, and he feels the ground become solid beneath his feet.

Before he opens his eyes, he knows where he is. It's not the icy chill in the air or the sounds of the city that give it away; it's the smell, the wonderfully horrible combination of pizza, bagels, and subway rats that can only belong to one place—New York City. David is home.

He's standing on a sidewalk in Manhattan, across from Central Park. It's nighttime, and from the relative inactivity on the streets, it's pretty late, three, maybe four in the morning. The last thing he remembers, he was in the South Hoover Galleria, getting into a fight with Cliff Wiggins and some linemen. There's no way he can be here, at least under normal circumstances, but nothing is normal these days. He thinks this might be another version of his vivid dreams, a vivid dream with a twist. So far, there's nothing fantastical about it. The asphalt, the potholes, yellow cabs, and the city trash cans overflowing with evidence of the previous day—he knows New York. And this place is gritty and raw, and every aspect screams at him: *this* is the real world.

Every detail of this place rings true. A chill wind is blowing and he's freezing his tail off. He has on the same jacket and hoodie he was wearing at the mall. You can get away with that during December in Birmingham but not New York.

He's trying to stay calm and keep his head clear, but despite the cold, his palms are sweaty, and he feels each heartbeat pulsating in his brain. David's petrified to his core, even more than he was a month ago. He wonders if he lost time again and pulls out his smartphone. It's dead, no juice; of course, it is. And that means no contact—with Edie, B.J. and the rest of the world.

Oh, man, this is not happening!

David hears what sounds like a woman's voice coming from the park, crying for help. He tries to ignore it; it's probably his imagination. All of this is, right?

Just keep walking, David.

He's lived down south too long. If this is New York, someone is always screaming. He puts his freezing hands in his pockets, keeps his head down, and minds his business. That's the New York way. He can catch the one train to his aunt's house and figure it out from there.

But the screams continue. She seems terrified, and the screams are getting louder and more desperate. David picks up his pace and starts walking toward the park entrance. He doesn't see where he has a choice. It's not in him to ignore someone in trouble. He will never be able to live with himself if he doesn't try to help. His brisk walk has now become a dead sprint in her direction. He's been running for a while, and the distance between what he thought he heard and how long he'd been running doesn't fit. David's now fairly deep into the park, off of the lighted main paths, with the clouds and the trees obscuring the moonlight. It's already dark and getting darker. He's been following the sound of her voice and he hasn't heard the cries for a couple of seconds. But somehow, he still knows where he's going. He turns onto the next path, and his heart stops at the image in front of him. Nothing in his life has prepared him for this.

A blonde-haired woman in her twenties is sitting on the asphalt, petrified, mouthing a cry that refuses to come out. Around her are the remains of what looks like a young man who has been torn to shreds. About fifty feet behind her, a man dressed in black is fighting off five or six animals. He's wielding what appears to be a glowing, yellow sword of light, but the animals are too large and powerful to go down without a struggle. They're not dogs; they're too massive to be anything you'd find outside of a zoo. They are standing upright and wearing shredded clothing. Whatever they are, they are predators, hunting as a pack, communicating with grunts and howls that sound more like a sophisticated language than any sound you'd hear on the Discovery Channel.

A hulking guy with flowing, blonde hair emerges from the shadows, joining the fray, swinging a fiery red scimitar at the warrior in black. Why would the newcomer be fighting on the side of the beasts that have just torn someone apart? What kind of creatures are these? Again, he remembers his first encounter with the dark, during the "big storm", and he senses that presence here, oozing out of the new arrival. He thinks this Mr. Red Blade slashes or injures the man in black in some way, momentarily giving Mr. Red and the creatures the upper hand. It is all happening fast, too fast, but somehow David's following along. It's all both foreign and familiar, like his dreams but darker, scarier, and hopped up on steroids. But each morning he wakes up from his visions. One glance over at the woman's pale face and the shredded body and he knows the truth. There is no waking up from this living, breathing nightmare. Whatever this is, it's real, and if he does not wrap his head around that fact and act quickly, he will stop being a spectator and become a victim.

Then, David hears something, a whisper, faint but near, telling him to run away. He tunes it out. He has to do something to help. He takes a couple of quick steps forward and reaches out for the woman, grabbing her hand and pulling her up. He moves her behind him, hoping that somehow he can get her to safety, but one of the creatures breaks away from the struggle and heads toward them. Before it can pounce, the man in black cuts the fiend down, saving their lives, buying them time. Their hero turns to chase off the rest of the beasts, but they run off as though through a portal, into nothingness, and his blonde-haired adversary disappears into the darkness.

David turns to console the woman, and for the first time realizes that there's something vaguely familiar about her.

"What's your name?" David asks.

"Tricia," she whispers trembling, "Tricia Morningstar."

"It's over, Tricia. You're going to be OK. We're safe."

Suddenly, there is the smell of burning flesh and a sharp pain that slices through David's back and then his stomach. The blazing scarlet sword stabs straight through him. He clutches his wound and collapses to the ground. All light fades, instantly replaced by darkness, only darkness.

David is fighting to keep his eyes open and remain conscious. He sees shadows move against the backdrop of the night, silhouetted by the spotlight provided by the moon. He squints, trying to focus, and sees them dancing, swaying to the fading downbeat of his heart, bobbing to his wheezing as he gasps for air. The shadows are gyrating frenetically, feeling the syncopated rhythm of David's agony, feeding off his burning pain. He's sweating profusely and the odor of charred flesh from his gut is overwhelming. David's muscles spasm. His heart is beating furiously, losing its battle. Inside he screams, but he does not hear the sound of his own voice. His perception of time has become distorted, and he has no idea how long he's been lying on a path in the heart of Central Park, fighting for his life. He can't believe this is really how his life ends.

Please, God, let this be a dream after all, a terrible nightmare. All I need to do is wake up. Wake up!

Unfortunately, he knows better. His hands are folded across his stomach, over his wound, and they feel warm when they should feel cold in death. They are glowing. David's senses are distorted and he isn't sure of what he's seeing, feeling.

The woman is screaming again and the police and paramedics are arriving on the scene. He hears sirens and voices all around him, but they are faint. They may be standing right next to him, but they seem as far away as distant thunder.

But there are other voices, and they are loud and clear. They belong to the shadows. "You are going to die here," they say. "You are a fool, like your father, trying to be a hero—a dead fool." They laugh and flutter about him. "Chosen one," they scoff. "Chosen for nothing but death." They are dancing in the darkness and staring out of the bushes with the same menacing red eyes he remembers, the same eyes B.J. described, waiting in expectation for his end to come.

My name is David Stone, and I'm only eighteen, and I'm about to die.

Now, there is no pain. He no longer feels his body at all. He feels nothing; hears nothing, not even his own heart. It's like he's slowly drifting away. They say that when you die, you see a tunnel of light, but they are wrong. Now, David knows better. He knows that when you die, the shadows dance, and when they're finished, everything fades to black, and then there is nothing, nothing at all.

Darkness. Until recently, David never knew that darkness could be alive, that it could breathe, move, and speak, that it could be so beautiful and yet so completely terrifying. He's enveloped in a thick ebony fog that appears endless and simultaneously confining, even suffocating. The blackness whispers to him in the silence and then raises its voice, shouting at him, overwhelming his senses. His mind shuts down and David is numb, like someone poisoned with hemlock—able to see and hear but unable to move. He is empty, alone. He is dead. But death didn't come as advertised. He had gone to church and Sunday school his whole life, but he doesn't remember the chapter covering this. This can't be heaven, can it? It's peaceful and still, but there is nothing, no activity, no sign of anything, no sign of his father, or his grandparents, only empty space and silence.

Of course, there may be a really simple reason why they're not around. As horrifying as it is to consider, maybe he just doesn't deserve to see the pearly gates. Maybe his past has caught up to him. He got through his birthday pretty much unscathed, caught up in the Semi drama, but that's his trick. He stays super busy with positive activity, other people's problems, all sorts of stuff, never slowing down long enough for his inner demons to grab him. The truth is David doesn't need an anniversary to remind him who he is. He carries it around every day. If he's honest, he hasn't had a moment of peace since the day his father died. Why should he? David is the reason his dad is dead.

So, if this is his life after death, just him, the darkness, and his thoughts, how long will it be before he cracks? His guilt is always bubbling under the surface, threatening to drown him the way it did before. He took his family and more than a few people down with him before he finally found his way back, but even on a good day, his footing is precarious at best. He's always guilty, so guilty. David knows what he did; his dad knows it too. All the good deeds that David's done these last few months, all the good deeds that he might ever do, will never be enough to wash that stain away. The wrong person got buried a year ago. Anyone who was paying attention knows that. Even if David lives to be a hundred, he will never be able to outrun that truth, so if this is the end, well, that's OK. Standing in the darkness alone is a terrible thing, but it's still more than he deserves. Maybe this is justice.

He hopes he's wrong, though. He prays that the preachers were right, and all their talk of grace and forgiveness is true. He could really use some of that grace right now. Who knows, this might not be his final destination. Maybe he's in a lobby, some kind of cosmic waiting area.

Suddenly, in the distance, he sees a lone light. David rushes toward it, hoping to find some answers.

It's like a spotlight, and as he approaches, he sees a body lying in the center on a slab, dressed in a white robe. It's the body of a young man about his age. No, it's him; the body is David's. With that recognition, suddenly everything changes. Now, he's no longer outside of it looking down but inside the body, fighting to get out. He comes to the horrific realization that his body is his inescapable tomb, and the dark empty space is what lives inside him. If David could move his mouth to speak, he would cry out with all his might, but even if he could, who is here to hear him?

At this moment of despair, his silence is interrupted by something far more powerful than a scream. He hears a hushed tone, soft and warm—her voice, gently calling to him.

"David, my David, it's time to wake up."

"I can't. I'm dead."

"No, not dead, my David, never dead, not now, not while hope lives. When it is time to take the great sleep, you will lie in my arms or I in yours. You were merely in a memory, drifting in the memory of another, like a lone leaf in an endless sea, but that past cannot take you where you need to go tonight, not yet. Open your eyes, my David, my chosen. Now is not your time to sleep, child of Adam. Now is your time to rise."

The sweetness of her aroma—the smell of freshly picked jasmine with a hint rose petals—fills the room and gives David strength. Her delicate hands caress his cheek tenderly. Slowly, his eyes begin to open, and as they do, they are blessed to gaze upon her transcendent beauty. She smiles, and a warm glow radiates throughout him, energizing every cell, bringing him to life. He looks into her eyes, filled with love and framed by her flawless mocha skin. He watches as they change colors from ebony to hazel, to blue, to green, to perfect orbs of incandescent gold.

"Hello, my chosen." She uses those words again, in a voice that is less speech than it is melody. It speaks straight to his heart and his soul hears.

"Hello, my love," he answers. "Semi, is that you?"

"We are your future," she answers. "We are Semi, and we are more."

"What is your name?" he asks.

She takes his hand and gingerly runs it through her hair.

"You know our name, my love."

David smiles and says, "Isis. Your name is Isis."

He sits up and they lean toward each other for a romantic kiss, but as their lips touch, she begins to fade away.

"You made a promise. Come find us, my love," she calls out as she vanishes. "Only you can make us possible. Come find us."

"I will," he answers, with all that is in him.

As she fades, the light slowly dims until there is only one speck of light in the darkness, and then it is gone, and there is nothing, nothing at all. All that remains is the scent of jasmine and knowledge burning in David's soul, filling every part of his being. He made a vow in love, and he will not rest until it is fulfilled.

Salioth Algo Daymon. In this life or the next.

THE OTHER —EDIE

I'm worn out. I've cried and I've prayed, and I've cried some more. I don't know what else to do. This is so freaking crazy.

Edie's eyes have finally stopped raining, but they're red and still raw from the near-constant parade of tears. She should be stronger. She's spent far too much of her young life in hospital rooms, praying desperately for people that she loves, but she never imagined that David would be added to the list. Reckless as he is, he's never had a broken bone, rarely caught a cold, and even during his wild D-Rock prime, he never missed a snap, no matter how irresponsible his behavior was off the field. But now, here he is, unmoving, undiagnosed, and his future very much undetermined.

David get up. Please, get up!

She keeps expecting him to pop up miraculously, good as new, but it was 5:30 when he fell out at the mall. It's 9 at night now, and David still hasn't moved. Three and a half hours. To Edie, it feels like an eternity.

David is in some kind of catatonic state, but there's no word on why, and they can't say how long it may last. They just don't know. Mama Stone, B.J., and Edie are waiting in his room at Parkwood Hospital, watching over him. There's talk that he may have been injured in the fight. But they were there. David wasn't touched! The doctors don't know what Edie and B.J. know, didn't see what they saw, superhuman speed and strength, glowing hands, levitating earrings. She's sure that David's condition is tied to that paranormal event, and all of it must be linked to everything that they've been experiencing over the last four weeks.

So how can this information be used to help David? Edie has no clue about what to do, no plan A, B, or C. Knowing about all that, witnessing it, doesn't make any of this better.

It's not going to open his eyes or get David out of this bed.

The best Edie can hope for is that the paranormal things will make another move soon.

There's the light, the glow—it seems to be positive. I need to figure out how to get that light to help me—to help David.

She glances over at B.J. Between the weirdness at the mall and his genuine distaste for being in hospitals, he's a nervous wreck. He's been on his phone relentlessly looking for chatter about what happened. Surprisingly, there's been nothing but a Facebook post by Cliff saying that he's been in another car accident—the same story he told last time he crossed paths with David. B.J is trying to find a video featuring David's Iron Fist imitation. He's thinking it should be all over the Internet by now, but there's not one clip. B.J. is freaking out about that along with everything else, but Edie can't afford the luxury of losing her head. She's always been the mama of their little group, and because of her aunt and mom, spending time in hospital rooms is nothing new.

The same single rooms, nothing's changed. All cookie-cutter: cramped, florescent lighting, white walls, cheap curtains, a whiteboard on the wall for the nurses, a small half bathroom, and a feeling of gloom and sadness that seems to permeate the walls. Edie doesn't have the answers, and she knows the doctors don't either. She and Mama Stone are sitting next to David. They've been praying nonstop. B.J. is staring at them as if they're wasting their time. They need a freaking miracle, and Edie doesn't intend to stop until the heavens open up and make her lil' bro well.

Mama Stone steps out to try to grab a doctor for an update. Edie picks up her smartphone to update her parents and buries her nose in texting. B.J. shocks her from her focus.

"David, it's David!" He's screaming and pointing.

Edie looks first at B.J and registers the shock in his eyes, almost simultaneously seeing David sitting up in the bed, eyes wide open, pulling his IV out of his arm.

"David!" she says excitedly. She grabs his arm. "Lie back down. Let's get the doctor ..."

She got her miracle. Edie's heart is leaping, filled with so much joy she'd be giggling if she weren't so concerned about her newly awakened brother hurting himself. He casts her arm away and springs out of bed.

"I can't be here," he mumbles. "Where are my clothes?"

Something's not right. Is he in shock?

With a grunt, she uses her legs, both hands and every ounce of strength in her body as she tries to maneuver him back to the bed, but pushing his body is like pushing a wall.

"B.J.!" she calls out. "Go get some hospital staff. Tell them we need help."

"No," David utters, commandingly as he gestures in B.J.'s direction.

"I can't move!" cries B.J., his eyes popping out of his sockets. "He's doing it. He won't let me move."

B.J. is struggling to get up, as if some sumo wrestler is sitting on him and another is holding down his arms.

"I can't move!" he screams louder.

"No," David says again, once more gesturing in B.J.'s direction.

Now, B.J. is mouthing words and no sound is coming out, and as much as Edie would love the ability to switch off his mouth upon command, seeing it actually happen is horrifying, even by their new standards for tolerating the unexplained and unimaginable. She freezes, gasping for air, on the verge of hyperventilating, stifling a scream of her own out of sheer willpower fueled by her desire for self-preservation.

"David...what are you doing?"

"My clothes, Eden Grace...now," David commands. "And I need to borrow your silver earrings as well."

She is stunned by the coldness in his voice and his expressionless face, but seeing no alternative, she reluctantly hands him his clothes and her shiny, beautiful, creepy earrings. Her hands are trembling, despite her best efforts to stay calm.

"You may look away, now," he states, with the tone of royalty directing a servant.

She quickly looks away for a variety of reasons. Yes, it's the appropriate thing, but part of her expects an alien to spring out of her brother's stomach at any moment, and she'd rather not see that. This much is clear, the voice is David's, but the cadence and the tone are all wrong. It's his body, but the movement is off; it's regal, elegant, perfect posture as if he grew up carrying books on his head. He has the presence of a king or a great military commander, not like himself at all.

"We need to go," he orders. "Eden Grace Garcia, Brantley James Scott, follow me."

Not seeing much choice, his friends grab their stuff and his and follow him. There's got to be a way out of this, but right now, Edie can't think of one. Besides, if David's still in there somewhere, he needs them. Maybe they can help him resurface.

Although B.J. can move again, he still can't talk, but that doesn't stop him from trying nonstop. When they get to the corridor, David walks over to the attending nurse, grabs her hand, and whispers something into her ear. Her eyes seem to glow momentarily, and then she walks past them as if they're not there. In fact, that's true for everyone they pass in the hospital. The staff are unable to see or hear any of them, even though Edie and B.J. are desperately trying to get their attention. Eventually, they bump into Mama Stone, Edie's mom, and Dr. Matthews, David's doctor. Edie and B.J. wave and stomp, trying to get them to notice, but the three friends remain invisible.

David waves his hand in front of Dr. Matthews and then places it on his shoulder, saying, "Dr. Matthews, David Stone was never here tonight. You will personally supervise the deletion of all records concerning him. Anyone you touch will remember things identically to how you do now. Either you or Nurse Sanchez will personally touch all staff who interacted with him and his family. Do you understand?"

"Yes," he replies.

"Mrs. Stone, Mrs. Garcia, David is fine. He was never hurt, and he was never here. Mrs. Stone put him on a plane this afternoon to spend the weekend with her sister in New York. Your social media accounts were hacked. There never was an emergency. Go and tell your family and friends the news. Everyone you touch will remember the events the way that you do now. Do you understand?"

"I do," they reply. It's clear they are in a trance.

He turns and walks toward the hospital exit with Edie and B.J. in tow. They exit and he turns to them.

"You two are free to go. You cannot follow me where I am going. I am not allowed to alter your memories, but I do not need to impress on you the importance of keeping the truth about today's events a secret. The truth is a perilous burden in this matter and must be guarded. David will contact you when the matter is complete."

David? In the third person? Edie doesn't have time to process it because David is walking off briskly, and though she should be relieved and running toward freedom, she can't. She can't abandon David. She scurries behind him, determined to keep up. B.J. is so busy testing out his newly returned speech that he doesn't seem to notice.

David goes to the parking deck, stands in front of a random car, concentrates, and then raises his right hand. After a few seconds, a set of keys comes toward it, whizzing through the air. David catches them and unlocks the vehicle in one smooth motion. Full-blown, long-distance telekinesis, with a dash of teleportation, OK, that was cool, cool in a terrifying, this can't be happening sort of way. Edie covers her mouth, once more stopping herself from screaming at the smurfing insanity of what she's seeing. She doesn't want to do anything to startle Creepy David, so she forces herself to keep her composure and pretend that this happens every day. Fortunately, up to now, he's ignored the fact that she has tagged along. But that reality quickly changes. He turns toward her with regal annoyance. She gazes into his eyes, and despite his alien behavior, she still sees her bother. She trusts in that.

"I told you that you were free to go," he says, sternly.

"Yes," she replies, swallowing hard and balling her fists to steady her hands, "and I've decided to come with you, freely."

B.J., out of breath, has caught up with them.

"What's going on?" he asks. "Edie, I thought we were leaving."

"No," she answers. "We're going with David."

"We are?"

"Yes," she replies, adamantly fixing her eyes on David's.

"No, you are not," David answers sternly. "I will not allow you to..."

He stops mid-sentence as if he were just interrupted by a phone call that no one else can hear. He nods his head, pauses, and then turns his attention back to them.

"David says that you may come," he states, reluctantly.

"David says?" Edie asks, leaning in and locking eyes with him. "So, you're not David."

"I am not."

"S—so, who are you?" she asks. Every cell is quivering as she braces for the answer.

"I am someone else," he says, matter-of-factly.

Something about hearing it out loud has her wanting to puke.

Hold it together, Edie. You're the beautiful female lead, remember?

She grabs hold of B.J., who looks as if he's about to pass out, or worse, start screaming again. All she can do is steady B.J. and stare at this "other guy" in disbelief.

"The choice is yours," says The Other. "But I must warn you that this is a specific path full of danger." He pauses ominously, piercing them with his gaze, and like the great OZ, his voice sounds like it's coming through an electric megaphone, hollow, with a reverberation that sort of hangs on the air. He then continues. "If you choose this path, it will choose you. What will be seen cannot be unseen, and what will be done cannot be undone. Do you understand?"

"Yes," she answers.

"He wants to know if you are sure," The Other replies.

She replies with a confident smile, saying, "Tell David that I'm with you till the end of the line."

"Winter Soldier," squeaks B.J., suddenly sounding like he's reliving puberty. "Good choice."

"Does she speak for both of you?" asks The Other.

There is a long silence. Eden Grace knows that B.J. is terrified, so is she for that matter. But she also knows that B.J. will never be able to live with himself if he stays behind.

"Yes," he replies, tentatively, breaking the silence. "I'm in."

"Get in the back seat, expeditiously," The Other instructs.

She grabs B.J. by the arm, pulling him along. Once in, The Other gets in the driver's seat, starts the car, pulls out, and heads north on Hwy 31.

"Where are we going?" Edie asks.

"Georgia," he replies.

"Why?"

"Sleep now. Questions later."

Edie tries to open her mouth to ask another question, but her words become a great, big yawn. All of a sudden, neither of them can stay awake. She's fighting it, but her eyes are very heavy, and she quickly fades into the twilight where her numerous unanswered questions are grazing with the sheep inside her mind.

PENFIELD —DAVID

David's skin tingles, and his brain feels like it's vibrating inside his skull. His body responds like it's running a little off, maybe a touch fast, like a thoroughbred getting used to a different jockey. Part of him wants to say that he's still a little groggy because he just woke up, but he knows that's not entirely accurate. He was never actually asleep. He's been awake since right after his vision of Isis. He was alert at the hospital but was regulated to being a passenger in his own body. The Other has been the one driving for the last two hours. It can only be in control of David for so long before doing damage to him. It's David's turn to drive and he simply wants to get on with it.

The sooner we get where we're going, the sooner I can rescue Semi, and Jiminy Cricket can get out of my head and go back to wherever it came.

He parks at a twenty-four-hour gas station at the Tallapoosa exit off I-20. David's been here more times than he can remember during road trips with his family, and it's hard not to feel something being here now. Memories of his family packed in a minivan and his father's belly laugh fill his heart. He fights to block them out. He doesn't have room for it tonight because, for him, reliving past joy just creates breadcrumbs that lead to bitter memories of his failure, and nothing good waits for him in that gingerbread house. There's enough drama ahead of them without it. Focus, he needs to focus.

This is the first exit after you cross the Alabama/Georgia line, and if you're from Bama, a state with no lottery, it's the closest place to go if you have an itch and you feel lucky. David hopes he's lucky. He has glowing hands, an alien inside his head, and he's a black man driving a stolen car across state lines. Yes, a little bit of luck would be great.

He checks on B.J. and Edie who are still asleep in the back from the whammy that was put on them. David turns around to wake them up and see if they need anything. If all goes well, this is the last time they'll stop before Penfield.

"Edie, B.J., wake up," he calls out. "Rise and shine, guys."

When neither stirs, he pokes B.J.

"Hey, wake up. We've stopped."

"It depends," he answers, opening one eye. "Is this creepy David or the regular David?"

"The regular David," he answers.

"Good," they answer in unison, both popping up.

"How long have you two been awake?" he asks.

"I woke up fifteen minutes ago," Edie answers. "B.J. about five minutes after me. Looks like we both had the same idea—fake being asleep until we figure out which David we'd be dealing with. So, how are you feeling?"

"I feel fine."

"So, is that other guy gone?" B.J. asks.

"Not exactly. It's kind of like a timeshare thing."

"And that doesn't freak you out?" he asks. "Because, dude, it totally freaks me out."

"If I stop to think about it, absolutely. But she's helping me, and I need her help to find answers and to get to Semi."

"She?" Edie asks. "You called it she."

"I did?"

"Yeah," she says.

"Huh," replies David, furrowing his brow. "I didn't realize that I said that. I'm not sure how I know, but yeah, it's a she and—her name is Sothis."

"Like from Semi's diary?" Edie asks.

"One and the same," he answers. "Sothis needs my help, and I need hers."

B.J. raises his eyebrow skeptically. "And we should trust this weird, powerful, body stealing, alien woman because?"

"First, it's not like that. Sothis didn't hijack my body. I agreed to this, and she's not forcing me to do anything. Look, I know a lot more than before, and new information is flooding into my brain by the second. But it's still a little scrambled, OK maybe a lot scrambled, so I'm definitely not ready to explain it all. I don't understand it all yet, just pieces of a much bigger picture, but I know we have a chance to help Semi if we move fast. Time is running out. All I can tell you now is that there's more going on here than even B.J could have imagined, and Sothis, well, she's one of the good guys. But I'm not asking you to trust her. I'm asking you to trust me."

"We trust you, David," says Edie. "Isn't that right, B.J." Her tone makes it clear that it's a statement, a directive, not a question.

"Yeah, sure," he answers, unconvincingly.

"So, David, where are we off to?" asks Edie.

"I'll give you one guess."

"Penfield," she answers.

"Yep," he replies. "Look, guys, this is the last stop. I'm going to fill up the tank. If you need a restroom break or some munchies, I suggest you take care of it now."

They get out and start toward the convenience shop inside. "So, on top of all the other stuff, you're not worried about driving a hot car?" B.J.'s question is half serious, half sarcasm.

"Of course I am, but it came to me a few minutes ago why Sothis took this particular vehicle. It belongs to an employee pulling the night-shift. He won't miss the car until 7 a.m., and it won't be reported stolen until sometime after that, so that's something."

"Wow, your green friend thinks of everything, doesn't she?" he says, sarcasm dripping from every word.

B.J.'s cynicism is both annoying and understandable, so David decides to ignore it. He goes inside to get some munchies. This place functions as a gas station/rest stop, and between its twenty-four-hour

status and the fact that it sells lotto tickets until midnight, it stays relatively busy.

While chomping on a Twinkie and walking out to the parking lot,
he walks past two truckers and...and they're glowing. An energy field or
aura is surrounding them like images he's seen in anime. He turns and
looks back inside, and he sees it around everyone, including B.J. and
Edie. But they're all different colors: varying shades of red, blue, gray,
and violet. But Edie's is unique. Hers is golden, not a pale yellow but a
true gold, the only one of that color on the premises.

Suddenly, before he can process this, he sees other images, creatures
surrounding the people in the store. They seem to be a graphic illustra-
tion of each person's personal story. There's a handsome, scantily clad,
dove-winged charmer whispering in the ear of one of the female cashiers
and a half-naked seductress draped over one of the truckers who's just
entered. He takes off his wedding band, puts it in his pocket, and walks
over to the cashier with a big, "Whatcha doing later," grin on his face. A
desperate-looking, older woman is sitting down at a table filling out
lottery tickets. Several foreboding shadow beings are whispering to her,
and a dark green, bat-winged goblin is hovering above her head supervising it all. Shadows are everywhere, with ever-changing forms and the
same glowing red eyes he witnessed on his first encounter with the darkness weeks ago. But there are beings of light as well. Blindingly-golden
humanoids, crackling with incandescent fire, some are merely watching
while others push the shadows away and whisper in the ears of the
customers. In Edie's case, they are providing a wall around her, actively
keeping the shadows at bay.

David hears a sinister hiss as Edie's guardian physically removes the
shadow that's trying to influence her, and he watches it float up toward
the ceiling. Up there, he sees the scariest ones hanging, impatiently
observing all the activity that's happening below. They are huge, ghastly,
horrid creatures, with wings like gargoyles, protruding fangs or tusks,
and merciless eyes, sometimes red, sometimes yellow, fixed on the
humans below, waiting for the opportunity to pounce.

What's holding these beasts back from attacking? There's palpable
tension. He can tell they want to strike, but maybe the watching
glowing beings are acting as a deterrent. And it's cool that the light

beings are protecting Edie, but why aren't the golden guardians more active in helping in every situation? He's trying to process this confusing, new "gift" of sight, and as he does, David senses something else, something even more deadly and infectious. The sky is at war. Thousands of monstrous shadows with bat-like wings and fiery weapons cover the night, blocking out the moon. Battling them are cosmic, saffron soldiers wielding weapons of light. War fills the heavens, and David can't help feeling like he's watching a movie about the end of days. But this is real, and no one here can see it but him.

Edie pokes David in the side. "What are you doing? I've been watching you stare off like you're high on something for the last few minutes."

"Well, I..."

"It doesn't matter. Give me the keys. I'm driving."

"But..." he answers, pointing upward.

"Look, lil bro, I believe that you're seeing stuff, and I trust that it's real, but it doesn't matter. The last thing we need is to have you driving down the highway at eighty-five miles an hour, staring off into space. I'm driving. You're riding shotgun. B.J., you're in the back."

"Hey, I can drive," says B.J.

Edie and David both stare at him.

"No, you, really, really, can't," she answers.

"Kid," David replies, "we owe it to the car's owner to get it back to him in one piece. Edie's got this."

Ignoring B.J.'s protests, they load up the car and head off. Edie has a bit of a lead foot, so they make better time with her at the wheel, and she's right about David. He couldn't have driven. He's having throbbing head pain, intermittent but excruciating. It's like a person is stepping on the back of his cervical spine while a vise is squeezing his brain. Whatever is happening, it's becoming more intense. All he can do when it comes is grit his teeth, close his eyes, and lean his head back. And even with his eyes closed, he sees flashes of colored dots, images of memories not his own, and hears voices, so many voices. And then it passes, at least for a while. With each wave, the agony increases, like the data being crammed into his head is too much for it to handle.

It's been a few minutes since he's had an attack. Hopefully, they've stopped. Even so, right now, it's hard for him to focus on anything with all the new sensations and information flooding him—stuff he can't make sense of and pieces he's starting to put together. He feels like someone is downloading the whole supernatural Internet into his brain, and David doesn't think it's all coming from Sothis.

As crazy as it sounds, she seems to be acting as his personal librarian, sorting the information and trying to keep him from being completely overwhelmed.

There's a third party at work, and maybe he's been at work for a while. It's the katana-waving, burning man from David's dreams. Before Isis appeared, it was that warrior's memories David was stuck in. Now, all the waves of memories and information that are streaming in, nonstop, are stirring something new in him, a dormant power awakening. It's rising with each passing moment. David's not sure that he wants it, but it's coming regardless, and there's nothing he can do about it.

When B.J. tires of defending his indefensible driving skills, he and Edie switch the topics to music, to religion, to movies, to sexism in pop culture. David's not really paying much attention to the conversation. It's background noise. He is unapologetically in his own world, trying to hold it together and trying not to do or say anything that will add stress to an already tense situation.

He's gazing out the window, fascinated by his new vision. The sky battle stretches on as far as he can see, in every direction. On land, it's been interesting to witness the type of crowd certain buildings attract, particularly churches. There's a church on almost every corner in the Deep South. To David's surprise, many of them are overrun by shadows. Even more disturbing, many of the larger places of worship have huge gargoyle creatures perched on them as if they and their shadow lackeys have staked their claim. Eventually, they pass a smaller church, and it is enveloped in light, protected by powerful guardians. The shadows give it and them a wide berth. David's not entirely sure what all of this means, but he's pretty sure that if he were church shopping, he'd rather attend this congregation than some of the others they passed tonight. As decisions go, that would be a pretty easy one.

"Hey, Stargazer." Edie interrupts his thoughts. "I can use your help. I always forget which turn it is."

I guess time flies when you're surfing the supernatural web. I can't believe we're already in Penfield.

"OK," David answers. "It's close, on the left, right past this creepy church, riiiiight here."

They take a left down a dark, winding, gravel road.

"Left another left...here," he instructs.

She does, and they travel a bit and arrive at a locked front gate. The camp is still closed due to the damage from the "tornado."

"Park here," David says, pointing to a spot on the right. "We can go the rest of the way by foot."

The main camp is only about a mile from where they are, but it's nearly three in the morning and the camp's abandoned. It's pitch black and a little spooky. The darkness is making them feel that they are traveling farther than they actually are.

After a while, B.J. quips, "So, this is Jesus Disneyland, huh? I have to say that after all the hype, this is a little disappointing."

"This is what?" David asks, feeling a little offended and a tinge of déjà vu.

"I'm sorry," he answers. "When we were kids, I heard you and Edie brag about this "amazing" church summer camp so much that I came up with my own little nickname for it—no offense."

"That's just weird," Edie fires back.

"Hey," he replies. "In my defense, I was twelve and in the middle of a long boring summer at my cousin's house. Anyway, I'm just saying I expected mo ... Oh, man ... Oh, man."

Silhouettes have darkened the sky, towering above them like dismembered giants broken in war, once mighty, now fragile, bowing to the winds they once used to defy. As David and his friends draw closer, it's clear these are trees, enormous oaks and pines snapped like twigs, some uprooted, some even shattered into kindling. Others are charred and sliced into pieces by something sharp and hot. The stillness and devastation is closing in. They huddle together as they slowly make their way through, relying on the light from their smartphones and the moon to guide them.

As they pass the broken tree line, they stumble upon a large, open field where there are numerous burned patches of grass and craters and sizable trenches that seem to have been made through forceful impact. There was a fierce battle here, and its fingerprints are everywhere.

"Um ... I ... I love what they did to the place," quips B.J. His words are a welcome relief that pierce the unbearable silence.

But no one laughs or even smiles. That would seem almost sacrilegious. This feels more like they're disturbing a graveyard than walking through a camp, the stillness and gloom in stark contrast to the laughter and joy from David's memories of this place. There's no joy tonight. Sneaking out of the cabins under the cover of moonlight and getting into mischief was always part of the appeal of camp week. It felt dangerous in a fun way, not like this. His heart is in his throat, and his steps furtive as he leads the way. He's trying to be strong. He doesn't have to see his friends' faces to feel their amazement and terror, confronted by the diversity and scale of destruction and its implications. Still, however foreboding the images are that all three of them can see, the ones available exclusively through David's extraordinary sight fill him with far more dread. Death has been here. Her essence still lingers on this parcel of land, like a passionate kiss from a beautiful but dangerous lover. She has bathed herself in blood and danced on the bodies of the spirits she ferried to the world beyond. There is a chill that remains everywhere she's stepped, and the coldness makes David shiver and makes him grateful that only her memory is here and not the mistress herself.

Pain leaves an impression that does not quickly fade. Even after the spirits cross over, their agony lags, leaving the equivalent of a sensory aftertaste. He can see glimpses of their final moments, spectral reenactments drifting like smoke across the battlefield. David can feel it in his gut and in his heart. He can hear the shadows laughing as most of the victims breathed their last. Most but not all. It is clear that not every passing gave the shadows joy. All deaths, it seems, are not created equal.

There are still a great many shadows present. Above them in the treetops, crouching in the tree line, cursing at them from the darkness, peering out with their red eyes and gnashing their teeth as they scurry about, flitting from limb to limb, following the friends' passage. They seem unsteady, tremulous, but it's not the teens they're afraid of. David and his companions are encircled by a wall of golden warriors, fearlessly walking with them. They are humming, and their voices exude a sense of hope that pierces the darkness and lifts David's spirits. The shadows give way to the guardians and their song like vampires reacting to a cross.

Something is stirring within him. They reach the center of the field and things are starting to become clear.

"This is it, guys," he says, breaking the silence. "This is the spot."

"Spot for what," B.J. asks.

"This is where it happened."

Before they can ask any more questions, David places his hand on his chest and pulls out a small aureate sphere, about the size of a tennis ball. Edie and B.J. gasp. David then holds the orb up to the night sky, and as it hovers, a life-size, resplendent image of a woman projects out of it, floating above them. She is the personification of elegance and beauty, gleaming with amber energy.

"Sothis!" Edie exclaims.

"Yes," she answers, in a voice that resonates through them, loud and clear, but soft and soothing, like a melody. "I am she. Children, I have much to show you and very little time. Listen and observe carefully." She points to the sky directly above her. "This is where the Dark Star fell four weeks ago."

As she speaks, images are materializing illustrating her words. Everything appears as it did four weeks ago, and a black vortex swirls in the heavens, comprised of a dense cloud of bat-winged creatures. In the center is a yellow speck, a man falling to earth. He begins as one of the golden warriors that David has been seeing. All of them are male, hairless, muscular, and burn with living, breathing saffron fire that comprises their armor and flows from every fiber of their being. The falling man starts out the same, but as he gets closer, his appearance changes. The light begins to fade, and he becomes more human. He grows long brown hair, including eyebrows and stubble, and his fiery armor transforms into tattered robes. As he draws near, the golden glow turns dim and eventually morphs into an eerie dark light, a gray-black flame emanating from his skin. He lands gracefully on one knee, with no sound or impression, and stands slowly, rising to a towering nine feet of chiseled muscle. He is as handsome as Sothis is beautiful, with a strong chin and defiant eyes that glow with crimson fire. The image freezes as Sothis resumes her commentary.

"It is essential that you understand what you are seeing. He was the last of the Dark Stars to fall. From a human perspective, the first Dark Stars came in a great wave before the Great Deluge, and the second wave came shortly after it. Since then, a handful has fallen over a period of five thousand years. But our reality tells a different story. Two large groups left the eternal kingdom milliseconds apart, and in a matter of seconds, several stragglers followed. Since their creation, they had lived their whole lives connected to the voice. The voice sustained them, directed them, empowered them, gave them purpose and love. Traveling from our world to this one through the voice is precise and instantaneous. The fallen left the voice when they left their home, and they did not realize the enormous time gap that would occur traveling without it. Ignorantly confident in their power, their wisdom, and their limited knowledge, they were not aware that a difference in milliseconds on one side of the barrier became centuries on the other, and seconds became millennia. Their unified defection became a disorganized graveyard of failure, regret, and loneliness.

"Furthermore, they could not foresee that the transgressions which had been tolerated since before the time of the Nazarene would not be indulged after. They took the form of human giants, indulged in man's pleasures, and coveted the gifts of procreation and family, forsaking their post, their home, and their purpose to do so.

"The first ones lived among men for two decades before they were dragged off by the messengers and put in chains and darkness; the next wave lived free for less than five years until they were similarly imprisoned. The stragglers since, like the one you see, have arrived alone and been taken within hours, a sad end to a once glorious existence. That is the lot of all the fallen.

"The children of the fallen are the Nephilim. The oldest of them were born long ago when the world was young, and the last was born over five thousand years ago. They are the fallen's oversized, half-caste progeny, who roamed the ancient earth as the giants of legend, learning over time how to cheat death by appropriating human bodies when theirs wore out. They were the heroes of old, the men of renown, and the source of so many of your myths. But they are no myth. They are among you, hidden in plain sight.

"They are not all the same, and they are not the only creatures who creep in the darkness. The Nistarim consists of noble Nephilim, called watchers, and their allies, who fight for humankind to keep you safe and free, but there are other Nephilim who conspire with dark forces that wish to see humankind's reign on earth end. This Dark Star that you see is significant because the newly fallen contain great knowledge, a knowledge that can be used to tip the balance of power. The Nistarim formed a wall around him when he appeared to prevent any from approaching him until he could be secured by the messengers, but he came suddenly, and they arrived too late."

"The bad guys got to him?" Edie asks.

"Watch and see," Sothis responds.

They watch, and the images begin to move forward again. Seconds after the Dark Star lands, three teenagers come out of the woods onto the field. It's David, B.J., and Edie from four weeks ago. They are emerging out of the brush on the far end, oblivious to the presence of the Dark Star. David remembers now. After he couldn't find Semi outside the diner, they decided to go on to the camp while he waited for her to call. From this point, it is less about watching images than about reliving memories.

"Just a little further," the image of David says, "and we can cut across to the cabins and then to the welcome center."

"So, this is Jesus Disneyland," responds B.J. "I have to say it's a little over rat ... W ... What's that?"

Suddenly, the three of them see him there, towering over them in all his glory, looking like a giant-sized version of one of those romance novel covers, his clothes still smoldering from his fall.

"He's beautiful," Edie says, utterly mesmerized, "terrifying but beautiful."

"Let's get out of here." David is fearing the worst. "Whatever this is can't be good."

He grabs Edie's arm and tries to lead them away, but he can't move, and neither can anyone else. They are stuck in place, staring at this alien giant, helpless.

"There is no need to run, children," he bellows in a voice like rushing waters. "I mean you no harm. Besides, if I did, there is nowhere you can run from me. I sense warriors coming. I have little time before battle comes my way. Bring the lovely lady here. Perhaps the three of you can amuse me before I vanquish the ones silly enough to challenge me, and if she finds me desirable and my exploits impressive, perhaps your lady friend will allow me to amuse her later."

Despite his welcoming smile, there is something nefarious behind his red eyes and extremely creepy in his invitation. But what choice do they have? David is trying to distract him so B.J. and Edie can make a break for it. David signals for B.J. and Edie to stay put and starts walking slowly toward the image. Of course, Edie being Edie, she follows behind him anyway and B.J. too, against his better judgment.

Whatever the giant's original intentions concerning them, something changes in him as they draw closer. The Dark Star's initial posture was arrogant and defiant as if he fancied himself a god among mere mortals. But as David approaches, the fallen one seems preoccupied, distracted, like David in the car, taking in large amounts of new data. Whatever he is experiencing has a traumatic effect on him.

Sothis, David, Edie, and B.J. continue to watch the past unfold before them.

The giant falls to his knees and covers his face, his reason for calling them over no longer ruling him.

"Oh, no, no! It's been over twenty thousand years," he whispers mournfully. "I see it in your mind. I hear it in the whispers. So many years have passed since we leaped and the first of my brothers arrived. They are all gone. How is this possible?"

He shifts his gaze to the sky, his eyes moving as if he's watching a movie in fast forward. Several minutes pass with him watching in silence. Whatever he's seeing is making him increasingly emotional.

"So much time has passed. So much has changed," the giant continues. "We were so wrong, so much hurt, so much pain." He pauses, letting tears stream down his face, and then continues, wistfully. "We were not rebels, not like the Accuser and those beasts who fought against the Ancient. We simply thought that we deserved a reward for thousands of years of service. We knew the punishment for desertion, yet we foolishly thought that we could change his mind. We thought we knew best. We believed that the Ancient would see our great deeds, how we were a blessing to his beloved humans, and he would reward us for our initiative. We were foolish. We were anything but a blessing, so much blood on our hands—blood and chaos. We were lost and scattered. I see it all, the whole sordid history transpiring before my eyes. What have we done?"

His voice trails off, and he kneels, sobbing for several seconds before he continues "I am lost. Without his voice...without his voice, I am deaf and blind, stumbling in the dark. And...and I can never go back. I will never sing with my brothers again, never have his song in my heart, never again."

He wipes away his tears and rises back to his feet, steadying himself as he resigns himself to his fate.

"I am done," he says with an eerie calmness. "My former brothers in arms are coming here to drag me off. There is no escape from them. The other warriors drawing near are not here to fight me but to fight each other over me. They want a gift, some forbidden fruit from the last of the 'fallen'. I have seconds left." He turns to David commandingly, with gentle firmness.

David watches his own image walk nearer to the giant, unafraid, confident but not cocky. David remembers the moment. He remembers feeling a sense of pity, of wanting to accept the stranger with kindness. He feels it now as he watches the interaction.

"Come closer, child. What is your name?"

"David," he answers.

"A good name," he replies, "A name of substance. I would share mine with you, but it seems that I no longer have one." He smiles mournfully and continues. "I am Nameless. That is what you can call me, just another unexpected consequence of my actions." He pauses and gazes intensely into David's eyes. "Young David, you are all I have. I traded eternity...eternity for a taste of this world, and this moment with you is all that I will ever have to show for it."

A lone tear trickles down his face as he lumbers toward David, not bothering to wipe it away.

"There will be no progeny, no legacy for me. My name and the names of all my brothers have already been erased from the heavens. This...this moment is all there is. You are my legacy, and I am your cautionary tale." His eyes pierce David's soul as he continues his appeal, saying, "Do not trade eternity for a handful of dust. Do not run from your destiny. Do not shrink from your purpose. You have a great gift in you, child, a great power. Do not continue to bury it beneath your shame. You have been chosen, David Alexander Stone, but even the chosen must choose. Choose well."

David did not at that time know who the fallen was or what he was or why he considered David so important, but he clearly felt the gravity of the giant's words, and he knew even then that his charge represented a crossroads for him.

"Yes...yes, sir," he replied.

"Good," he answers. "Good. Now, I am going to impart to you a gift, and my hope is that you will use it well, use it in such a way that you make my brothers sing, sing their beautiful songs."

Without warning, he reaches out to David with impossible quickness, grabbing his right arm in his unbreakable grip. David's arm is swallowed up like a twig in a grown man's hand. Before he can utter a word, Nameless's hand becomes white-hot like a solar flare, and David's arm and his whole body catch fire, consumed by white flame. David screams as the burning cuts through his veins and courses through every cell of his body.

"I give you the gift of Barac Navaar," the giant proclaims in a powerful voice that reverberates and visibly buckles the atmosphere around him, swallowing David's cries.

But cry as he might, Nameless does not let go.

B.J. and Edie are standing nearby, unable to comprehend what's going on. They are in shock, motionless, speechless, defenseless.

Now, from their future position, they continue to watch.

The flame on David's skin ceases leaving it shining like bronze, but there is volcanic fury bubbling inside him, erupting through his eyes and mouth. The pain is so intense that even seeing it now, he feels it all over again, but the fallen would not release him. Eventually, Edie grabs David's free arm, futilely trying to pull him loose, and B.J. grabs hold of her in his attempt to help. The living fire simply spreads to them; the jolt from it shocks them into releasing David and renders them unconscious. Even then, Nameless does not let him go. Only after Nameless is spent and seems to have nothing else to give does he release Stone's arm. He falls back onto his knees, leaving David's scorched body writhing on the grass. He then lifts his left arm and opens his massive hand in Stone's direction.

"Now, go," he commands. "Others are arriving. They must not find you here. They will seek to undo what I have done, and I cannot allow that. Be safe, young David; watch over your friends." The fallen pauses, as if laboring to catch his breath, and David can't help but notice that Nameless's skin is losing color, and a gray mist has begun slowly emanating from his pores, absorbing all surrounding light. His eyes narrow, his mouth twists into a sinister grin, and his voice becomes a low menacing growl. "As for me, well, if these warriors truly crave secret knowledge, I have a prophecy to share that will shake the foundations of Avalon and the nine worlds."

The three of them watch as a spherical force lifts them in a rushing wind and sends them flying over the treetops out of sight. The vision of the past stays focused on Nameless and does not follow them.

The vision continues with warriors, men, women, and man-beasts with flaming swords appearing. The katana-wielding man from David's dreams is there, still dressed in black from head to toe. It's obvious that he's in charge. Next to him is a statuesque goddess with ebony skin. Somehow, he knows that this is Iset, Semi's aunt and Sothis' previous host. Shortly after they encircle the Dark Star, opposition arrives, and an epic battle begins.

With each new image, memories are awakened inside David, and reservoirs of esoteric knowledge bubble up from deep inside him, forcing their way to the surface, barraging his senses. David is so engrossed by what he's seeing and experiencing that he doesn't notice that Edie and B.J. have stopped watching.

"What the frak!" B.J. exclaims. "What was that? And what happened to us? Where are we?"

"This is insane," Edie gasps, shaking her head. "This really happened to us? I can't believe this really happened. What did he do to us, David?

What did he do to you? Sothis, before we see anymore, I've got to get some answers."

"That is permitted," Sothis responds.

"He gave David the gift of Borooc Noveau?" she asks.

"Barac Navaar," Sothis answers.

"Yeah, that," Edie continues. "What is it?"

"It is the blood of angels," David answers, solemnly. "He bathed me in the blood of angels, the last that he had left, and you two were touched as well."

"Blood, what blood?" B.J. interjects. "I didn't see any blood."

"Blood is the essence of life, the sum of the spirit, the chasmal, the Qi, the Odic force, the essence, that makes each being what it is," Sothis replies. "There are trace amounts in physical blood, but in its pure form, it is living energy. The fallen's was becoming corrupted, turning dark. He passed on to David, all that remained from who he had been before. It is an extremely potent gift, a troublesome gift that can be used for good or evil. If David did not possess latent power of his own, the touch of the angel's blood would have killed him and you instantly, but his gift was a filter for him and for you."

"And how will it affect us?" Edie asks.

"It has and will continue to have a profound effect on David," Sothis responds. "For the two of you, it remains to be seen. Presently, it is mostly dormant within you, but with the right—or wrong—catalyst, it may create changes. More than this, I cannot say."

"Angels?" B.J scoffs, incredulous in his disbelief. "What do you mean, angels?"

Sothis replies gently, "They are messengers, ministering spirits, and mighty warriors for the Ancient, led into battle by their commanders and archangels. It was some of their order that deserted long ago and became the fallen. The messengers are connected by and empowered by the voice of The One. They are nearly everywhere, all the time, even here, even now."

"Are you an angel too?" Edie asks.

"Yes, is the simple answer. But I am a Throne, and we are different than other angels in ways that are significant. We are both angelics, but the Malakhim are common angels, sort of the infantry. We generally refer to them as messengers, and they always appear as males and have very specific roles and powers. Our order is older and can manifest as either male or female deriving what we are from the presence, not the voice. Our roles are more nuanced. In human terms, we are of the same genus. I am a Seraph, and I and the other Thrones are to messengers as wolves are to dogs. They are soldiers, and we are Mossad; we are MI-6; we are many things. I and the one hundred and forty-three under my command have become earthbound. We are not fallen, far from it, but we are each anchored to and constrained by a talisman. Only by sharing this talisman with a human host and forming a symbiotic union can we move freely within the nine worlds of earth."

"That's why you need Semi?" Edie asks.

"That is why we need each other,' Sothis replies. "I know that you have many questions, but to quote a great man, 'Time is not our friend.' There is more that you must see, and then we must move. Coming back to this location has helped me locate Semi. I know where she is, and I know where she will be. But first, we must shift the scene ahead one hour and roughly five miles away, where you three landed."

Their personal movie continues, shifting from the battle to the three of them waking up an hour later, on a gravel road on the backside of the camp. As they begin to stir, a great burst of light illuminates the sky, and an enormous feeling of sorrow seizes David's heart. He can see it in his face and his demeanor, although at the time, he did not know why he felt that. Now he does. A great light disappeared from this world. Iset crossed over, sacrificing herself to save their next guest.

An incandescent sphere crashes to Earth a hundred yards from them. They run over, and emerging from the center, unharmed, is Tricia, the blonde woman from David's encounter in Central Park.

"Are you OK?" he asks as he approaches her.

From behind, he hears a familiar voice call his name, saying, "David, you shouldn't be here. It's not safe."

It's Semi. She pops out of the brush carrying a sword of blue fire. Her clothes are torn, and her face smudged with dirt.

"It's good to see you," she says, flashing her irresistible smile, "but if you're going to stay alive, I need you to listen carefully to me. You and your friends stand with Tricia, behind me. I'll keep you safe."

Oh, no, David remembers now, and he knows how this ends. He stiffens, heart pounding, eyes burning, shaking as he fights back tears. He can't watch this, not again, but he has to. He needs to.

Three nasty looking thugs show up, a seven-foot lizard man with a red fire blade and a man and woman. The man is short and stocky, with a blue flaming ax, and the woman is a tall, sinewy brunette, with two glowing blades. The woman launches at Semi first. Semi deftly parries her attack and beheads her with three, lighting quick moves, but before she can catch her breath, the blue ax man and the lizard guy attack simultaneously. Her arm is slashed. Barely taking time to wince from her injury, Semi kicks ax guy in the face, dodges lizard man's sword, and cuts off his sword hand. He screams, but with his other hand, he runs Semi through with his six-inch claws. Once again, David witnesses as all five nails cut through Semi's gut and protrude out of the small of her back. She doubles over in pain, but she does not scream, not once. The scream belongs to Tricia, but it is less a cry of fright than a battle cry, the sound of a lioness protecting her cub. She releases a blast of purple energy that consumes the two remaining foes before they can finish the job, and then Tricia collapses. Before all light fades, David moves over and grabs Semi's slumping body, and the shriveled corpses of her enemies fall to either side of her. He doesn't even remember Edie and B.J. being there at the time, and he barely notices their reactions now. All he sees is Semi.

"It's going to be OK," he lies as he holds her gasping in his arms. "We're going to get you help."

"I ... I told you," she says, breaking David's heart with her smile. "I told you I'd keep you safe. Y ... you don't get to save me, Prince Charming. I'm not that kind of princess."

She clenches her teeth, grasping his hand as spasms of agony wrench her body.

"H... Heck of a way," she replied, panting heavily. "Heck of a way to end our first and last d... date."

"Not our last," he answers, weeping, "Never our last. Hang in there, Semi. I hear people coming."

She reaches out and places her bloody hand on his chest, fighting hard to say something.

"Please, save your breath," David pleads. "Hang on just a bit longer."

"S ... Something is happening," she whispers. He places his ear next to her mouth. "S... Something different ... I ... I feel it." She opens her eyes and peers into his. "Come find me." Her words are carried on her last bit of strength.

"I will," David promises.

Semi breathes her last, and David holds her in his arms, cheek to cheek, sobbing. Some men show up, friends of hers. He vaguely hears them talking about securing Tricia, someone breaking the sad news to Ra, and a cleanup crew, getting the civilians to safety and erasing their memories. He can't really hear them, not then and not now. David does notice that his chest glowed for an instant as he made his promise to Semi. That was the moment that Sothis placed the talisman in him and chose him to be her caretaker, holding him to his promise.

B.J. and Edie have started asking questions again, but he's still watching Semi, reliving his pain.

B.J. grabs his shoulder. "David, man, we need you here. The movie's over, dude." Then he turns to Sothis. "I don't want to sound cold, but if Semi is dead, how are we supposed to help her?"

"She's not dead," David answers sternly.

"Dude, we just saw ..."

"Amesemi did not die that day," Sothis interjects forcefully. "Through an unusual circumstance, her soul was transported to another body when she breathed her last. I have just found her, and even now, I am strengthening her shell, preparing it for our union, but now that she has awakened, she will be hunted, and she is far too weak to protect herself. My host is destined to be the afreet, the queen of the Earth-bound and our descendants. If our enemies discover her, she is an extremely vulnerable target. We must go to her. I'm sorry, children. I must conserve my energy until we arrive."

With those words, Sothis disappears, returning into the talisman like a genie returning to its bottle. David places the orb back into his chest and starts walking back to the car.

"C'mon guys," he says. "I know the way. We need to hit the road."

Edie starts following behind, but B.J. doesn't budge.

He crosses his arms and juts out his chin defiantly. "Why? Why should we go? How can we trust what she's shown us? All she's done is lie to us. Angel blood, really? There's no such thing as angels. If the glowy alien lady is going to lie about that, how can we trust anything she says?"

"She was telling the truth," answers Edie. "You saw it, same as me. Couldn't you feel it in your spirit? We're part of something big."

"Feel it in my spirit, really?" he fires back. "Here you go again, all about feelings and faith. Where's the science behind this?"

David steps toward him, confident his words will convince B.J. that what's going on here is real, with or without 'science'.

"You want facts, B.J.? This world is full of mysteries that we cannot explain. And believing or not believing in them doesn't make any of it less real. That lizard creature that gutted Semi is called a sirrush. They're half Amar and half alitha with steel-hard claws and skin, and they can throw a truck like it's a beach ball. The woman who attacked was an udar blood slave, a half ravager/half Amar, who was controlled by ravagers through her blood. And that short merc is called an asura. He's a gifted human who's been trained to use his gifts from birth. Their kind and worse are out there in the shadows whether you like it or not."

"How do you know any of this, David?" he protests. "How can you trust any of the knowledge that she has put in your head?"

"Fair enough," David answers. "But it's not just about what I know. It's what I see. Do you two want to see what I see?"

They nod and he places his hands on their foreheads for a second, then removes them.

"Now what do you think?" he asks, stepping away.

They see through his eyes now, the shadows infesting the woods, the demons in the night sky, and the wall of angels surrounding them. Edie walks around, mouth agape, soaking in the wonder of it all while B.J. stumbles about and keeps rubbing his eyes, hoping it will all go away.

"T... This is amazing," Edie gasps.

"Welcome to the eternal war," David proclaims. "To paraphrase Sothis, 'What is seen cannot be unseen.' You can do with it what you will. I'm going to find Semi in Atlanta. If anyone wants out, I under-stand. I can drop you off at a bus station when we reach the city."

"Don't look at me," says Edie, laughing. "This is waaaay cool. Besides, I took the Winter Soldier vow. I'm in."

"I... I," B.J. stutters. "I guess I'm in. Just get me out of these spooky woods."

They walk back to the car in silence, and David observes Edie and B.J. desperately trying to digest tonight's events and the images before their eyes. After a few minutes, his skin tingles as his friends' borrowed gift of sight fades, and B.J., true to form, is the first to break the silence.

"So, you survived the touch of Nameless and did not die, huh" B.J. chuckles. "So, does that make you Harry Potter?"

"That's funny," David replies.

"So, what does that make me?" he asks. "Please, don't say Ron."

"You're definitely Ron," Edie responds. "What's wrong with Ron?"

"Ron was useless," B.J. answers. "What did he do?"

"If you ask me, Hermione was the real star of the series," David replies. "She saved the day almost every time."

"Her character is a perfect example of the male patriarchy," Edie interjects. "The woman does all the work, and the man gets all the credit."

"Oh, no, look what you did now, David," says B.J. "You've got Hilary Clinton stirred up."

Those two debate back and forth, and for once, David doesn't mind, not at all. That's normal for them, and right now, normal is in short supply. Normal is underrated.

As he walks along, his mind drifts back to the images of swirling darkness and the attack of living shadows he experienced as he woke up in his truck a month earlier.

It wasn't a dream.

David thought it was a dream, but he understands now. Semi's friends wiped David's mind but not completely. Thanks to the Barac Navaar flowing through his veins, there is a part of Stone that knew the truth, helped him cling to his promise, and wrestle with the horror of Semi "dying' in his arms. And that same piece of him remembers receiving "the gift" of vision as Semi breathed her last. Because of it, he was able to see it all. David witnessed the messengers hanging their heads, the twister of shadows cackling as they filled the sky, the sinister red eyes of the whisperers as they lurked from the brush, and their fangs. He remembers their chortles over his anguish as Semi's eyes turned dark, his heart breaking, and all hope being lost. He remembers now. They were ecstatic as they came to him, surrounded him, and devoured David from the inside out. David doesn't know what it all means, but that agony was his last experience before his memory was edited, and the first image before his eyes opened almost a day later.

What did they do to him, and has it truly ended?

Those answers are going to have to wait. David has enough present drama in front of him and all around him to occupy his thoughts, starting with the fact that tonight's Penfield shadows haven't gone anywhere. They are still hurling taunts at him, telling him that he will die a failed hero, like his father. They are saying all types of things. But David's not alone. He utters a silent prayer, and the angels' singing seems to grow louder with every syllable, drowning out the noise, vanquishing the shadows with incandescent light. Stone walks confidently, swaying to their tune, with the words of Nameless ringing in his ears. "Choose well," he said. Well, David's chosen to keep a promise he made to a princess. As choices go, he's guessing he could do a whole lot worse. All he knows for sure is that Penfield has left its mark on them. Nothing will ever be the same.

Avalon —David

"Time is not Your friend," says a voice from deep inside.

As they near the car, it's no longer shadows and messengers that he hears. But this sentence keeps reverberating in David's mind, first like the hook of an annoying song you can't get out of your head, then as something else, something ominous. It's causing a growing, sinking feeling as he picks up his pace. Is that Sothis's voice? It doesn't feel like her. She seems to have gone radio silent. This message appears to be coming from another source, maybe the Burning Man. Whoever it is, he seems intent on further stressing David out, not exactly the most helpful thing at the moment.

When they reach the vehicle, Edie jumps into the front seat, forcing B.J. to sit in the back, the two still going back and forth with their never-ending series of debates. David smiles at them, shaking his head as he slides into the driver's seat and...

Flashes of yellow fire, rainbow speckles of light, then everything goes dark, his stomach is in his throat, and muscles, bones, and tendons feel like he's been pulled apart and put back together, none too gently. He's on his knees dry heaving when he slowly opens his eyes and looks around. *What happened? Where am I?* The car, the camp, B.J., Edie, the ground itself, it's all gone. He's just floating in the middle of a misty, white void, alone, all alone. This can't be happening again, not now. It's like the episode in the mall when he fell out, and his mind was transported to Central Park, living out someone else's memory. That was "fun," and he was out for hours before he woke. They don't have hours or even minutes to waste right now. Semi needs them, and well, like he keeps getting reminded, time is not his friend. He's got to get out of here.

So, where is here, exactly? He feels tingling on his skin, and the hairs stand up on his arms as he senses unseen energy swirling around him. He grits his teeth and quickly whips his head from side to side witnessing silhouettes beginning to appear and take form, and he experiences the uneasy sensation of the ground solidifying beneath him. The mist is dissipating, and images are beginning to emerge.

He's in a crowd standing on a massive rooftop, and as a clearer picture of the individuals surrounding him comes into focus, David's jaw drops, and he stumbles backward into one of them, well, actually, through one of them. Unlike his time in the Central Park dream world, this time, he can see, hear, and feel everything around him, but evidently, no one seems to be able to see or touch him. He's invisible, and although he can experience this reality with all five of his senses, none of theirs are registering him. At least, not yet. He's a wraith, haunting this plane. In a way, it makes sense. He's in a memory, after all, but it begs the question of why the New York experience was so interactive and scary. But that's a question for another time. He needs to find a way to get back to reality, and if there's purpose guiding these events, it's likely the sooner he learns what he was brought here to learn, the quicker he gets back.

David slowly rises to his feet and takes his time taking in his surroundings, especially the creepy people that startled him earlier. He's in the middle of an extremely unusual and eclectic group. There is a barefooted, old man, in white robes, with long white hair and a matching beard. This gentleman is speaking to an extremely tall woman wearing a black and gold hooded robe. Her skin is translucent, she is hairless with small ridges on her face, and she has penetrating blue eyes, featuring a vertical third eye in the middle of her forehead. They are flanked by a fashionably dressed, cute young woman with flamboyant, iridescent, purple and black hair and an energetic demeanor. Within seconds, even more, two dozen or so, gather around them, speaking various languages. English and that ancient language from his dreams are among them, but several others are being spoken that are entirely unrecognizable.

They vary in appearance from short, tall, slim, round, cool and modern, stuffy and corporate, ancient and exotic, girl next door, and an eight-foot, furry monster from the most hidden world. They seemingly have nothing in common but an unspoken but obvious connection and their spooky eyes. Their gazes are penetrating and hypnotic as if instead of looking at those around them, they are reading their lives like a book, from beginning to eventual end. David has been in his share of alien environments in the last twenty-four hours, but this gathering may be the most unnerving. He's just glad that they can't see or touch him. Even so, he makes a point to avoid eye contact with whoever these guys are.

"Oracles, they are called oracles," says the same voice as earlier but clearer, a smooth baritone that sounds as if it's being spoken by someone standing next to him, not coming from inside him like before.

David spins around, frantically looking for the source, but doesn't see anyone that feels right.

"Do not waste time with that," the voice answers. "Neither of us is truly here, not now. I am Amon Ra, the voice inside your head, and you, young man, have very much been inside mine. You are presently in my memories from earlier today. Pay very close attention to everything around you, everything you hear and see. There is wisdom you will find here, knowledge that you will need to succeed in your mission. Listen and learn.

"The oracles are individuals from across the nine worlds with the gift of glimpsing the future. Today, they weighed in on the accuracy of a prophecy spoken by the Dark Star a month earlier and shared their findings with me and select leaders within the Nistarim."

"What was the prophecy? "David asks. "What were their findings? I have so..."

"Be silent. Listen and learn. Follow the oracles as they return to the meeting from their break. The rest will become clear."

"But sir, I have so many questions, and I'm kinda in a hurry. You could just tell me what I need to know, and I could get on my way." There is total silence. "Mr. Amon Ra, sir. Sir?"

Nothing, nada; David's on his own once again. He inhales slowly and exhales a deep, cleansing breath. *OK, I can do this.* David slowly scans the area, attempting to take all emotion out of the exercise and just focus. They're high up. He's not sure exactly how high, but it reminds him of the view from the Empire State Building, so it's up there. The picture is breathtaking, and he can see some landmarks in the distance that are familiar, landmarks from Washington D.C. They're not far from the nation's capital.

Gray clouds have moved in, and it's starting to snow. He sees the snowflakes falling, but somehow, they stop before they reach the roof. How is that? And it's December in the DMV, but the weather is perfect up here, not cold, not chilly, not windy, just perfect. He glances up again and thinks he sees something shimmering briefly above him. He closes his eyes and reaches out with his mind, and with his mind's eye, he sees waves of gold and blue light above, to each side, and completely surrounding the tower. He gets it now. Some kind of energy field protects this place. Knowledge, knowledge from Ra, invades David's mind. He is standing atop the tallest of the three towers of Avalon, and the energy sphere protects the complex from weather, from attack, and from prying eyes, creating an illusion allowing Avalon to hide in plain sight. Wow, so this is the place from Semi's journal. OK, so now he knows where he is. What's next?

"Thoth, Osiris, Iset, Bast, Nephthys, The Great War," David winces and grabs his head, almost falling as names and seemingly random phrases boom in his head, courtesy of Ra. It continues, "Cole, Sarah, Tricia, Maat, Athena, the prophecy, Thoth's equation, The Great Lie."

Details, so many details are flooding David's brain, too much, way too much. One thing is clear through the muck. Thoth is the big bad, the Nephilim who inspired all the rest to believe that they are meant to rule the earth. Osiris joined Thoth's cause later, creating a rival faction with the same wicked agenda. For millennia, Thoth, Osiris, a host of copycats, and random dark entities have waged war against the Nistarim, and they've always lost. Led by Amon Ra and his sister, Iset, the

Nistarim has been the line that cannot be crossed, the protectors of humanity's freedom, and they've never failed, never wavered — until now.

Thoth has reemerged with a new scheme, and he and his equation have changed everything. He claims he has predicted the end of the nine worlds precisely, to the year, to the month, to the day unless the current path is abandoned immediately, and humankind is overthrown from ruling the earth. Fear of the end is a powerful drug, and many have rallied around Thoth's flag, even some in Avalon's halls. The Dark Star's prophecy has only compounded matters and could not have come at a worse time.

The barrage of information has stopped for now, and David's head is clearing. *What does it all mean? What is this prophecy, anyway? And what am I supposed to do about any of this?*

"What's going to happen now," whispers a stocky, gruff-looking man to a petite, raven-haired woman standing beside him. "What now?"

They and several others are standing on the opposite end of the roof, purposely avoiding the oracles and their creepy interactions. They should be too far for David to hear them, especially as softly as they are speaking, but these are Amon Ra's memories. Even though Ra is nowhere to be seen, he must have eavesdropped on their conversation somehow. That's why David's able to hear them now.

Shoulders slumped, his voice trembling, the man continues, "Ra and Iset have been the heart and soul of the Nistarim for so long. We lost Iset a month ago at that blasted battle of Penfield. And now the oracles are saying the prophecy is true. It can't be. We can't lose Ra too."

"There're still some oracles that haven't spoken," she replies. "Maybe they'll..."

"Maybe they'll what, Savina? Over two-thirds of them have shared, and so far, they all agree. The prophecy is true. Sometime within the next three years, Amon Ra, our majestic, will breathe his last breath. So, this is our future, Thoth back, no Iset, no Ra, and Sothis has completely disappeared. What happens, Savina? What happens next?"

She leans in and whispers words of hope. But their voices are fading, and David can no longer hear them.

Instead, he is drawn to another interaction, one on the opposite corner of the rooftop. Two young women are having a conversation in hushed tones.

One is a bronze-skinned brunette, immaculately dressed in a classy, charcoal grey, belted pants suit and heels. She wears it well. Instinctively, David knows she is a watcher in a human host, and by appearances, her host had been a model or a pageant queen or something similar when she was alive.

The new library of information inside David identifies her as Maat, one of Ra's daughters, and she is talking to another daughter of Ra, a niece that he later adopted. Her name is Nephthys, and while Maat is a watcher in an attractive human shell, Nephthys is something else entirely.

She is a shapely, statuesque, ebony goddess, clothed in an elegant white gown, with flowing dark hair and otherworldly pulchritude that rivals Semi's dream avatar. She's not human, and she's not a watcher. She is something else, something ancient and powerful. Could she be an Earthbound?

"How are you, sister?" Nephthys asks tenderly.

"Father dying, it seems unreal, and it really hasn't registered. I guess in my heart, I fully expect him to cheat death like he has so many times before."

Nephthys cracks a slight smile. "I know what you mean. I've been floating on the river of denial myself. Mother, Semi, now Father, it seems like a bad joke. The light will provide. That is the one truth to cling to above it all."

"I know. You're right. It's just that on top of it all, I still haven't digested Penfield. I'm just so angry. What was Tricia even doing there? She was supposed to be a normal human. When did she get powers? Iset and S... our little Semi..."

A tear trickles down Maat's cheek, and Nephthys wraps her comfortingly in her arms. "I know, sister. I know."

"They gave their lives for her...for Tricia," Maat continues, clenching her teeth. "She better be worth it."

Maat takes a beat, steps back, and composes herself. "So, you're not attending the rest of the meeting, are you?"

"I'm not, nor will I be attending the intervention after. I've been sent on a mission."

Maat furrows her brow, leaning in even closer. "Is it concerning the rumors about returned warriors?"

"I fear it may be more than rumors sister. I cannot say more."

"Understood."

"Be gentle with Father."

Gentle with him?" Maat laughs. "A handful of us trying to get Father to open up, trust me, it's far scarier for us than for him."

Nephthys grins, rolling her eyes sarcastically. "Yes, and I am oh so disappointed that I'm going to miss the fireworks."

"You're awful."

"I'll be back by sundown. Take care, little warrior."

"Be careful, old lady."

Nephthys's dress morphs into golden, form-fitting armor, equipped with both sword and spear, and fiery golden wings sprout from her back. She unfurls them, touches some device on her wrist, and looks skyward. In a flash, she disappears beyond the clouds.

Suddenly, David is drawn to an interaction behind him. A cute woman dressed in a white blouse and black slacks, with shoulder-length, strawberry blonde hair, is approached by a man wearing a stylish, gray sports jacket and jeans. The man has fashionably cut, sandy blonde hair and a face covered in perfect, action hero length stubble. He kisses her on her cheek, and as they talk, another woman joins them. Dressed in conservative business attire, she's taller than the first, with dark brown skin, long braided hair, and preternatural beauty, similar to Nephthys's. The blonde woman's name is Sarah Cole. She's human, and the gentleman next to her is her husband, Cole, and he definitely isn't human. The second woman is Athena, another daughter of Ra, and like Cole, whatever she is, she's not a normal homo sapiens. After a few words, she collapses into Sarah's arms, her hair shifting colors from dark brown, to sepia, to umber, to auburn, coinciding with the grief raging inside her.

All around David, people are filing toward the exits. Evidently, the break is over. Cole lingers for a minute and then says something to

Sarah, squeezes Athena's shoulder comfortingly, and heads back to the meeting. David follows behind him.

He hadn't taken time to notice before, but it's more than the view from Avalon's rooftop that is impressive. Avalon's futuristic ambiance makes David feel like he is walking in a luxurious starship straight out of science fiction. And now, he and Cole are headed to the meeting aboard an insanely fast, transparent, omnidirectional elevator that makes any ride from Six Flags seem pathetic. To him, it feels like this place is the love child of Wakanda and the Starship Enterprise, and no matter how hard he tries, he just can't stop his inner nerd from doing the happy dance. He wishes he had time to take it all in, but he doesn't. Unfortunately, sightseeing is not on his agenda.

As he steps out of the elevator, his vision blurs, his knees get wobbly, and his stomach does summersaults as everything starts moving around him and through him quite rapidly. When it stops, and his head stops spinning, he's standing in the lobby outside an empty, circular conference room, and all the meeting's participants are mingling and exchanging goodbyes. The meeting is over.

Standing next to David is Cole, and next to him is a handsome African American man in a blue business suit and red power tie. He's roughly David's height but thicker, and simply standing there with his arms crossed, he shows off his guns bulging through his sleeves, courtesy of an intimidatingly chiseled physique. But that's not what gives him away. It's his piercing, dark brown eyes. This is Amon Ra, the voice in David's head, the line that cannot be crossed.

"Any concerns?" Ra asks.

"Not among the Oracles," Cole answers. "They're afraid, terrified even. They reek of fear, and there are whispers surrounding them, speaking to the terror in their hearts. The smell was unbearable after a while, but I don't think there's a traitor among them. They're not with Thoth."

"Good."

"It's not all good. Nabu concerns me. I know you two go way back, and he's married to Amaunet, one of your best friends and one of our most powerful warriors, but something is off with him."

"Are you sure?"

"Like all of the Rephaim, his mental defenses are superior, but I don't need to read someone's mind to know what's in it. Long before I got these powers, I was a detective, Ra, a good one."

Ra smiles, "I remember."

"His body language was off, his pulse fluctuated with key words, scent as well, and a dark shadow was following him. Whispers aren't speaking to him. They've set up shop. He's harboring a big lie and weighing a very dark decision."

"Amaunet is a sila of the Earthbound, and he holds her tzohar. If he were to turn..."

"I know."

"Is he still here?"

"He jetted as soon as the meeting neared closing, but I've got people with eyes on him. We'll track him down."

Ra and Cole exchange a few more words, but David finds his focus drifting, distracted by his eyes. They're playing tricks on him. One second, he sees Cole and his gray jacket. A second later, he sees Cole in a black T-shirt, a tight, brown leather jacket, and matching pants, wearing holstered sci-fi blasters and a sword and big gun on his back. David rubs his eyes and looks again, but the image still flickers back and forth. He scans the foyer, and with at least half of the people, he sees similar image fluctuation.

A quote pops into his head, something his dad used to say in sermons about wisdom in relationships. He'd say, "Books and covers, it's always best to read the book because covers lie. Like dating profiles and fast-food ads and first dates, Teflon smiles, insincere laughs, charming, shallow conversation, pushup bras, and flashy cars, they're tools that obfuscate by design, distracting from the raw truth. They allow the true character of things and people to be hidden in plain sight."

Thanks, Pop.

The Nistarim, aka the concealed ones, not just Avalon, everything about this world is hidden in plain sight. Nothing is what it seems. His eyes aren't playing tricks. He's seeing through illusions. He needs to trust it, to let it happen, see beyond the covers.

He takes his time and slowly scans the room once again. Half of the inhabitants are what they seem. The other half isn't. Most of the ones using an illusion are using it for their clothing. Under the disguise of standard attire are skintight, sci-fi looking leather outfits and weapons.

"Velecor," says the voice, and just the mention of the word unlocks hidden knowledge.

It's not leather. It's velecor, some kind of hi-tech body armor. It makes sense that soldiers would wear protective armor and carry weapons, and it's reasonable that they would want to make their oracle guests feel at ease by masking them. But some of what David's seeing defies explanation. More than a few are transforming more than their clothing. They are altering their appearance as well. In fact, David can divide the soldiers in the room into three categories. All are wearing hidden armor, but one type leaves their physical appearance unaltered, one type enhances theirs, and a third type, in the spirit of Nephthys and Athena, has legitimate supernatural beauty.

In the middle of the foyer stands an Asian woman with long, lustrous hair who emphatically falls into the third category. She looks stunning in a black halo sheath dress with three-quarter sleeves. But this is just a disguise hiding a sheathed sword strapped to her back and her form-fitting, black, velecor bodysuit, one that makes her look even more spectacular. She is Bast, the oldest of Ra's daughters, and David has just realized that the source of the otherworldly physical gifts that she shares with several of her siblings has a name. It's called azaira, the deadly flower. Certain types of Earthbound possess it, passing it on to their offspring. They believe that beauty is a weapon, especially for women. It has the power to make other women insecure and men stupid. Well, if that's true, Bast possesses that weapon in overwhelming abundance. David is just going to keep his eyes focused on hers. Anything else might get him in trouble.

Only a handful of others present seem to have this gift legitimately. What intrigues David are the ones who fake it. There is one man, the life of the party, a massive, tanned, bearded mountain of muscle with the face of a movie star and marvelous hair. But it's all smoke and mirrors. Beyond the veil, he's a short, stubby, middle-aged, balding warrior. Another is a beautiful blonde bombshell, whose exaggerated, pinup girl proportions seem to be bursting out of her tight blouse and short skirt.

But in reality, she's a lanky woman with brown, stringy hair and a nose that seems much too large for her face.

Why the illusions and all this attention to faux appearance? David doesn't know, but he has learned something important. If he wants to stay alive in this dangerous world he's been drawn into, he has to keep one simple rule. Never trust your eyes.

As the oracles begin to leave, Bast whispers in her father's ear, pulling him into a side chamber. Cole and a short, muscular Asian man in a horrendous blue sportscoat follow them. But Cole seems a little uneasy and less than enthusiastic as he trails behind.

This is it. David knows it. Behind this door is the bulk of what he was brought here to see. As he walks toward the entrance, his hands shake with nervousness that is quickly escalating to full-fledged panic. There have already been so many life-changing revelations. What could possibly be behind this door? Every new choice seems to lead to more danger. Can he handle more? Does he want to? He put his fear in a box a while ago so that he could do what he needed to do. But it's out now, out with a vengeance, and everything in him wants to run away screaming— a normal response, a logical response.

He closes his eyes, and he glimpses it, his why. He's back in the diner, and he sees Semi's smile, gazes into her eyes, and hears her voice calling to him, softly, so softly, but it thunders in his heart. Like when they first met, a warm glow radiates through his body, casting out all doubt, filling his heart with courage. He fell in love with a girl after one conversation. That doesn't make sense, and it's not remotely logical. Edie's humored him, and B.J. has tolerated it, but it's never made any sense to either of them. David's not stupid. He knows that, how it looks, how it sounds. But he's in love, and no matter what anyone thinks, he knows it's real. And Semi needs him, so he'll risk everything for her and gladly run into the fire, again and again, if necessary.

David balls his fists tighter and tighter until they stop trembling. He breathes in deeply, slowly puts fear back in its box, and takes one massive step forward— one step for love.

THE PHOENIX CHILD —
DAVID

David's played on teams and been the best player on most of them for as long as he can remember, mainly basketball when he was in New York, and football slowly took over when he moved down south. There have been a lot of big games, and before every one, he'd feel the pressure, no matter how much he denied it. Blood would rush to his head, adrenaline would surge, and he'd straddle the line between nervous anticipation and crippling terror. Before most of those moments, his dad would give some variation of the same pep talk.

"You scared, son?"

"No, Pop," David would answer, "never scared."

His dad would lean in and gaze into David's eyes, smiling.

"Maybe a little," he'd say. "Everyone feels it at least a little. Fear's a beast, son, and it's always there. Either you tame it and ride it, or it will trample you, trample you every time. Here's the key. Don't make this moment bigger than it is. It's just the next test, that's all, and you know all the questions. You've got all the answers, just got to trust in that. You hear me."

"Yes, sir, I'm ready."

"Yes, you are, son. Yes, you are. You see your opponent, you know what's coming, and you're prepared. What's really scary is when you can't see, walking in the dark with no clue, no idea what to expect or what's happening. The only chance then is to believe in something bigger than yourself. But this ain't that, not even a little."

For the most part, that talk would help. David never got the very last part, but he'd tune that out and focus on taming the beast. He never understood what his dad was saying about the dark, the unseen, the unexpected, not until that night, the night Dad died. A part of David has been running around in the dark ever since. Entering this room is just the next step of his journey into the shadows.

He walks into a relatively large and fancy office featuring a spectacular view from the eighty-ninth floor. It's tastefully furnished, with an impressive executive desk, an overpriced couch with matching throw pillows, hardwood floors, an expensive hand-knotted rug, and five leather chairs, one behind the desk and four against the walls.

Everyone in the room but Ra looks a little jittery. From what David heard on the roof, this is supposed to be an intervention to get Ra to share how he's feeling, so, understandably, everyone gathered seems a bit nervous. Including Ra, there are five people inside, and as David enters, information about each of them surfaces from his mind clutter.

On the desktop, Maat is seated, waiting impatiently, legs crossed and arms folded. She runs her hands through her long brown hair and fixes her piercing brown eyes on her father. Of his children, Maat is generally the positive one, the peacemaker, never getting too up or too down. She's skilled with the flaming sword, the most common version of a lorenth. But more importantly, Maat is the Nistarim's most talented telepath, adept at psychic interrogation, memory manipulation, illusions, weaponized telepathy, storm watching, and every other type of mind voodoo out there. If anyone in the world could sneak a peek into Ra's brain, it would be Maat. She can't, and that's part of the reason why they're here.

The guy standing next to Maat is the muscular Asian man with the hideous blazer and outdated pants—real, by the way, not illusions. His name has popped into David's head. He's Gilgamesh, and like Ra and Maat, he is a watcher in a host body. He is a legendary warrior, Ra's dear friend, and Ra's second in command.

Next to Bast is Thomas Jefferson Cole, Cole for short. He was an NYC detective who sold his soul, number one on his list of horrible choices. He sold it and became a ravager, the closest thing the real world has to vampires and werewolves. But Ra interrupted the ceremony before it was complete, and Cole was able to hang on to his soul—with conditions—and become a danag, a ravager who retains his humanity. That was five years ago, in the middle of a case that involved Amon Ra and a seemingly helpless grad student named Tricia Morningstar. She was attacked in Central Park, Ra saved her, and Cole investigated. The three have been intertwined ever since, and Ra and Cole have been inseparable. Hopefully, Ra remembers that today if things get a little heated, but if it all goes south, at least Cole's a quick healer. That's something.

As David noticed earlier, no one would ever accuse the woman standing between Gilgamesh and Cole, Bast, of being a poor dresser. She's quite the opposite. A legendary warrior, Bast is Ra's oldest living child and the closest to him, sharing a relationship that often borders on brother and sister rather than father and daughter. They've forged this bond through a tumultuous and interesting history. Bast was there almost from the beginning, seeing Ra at his best, his worst, and everything in-between. For centuries, the two have been inseparable. Hopefully, their connection will help Ra today.

It's not looking good, though. No one has said one word, and that much is already clear. Amon Ra stands arms folded, chin jutted out, and his handsome mug fixed in a scowl, and someone doesn't have to be a mind reader or Dr. Phil to know what he's thinking. Ra is doing his talking with his body language and his face. He's emoting, so maybe that's something; it's just not happy thoughts.

"OK, old man," Bast says, jumping right in, "you need to talk to us. What's going on with you?"

OK, so much for small talk. David didn't know what to expect, but evidently, subtlety is not a great strength of the House of Ra. It produces a significant number of warriors and heroes, but there doesn't seem to be a diplomat among them.

"Look," Maat interjects, "before you get defensive with your standard answers and deflections, we all know something is going on with you, and you know that we know. All of us are still grieving Semi and Iset, and this death sentence that the oracles have confirmed cannot be easy to hear, even for you. So, talk to us."

Ra looks back at her stone-faced, evidently having little intention of sharing anything of substance. Cole opens his mouth to make an appeal, but before he can spit it out, Bast takes a step toward her father and continues her plea, softening her tone.

"Dad, you know if Iset were here, she'd give you that look." She pauses, scrunching her face, doing her best imitation of her aunt's "Let's get real" face, and then continues. "Then she'd say, 'C'mon Mumbles, spit it out. I'm not going anywhere until you do.'"

Despite himself, Ra cracks a smile at Bast's dead-on imitation.

"Dad," she continues, her voice quivering with emotion, "we miss her too, and I'm not trying to replace her; none of us are, but we love you just as she did, and we are all we have. So, we are not moving from this spot until you talk to us."

Ra drops his head and lets several seconds pass. Then he lifts it again, and the wall that he has built around himself seems to melt as he does.

"It's complicated," he begins slowly. "Losing my sister, Iset, was a big blow, but we are warriors. Neither of us ever imagined that we would live this long, and I am grateful for the time that we shared, especially since so many others we have known along this path were not so fortunate. I miss her. I miss her terribly, but she lived long. She lived well. I will see her again.

"Semi...Semi is something else. I lost everything on that day long ago, during The Battle of Taliath Garr. It was a day of our great glory, a day of our great loss when lifeless Barac Navaar and humans filled that valley until there was no room to stand. I made hard choices there, choices that helped to free this world. In a span of hours, Horus, Aqen, and Hathor died, and our newborn baby, Amesemi, disappeared and was presumed dead. The world was freed at the cost of my own. I have lost many before that time and since, but for reasons you all know, that day weighs particularly heavy, and though I am not so dull as to question the wisdom of the Ancient, it seemed a steep price, a very steep price to pay in service to him.

"Eighteen years ago, when Iset found Amesemi alive, preserved as a newborn in an erathipa sphere, it was like a kiss from the heavens. The Ancient gave back a piece of what was lost, a piece of what Hathor and I shared. I have never been happier than I was that day, with her 'second birth', when I removed Semi from the sphere's ectoplasm, held her in my arms, and blessed her before the angels and the one who is above all." He pauses. "I vowed to keep her safe," he says softly, voice trembling. "With this wonderful second chance, I vowed to keep her safe ..."

His voice trails off, and there is not a dry eye in the room, including David's. He wishes he could comfort him and tell him Semi's alive, but he can't. No one can hear him.

Bast walks over and grabs Ra's hand. Cole rubs his fingers over his stubble, fighting back tears of his own and places a hand on Ra's shoulder. He clears his throat and takes a second to compose himself before continuing.

"I planned to give her a normal life, far from this war. But Sothis touched her when she was three months old, and that door was closed to us. But I still vowed ... I failed her ... failed her again. That guilt has been eating me. It's still difficult to believe that I could not have done more. There must have been something..." He now has a distant far-off gaze, as if speaking to no one but himself. "The whispers from that guilt grew louder, drowning out all else. The prophecy was merely noise... noise in the background.

"But something has happened since, something amazing that I dared not believe. I was hesitant to speak on it, to share before ... befor ..."

Ra freezes in mid-speech. His eyes roll to the back of his head, his body shivers, and he begins to collapse. Cole catches him before he hits the floor.

"Dad!" Maat exclaims.

"Dr. Senaat is in the building," Gilgamesh says, heading for the door. "I can have him here in three minutes."

"Hold on," Cole interrupts.

"What is it, Cole?" Maat asks nervously.

"Bast," he replies, directing his response to her. "Do you feel what I feel?"

She clutches her father's hand tighter and caresses his forehead with her free hand as she responds, "I think so."

Cole focuses his blue eyes on Ra's brown ones as if he's looking beyond the physical and into his soul.

Cole glances over at Gilgamesh. "I don't think this is physical. I don't believe he's sick. Ra's in there, but it seems like somebody's in there with him."

"A telepathic attack?" asks Gilgamesh.

"No, not telepathic. There is a second presence," Bast replies. "It's like he's in communion with someone else."

"So, what do we do?" asks Maat.

"We wait," Bast answers, kissing her father's forehead.

They prop a pillow from the couch under Ra's head and put him in a more relaxed position, opting to make him comfortable where he is rather than moving him. Maat and Bast sit on either side of him, each clutching a hand, Maat using her formidable telepathic skills to search for activity. Gilgamesh and Cole pace the floor, trying to see who can wear a hole in it first. David thinks Gilgamesh is ahead.

This is crazy, so crazy. It seems silly, but David didn't put it together before now that Semi's dad has been the one in his head since...since. David's not sure when it started. And it's mind-blowing that Semi was born thousands of years ago and placed in a type of suspended animation. That really happened? And what's going on with Ra? Is he dying? Is he in a coma, and if he is, is David trapped in there with him?

Long minutes pass, then out of the blue, Ra sits up suddenly, startling all of them.

"How long?" he asks before any of them can say a word.

"About fifteen minutes," Maat answers immediately. "Get Father a glass of water."

"I'm fine," Ra states as Bast helps him up to the couch.

"This isn't the first time, is it?" she asks.

"No."

He extends his hand, silencing her before she can get out her follow-up question.

"I've been drifting."

"Drifting?" Cole asks.

"Yes," he responds. "When a new majestic, the herald of the nine, appears, the old herald will begin drifting, establishing a soul link, an intertwining of spirits. The initial interaction can be traumatic and involve a temporary loss of consciousness, but once the young one is truly awakened and the bond fully established, it is not at all invasive. The link is a great benefit to the new majestic, allowing him to access and learn from the memories of the ones who came before. Once drifting begins, it is a sign that the old majestic's days are numbered. I started drifting roughly three months ago."

"Why didn't you tell us?" Maat asks.

"Initially, I didn't know. It took me some time to discover the truth. I had never experienced the sensation before. The duration of overlap between two majestics can be as short as a few days to well over a century, but my case was different. The herald who preceded me was murdered before I was anointed, so I was aware of the concept of shared memory but had difficulty recognizing it when it actually occurred. Most of the early experiences happened while I slept, so I believed that they were some type of unusual dreams. It was seven weeks before I understood that I was beginning to drift. Even then, the images were so fragmented that it was a challenge to decide on the next step. Iset and I determined that I was drifting on the same day that the Dark Star was discovered. We thought it best to wait until the incident passed before sharing it with our inner circle."

"And then Penfield happened," says Bast solemnly.

"Yes," he replies.

Cole scratches his stubble and runs his hand through his hair. "What you're saying is that the Dark Star's prophesy... it wasn't really news for you other than giving a more specific time frame. Wow. So, before you drifted just now, you said something amazing happened. Is this it?"

"No," he answers, "but it is connected. I am going to need all of you to keep an open mind. Even by our standards, what I am about to share seems incredulous. The drifts have been more regular, more vivid, and more violent since Penfield. He's not awake yet, this young majestic, but he is getting stronger. He's young, very young ... and human."

"Human? Are you sure?" asks Gilgamesh. "Humans have their own heralds. There has never been a human herald of the nine before."

"He's human, Gilgamesh," Ra answers, "and very powerful, although he has no idea just how powerful he is or how to use that power. He has not begun to tap into his gifts. But she has."

"She?" Bast asks.

"Yes," he answers, "she. He has been visited by Sothis."

"That's not possible," mutters Maat.

David's mouth is agape, and his heart is pounding through his chest. The person Ra's proclaiming, no, he can't be talking about him, can't be. He's not a herald or the majestic or whatever Ra is describing. He's just a kid who was in the right place at the right time when he met Semi and in the wrong place at the wrong time when the Dark Star fell. He's not special. It can't be him. Ra must be talking about someone else.

"I haven't gotten to the impossible part yet," Ra chuckles. "Sothis has been visiting him for a few weeks now in his dreams. It took a while to see it clearly, but it's real. It's her, and she needs his help. But she's not alone. There's someone with her. A glimmer of hope has stepped out of the darkness. I have heard her voice. I have felt her, as the brilliance of her spirit caressed my own, first as a flicker, now as a flame. It is Semi. She has returned."

David looks, and Cole's jaw drops. In fact, all of theirs do, and it doesn't seem to be because they believe what Ra is saying. They seem stunned by the very fact that these words came out of Ra's mouth, the last words they thought he'd ever say. And David doesn't have to read their minds to know that they're wondering if Ra's lost his grip, and he can tell that Ra can see it too. David wishes he could speak up and assure them that Ra's right. Semi is alive.

He watches as Ra scans the room, looking into each of their eyes, attempting to chase away their skepticism through the sheer power of his earnestness. Ra ignores their stunned expressions as they all seem to vacillate between embracing hope and proclaiming him insane.

"Father," Bast says, breaking the silence. "We all desperately want this to be true, but surely you realize how ridiculous this sounds. There are no facts to support it, and it goes against everything we know about cheating death. At the end of the day, that's the bottom line. Only the

Ancient has the power to raise those who are truly dead. We Barac Navaar merely specialize in creative ways to cheat it.

"But humans, even powered humans, like Semi, have much fewer options, and none can leap into bodies with souls or reanimate the recently deceased. A very gifted human can sometimes jump into a weakened ravager, seizing its soulless body and changing it from a ravager into a skin-walker. That's rare and difficult to master. And none of this applies to Semi. Cole investigated her death himself." Bast pauses, holding back the tears in her eyes and steadying her emotions from fresh wounds reopened by this discussion. She composes herself and continues. "They found her body shortly after she was brutally murdered, and her murderers died beside her. Even if she could have leaped, there was no one to jump into and no time to think about it. Her death was violent and sudden. Maat pulled the record of the event from the mind of the only living eyewitness to Semi's demise: Tricia Morningstar. While Tricia's account has numerous unanswered questions, her memory of Semi's end was vivid and irrefutable. We all want to believe, Father, but what you're saying is just desperate hope from a grieving parent."

Ra smiles wryly and speaks in a voice both calm and forceful. "Look at us, the five of us, a fae, a vampire, and three children of the fallen— beings of myth and legend all. It always amuses me that creatures like us, whose very existence defies credulity, can use terms like impossible or unbelievable when every breath we take is evidence that there is no such thing. I know how this sounds. Ignore the voices that say that this is nonsense, mere fantasy and that it defies the way we know things work. Who told us that we know how things work? We know more than humans; this is true. But all of our knowledge is still next to nothing. Even as I speak, the shadows of despair and doubt are whispering, telling you that this is impossible, that I have let my guilt fuel my imagination, and that may be the more probable explanation. But let me remind you that the mind of the Ancient is an awesome wonder, probability dissipates in his presence, and miracles are merely his fingerprints upon creation. I have seen a miracle in the drift. I have felt her."

He pauses, letting the impact of his words settle in, once more gazing into their eyes, allowing his unwavering conviction to pierce their hearts and quiet the whispers before he speaks again.

"Semi is alive."

With those three words, David feels turned inside out once again as everything around him speeds up and passes through him. This time his disorientation is exacerbated by a highspeed commentary moving through his brain like a bullet train, providing a synopsis of the events zooming by. In his current state, he can only hold on to bits and pieces. The rest is either lost or buried in his subconscious somewhere. Eventually, there's a pause in the commentary even though things are still zipping around him, and it gives David a chance to close his eyes and collect his thoughts.

From what he can make out, after a few hours of discussion, everyone was persuaded to believe Ra about Semi. It didn't hurt that Nephthys returned from her mission with a prisoner, one that Maat, Gilgamesh, Bast, and Ra immediately recognized— especially Gilgamesh. The prisoner's name is Zaqar, and he was beheaded by Gilgamesh five thousand years ago during the battle of Taliath Garr. After seeing him, the group was pretty open to just about anything.

After everyone got on board with Ra and accepted that Semi somehow survived, that led to a slightly larger meeting involving the first group with the addition of Athena, Nephthys, Tefnet, who is yet another daughter of Ra, and two ancient Earthbound, Qetesh and Apedemak. After some discussion, Ra gave everyone their marching orders. David doesn't remember much about that other than two assignments.

Qetesh and Nephthys were charged with studying Iset's notes on something called the Naka Surr, also called the Phoenix Curse, rumored to be an extreme method of cheating death through blood magic. Evidently, it's ancient, forbidden knowledge that Iset was researching before she died, but for some reason, she did so in secret and only revealed this fact to her daughter, Nephthys. It's possible the Phoenix Curse might explain why Thoth has been pursuing Tricia, why long-lost warriors are seemingly rising from the dead, and perhaps, how Amesemi herself cheated death. Semi may be a phoenix child.

Bast and Cole were given the high-pressure assignment of finding

Semi within the next twenty-four hours. Obviously, the sooner, the better. Once Semi joins with Sothis, she will become the most powerful person in the nine worlds and Thoth's primary target. It seems the myths about the genie in the lamp were inspired by tales of the Earthbound. If their talisman, formally titled a tzohar, is stolen, they become subject to whoever controls it. Thoth capturing Semi and seizing her tzohar could very well tip the balance of the war. Ra instructed them that finding the young herald might be the key because he, Sothis, and Semi are linked somehow.

David smiles broadly. They were talking about him, and for once, that's excellent news. He's not buying all this young herald foolishness, but they're right about how to find Semi. David, Sothis, and Semi certainly share a bond. If only he could contact them and let them know where he is.

He opens his eyes and notices that things have stopped spinning around him. As he steadies himself, he looks up and realizes that it's night, and he's back on Avalon's rooftop. He sees Amon Ra standing alone, deep in thought, and somehow, David knows that this memory is very recent, less than an hour ago.

With a golden blur, Nephthys appears, and she and Ra have a private conversation.

"You summoned me, Father?"

"I did," he answers. "How is the research coming?"

"Well. We should have something to show you sometime tomorrow."

There is a pregnant pause as Ra carefully measures his next words.

"I know why you kept your promise to your mother, my love. I respect that. What I cannot comprehend is why Iset kept this secret from me. That is not who we were, Iset and I. We might keep secrets from the whole world but not from each other, never each other. I know her. She was trying to protect me from something in her research, a theory concerning the Naka Surr with dark implications. I cannot help but wonder. What could she possibly have been investigating that caused her to fear for me?" He leans in closer. "You know, don't you? I know you do."

Nephthys caresses her father's cheek tenderly. "I do." She pauses a beat, sighs, and then continues. "Father, I kept my mother's secret because I trust her. At this moment, I ask that you do the same. If her actions were extreme, we both know that it was for good reason."

He nods his head in agreement.

"Let Qetesh and me finish her research, prove or disprove her theories, and I promise you that I will tell you all, just like she always intended."

"Let it be so," Ra replies and then smiles and kisses her forehead gently. "You are very wise, child of light. Iset could not have said it better."

With a twinkle in her eyes, she kisses his cheek and whispers in his ear. "I had excellent teachers."

And like lightning, she disappears into the night air.

For some reason, David is drawn to Ra, who once more stands alone peering into the darkness, and though he is still and the night is peaceful, he does not seem at peace. Eventually, David's focus shifts to the opposite end of the rooftop as he sees Bast and Cole arrive together. As they walk toward Ra, he turns and nods.

Cole whispers to her. "Just once, I want to be able to sneak up on him."

Bast laughs. "I've tried, and I've tried, and I've given up. I honestly don't think it's possible."

"You two seem upbeat," says Ra slowly turning around. "Any news?"

Cole answers, "Not on Semi, directly, but we may have located a young man with connections to Semi. He could be the young herald you mentioned."

"He says we," Bast interjects, "but it's mainly been Cole with a major assist from Sarah."

"I'm intrigued," Ra replies.

It's not conclusive," says Cole, "but this is what we have. It seems like the trio of soldiers that found Semi left out a detail in their initial report. They mentioned that they found three civilians on the scene, but they left out that one of them, a guy, was cradling Semi and weeping as if they'd been close. I knew it was something but didn't know what to make of it at first, but when I stopped by the house to check on Sarah, she was awake and very emotional. She'd been tasked with clearing some of Semi's accounts, and today she finally got around to her personal phone. Sarah got choked up listening to voice mails and reading text messages to Semi from some guy. She seemed to have a boyfriend or something."

"Semi? My Semi?"

"It gets better. They met at a diner in Penfield the day of the attack, and then he texted and called every day trying to find her, most days multiple times. And he did it every day for four weeks as recently as yesterday. Sarah said some of his voice messages were so moving she couldn't make it through without tearing up. He fell for her hard. Assuming he's the same guy they found on the scene, he and his friends had several hours of their memories erased, so he didn't have any recollection of Semi dying. But the feelings he experienced when she passed are harder to delete and evidently, still very strong."

"Have you been able to identify him?"

"Oh Yeah, and more. The teen's phone is still on him, and he's on the move. The phone's in his mom's name, but I can track it, and yes, I was able to get his identity. I have recent pics from his social media accounts and information on his primary associates. He's a New Yorker, like me, born in the Bronx but moved to Alabama at twelve. Now, he's a senior, a music major, at some school called the Alabama Academy of Fine Arts, but he's an ex-jock, a big-time former high school QB who suddenly quit the sport about a year a..."

"Cole," Ra interjects, folding his arms impatiently. "I don't need his whole autobiography. What is his name?"

"OK, OK," Cole answers. "The kid's name is David, David S..."

"David Stone," Ra interrupts, wincing as if suddenly fighting a migraine. "David Alexander Stone. His father, Anthony, passed away last year, and young David carries a great deal of guilt concerning this."

"How'd you ..." Bast attempts to ask.

"You are correct. He is the herald, the new majestic, and the child and I are linked. Hearing his first name unlocked a rush of memories concerning him. He's just turned eighteen, he's courageous, and he's in love with your sister, literally love at first sight." Ra smiles and pauses before continuing. "I'm not exactly sure how I feel about that, but he's the one, and he can find Semi. If we find him, we find them both."

David jumps up, pumping his fist. They figured it out. They're going to find them and come to the rescue. He's so happy. He'd hug them if he could.

Ra leans in closer and continues. "Listen to me carefully. In David's mind, he and Sothis are on a quest to rescue Semi, and he is willing to lay down his life to do it. As admirable as that sentiment is, we must not allow that to happen. As much as I love my daughter, keeping him safe is as much of a priority as securing her. We cannot risk the enemy discovering who he is."

"How much do you think Thoth knows?" Cole asks.

"It is difficult to say. Thoth has been two steps ahead of us since he resurfaced five years ago. He has been planning for decades, and we still know very little about his grand scheme. We do know that he has eyes and ears everywhere. This equation that he has developed has deceived many, some in the highest levels of the Nistarim. At the minimum, we have to assume that he can track the Naka Surr energy surrounding Semi and that he has discovered that she is the new afreet. Time is not our friend. It's a race right now, one that we cannot afford to lose." Ra's eyes become slits as he turns to Bast, his oldest, his rock. "Bast, I need you to assemble a small strike force immediately. This group is charged with finding Semi and the young majestic before our enemies do. Its members must be extremely capable and unquestionably loyal, and I need you to be ready to leave five minutes ago."

"Understood," she answers. "Cole, you're with me as my second. We have a team to assemble. Telepathically send me your suggestions, then gear up and meet me at Fasson transporter two in ten minutes."

"I'll be there, boss lady," Cole answers.

"And Cole," she adds, "be careful tracking David's phone. As we get closer to him, the enemy can use that tech to track us. Once we get a general location lock, shut it down. With our heightened senses, we can track him from there the old-fashioned way."

"Consider it done."

Ra kisses his daughter, rises to his full height, crosses his arms, and bows slightly, interlocking his thumbs, palms outstretched, forming the traditional symbol of the Barac Navaar. Bast and Cole do the same.

With his head bowed, Ra says, "Be smart, pray continually, move quickly. Salioth Algo Daymon."

"Salioth Algo Daymon," they reply.

Cole gives his friend a bro hug, whispering in his ear. "Ra, buddy, I promise you, we will bring your daughter back."

"I know," Ra answers.

Bast and Cole quickly exit, but to David, Ra's gaze lingers, not on them but straight ahead as if he's looking directly into David's eyes. Is he? Can he see him? C...

What happened? Avalon is gone, and he's back seated in the "borrowed" car, key in the ignition and his trembling right hand on his key. His heart is racing, but he feels good. He feared coming back might be more traumatic, but it feels like he just woke up from a dream. He's fine physically. There's just so much bouncing through his mind. The good news is that help is on the way, but the challenge is that the heroes may not find them in time to help Semi. David can't wait for them, so hopefully, they'll meet up with them on the way to her. And all that stuff about being a herald, whatever that is. That's nonsense, some kind of mix-up. He doesn't know much, but one thing he's sure of is that he's not the one. David's just going to put that part out of his mind because he has enough real challenges facing him and chasing him. He doesn't need made-up ones too.

"Are you OK?" Edie asks

Man, for a second, he forgot that Edie and B.J. were in the vehicle with him.

"Why do you ask?" he replies

"We're in a rush, but you haven't started the car, and you've been just sitting there staring at nothing."

"How long has it been?"

"Only a few seconds, but..."

"A few seconds," he says in barely a whisper. "It felt like hours."

"OK, mano, now, I'm officially worried. Get some rest. I can drive."

"No, I've got it."

Are you sure, dude?" B.J. chimes in.

"I'm fine," David replies as he starts up the engine and quickly backs up. "I can find Semi, but it's by feel. I've got to be the one to do this." He radically accelerates the vehicle as they reach the main road. "Anyway, like Edie said, we're in a rush and time..." He pauses and smiles mischievously. "Time is not our friend."

Edie gives him a side-eye, and he can't blame her. He'll explain the reasons for his odd behavior and corny catchphrase to her when he has more time, something they definitely don't have now. He needs to focus, and he's still reeling a little from his stroll down Ra's memories.

One-eyed, two-eyed, and three-eyed oracles, a death sentence for Amon Ra, and warriors seemingly returned from the dead. How is any of this possible? He can't think too hard about how or why or his brain will explode. Those answers are a problem for another day. For the moment, they have a phoenix child to save and a race that they must win. With any luck, they'll get there just as Semi's rising out of the ashes, and they'll welcome her back to the land of the living with open arms. It should be simple, right? But it never is. After a day of surprises, the odds are there's at least one more waiting for them, whether they like it or not. And that's the part that makes David nervous.

THE NIGHT HUNTER —
EDIE

David's "borrowed" car has been racing down the highway for well over an hour, but it's still not racing as fast as Edie's heart. She's interlocked her hands to stop them from shaking, and silently, she's singing every comforting song she's ever heard. Eden Grace is petrified, and it's taking everything in her to try and mask it, going out of her way to appear like some version of normal. She doesn't want to give her lil' bro an excuse to switch to his default setting and go this alone. Whether he realizes it or not, David needs her. He needs them both, so she's just going to have to woman up and hold it together. Women are stronger than men anyway. If David can do this, it should be a piece of cake for her, right?

Since they left Penfield, David has been behind the wheel, driving with laser focus. Edie's riding shotgun, and B.J.'s in the backseat, being his usual chatty self. Honestly, they should all be knocked out. They've been going all night, and it's after four in the morning, but adrenaline is a funny thing, and they have a bunch pumping through their veins. Edie doesn't see any of them falling asleep again any time soon. And even if her body wanted to, her brain won't shut down. It's spinning, intoxicated from the double shots of crazy she's been drinking all night. Yeah, she really needs to cut down.

Angels, demons, and the fallen, for starters; Edie doesn't know if she's more inspired or terrified. The only memory more enduring than the sinister, crimson eyes of those evil spirits in the shadows is the glory of the angels' song. She still hears it, feels it somewhere deep inside of her. It gives her hope, and it may be the only reason she hasn't lost her freaking mind and jumped out of this car, screaming in the dark. All this and she just saw what she saw for a few minutes. She knows that David has been seeing spirits for much longer and wonders how he can keep it all together. She's worried about him. Edie's pushing through her fear as is B.J., in his own unique, loquacious way, but David, well, she thinks that he's been in firefighter mode since they stopped for gas. He's running straight to the fire, and he doesn't even seem to notice the flames. For Edie, his steely focus may be the most inspiringly terrifying thing she's seen all night, angels, demons, and fallen included.

During the ride from Penfield, they've all been processing their experiences in their own way. In B.J.'s case, that means he's come up with a way to rationalize away the undeniable truth of what he saw and devise a complicated theory more to his liking. It's irritating but predictable.

"So, I think I've got it figured out," B.J. says as he continues to ramble. "One of Clarke's three laws states ..."

"Who?" Edie asks.

"Famous British science fiction writer Arthur C. Clarke. Anyway, he came up with Clarke's three laws. I don't remember the other two, but the most widely known one states that any sufficiently advanced technology is indistinguishable from magic."

"Oh, no," I see where this is going," David chimes in, chuckling.

"Yes," says B.J., gleefully. "You see it because it's logical. Sothis, the winged creepers, and the glowing things fighting in the sky, all of them are some kind of alien species. It only seems supernatural to us because they are so much more advanced than we are. Now that I think about it, my alien theory was right all along. People have been mistaking them for some kind of divine being for thousands of years."

"Or, here's a crazy thought," Edie counters, "maybe the simple answer is the correct answer. We just saw angels and demons, the fallen have offspring on earth, and the three of us have been touched by the blood of angels."

"I cannot accept that," he replies stubbornly.

"Well, that's the thing about the eternal war," David says. "It goes on above you, around you, and inside you, whether you believe in it or not."

"That's the second time you've mentioned that, the eternal war. What exactly is it?" Edie asks, not exactly sure that she wants the answer.

"Edie, in the words of the immortal Meek Mill, 'There are levels to this,'" he replies. "I'll tell you everything I know, but let's get through the night first. We all have enough to digest for one evening."

"OK, that sounds ominous," replies B.J. "Well, on the lighter side, David has superpowers. How cool is that? We need to come up with a code name for you."

"No, that's OK. I'm fine."

Edie replies, "Yeah, well, if he gets one, I hope we come up with something better than the lead hero's name from that comic B.J. created back in the day. What was his name?"

"Jace, Jace Rider," answers B.J., defensively. "And that's a very cool name. If I ever get powers, I would proudly call myself Jace Rider, man of mystery."

A needed release comes as they laugh for a moment and take a few minutes to reminisce about being twelve, hanging out, and reading B.J.'s awful comic, *The Adventures of Jace Rider*. Hero, adventurer, ladies' man, Jace was James Bond in tights and a cape. A very bad comic book, but those were good times, simpler times. But what's going on with them is no graphic novel. It's real, with real consequences.

"So, David, how are you feeling?" Edie asks. "These new abilities of yours have to be a jolt to your system."

"Yeah, it's strange and rapidly evolving, but in a weird way, it feels natural, like they've always been a part of me. It's been more of an adjustment getting used to the voices in my head."

"Voices?" Edie asks. "As in more than one?"

"Uh, yeah," he answers sheepishly. "I didn't mention the other guy?"

"There's another other guy?" B.J. asks. "Really? How many voices are there?'

"Just two, there's Sothis, she's kind of like my guide, and there's this other guy. His name is Amon Ra, and it's different. He's not here with me like Sothis. He's physically somewhere else, but we're linked some-how. Ra's a warrior, a good guy, and he's Semi's, dad. He's been giving me information and helping me use my abilities."

"So, can you have your warrior buddy come here and help us?" B.J. asks. "We could use the assist."

"I wish he could, but it doesn't work that way, at least not yet. We really can't send each other messages or direct communication. He's looking for us, though. Hopefully, he'll find us before someone else d ..."

He stops in mid-sentence, and to Edie, he has the look of someone who has caught a whiff of a very strong, very bad odor. Based on David's behavior, Edie knows something is very wrong, and then she senses something as well. The hairs on her arms are suddenly standing at atten-tion, and there is a sudden thickness to the air. And she experiences a sensation as if invisible fingers are on her. They move up both arms before resting on her chest, applying pressure, making it difficult to breathe. Somehow, she knows this is a sign, the universe speaking to her. There's a dark presence around them, more than one actually.

They've driven as far as metro Atlanta on Memorial Drive, not too far from Stone Mountain. David quickly pulls into the parking lot of a liquor store and stops the car. He reaches into his pocket and pulls out Edie's silver earrings, and then steps out of the vehicle.

"David, what's wrong?" Edie asks.

"Be quiet and very still," he warns. "No matter what happens, stay in the car—no matter what."

"Dude, seriously," B.J. blurts out, "What's going o..."

"This isn't a game, B.J. Shut up and stay in the car."

He gently closes the door and quickly walks around the store to the back alley behind it. B.J. shoots Edie an exasperated look as she opens her door quietly to follow David.

"Really?" B.J. whispers.

She shrugs, grabs her Taser out of her purse, and exits the vehicle, leaving the door slightly ajar in case they need to make a quick exit. As she gets to the back of the building, she sees David standing with his back toward her. He's about ten yards ahead facing some creepy dude, crouched over an old, homeless man, doing God knows what.

Oh no, I know what he's doing. This is so frakking insane.

She didn't want to admit it to herself. The creep's lips are covered in the homeless man's blood as if he's been drinking it. Every part of Edie is shivering. *This can't be happening; it just can't.*

David places one of Edie's earrings in his right hand, between his index finger and his thumb and inches toward the crouched man. As weapons go, earrings don't seem like much. He calls out to the hunched-over man.

"Leave him alone. I'm not going to let you feed on him."

"Go home, child," the bloodsucker cackles, "or you will be our dessert."

David calls out to him again, this time speaking a hideous, grating language that Edie wasn't aware he could speak. Whatever he said gets the full attention of the other man. He rises and utters what seems like some choice curses in the same tongue. Edie gets a decent look at him. He's a dark-haired, unassuming man of average height, casually dressed in a jacket and hoodie. What's notable about him are his pale skin, glowing red eyes, fangs, and claws that seem to pop out of his fingertips as he comes forward. He sees Edie watching them and gives her a wink as if to say, "you're next." He's a hunter, and suddenly Edie and David have become the prey.

The night hunter brandishes his fangs and charges David, and as he does, Edie gets the same feeling she used to get watching David play QB, but this time on steroids. It's like David sees everything at once and is one step ahead. His adversary is moving inhumanly fast, and David is faster. He treats it all like he's watching it in slow motion. And Edie's sight has changed too; she can follow along easily. She sees the predator, his buddies crouched in hiding, ready to pounce, something she didn't notice before. She sees the shadows, surrounding them in the alley, angels and demons battling in the night sky, and a trail of living darkness surrounding David's assailant. This individual is pure, living evil. Two things Edie has figured out: Revelation one, this being is an it not a who, and secondly, her Taser isn't going to cut it. Maybe, just maybe she should have stayed in the car.

Her body is rigid, and a scream builds from her gut, threatening to erupt out of her throat and pierce the night. She feels a burning sensation as she holds it back, fighting against her terror and a powerful fight or flight instinct to stand her ground, shaking as she watches silently.

Fang Face comes at David, and yes, he's fast, but David's faster. David spins and kicks it, knocking it backward, and when it charges again, David flips it over on his back toward Edie. The bloodsucker is about to charge again when a second one jumps from the rooftop behind David. It's leaping toward him. The earring in David's right-hand turns into golden fire, and without looking, he flicks it at the leaping hunter. It strikes the monster in the forehead, burning a hole through its skull as if it were a laser. The creature falls hard, falling to the pavement, howling in pain. The first predator charges again. David flicks the second earring, and its golden light burns a hole through the attacker's chest. It falls backward, howling as it runs off, disappearing into the night.

There's no time to celebrate, though. Edie was so caught up in what was happening in front of her that she didn't realize that B.J. is screaming back by the car. Edie hears him before David and has a head start as she runs around the building toward the sound. When she gets there, she sees B.J. being dragged out of the car by some vampire pretty boy in a leather jacket, and despite her efforts to get there, she feels like she's running in quicksand. David blows by her, racing for the car, but he's not going to get there fast enough. Now, the vampire is on top of B.J., and B.J. is fighting for his life, trying to push him off. David grabs the hunter from behind, but there's a burst of red light, and David is forcefully repelled, crashing into the store's front wall. Edie puts on another burst of speed, Taser in hand, but she notices something odd as she approaches. B.J. is no longer the one screaming. The attacker is the one hollering in pain, frantically trying to escape, and B.J. won't let him go. That doesn't seem right. Whatever, she'll figure it out later. David zooms by again and leaps on top of the scumbag, her brother's eyes aflame and his whole right arm burning with the same saffron fire.

He forces his right arm through the red fire and grabs the hunter, saying, commandingly, "Get off of my friend."

David pulls him, squealing, off of B.J. and flings him hard into the front wall of the building, forcibly enough that Edie hears bones break as he crashes. Yet, he still manages to stagger to his feet and hobble off.

David pauses for a minute, making sure the threats are all gone, and then holds up his right hand as both earrings come back to him, flying through the air.

"B.J., are you all right?" David asks.

"Uh, I...I'm not sure. Is it normal for your heart to be in your throat?"

As David helps him to his feet, Edie asks, "So what happened?"

"This... This boy band looking guy, with fangs and all, pulled me out of the car and was trying to eat my face, and all of a sudden, my hands started to glow, and red fire started shooting out of them. Then I was screaming, and he was screaming. It was crazy. Thanks for the save, dude. I thought I was done."

"Hey, what are buds for?" says David, in his macho, corny way. "But we've gotta get going before those things come back with some friends. Guys, come this way."

David elbows Edie.

"I thought I told you to wait in the car. You could have gotten hurt out there in the alley."

"How long have you known me, David?" she answers, shrugging her shoulders. "You had to know I wasn't staying in the car. I'm not the staying in the car type."

"Trust me," B.J. adds. "Staying in the car's not all it's cracked up to be."

"Yeah, I guess," David concedes.

David walks over to the old man who was attacked and checks his pulse. After a few seconds, he gives the guys a thumbs-up sign. Evidently, the old man's pulse is strong or at least strong-ish.

As the old man starts to stir, David places his hand on his forehead, saying, "It's OK, sir. It's going to be OK. You lost a little blood. You just need to get some rest."

On command, the gentleman falls asleep, so David picks him up effortlessly and lovingly and starts walking toward the car.

Seeing their perplexed expressions, he explains, "We can't leave him here. They're not done hunting, and they love to feed on runaways and the homeless. We need to find a shelter for him. He says there's one nearby that he's tried to get in before. We can bring him there."

"Said?" is B.J's stunned response. "You put the whammy on him and knocked him out. When did he have a chance to tell you any ... Oh, I get it. You're reading his mind. You read minds? Wow, what am I thinking right now?"

"Kid, I'm still learning about this power stuff," he replies. "But I know enough to stay out of your head. That's a very scary place."

When they get to the homeless shelter, they're told that it is full and that their friend will not be allowed in. David does some kind of Jedi mind trick vodoo on the guy in charge, and the next thing Edie knows, not only is the old man allowed in, but he's also getting five-star treatment. Where was that ability when Miss Shruggs gave a pop quiz in theory last Wednesday?

Back in the car, Edie asks, "So, what were those things, and how'd two of them manage to get back up after you burned holes in them?"

"David burned a hole in somebody?" blurts out B.J. "I knew I shouldn't have stayed in the car."

"They're called ravagers. The Nephilim created them. They've been on earth for thousands of years, and they're the source of most of the myths about vampires and werewolves."

"Vampires and werewolves?" asks B.J.

"Yeah, when they're young they turn into man-beast to feed, they eat their victim's raw flesh and lap up their blood. Once they mature, they only consume blood and maintain a mostly human form when they hunt. They are strong and fast, they don't age, and they are rapid healers, with all these abilities increasing the older they get. Most importantly, they're soulless."

"Soulless?" B.J. asks, frowning. "What does that mean?"

"Everything, Kid, everything," David says grimly. "Look, we've got to get moving. Our situation has gotten more intense."

"OK," Edie replies. "How far are we from Semi?"

"About ten or fifteen minutes away, maybe less, but we're not going there yet. We can't."

"I thought that was the whole point, what gives?" asks B.J., dumbfounded.

"Sothis hoped we could get to Semi and get her out of here before she attracted unwelcome company. That's gotten less likely. Those ravagers weren't the only dark beings I sensed in Atlanta. There are hunting parties looking for her. They haven't found her yet. They're still looking in the wrong areas of town, but it's only a matter of time. "

"Isn't that even more of a reason to go straight there?" Edie asks.

"No, once we wake Semi, they'll be on our heels. A confrontation is more likely than not, and they won't be carrying flaming earrings. I've got to make a stop before we go to her."

This revelation leaves the car deathly silent. And just like that, her brave façade crumbles. She doesn't even bother to reply because she might start balling hysterically in mid-sentence. Her left hand has the shakes, so she grabs hold of her wrist with her right and turns to face the passenger side window so that David won't see the sheer terror on her face. They almost died a few minutes ago. Now, they may be racing headlong to face more real-life monsters, and David's talking about it as calmly as if talking about taking out the garbage. She finds herself short of breath; Edie has to remind herself to breathe, just breathe. By the time she's somewhat pulled things together, they are in SW Atlanta, at an abandoned building not too far from Morehouse College.

"I would ask you two to stay in the car, but we saw how that worked out," David says, grinning. "Come on, follow me."

Humor? Really? She smiles a tight smile and steadies herself as she eases out of the truck and follows him. They walk up to an ancient, brick building, with a dilapidated wooden door that looks like the Big Bad Wolf could blow it down, even after smoking two packs of cigarettes. Edie can't help but wonder what could possibly be in here that could help them, but in this brand-new insane world, she's beginning to realize that anything is possible.

David removes one of the bricks on the front of the building to the right side of the door, revealing a high-tech keypad. He enters a code, and the appearance of the entrance changes into a space-age looking metal door that opens from the center, allowing them in. As they enter the pitch-black foyer, the doors close quickly behind them, and lights automatically start coming on, revealing an elevator. They get on it warily and travel down ten or more levels until the elevator stops and the doors open up again, revealing a secret lair straight out of a Bond movie, high tech computers, holographic monitors, and futuristic weapons included.

"Where are we?" Edie asks breathlessly.

"It's a private safe house belonging to Amon Ra, the guy in my head. The link we share is working better. That's how I knew it was here and how to get in."

"So, you brought us here to weapon up for the big rescue?" Edie asks, trying to sound courageous and working hard to ignore B.J. as his expressions vacillate between wonder and horror.

"No, I'm here to weapon up. You guys are here to stay, at least until this is all over. You'll be safe here, and there's plenty of food and a place that you guys can rest a little until I come back for you."

She exhales. Edie should be relieved, but she's not. She knows what she has to do. She silently prays for courage, takes a deep breath, and turns and faces him.

"No, no way," Edie answers, arms crossed and shaking her head defiantly. "Mano, I'm not leaving your side."

"Sis, I appreciate your old school, ride or die spirit. I really do. DMX would be proud. I appreciate both of you, but this has switched from a weird adventure to a warzone. You two could have died tonight, and it's only likely to get worse."

"Yeah, I'll be the first to admit that this scares me to death, but you don't get to make this decision for me or B.J. Lil' bro, the two of us have had each other's backs since we were crawling on the floor, jacking kids' toys at Miss Ione's daycare. Nothing changes that, and you and I both know that if it were reversed and I was the one with spooky powers and not you, that wouldn't be enough for you to leave my side. We're family, mano. You're not walking out that door without me. If the worst happens, and something bad happens to you, I'm not going to look your mom in the eyes or my mom for that matter, knowing I wasn't there to at least try to help."

Edie half expects David to force her to sleep again and make the point moot when suddenly his attention diverts to B.J., who has been uncharacteristically quiet. David's drawn to something different about his face and starts walking slowly toward him.

"B.J., have you gotten taller?" he asks.

"And your face and hair look different," Edie adds. "What the...?"

David drops his head somberly. "I'm sorry, buddy. I should have listened better earlier. You said that red fire was coming from you, not the ravager. That's why he was screaming. You absorbed something from him, someway, somehow, and it's changing you."

"What?" B.J. gasps.

"How are you feeling, B.J.," David asks.

"A little light-headed, but overall, pretty good and strong, really strong." He squeezes his left bicep and smiles. "I think I have muscles for the first time."

"Edie, come here," David says, touching B.J.'s chest with one hand and summoning her with the other. He grabs her wrist. "The blood of angels is no longer dormant in either of you. It's just starting to stir in you, Edie, but B.J., you're about to erupt like a volcano. B.J., I think that ravager attack was your catalyst." David puts his hand on his face and sighs. "Oh, man, this is bad timing."

"What's it mean?" Edie asks. "Are we changing?"

"Yeah, in what ways and how much, I can't say, but changes are coming and probably new abilities if they haven't started already. Have they begun for you, Edie?"

"Well, now I'm able to see the way I was able to at the camp on my own. So much was going on, I didn't think to mention it."

"So, what's this mean?" asks B.J.

"This is way above my pay grade," he answers. "All I know is that it's not good for you two to be alone here while this is going on. Edie, you win. We stay together."

"Don't I get a vote?" asks B.J., nervously.

"No... not really," David answers, only half-joking. He pauses, massaging his forehead, obviously struggling to figure out how this is possibly going to work, and then his eyes light up. "Both you guys are pretty good with handguns, right?"

"Dude," B.J. replies, "I was born and bred in Warrior, Alabama. I fired my first gun when I was eight years old. Shooting stuff is the one sport I'm good at."

"Yeah, you know my story, David," Edie answers. "I've been hunting and going to the range with my dad and uncles since I was twelve. Why do you ask?"

He pulls two sci-fi looking blasters off a gun rack nearby and hands each of them one.

"These are called vipers. They shoot plasma burst. They handle like a Glock but with no kick. I'll set them to your brainwaves, and your thoughts will work as your safety. If your charge runs out, you wait sixty seconds, and it will reload."

B.J.'s eyes light up, and he blurts out, "Blasters, real-life blasters!"

"Chill out, Mr. Solo. This is really important. I don't want you to pull that trigger unless your life depends on it—seriously. Right now, you're both civilians, but the moment you pull that trigger, you're part of this war, and there's no going back."

"What will be done cannot be undone," Edie mumbles.

"Yeah," David agrees. "That's right. Hopefully, it won't come to that. Help should be arriving soon. Ra monitors this location, and I'm sure he's noticed that somebody's used his personal code to enter and figured out that it's me. If he didn't know before, he now knows that I'm in Atlanta, and Semi is too."

David tells them to wait one second and then goes to another room. As he leaves, Edie allows herself to push past the fear and bathe in the wonder of it all as she takes a good look around. She's not a techy, but this technology does not look like it could possibly be from this world. It looks far too advanced. The weapons look space age, the holograms are lifelike and seem interactive. Very *Blade Runner 2049*. And the displays all feature writing which resembles what Edie saw in Semi's journal, with some showing images of places that do not exist on Earth. She wants to take a closer look, but the computers appear to be protected by some type of energy shield. Why take the risk? Besides, she's having too much fun getting used to her new weapon. Her blaster is sleek, lighter than a Glock and, right or wrong, just holding it makes her feel safer, like a futuristic security blanket. Of course, that feeling is kind of offset by watching B.J. pose and clumsily try to twirl his weapon. That image should terrify the whole human race.

Like Q from the James Bond movies, David comes back with more stuff: three large, black backpacks, two holsters, two metal poles with unusual markings on them, and several sets of what can best be described as shiny, black, skin-tight, unisex cat suits.

"I am not wearing that," B.J. says, shaking his head defiantly.

"You will if you want to live. It's lightweight body armor, made out of this stuff called velecor. Don't worry about the size; the nanites in it will make it form to fit. Once in contact with a supercharged aura, like yours, it's bulletproof, claw resistant, and can save you from a glancing energy blast. It will keep you warm or cool, insulating you from the elements, and you can wear the pants under your jeans and wear the top either by itself or under a top. It's not fashionable, but it can save your life."

"And those poles?" Edie asks.

"They're for Semi and me."

"Dude, what are you going to do with a steel pole?" asks B.J., sarcastically. "Pick up trash in the neighborhood?"

David puts one pole inside a backpack and holds out the second, pushing a small button on the side. A long blade pops out of it, turning the metal rod into a specific type of sword. As soon as this happens, the whole object becomes blue and yellow fire, an actual flaming sword.

"It's called a lorenth. It's not made out of steel, but silver, like Edie's earrings. Silver is one of the best conductors of the focused Qi that a shadow warrior can generate. Silver blades, silver arrows, silver bullets, it's all the same, but the sword is the most common form."

"So, can this velecor stuff protect us from that?" B.J. asks.

"Kid, nothing on earth can protect you from a lorenth but another lorenth. If you see one, your best bet is to run.

"Suit up, and don't forget to put some food and drinks in your bags, no more stopping. We need to pack up and get out of here quickly. I'm not trying to be a jerk about this, but I've got the world's greatest warrior downloading his playbook into my head, so I need you to listen to me out there. Do exactly as I say, unless we come across an experienced hero, then we all need to listen to him."

"Or her," Edie adds.

"Or her," David agrees, smiling.

Despite the seriousness of their situation, Edie's inner nerd is giddy as the parade of gadgets continues. He supplies all of them with metal collars to fasten around their necks to function as psi-masks to disguise their identities. Theoretically, people won't see their actual faces, but the image that they imagine. He also gives everyone little silver stickers to put on their smartphones so they can't be traced. When he's done, they put on their new super suits and grab their gear, with the guys staying where they are and Edie going to a side room to get some privacy.

So, now they're soldiers in a rescue mission; their strange, endless night continues. This is crazy. It's all freaking crazy, but Edie's trying not to focus on it too much or she will completely spaz out. As she puts on her suit, Edie is once again desperately trying to steady her hand and quiet the sheer panic in her thoughts. She can't believe that she was lobbying to come along, but she did, and the truth is, she'd do it again. She can't run from this, no matter how she's feeling. Whether it's their world getting bigger, B.J. getting taller, or all of them seeing with new eyes, they are all changing in wonderful, unpredictable, horrifying ways as they adapt to their perilous new reality. But they have to adapt, and she has to do her part to help hold this group together.

Truthfully, she's even more terrified for David than she is for herself. It's not lost on her that David's been trying to keep them safe and sheltered but hasn't considered doing the same for himself. She knows he's getting help from Sothis and Ra, but she can't help but feel that a lot of this is just him. It's like the quarterback switch David used to flip; he'd become a totally different guy, a laser-focused, ruthless competitor. Edie thinks he's flipped a switch into warrior mode, and even more than football, in a strange way, this world seems to suit him; he's in his element. She saw it in his eyes in the alley. Those ravager things were predators, but to her, David was the real hunter. He sensed them, stalked them, and she believes that he would have killed them if he hadn't been worried about her. Her lil' bro, the guy with the big smile, the huge heart, and unshakable determination, is also a very dangerous man, and she doesn't know how she feels about that or how she can reconcile it. She's more terrified for David than she is of dying. Edie's not going to leave his side, no matter what. No matter the risk, she's going to make sure that he doesn't lose himself in the process of finding Semi.

As she puts on her "Black Widow" outfit, she prays a silent prayer.

She prays for their safety, for the courage to do what needs to be done, and that somehow, someway, they don't lose the best parts of themselves along the way. She hears the angels begin to sing as she prays, but it's a different song than before, a song of war, and Edie realizes something that she didn't understand before. Angels are messengers, servants, and guardians, but they are warriors and hunters as well. Whatever waits for her and her friends out there in the night, they are not alone.

They are among us.

THE SLEEPING
PRINCESS —EDIE

oly friggin' shiitake, we are in a hot mess.

It's 7:30 a.m., and for the last two hours, they've been somewhere in Stone Mountain, driving in circles. Lil' bro has managed to track Semi to about a two-mile radius, but he's having difficulty narrowing it down from there. So instead, David's driving around like a dad on a family road trip with a broken GPS who's too stubborn to ask for directions. Yeah, it's that bad. They are so completely screwed.

Edie was raised in a religious household, so technically, she never swore. but all that meant was she had to be careful not to use foul language in front of her parents and beyond careful in her second home with the Stones. Mama Stone is no joke. Everywhere else, she cursed like a sailor, and because her grandmother made sure she spoke Spanish, Edie had a really extensive, bilingual swearing vocabulary, a potty mouth second to none. Two years ago, Eden Grace made some changes in her life, and foul language was one of the things she cut out. Edie thinks it's made her a better person, really, but this day is tempting her to fall off the wagon. Her finite collection of stand-in words just doesn't seem to quite express the freaking magnitude of their predicament. As the insanity they're in increases, she's inching closer and closer to completely losing it.

Smile, Edie. Hold it together. Remember, I'm the rock of this group, the fearless, beautiful female lead. If I lose it, we are beyond screwed.

David is pressing hard. He's trying to force his connection, and the more he pushes, the less these abilities seem to be working. He's frustrated and edgy—characteristics that are not like him. Edie's trying to get him to calm down and take a breath, but like a typical man, he's zoning her out. He's worried about Semi and feels like time is running out to find her before something terrible happens, so the last words he wants to hear is someone telling him to calm down and relax. That's the funny thing about the truth. Truth is truth, whether we want to listen to it or not. Edie's trying to be chill and supportive, but if he keeps up and says one more snarky comment, she's definitely going to clap back.

Cool down, Edie; cut him some slack.

Under the best circumstances, her lil' bro puts too much pressure on himself. He grew up that way. Being a PK and a football player, who happened to be the son of Alabama football legend Anthony "A-Train" Stone, can do that to someone. He went a little crazy with his D-Rock celebrity for a bit and went totally to the dark side for a few months after Pastor Stone's death, but since coming back to his senses, he's taken on even more responsibility. David's trying to be the perfect son, the super big brother/surrogate father, the model student, the inspiring friend, everything for everybody. He's riding the guilt train over his dad, and no one can talk him off of it. It compels him to be the one to swoop in and fix every situation. Some of that he gets naturally, but that part of him has been on steroids lately. You combine his guilt, heroic nature, and adorable love-at–first-sight passion for Semi, and you get an uber-focused David 3.0, with crazy eyes. Calm simply isn't an option.

But he's not the only one stressed. David and Edie are both worried about B.J. When they got into the car, B.J. ate a boatload of food and then fell immediately asleep or something that looks like sleep. They keep hearing noises from inside him, rumbling, groans, murmurs, and what sounds like bones breaking and resetting. His face has changed to the point that he's unrecognizable, and his hair is darker and longer. He's sitting in the back seat with his head slumped over against the window, so it's hard to tell, but it seems like he's grown a few inches taller since they left the safe house, too. His body type has changed as well. He's gone from skinny and scrawny to an impossible combination of slender and sinewy. And he's acquired a six-pack that looks like it's been drawn on, a really sexy six-pack.

Did I just think that about B.J.? I must be more stressed than I realize.

She's switched to the back seat to keep a closer eye on him, but it's freaking her out. Is it a permanent change? What does it all mean? Is she freaking next? To say that this is a tense situation would be a gross understatement.

"How's B.J.? Any change?" David asks, between frustrated mumbles to himself.

"It's constant change, David," she says, using her calm, mature voice. "Is this going to be permanent? I'm really worried about him."

"I don't know. We need to get him some help if and when the cavalry shows up."

"Any luck locating Semi?"

"We're close," he grunts. "It's just so frustrating. The closer I get to her, the stronger her presence, but it's too strong. I feel her everywhere. Short of going house to house, building to building, I don't know if I can do this."

"Flowers," B.J. mumbles.

"B.J., you're up. We thought you were knocked out," says David, excitedly. "We've been worried about you. How're you feeling?"

"Haven't been asleep." He answers in a voice strangely deeper than his screechy old one. "I've been trying to shut everything out. Everything's so loud. Everything smells. It's too much, and you and Edie keep shouting."

"We haven't been shouting," Edie replies, defensively.

"I don't know," he answers. "It just seems deafening. All I know is right now I smell an overwhelmingly intoxicating scent of flowers, very strong and very unique. I don't know anything about them, so I can't tell you what type, but it's an overpowering scent, and it' s close, extremely close."

"Is it jasmine and rose petals?" asks David excitedly.

"Could be."

"Can you track it?" David responds.

"Maybe," B.J. answers, shrugging.

"What's going on, David?" Edie asks.

"It's a long shot, but in one of my visions, Semi's avatar had the most wonderful aroma. She smelled like jasmine, with a hint of roses."

"OK, that's weird and oddly specific," she replies. "But by the standards of today, I guess that makes it normal."

"It's fading a little," B.J. interjects. "We're moving away from it."

As David makes a U-turn, it dawns on Edie where Semi is.

"She's in the hospital," she blurts out as B.J. covers his ears, wincing. "We just passed the sign for one. It makes sense. Sothis said she'd be weak. There's the sign. Take a left, here."

As they pull into the parking lot of Stone Mountain Memorial Hospital, David says, "Yeah, this is the place. I feel her. Good call, Edie. She's somewhere on the third floor."

David eagerly hops out of the car. B.J. starts to follow, but she puts her hand on his shoulder.

"B.J., before you go out there, I've got to warn you..."

"That I look totally different. Yeah, that's all you kept thinking, very loudly, over and over again. That's part of what I was trying to shut out."

"You read minds too?"

"I guess. Right now, it's all pretty scrambled," B.J. answers. "Let me see what all the big fuss is about."

He stands up, outside the car, and looks at himself in his phone's camera. Edie braces for the worst, expecting a horrified reaction at seeing such a drastic transformation.

"Wow! This is radical. I look exactly like that vampire guy who tried to eat me. This is his face."

"I'm sorry, B.J.," she replies.

"Sorry? What's there to be sorry about? I look like a lead singer from a boy band. I love it. No more geeky B.J. I'm a total stud—with powers. This is a dream come true."

Seeing that they're not behind him, David walks back over to them. This is the first good look he's had of B.J.

"You've got to be about six feet tall, not that much shorter than me.

This is crazy," he says. "You look just like him." He leans in and looks B.J. in the eyes. "B, are you sure you're OK?"

"Never better," he says, beaming as he runs his hands through his now fabulous hair, "but don't call me B.J. anymore. No more, wimpy, nerd boy for me. From now on, I'm Jace Rider."

David and Edie look at each other and bust out laughing.

"We are never going to call you that," Edie replies.

"We'll see," he answers.

"C'mon guys," David calls out as he starts to jog toward the entrance. "We've got to get moving. We can debate about B.J.'s extreme makeover later."

"Hold up, we can't go like this," Edie says, pointing to their outfits. "We look like we just lost a cosplay contest."

David is wearing his skintight velecor shirt and jeans, but B.J. and Edie had chucked their jeans and are wearing the full velecor cat suit, superhero style.

"Yeah, it's not exactly blending in," David concedes. He puts his hand on each of their shoulders and says, "Now think of your favorite outfit."

They do, and suddenly Edie's in heels and wearing the yellow-flowered dress she wore at her ex-boyfriend's junior prom last year. The date was a disaster, but the dress was fire. B.J. is now in a black suit, black shirt, a black tie, and shades, with his hair slicked back as if he's joined the mob. Meanwhile, David is dressed in the identical clothes he was wearing when he first met Semi: his favorite jeans, his jean jacket, and his dad's old FDNY T-shirt—sans bloody handprint. Unlimited choices, and this is where he lands. Her lil' bro has many wonderful qualities. Unfortunately, fashion is not among them.

"How?" she asks.

"The short answer is that it's an illusion created by your armor," he answers. "It'll keep generating unless you decide to change the image. Let's go."

They move quickly through the front entrance and then up to the third floor, following behind David, who seems pretty sure of where he is going.

When they get off the elevator, David looks to his left. "She's this way. I picked up a stray thought from a nurse about a Jane Doe in room 312. Jane Doe's non-responsive. They say she's in some kind of catatonic state."

They slow down their pace, to blend in and head toward room 312. When they get to the doorway, the first thing that strikes Edie is the fabulous aroma emanating from it, not the kind of thing that you usually associate with a hospital room. And then she looks over and sees Semi, and she's absolutely stunned. Semi's ...

"She's soooo hot!" shouts an overly excited B.J. "Are you sure we're in the right room? She doesn't look like Semi at all."

"This is her," says David, with a tone that reflects that he is relieved, awestruck, excited, and more than a little nervous. "This is exactly how she looked in my dreams and in my last vision."

"Wow, she's hotter than anyone I've ever seen, in person, on a website, in a video game, anywhere. David, I'm sorry to inform you that this girl is officially way out of your league. She's so hot. I ..."

The next sound is Edie's hand slapping B.J. upside his thick, misogynist, pervy head.

"Hey," he whines. "You've got to stop doing that. I'm Jace Rider now."

"B.J.," she replies. "You can call yourself anything you want and grow to seven feet tall with lasers coming out of your butt, but as long as you're going to say stupid, insensitive, sexist things, I'm going to be around to slap you upside the head. She's not an object, B.J. She's our friend."

B.J. starts to open his mouth to defend himself, proving that, despite appearances, he is the same old B.J., but Edie glares at him, puts her finger to her mouth, and shushes him. She looks over at David and sees that her friend is trembling. D-Rock is long dead, and his warrior mode can't help him now. He's just a kid, her little bro, and he's in love for the first time, wondering if the post glow-up Semi is going to feel the same things for him that the old one did. He's stolen a car, partnered with angels, fought vampires, and risked running blindly into a battlefield in order to be here for her, and he's done it all without a hint of fear. But now, before his sleeping princess, he's terrified. Edie's two feet from him, and she can feel his heart racing. Love can have that effect on people.

"So, she's the new Iset, now?" she asks, less because she wants the answer and more because she's trying to break the ice.

"She will be," David answers, "As soon as I give her the talisman, but I think she's going to end up calling herself Isis. That's what she called herself during my last vision."

Edie grabs his hand tightly, just like she did on their first day of kindergarten when he was afraid to go in, just like he's done for her on more than a few occasions.

"Then what are you waiting for, Romeo?" she asks gently. "Go to her. Just like Boy Band Dude over there is the same old B.J., she's the same Semi from the diner; trust me. You two are meant to be together."

David steps forward slowly until he is standing over Semi, and then puts his right hand on his chest and summons a baseball-sized, resplendent sphere. He then slowly places it in Semi's chest and quickly backs away. She inhales deeply as it enters her. Her body glows briefly, but then it quickly fades, and there's nothing, no fireworks, no light show, no movement. She continues to lie there as if she's in a deep sleep.

"Is that it?" Edie asks. "Shouldn't something be happening?"

"I don't know," David answers. "I was told by Sothis to put it in her chest when we got here. That's all."

"Can't you ask her?" asks B.J. impatiently.

"No," says David. "Ever since we parked, I can't hear her anymore. We're just going to have to be patient."

Stone Mountain Memorial is an older hospital, desperately in need of updating, and Semi's small, dingy room is starting to feel suffocatingly small. Edie feels as if the darkness is closing in around them. She hears a chilling hiss coming from the window on the far wall, and it's not coming from the creaky old radiator beneath it. They've got to find a way to get her up and out of here fast.

Edie walks over and grabs Semi's hand, whispering gently in her ear, "C'mon Semi, get up. We're here now. You're among friends."

"I know," interjects B.J, excitedly. "David needs to kiss her, you know, to break the spell and all."

"No," Edie responds. "That's a terrible idea. The last thing she ne ..."

Boy Band B.J. interrupts. "No, this is brilliant. You know, the power of true love's kiss from all those princess movies. C'mon David, just kiss her. What do you have to lose?" Seeing David hesitate, he adds, "If you're too scared, I will. I mean, who wouldn't want to kiss this face?"

No saber ni papa de algo. That's what Edie's grandmother would say about B.J. if she were here, and she wouldn't be wrong. B.J. doesn't have the sense of a potato. Her potato headed friend has no idea what he's talking about. Edie starts to explain to her two male associates that this may be the most horrible of all B.J.'s horrible ideas, but she saves her breath. She's too late. She learned something over the years watching the male species. One on one, you can possibly reason with a man, but there's something about testosterone. When there are two or more, their hormones interact, making them increasingly stupid, the stupidity growing exponentially with every male who enters the room. This stupefying testosterone elixir is as combustible as gasoline, and there's nothing like a challenge or a dare to ignite it and eliminate the slightest possibility of a reasonable outcome. In keeping with the fragile nature of masculinity, in the face of B.J.'s challenge, her dear brother has been transformed into a moron, intent on accepting romantic advice from the least qualified person on the planet. Princess movies? Please. All of B.J.'s knowledge about women has come from anime and porn. This is not going to go well.

David walks to the opposite side of the bed and leans forward for his Prince Charming moment. Still clutching Semi's hand, Edie mouths the words don't do it, but he is too far gone. He puckers up and slowly moves his lips toward hers.

Semi snatches her right hand out of Edie's and it erupts with golden flame. Before David can un-pucker, she punches him in the jaw with so much force that she knocks him across the room and through the wall, barely missing the window. David falls three stories.

"David!" Edie shouts. "Is he ...?"

"He's OK," says B.J. "I sense him. He's seeing stars, but OK."

Her attention is immediately drawn back to Semi, who is sitting up straight, gazing right at them, eyes blazing and veins of golden fire glowing beneath her skin. Golden energy starts to crackle around her, causing her hospital gown and her beautiful, long, black hair to blow from some kind of invisible force, moving around her like a not so gentle breeze. She springs out of bed and glares at them ominously, obviously confused and frightened. But as they saw with David, when faced with a fight or flight scenario, Semi's instinct is to fight.

Edie's heart just stopped and fell into her stomach, but there's No time for nerves. There's only time to act.

Edie steps in front of B.J. before he can say or do anything stupid and stretches her palms out in front of her, saying, "It's OK, Semi. I know you're confused, but we're not here to harm you."

She turns from them, and with one effortless, hyper-accelerated motion leaps over the bed and out through the hole in the wall, landing three stories down into the parking lot below. B.J. and Edie rush to the hole and look down. David is sitting up, trying to clear his head. Semi gracefully lands near him, gets her bearings, and then starts sprinting off, barefooted.

"Man, is she moving," says B.J. "She's got to be going forty ... fifty miles an hour."

"C'mon, let's get to the elevators," Edie answers. "We've got to get down there and check on him."

As she tries to head for the door, B.J. grabs her arm and asks, "Do you trust me?"

Still miffed at him for spurring on David, she answers, "No, Mr. Potato, not at the moment."

"Mr. What? Whatever, I'm sorry to hear that. That makes this harder."

Before she can ask him what he's talking about, he scoops her up effortlessly in his arms and jumps through the hole in the wall. Edie tries to scream on the way down, but her stomach is in her throat. He lands cat-like and places her gently on the ground, where Edie proceeds to puke her guts out. This type of thing is so much cooler in the movies. While she's having her moment, she hears B.J. apologizing and explaining himself, sharing how he figured out that he has all the powers of his vampire look-alike and somehow instinctively knew that he could make the jump and that he didn't have time to explain his plan...blah, blah, blah. She's still going to kill him. If she ever stops puking, that definitely tops her list.

While she's still in her glory, B. J. helps David to his feet.

"You OK, man?" B.J. asks.

"Yeah," David answers, "A little groggy, but OK."

"No offense," Edie chimes in, "but how are you still alive?"

"My body instinctively generated some kind of telekinetic shield when Semi attacked. It took most of the impact."

"A TK shield, wow, that's crazy," says B.J. "I need one of those."

"You seem to be doing OK," David answers. "That was quite some jump."

"So, what are we going to do now?" Edie asks. "Semi is long gone."

"We can catch up to her in the car," says David. "Because of our contact upstairs, our connection is really solid. I know where she's going."

"We're drawing a crowd," says B.J. "We need to get out of here. I'm fast, and you're still groggy. I'll run and get the car. Throw me the keys."

Seeing David hesitate, he adds, "C'mon David, I can do this. My driving is much better now."

David tosses the keys and B.J. speeds off to the other side of the building.

"So, are you really, OK?" Edie asks.

"Just a little punch drunk, but I'm getting there."

"Good. So, do you have something to say to me, Romeo?"

"Huh?" He feigns ignorance.

"You know, something like, 'Edie, you were ...'"

"OK, OK, already, you were right, and I was wrong."

"So, very wrong," she chuckles. "What were you thinking, taking advice about women from B.J.? Seriously though, she's confused, traumatized, not quite in her right mind yet. When we catch up to her next time, you can't come on too strong."

"Trust me," he says, rubbing his jaw. "I've learned my lesson. That girl punches like a superpowered Tyson."

As if on cue, B.J. skids to a stop inches in front of them. They jump in, Edie in the back and David in the passenger seat, and take off, flying out of the parking lot, down Memorial Drive and onto Hwy 78, headed toward Stone Mountain Park. So, here's the thing: they've faced vampires, talked to an angel, and jumped out of the third floor, but

B.J.'s driving is by far the scariest part of their journey—so far. They narrowly missed three crashes before they left the parking lot. He's horrible, and if anything, his powers have made him worse, if that's even possible. Edie finds herself praying hard. On top of it all, the whole powers issue is causing her to have mixed feelings, now that she's the only one of them who hasn't manifested any useful ones. She's not sure if she's relieved or envious or maybe a little bit of both.

This is not the time to figure it all out. They're at the gate of the park entrance. David puts the whammy on the guard and uses his TK to open the gate. In stark contrast to earlier, he seems to know precisely where Semi is. After a couple of quick turns, he tells B.J. to park, although B.J.'s version of parking more closely resembles a controlled crash.

"See, that wasn't that bad," says B.J., after their whiplash-inducing stop.

Edie glares at him. "Give me the keys. You're officially retired."

David looks around pensively.

"She's just a little ahead. We can walk to her from here, but others are close, real close."

"Good guys or bad?' B.J. asks.

"I'm not sure. It could be either or both. We've got to move quickly."

He takes out his silver pole weapon and slings his backpack over his shoulder. "Take out your weapons and bring your stuff. Remember, don't fire unless you have no choice, but if you have to shoot, don't miss. This isn't a comic or a movie. These things play for blood."

"So, I guess staying in the car's not an option?" says B.J., half-joking.

"No, not this time," David answers. "There's not a safe place in this park. We're already too deep in the woods. The only way out is through."

David leads the way, and B.J. and Edie trail behind a bit. She clutches the handle of her pistol, but her hand is so sweaty she's scared it may slip out. Every part of her is shaking with fear.

Looking equally nervous, B.J. whispers to her, breaking the tension. "Soooo, yellow, huh, you decided to go to war in a flowered prom dress?"

"I was going for elegant warrior. So, what are you, an extra from a De Niro movie?"

"Nah, I was going for a Neoish vibe from the Matrix, an oldie that never gets old."

"If you say so, Vinnie," she answers. "Shhh, I think that's her."

They see her sitting cross-legged about seventy yards away, on a path at the base of the mountain, rocking back and forth. David motions for them to stop and starts walking toward her alone. Edie mouths to him to be cool. He nods his head affirmatively and walks toward Semi slowly.

There's light around her. It's almost 8 a.m., but what they're seeing is way beyond regular sunlight. It's an angelic glow. Edie focuses and sees several messengers gather around her humming. Their soothing song is helping her, but Edie doesn't know if it's working on Semi. Edie's starting to feel better, but then she feels something else. A chill breeze from behind her radiates through her, right down to her bones, making her feel dirty and desperate. Darkness is near and closing fast.

"David, hurry," Edie whispers. "Please, hurry."

Semi sees him and startled, rises quickly to her feet, both hands bursting with resplendent flame. Undeterred, David continues to move forward, pole in hand, both arms raised high above his head. Now, her hair is a yellow flame, and her whole body is glowing. Edie can feel her power from where she stands. If she hits him again, Edie doesn't think there's a TK shield that he could possibly muster to stop him from becoming scrambled eggs. This could be bad, really bad.

David approaches at a snail's pace. Semi is clearly frightened. The golden fire around her is growing; the earth is vibrating and stones are rising from the ground.

"It's OK, Semi," he says. "It's me, David."

She grunts aggressively, obviously confused, but he keeps coming.

"I'm sorry I spooked you earlier. That was stupid," he says, inching closer, "But it's me. You know me. You both know me. You know that I would never harm you. I'll never let anyone harm you. You can trust me, Semi. You know that. Look into my eyes. You know me."

As he draws close, he kneels before her and lays the pole at her feet. She raises her hand in the air as if to strike him but hesitates. Her confusion seems to have melted away. The ground stops shaking and the fire fades. She places her hand on his head and then gently caresses his face.

"David, is that you?"

He stands up and takes her hand. "Yes, it's me."

She smiles weakly, clasping both his hands with hers. "You did it. You found me."

With those words, she collapses into his arms, conscious but very weak, leaning on him for strength.

"Pick her up," Edie calls out. "Let's get back to the car and get out of here."

Initially, David nods in agreement, but then he hesitates, furrowing his brow. He motions them to stay back, leans Semi against the mountain, and with one blinding motion picks up the silver pole, releases the blade, and it turns into a sword of yellow and blue fire. David lifts it just in time to parry a red fire blade belonging to a muscular man who seems to have materialized from the air. He's big, with shoulder-length brown hair, wearing what looks like leather pants and a sleeveless leather shirt. David blocks several thrusts, but he's obviously overmatched. He needs help. B.J. lifts his gun to take a shot at Leather Man and has him dead to rights, but he hesitates, freezing up. Meanwhile, David's attacker makes a slick move and disarms him.

"You've got heart, boyo," he says mockingly "But you are way out of your depth. Black Shuck has been taking heads since long before your great-grandpappy was born."

He lifts his blade for a killing blow when, without thinking, Edie raises her viper and shoots three shots. The first strikes him in his sword arm, causing him to drop the blade, the second misses, and the third burns a golf ball size hole in Black Shuck's torso. But instead of falling to the ground, Shuck turns in her direction, bares his fangs, and three-inch claws pop out of his fingers. He's ready to pounce when David grabs him.

"Hey, ugly," he says, "We're not done."

David's hands are now radiating blue energy and he strikes Shuck several times in the gut, lifting him off his feet. He then grabs his muscle-bound opponent by the hair, pulls his head back, and strikes his windpipe with bone-crunching force. Unable to breathe, Black Shuck collapses to his knees, clutching his throat.

As David attends to Semi, Edie and B.J. start to run toward him, but they're grabbed from behind. Edie spins around expecting the worst, but instead, she finds a smiling, handsome, twenty-something man with brown hair, just the right amount of stubble, and dreamy blue eyes.

"No need to shoot," he says. "My name is Danny, Danny Vision. I'm one of the good guys and a friend of Semi. Grab my hands, and I'll get you two out of here."

"What about our friends?" Edie asks.

"They'll be fine. The rest of my team should be here any second to help them," he answers. "When the boss lady realized that David and Semi brought friends, I was told specifically to find you two and keep you safe."

"No," Edie answers, sternly. "I'm not going anywhere without David and Semi."

B.J., who has already grabbed hold of Danny, interrupts excitedly, saying, "Hey Edie, listen to the nice man. They'll be OK. We should definitely go with him."

What an idiot.

"No way," Edie replies. "I'm not leaving them, and how do we even know we can trust him? How does he know our names? I ..."

"*Go with him now!*" a voice, David's voice, bellows in Edie's head. "*He's on the level. We'll be fine. Go.*"

Reluctantly, she grabs hold of Danny's hand.

"Okay, now what?" she asks.

"Stay in physical contact with me and keep conversation to a minimum. This is going to feel weird. With any luck, we'll be long gone before...they're here. Hold on tight."

An eerily pretty, Goth-looking woman clutching a blazing red sword, appears behind them, leading a crew of four fearsome-looking dudes. They're right on top of Edie and the guys. She lifts her gun, but Danny shakes his head, and Edie feels her body tingling in waves as the group walks right through them. Somehow, the three of them have become mist, and from what Edie can tell, invisible mist.

"How...what?" she whispers.

"I'm an Earthbound," he whispers back, "a qareen. We have the power to transform inorganic matter permanently and temporarily affect living things. Because we can also create illusions by bending light and confusing the six senses, we are commonly called mindbenders. Right now, I've turned us into mist and blinded their sight, smell, and hearing to our presence although I wouldn't test that theory by continuing to talk. There are two ravagers in this group and a skin-walker. Their senses are very, very heightened. We're not going to be able to keep them fooled for long, so I'm not planning on hanging around. As soon as we get a big enough diversion, I'll get you out of here. I promise."

B.J. and Edie nod their heads affirmatively. Resigned to merely being spectators, they turn their attention to their friends.

About fifty yards away from David and Semi, the Goth woman stops and unleashes a ball of violet energy about twenty feet above David's head, striking the mountain behind him, a warning shot.

"Do I have your attention, shadow dancer?" she asks. "My name is Serafina. I've come to collect the young afreet. Step aside, and you can simply walk away. And yes, you can trust me. I'm a mercenary, and I am not in the habit of killing for free. I will be paid handsomely for finding the afreet and even more for collecting her, and I'll receive a bounty for every dead or captured Nistarim I collect along the way, but you are no one. No one wants you, dead or alive. Maybe you will accomplish something noteworthy at some point in your life, and there will be a price on your head as well, but this is not that day. Letting you go is not an act of mercy. It's an investment in that unlikely future. But I am not married to it, so if you do not leave in ten seconds, you will not leave at all."

With Semi leaning on him weakly and his flaming weapon in his free hand, David simply stands there with steely resolve. Edie notices small, black, bat-winged spirits have begun to gather around the scene, circling, their red eyes transfixed, anticipating something deliciously dreadful. Whatever is about to happen, this isn't good.

Finally, David responds, "No reason to count. I'm not moving. You can do your wor..."

Before David can finish his sentence, Serafina releases a mammoth purple fireball. It strikes David, and the explosion envelops him, Semi, and Black Shuck. The dark spirits shriek with glee and the mercenaries whoop with laughter. Edie's mouth is agape, and tears fill her eyes. She doesn't even have the strength to scream. All she can do is pray, pray that her eyes are lying to her, and she didn't just watch the death of her brother, David, while she hid here and did nothing. But unfortunately, Edie's lived long enough to know that prayers aren't always answered the way you want, and in the real world, Charming and Sleeping Beauty don't always have a happy ending. Sometimes dreams and dreamers are consumed by fire.

THE SECOND WORLD —
DAVID

David sees light, brilliant light, blinding but beautiful. Is it a tunnel? Is it calling to him? Was his body fried to a crisp or blasted into a million pieces? Maybe, all has been forgiven and his stains finally washed away, and he's on his way to glory, finally free.

So, if that is the case, why does he feel like he's been trying to dead-lift an incredible weight, and his body buckled and then collapsed under it? Pain is proof of life. No, he's not dead, but he failed. His defenses were crushed before the force of Serafina's attack. He remembers now. The light was purple, and it was not his friend.

He sees fire all around him. *What's going on?* he asks himself for the hundredth time since this whole thing began. He should be dead, not that he's rooting for that outcome, but he should be. According to the supernatural Wikipedia in his head, Serafina is both a skin-walker and a dark witch, and that eldritch energy fireball she threw was generated by a spell designed to shatter David's TK shield, incinerate him, and incapacitate Semi. David felt his shield crumble on impact, but here he is, still breathing, surrounded by purple flame yet somehow untouched. It takes him a second to notice that Semi, though barely conscious and leaning on David heavily, has her left arm outstretched. She's the one holding back the inferno.

She opens her eyes wide, and they blaze like twin suns. Pure, brilliant light radiates from her, engulfing David and consuming the flame, creating a wave of force that knocks their would-be attackers off their feet. As they scramble to get up, more bad guys arrive, but fortunately, so do five heroes, three women and two men. The good guys engage them and, though outnumbered, they are holding their own. That's the good news. The bad news is David can sense even more enemy entities drawing near. They are about to be overrun. Hopefully, that Danny Vision guy got B.J. and Edie to safety. At least, they'll be OK.

"Charming," Semi whispers weakly, collapsing into his arms. "Get us out of here."

With that, she loses consciousness. David instantly scoops her up, putting his super strength to use, but as much as he wants to oblige her and get them far away from here, he doesn't see how he can possibly get through this warzone without fighting his way out, and he's no match for these warriors. They make Black Shuck look like a Pee Wee Leaguer. Focus, just focus, it's just another obstacle. An enormous one, easily the biggest one so far, but there has to be a way around this. Despite the battle raging around him, fear isn't an option. It's there. It's always there, but he hasn't let it creep out of the cellar much since Penfield. It's just like it was on the gridiron: focus on the next move, the next play, the next challenge, and keep your eyes locked on the prize. That's all.

Suddenly, the words Gray Zone come to his mind. *What's a Gray Zone?* A voice, Ra's voice, is telling him that it's the key to their escape. So how does he get there? What does he do?

"Relax," Ra says. "Just relax. Close your eyes. Forget the battle; forget everything— breathe. Feel the earth, every bird, every stone, every blade of grass; let it touch you. Feel its essence; feel its pulse; hear its song. Experience the earth beyond what can be seen by mere men, the second world hidden from men's eyes since the time of the Corruption. Now, speak to it, call to it, with your soul, your spirit talking to the spirit of the nine worlds, the nine that form the one. Let it speak. Let it speak."

Ra repeats that last phrase over and over, his voice slowly fading until it becomes a faint echo that scatters in the eternal void. David hears him clearer than ever before. It's always been faint, more intuition than conversation, but this is different, and it's helped. He feels so at peace, so connected to everything, but he's not sure how it's going to help them get out of here.

What the ... What's happening?

David opens his eyes, and Stone Mountain is gone. Semi, his lorenth, his backpack, and David are in a golden sphere flying insanely fast through the air over...over... Where are they? This isn't Atlanta, and if the purple-red sky and the three moons are any indication, this isn't even Earth. It's hard to see exactly what's out there, but around them he sees mist and objects moving in the depths. He can't see much more than that because of the incredible speed of the sphere.

Am I doing this? How? If I'm the one driving, where exactly am I going, and how do I get us home from here?

The sphere is like a turbo powered roller-coaster, except one with no track, no anything, and his stomach is doing cartwheels. He's not normally prone to motion sickness, but he normally doesn't zoom through the Twilight Zone at a zillion miles per hour either, so all bets are off. It's odd. He just noticed that it's almost like the sphere has its own gravity. They're anchored, stable, not rolling around, and, unbelievably, they seem to be picking up speed. He wonders how fast they are going, and if he really is the one doing the driving, maybe he could put the brakes on and stop, get a chance to get his bearings and come up with a plan before he goes further. That sounds like the right thing to do. But he has no idea how to stop or land. He got here by relaxing connecting with the earth, speaking to it; at least, that's what he was told. But he really doesn't know how he did that. Maybe he could try, "Up, up, and away" or "Flame on" or something. It seems like the more he stresses about it, the faster they go. He just wants to make it stop.

Suddenly, the golden sphere vanishes, and they begin to fall, and in the middle of an adrenaline rush and his heart on the verge of exploding, it dawns on David that maybe he should have been more specific. He thinks they must be a mile up or more. Whatever, they are descending rapidly, and he doesn't have a parachute or wings or a silver surfboard, so this could get messy. His muscles tense; his heart pounds, on the verge of hyperventilating, and he feels a scream from down deep building, fighting to get out. *Don't scream. Stay frosty.* They are seconds from impact and a sudden end, but he can't panic. His dad always said, "Stay calm and work the problem. The only sure thing in a life-threatening situation is that the one who loses his head loses his life." Well, that may be true, but at this rate, David's going to lose a lot more than his head if he doesn't do something fast. He desperately needs to find a way to slow down.

Suddenly, he does. He slows down, and as they get about ten feet from the ground, they start to hover above it. He lets out the mother of all sighs and takes in several slow, long calming breaths. Good, very good. David thinks he's starting to get the hang of this. He tells himself not to overthink it, just relax, use instinct, and get his mind out of the way. OK, OK, he's got this. He slowly lowers his backpack to the grass below, and then he lowers Semi, who is still unconscious, resting her gently against a tree in the same beautiful field. Good, very good. David hovers above her, getting used to this whole flying thing, and after looking around to make sure that there are no threats, he takes a couple of laps around to check out the surroundings and get used to his powers.

David is stronger here than on normal Earth, a lot stronger, and he can do feats he can't do there, like flying, for example. Now, he doesn't even need a sphere. He's soaring Superman-style, practicing different heroic poses as he cuts through the air. Under different circumstances, hanging out here could be very cool. At least that's how it seems so far, but he doesn't know anything about this place. Something horrible could be waiting for them right around the corner.

Fortunately, David doesn't see any threats at the moment. The Gray Zone is breathtaking, with a gorgeous yellow sky, lush green grass and exotic flowers, fruit trees, blue deer, purple and pink bunnies, unicorns, and exotic, rainbow-colored birds. The colors are unnaturally vibrant, eye popping, as if the plants and animals are digital creations or a product of some psychedelic dream. And then there's the smell. It smells —peaceful. David knows peaceful isn't a scent, but he's bombarded by pleasant aromas that he can't place even though they seem vaguely famil-iar, and they all leave him feeling very, very calm. In fact, everything around him has that effect. This all looks awfully green and Garden of Eden-y to be a place called the Gray Zone. Then he sees them, portals that pop open and close in various places. They act as windows for him to view the Earth he knows. But through these windows, all objects on Earth appear in black and white.

Whatever this place is, it's incredible. David finds himself straining his neck, looking back and forth, zooming around, not wanting to miss anything. Unfortunately, he's spending more time sightseeing and not enough paying attention to where he's going. Without warning, the wind is knocked out of him as he face-plants into something, no make that someone, and fortunately, whoever it is catches David in massive, powerful arms and keeps him from hurting himself. His cheek smushes into the guy's chest and his senses are overwhelmed by the wonderful smell of vanilla and freshly baked cookies. David looks up and realizes that he's being hugged by one of those glowing angels that Sothis referred to as messengers. Startled, he pushes away, falling backward and plunging toward the ground. In his shock, David totally forgets how to fly. At the last second before impact, he instinctively surrounds himself with a TK sphere. It absorbs the collision, but he ends up rolling down-hill and falling into a ravine. *Real smooth, hotshot.* He's sure the angel is impressed.

The important thing is that he's OK. It's all good. David considers his embarrassing act of clumsiness a needed wake up call, telling him to get his head in the game. He needs to fly back up there and check on Semi, stop all this sightseeing, and get back to the business of figuring out how to get them to safety. He dusts himself off and rises to his feet, and then he realizes he's in a different place altogether. Gone are the lush foliage, pleasant aromas, and gentle, colorful animals. In their place is a desolate wasteland, a crumbling landscape of fissures and sinking streams. A heavy mist floats above shadowy crags and karst caves that smell like backed-up sewage and sulfur. Slithering, creepy-crawlies, gigantic cave crickets, and centipedes are everywhere. The sky, which had been yellow-blue with three suns, has darkened into a gray haze with two yellow moons. David's not in paradise anymore, and he has a bad feeling about this. He needs to quickly fly himself out of here before something or someone pops out of the mist.

As if on cue, he's suddenly surrounded by four beautiful, flawless, scantily clad humanoids with wings like eagles. Three of them are tall, studly men, two are fair-headed wearing loincloths, and one is dark-haired draped in a toga. The fourth is a statuesque blonde woman in a chain mail bikini, straight out of a sword and sorcery comic. To David, because of the wings, they kind of look like stereotypical pop culture angels, but there's nothing angelic about this group. Their demeanor seems like the opposite of angels. Instead of making him feel safer, their arrival sends spasms through David's stomach and a chill that crawls through his skin like a living thing. His Spidey sense is screaming stranger danger so loudly that he's getting a headache. He powers up to quickly fly away when Toga Guy puts his hand on his shoulder.

"There's no need to be afraid, son of Adam," he says in a smooth, baritone voice. "We're not here to harm you, friend."

David doesn't believe him. He can't put his finger on it, but there's something a little off. *Remember, covers lie. Never trust your eyes.* As he looks more closely, he notices something weird about the man's appearance. A small part of him is out of focus. David realizes they're projecting some kind of an illusion, masking their actual appearance. He steps back from Toga Guy and extends his right arm defensively. He left his lorenth next to Semi, so he's going to have to fight his way out of this the old-fashioned way.

Toga Guy starts chuckling and edges closer. As he does, his smooth voice changes, becoming rough and gravely, with a sinister edge as if the Cookie monster and Dikembe Mutumbo gave birth to a sociopathic child.

"You see it don't you?" he says with a devilish grin. "What a clever little monkey you are."

He morphs into his true form, becoming a slimy, green, eight-foot ogre with gnarly, yellow teeth and six-inch fangs protruding from the bottom row. Clothed in rugged, battle-worn armor, he has black talons coming from his fingers and toes and massive bat-like wings attached to his back, yet his creepiest feature is his, bulging, yellow eyes, filled with malice. David scans the other three, and their appearance has also changed. One has become a short, stocky, winged toad, another a seven-foot, horned, gray gargoyle. The female is now a lanky, red, horned, winged, lady lizard, with long, stringy, red-black hair infested by small colorful spiders. As they unveil their original forms, something else is revealed as well—their power. They have a dark force that is staggering, far greater than anything David has encountered thus far.

"You...you're de...de...demons," he stammers, hoping desperately for a way out.

When David saw the shadows and messengers on Earth, they appeared as apparitions, obviously functioning on a different ethereal plane. But it's different here. Here they're flesh and blood, same as him. The ogre leans in until they are face to face, and David is overwhelmed by the stench of his breath, a repulsive combination of rotten eggs and toe jam, so disgusting that David's eyes begin to water.

The ogre flashes a crooked smile and replies, "Demons? Really? That's such an unflattering term, perpetuated by the Ancient and his book of 'holy' fables. Yes, they call us demons, shadows, whispers, dark hearts, and worse, but none of that speaks to the essence of what we really are. We are truth-tellers. Don't let our appearance fool you. We are not inclined to harm you and wouldn't be allowed to even if we desired. That simply is not the way things work."

"Really, so how does it work?" David asks, full of false bravado.

"We simply, wholeheartedly tell the truth, our truth, at all times, in every way. The rest is up to you," he answers.

"Tell me what truth? You don't know anything about me."

"Oh, young David," the lizard woman interjects as she rubs her bony fingers across his cheek. "We know everything about you. Son of Anthony and Patricia, brother of Eli and Ellen, failed football hero, failed brother, failed son, oh, we know you far better than you will ever know yourself, and we know the lies you tell yourself every day just to make it through the day. Your faith is merely a crutch, a façade to cover up your truth."

"What are you doing here, son of Adam?" asks the winged ogre. "You thought you would sweep in and save the day? Really? You? We know who you are. You know who you are. You're no hero, David Stone. You know that, don't you? Do you need proof? What are the facts of this case?

"For the record, on the day you turned seventeen, there were drugs in your truck. Your dad, the late Pastor Stone, found them, you two argued, and you ran off. Your family threw a birthday party for you that night, and you never came, content to carouse with undesirables instead. Pastor Stone, bless his soul, went looking for you. He came across a house on fire while he was driving around, and called 911, but he heard people crying for help inside and knew that the fire truck would not get there in time. He saved four people that night, a couple and their two kids, but he never made it out. Pastor Stone died saving lives. He was a hero, a man among men, but not you, not you, never you."

The tall gargoyle chimes in, adding, "David do you remember your response when you found out? You came back after one in the morning, full of regret and smelling of alcohol, expecting to face the wrath of your pop, but it didn't happen. Instead, you saw your mom, the Garcia's, and your whole family waiting for you in the living room with tears in their eyes. The look on your face when you heard the news was priceless. You just stared straight ahead, frozen, with your mouth wide open, but you didn't cry, not then, not the next day, not even at the funeral. Your eyes went dark, and they stayed dark for quite some time. Do you know why, David? Do you? You were choking, suffocating under the weight of a truth that no one else knew, and you were too much a coward to admit. You killed your father. You know that. We know that. You are the reason that he died. You're no hero, David. You've never measured up, and you never will."

The toad-bat hisses, "You say you've changed, been born again— hallelujah. Merely more lies, son. The darkness never leaves. It lives in you. This kind of darkness can't wash away. You know what you are. The preachers lie. So many have said that you shouldn't feel guilty, that it wasn't your fault, but guilt is truth, the unedited story of your authentic self. There's no forgiveness for what you've done. Can you give your mother back her husband? Give Eli and Ellen back their dad? And there are more, so many more, aren't there D-Rock? Your fall from grace damaged many lives. There's no way to earn redemption, to wash away your stain, not for you."

Initially, David tried to have a stoic reaction to their words, but at this point, he's on his knees, covering his ears, fighting hard to hold back tears. He doesn't want to give them the satisfaction of seeing him cry. But covering his ears does nothing. It's as if the words are coming from inside him, and their mouths merely echo the truths that David already knows.

"No, no!" David cries out, but they simply laugh.

"Silly boy," sneers the lizard woman. "So now, you stumbled into the woods and were touched. They're going to come to you and tell you that you're chosen, chosen by the Ancient for some great task. Don't believe them. You were simply at the wrong place at the wrong time. It should have been someone else, someone better. Your father believed in you, David, put his faith in you and look what happened. So, tell me, how could you be the one to help this girl? Your father's fate is what happens to the ones who believe in the 'great' David Stone. You should have used the gun that night in the woods. You should have balanced the scales."

Now, David is weeping uncontrollably, hands covering his face.

"No," he mumbles. "No, my father loved me...no."

The eight-foot ogre puts his hand on David's shoulder again, this time gently saying in barely a whisper, "Yes, he loved you. He loved you, believed in you until the end. His last thoughts were of you, child, as his skin melted away. He died of a broken heart, finally realizing that he was wrong about you after all, that he had raised a great disappointment, bet everything on the wrong horse."

"No, it's not true," David answers angrily, finally finding his voice. "It's not true. Get away from me!"

They open their mouths to reply when suddenly the golden messenger that David bumped into earlier appears by his side, towering above him, looking down on even the biggest of the shadows. The messenger looks like a living, cosmic version of the Oscar award, bald and muscular, with armor made of aureate flame, and this same fire covers his body, flowing from inside him. The dark ones cower in his presence, backing away.

"You know the rules," he says in a mighty baritone voice that shakes the ground and fills every part of David with courage. "The child said, 'go,' so go or you will deal with me."

And just like the hyenas before Mufasa, the dark hearts flee, disappearing into the shadows. He extends his hand to David to help him up, but the son of Adam doesn't accept it. Instead, David prostrates himself before him. Everything happened so fast with Sothis, and when he bumped into the messenger earlier, David didn't quite grasp the significance. He does now. He is in the presence of a freaking angel. If he doesn't know anything, he knows he is unworthy.

"Rise, Chosen One," he commands. "There is much to do and little time. Follow me, and I'll lead you back to Amesemi. She is safe but will soon require your assistance."

David follows him without speaking. He feels heavy, his emotions still reeling from the shadows' assault. Eventually, he's the one to break the silence, finally mustering the courage to address the messenger. David asks him some general questions concerning where he is and what's going on but avoids the issues burning in his heart.

As they walk, the messenger answers each of David's questions patiently. The messenger explains that they are in Neter-khertet, the Gray Zone, one of the nine worlds of Earth, and that the Gray Zone functions as a barrier between the worlds beyond, the spirit worlds, and their own. It is the only place where humans can interact with spirits face to face in their natural form. Shadow dancers, the common name for Earth's gifted warriors, use the Gray Zone to teleport over short distances instantaneously and to travel great distances in a short period of time because time and space move differently here. The traditional name for this is Kefitzat ha-Derekh, the jumping of the road, but it is more commonly called shadow dancing. Because some warriors have a radical increase of power within its confines, the Gray Zone is also sometimes used as a place for epic, cosmic battles.

What humans call Earth is truly nine realms: Perinesa, the Earth that humankind sees, and eight worlds hidden from the eyes of men, each with unique properties. It was not that way in the beginning. Before the Corruption, the worlds were easily accessible, functioning as separate rooms in one big house. Afterward, they drifted apart, became hidden, and became corrupted versions of what they were.

David's Earth, Perinesa, is considered Earth Prime. The Gray Zone, the most accessible of the hidden realms, is the second world. The third world is Alchera, the next four, New Eden, Agartha, Nibiru, and Mu, are commonly lumped together and referred to as the four worlds. The eighth is Yaaru, and the ninth and most dangerous is Akert.

As the messenger shares about all this, it awakens information in David's internal, supernatural directory. Knowledge floods into his brain about these places, their inhabitants, and more.

David's learning so much, but he's only half-listening. The words of the shadows weigh heavily on his heart. After a while, he works up the courage to ask what he really wants to know.

"Why did you call me that?" David asks. "Why did you call me chosen?"

"Because you are, son of Adam," he replies. "You are descended from great lineage, were born with a unique gift, and destined before the beginning of time to be there when the last Dark Star fell so that he could activate your hidden power and bless you with more. You have been chosen, young one, picked by the light for this time, for this moment to do great things. This is only the beginning. Strigor Rey Perines, the nine worlds have waited a long time for your arrival."

"Strigor What Who?" David stutters. "That's not me. I'm David... just plain David."

"That is you for the moment. I speak to who you will become."

"You talk as if I have no choice. Is it destiny, or do I have options? You know, free will and all that?"

Up to now, they've been moving at a brisk pace, but suddenly, the messenger pauses, turns to David, and smiles.

"Yes," he replies. "The answer is yes."

"Huh? How can the answer be yes? Those two things do not go together."

He raises one eyebrow, obviously amused. "Really? The divine light specializes in things that his creations consider impossible, combinations that you may deem incongruous. Everything about the light's actions is too vast, too amazing, and too complex for us to comprehend, even for celestials. And humans are the greatest mystery of all.

"Humanity is unique among all that has been made, each one cast in the image of the divine's brilliance. Like all life, humans are a hybrid of nature, nurture, and destiny, but with your kind, free will was added to this mix, a gift so treasured that none are allowed to disrupt its course.

"Nature, nurture, destiny, and will, how these seemingly disparate elements function and balance is above the understanding of us all.

What we know for sure is that there is a unique power in every man and woman, a force in each individual's will that is so extraordinary that both nature and nurture bend to it. And at times, it even influences the course of destiny. Not even the greatest of celestials understand this, but we know this to be true.

"That is why the dark hearts fled. You acted upon your desire, your will to have them 'leave you alone', and they were bound by the Unbreakable Laws to do so.

"Free will is the most potent weapon given to the children of dust. Each choice shapes generations and echoes for eternity. So, know this, young one, life in the flesh is fleeting, a mist that quickly fades. Every breath is a precious gift, and each decision sends ripples that reach both the depths and the heavens, drawing the attention of celestial beings. As long as you draw breath, endless voices will sing to you. The light is calling, young David, but the darkness is never far behind. The eternal war, this war, is very real, and it is the only thing that will matter in the end."

He pauses, allowing the overwhelming truth of his words to sink in, then he puts his massive hand on David's shoulder.

He smiles warmly and adds, "So, to answer your question, you can decide on another path. Destiny is a choice. Many voices lay claim to you, but what you believe is who you will become. You have been chosen, young David, but even the chosen still must choose. The trick is to choose well."

"Yeah, well, that's the thing," David answers. "It's not that I'm unwilling. It's just that someone made a mistake. I'm not your guy. Those shadows may be evil, but they weren't wrong about me. If I'd done the right thing, if I hadn't run off, my dad would still be alive. And the people I hurt after— if I'd been different, stronger..." His voice trails off, and he diverts his eyes, finding it difficult to find the strength to continue. He swallows hard and lets a beat pass before he does. "I... I'm not cut out for all this chosen one stuff. Something this important needs to go to somebody better, a real hero."

"A hero like your father."

David nods his head affirmatively, sadly.

"You've failed. You've let people down, let yourself down," the messenger replies. "Once, you were sure that you could do anything, and now, you live constantly with the shame of your failure and the fear that someway, somehow, no matter how hard you try, you're destined to fail everyone again."

"Yes."

"Good," he replies, "then, you're ready."

"What?"

"The divine light specializes in the broken. Conviction is forged in the furnace of failure, wisdom is gained through tears and loss, and strength is birthed when frailty refuses to surrender. In the end, it is only the weak and the broken who are truly prepared for greatness. Do you understand?"

"I think so."

"Who you were, what you've done, your glory and your shame, it is all part of the journey that has brought you here, to this moment. And what happens next is not a question of worthiness or ability. It comes down to what you believe. Are you a mistake, a cosmic accident, brought here by chance and circumstance, or were you carefully and lovingly made for this very purpose? What is in your heart, young David? Do you believe that you were chosen? Do you trust the one who chose you?"

There is a long silence as David contemplates the questions with his head down, then he slowly lifts his head and gazes into the eyes of the messenger.

"Yes," David answers. "Yes, I do."

"Good, very good," he says, smiling.

"So, what do I do now? I have so many questions. Where are my friends? How can I get Semi and myself to safety? What's my next move?"

"This is my stop, young David. You'll find Semi a couple of hundred yards over that ridge. You'll know the rest when the time comes. Follow the light. Trust in the one who chose you."

He turns and walks away. David starts to call out to him, to beg him to stay and give him more specific help. The messenger turns his head and speaks over his shoulder.

"Oh, by the way, your father never stopped believing in you, never stopped being proud. He still speaks of you glowingly, all the time."

"You've seen my dad?"

"Do not mourn the living, young David. I saw him just today," he answers nonchalantly. "Job, Peter, your old neighbor, Mr. Assad, your father, and I were having the most stimulating conversation. Your father had a message he wanted me to give to you. He said, 'Talioth Sagana Sett Nava Say Algo Daymon.'"

David knows this language fully now. It was the language from his dreams and from Semi's journal. It is Kolu, common angelic, one of the 144 known angelic languages. This expression means, "Promise me you will cling to the path so that I will see you again." His eyes tear up at these words, but these are happy tears. A sensation washes over him like cool, cleansing water, and for the first time in over a year, he feels the massive weight of guilt lift and dissipate.

"I promise," David whispers, and then he calls out boldly to the messenger, "Talioth Algo Daymon, Tell that to him, please, for me."

"I will," he answers. "My men wait for me. Battle calls. Until next time, son of Adam."

"What is your name?"

"Commander Shamar," he answers. A brilliant blade of light appears in his hands. He bursts into golden fire, Human Torch style, and stands up straight, all nine feet of him, then Shamar flashes a smile and flies off, blazing through the now blue-purple sky.

David turns and starts walking toward the ridge. When he reaches it, he sees Semi in the distance, just beginning to stir from her sleep. *Good, she seems OK.* He picks up his pace, and as he walks, he can't stop smiling. Of everything he's seen and heard in the second world, all he can think about is the last part of his conversation with Commander Shamar. His father is alive on the other side, and he's waiting for David. He doesn't know what his future holds, what role he's supposed to play in all this, or what challenges he's going to face along the way, but if he clings to the light, he will see his dad again. That doesn't sound too bad, not too bad at all.

CROSSROADS —SHAMAR

This is what Shamar knows. During a storm like this one, humans see the flashes of lightning, feel the wind, and hear the sound of thunder, but they do not see and dare not comprehend the celestial fire behind each bolt or the awesome, divine power echoed in every rumble. If they did, they would fall on their knees and worship or cringe in the shadows in fear, for they would have gleaned the truth. The celestial divide is in their midst, and there is war in the heavens for the hearts of men.

For a moment, perhaps less, he closes his eyes and leans on his precious sword, letting the voice flow through him, renewing his strength. Three days have passed since Shamar met the young chosen one, and he has spent that time knee-deep in the blood of shadows as the battle of Nairobi rages on. Necronis, the dark prince of this city, has established a powerful stronghold here, and the dark hearts have overrun it, upsetting the balance. The prayers of the remnant that remains have summoned Shamar's celestial legion. So, here they are, waging war for the remnant's sake and for the sake of those who have not yet chosen their destiny. Shamar's forces are even more terribly outnumbered than usual, but the legion at his command consists of both messengers and virtues, and they have fought bravely, managing to push back the horde and break its spirit, at least for the time being.

He senses him, smells his putrid flesh. Even though their forces are retreating, a lone shadow attempts to sneak up on Shamar from behind, seeking to collect his head as his trophy. Silly rabbit, he will not be the one. With a twinkle in his eyes and one blinding motion, Shamar's stasial blade cuts through the air, its brilliance lighting up the midnight sky, leaving his opponent headless and separated from his physical form. He is eradicated, bodiless and depowered for now, and must endure the painful, century-long process of his form being reborn. Eradication is the worst that either side can do to the other. Celestials and shadows do not have the power to kill one another permanently. Only the Ancient can do this. This one's final end will not take place until the day he and his allies face the lake of fire that is the second death. That will be a glorious day. Casting him out of this dead shell will have to suffice for now.

Shamar surveys the battlefield, the clouds and the mists of the land between, where they rage their "endless" war, the broken and decaying bodies that litter the green-brown hybrid of ectoplasm and celestial dust that makes up the ground beneath them, and the bodiless spirits that pass beyond his reach. So many battles. He should be weary, but he's not. He loves this. He was made for it, and as long as the voice sustains him, he will never quit.

Eitan shouts out to Shamar. "Commander Shamar, the rats are fleeing, commander. The battle is over."

"Don't get ahead of yourself, Lieutenant Eitan. Ready your men. Necronis did not get so old and fat by being easy to defeat. This is far from over."

As if on cue, Gibbor, Shamar's second in command, approaches, obviously distraught. Above him, the winged virtue, Mehira, their best scout, departs. She has obviously passed on to Gibbor some crucial intel.

"Commander, Mehira has informed me that the princes of Kisumu, Mombasa, and Eldoret are approaching, each leading a large army. Our one legion cannot repel a force this size. We will soon be surrounded on every side, with no hope of retreat. This was a trap."

"Of course, it was."

Gibbor smiles. "You know, it's been one thousand years since I've been eradicated. I'd like to keep my streak intact. Please, tell me that you have a plan."

"How long have you known me, Gibbor?"

"Too long," he quips.

"When have you known me not to have one?"

"OK, so, do you care to share it with an old friend? Another two or three legions coming to reinforce us would be a welcome sight, but our intel says that the remnant is too weak to summon more."

"It's a surprise."

"I hate surprises," Gibbor mumbles, crossing his arms disgustedly. "I think the last time you surprised me, I got eradicated."

"Tell our forces to hold the line but not to initiate engagement. All will be clear soon enough."

Gibbor goes to carry out his orders, and a chill fills the air as a seemingly endless swarm of malevolent spirits approaches. As dark forces encircle their own, Shamar can feel Necronis's foul laugh vibrating in the depths of his soul. Necronis gloats, reveling in the hopelessness of the celestials' situation, counting down the minutes until his troops are in place and they descend upon them like locusts devouring a vineyard. Unfortunately for Necronis, he has failed to grasp a simple, significant truth. Desperate circumstances are when the light does his best work.

"Their forces are moving forward beginning to engage," says Gibbor as he returns. "Are you ready to unveil your plan?"

"Not yet," Shamar replies.

"But commander..."

"Wait for it," he says, lifting his hand, silencing Gibbor, and then after a seemingly unbearably long pause, Shamar begins to count down "Five, four, three, two..."

At one, he whispers the word, "Now," And she appears in the center of their legion, hovering above them in all her resplendent glory. Hair of white-hot fire, skin like golden gleaming bronze, eyes like twin suns, with six wings radiating golden flames. She carries no weapon in hand, but there is a reason for that. She is the weapon.

Gibbor calls out to his commander, raising his voice over the throng, the cheers of their troops, and the horrified screams of their adversaries, saying, "Adira... Adira here? I can't believe you had a throne for backup the whole time. Not just a throne, a Seraph at that. How?"

He grins. "The remnant is not quite as weak as the enemy has been led to believe. One warrior, in particular, Mr. Ondatto, has shaken the heavens with his pleas for this city. I was able to secure some help. Given the choice, knowing we were walking into a trap, I chose a throne over an additional legion, hoping we could set a trap of our own."

Shamar nods toward Adira. She nods back, flashes a confident smile, raises her right hand high, and simply snaps her fingers. Like a pebble cast in a lake, ripples of brilliant light emanate from her in every direction, becoming powerful waves of pure aureate energy that sweep over the battlefield. The shadows try to run, but though more pervasive, in the end, darkness is not more powerful than light, and it is certainly not faster. The waves comfort and energize the legion of celestials, but it burns the dark hearts, instantly eradicating them. Faster than the rest, Necronis vainly attempts to flee, but in a flash, Shamar flies in front, grabbing him by his massive throat. Necronis struggles furiously to break Shamar's grip, but he squeezes even harder, determined that the villain will not elude him as he has before. The waves catch up to them, and as they do, Shamar simply gazes into Necronis's dark eyes as the light consumes him, exiling him for one hundred years. The malevolent armies have been swept away. Other shadows will come to this city to fill the void, but the balance between whispers and hope has been restored. That is their part in this. What happens next is something that the humans of this city must decide. Hope or darkness, it is up to them.

Celebration ensues, and once more Shamar smiles as he surveys the rejoicing of his legion and the tens of thousands of steaming enemy carcasses before them.

Gibbor glances admiringly at Adira, who is hovering a few feet from them. "This is the closest I've ever been to a Seraphim when they unleashed. That was truly incredible," he remarks. "And the majestic way she hovers there, it almost makes me envious that I have no wings. Half the virtues have wings. Thrones have wings. Why are we Malakim the only ones without them? Seems odd."

"If you want to file a formal complaint, go right ahead, but I won't be standing next to you when the Ancient replies." Shamar chuckles.

"No, old friend," he continues. "We are what we are, made for battle out of celestial dust and white-hot chasmal, and we both know you wouldn't have it any other way." Gibbor nods his head, approvingly. "Besides," Shamar adds, "we messengers are the only ones who get to carry stasial blades. In my opinion, we got the better end of the deal."

As Shamar starts floating toward Adira, he issues an order to Gibbor, saying, "Organize the legion. I need to speak to Adira before she departs."

As he rises, Adira smiles. "Greetings, golden guardian. Brave Shamar, as always, it is good to see you. You and your legion did great things here today."

Like most thrones, in her typical form, she is short by celestial standards, at barely six feet, but she is regally stunning in her appearance, glowing with a brilliance gained by standing in the presence of The One. This makes her difficult to gaze upon for any length of time.

"You are too kind, mighty Adira, but we both know without your assistance, the conflict would have gone differently."

"We all play our role, commander, but it is not lost on me and others that this was your plan. Take the compliment. Many are always watching. You and yours have taken a unique path to get where you are, and there were some who secretly doubted the decision to give you the opportunity. The Ancient is proud of you and your work. Your example gives hope to the hopeless. He wanted me to tell you that personally."

"I am honored and grateful to serve."

"One other thing," she continues. "He has granted your request."

"Request? I made no requests."

"He knows your heart's desire, commander. He knows that you yearn to stay and witness the young majestic and his friends as they each encounter their next major crossroads, the nexus point where destiny and will converge."

"Word is that each of them experienced a defining moment after I left young David. They say that the impact of these choices reverberates across time and space," Shamar responds. "Yes, I would greatly appreciate the opportunity to witness this firsthand."

"I will take you there, to moments after you left, so that you can bear witness."

Shamar is both honored and somewhat confused by this. He does not need Adira's assistance to travel back. Daily, the voice moves him and those under his command forward, sideways, and backward through time and space, sending them where and when they need to be, to serve the Ancient's will. They slide in, and they slide out, experiencing the universe in pieces, and although they understand far more than humans, they know less than one might think. They experience the grand plan as random puzzle pieces scattered across time, trusting by faith that they all fit together perfectly and beautifully. Shamar knows that it is different for thrones. Their knowledge is much deeper, but he has never envied their position or questioned his. He goes where he is sent and serves where he is called. Why would he need an escort now?

"You worry that you are not trusted," states Adira, intuitively knowing his fear. "Nothing could be further from the truth, Shamar. Let me ask you a question. A few days ago, how was it meeting the young herald again— again for you, the first time for him? He was older in your other encounters, wasn't he?"

"He was. Seeing him, it was great, exciting, and if I'm honest, more than a little strange. I had forgotten how different things were then. David was so young, so innocent."

"For good or ill, what happens next will change that. You share a special bond with them, Shamar, especially young David and Amesemi. It will not be easy to simply witness what happens next and not interfere, even for you. It is a painful experience, and while none of us question your resolve to do what's right, you should not have to endure it alone. Allow me to be there for you as you have been there for me, so many times in the past."

Shamar bows his head. "It would be an honor, old friend. But first, let me give some instructions to my troops."

"No need," she answers. "I will have you back within minutes, and Gibbor and I can fill in for the brief time that we are gone."

Shamar looks up, and even while she is hovering next to him, she is standing next to Gibbor, giving him instructions. It's astounding. He'll never get used to it or understand it, how she and her kind can be in more than one place at a time.

Seeing his expression, Adira laughs. "It still freaks you out, doesn't it?"

"Honestly, it hurts my brain, Adira. You are there and you are here, and you are always standing in the presence of the Ancient."

"Yes," she replies.

"And simultaneously, you are the Earthbound that humans call Sothis, destined to live out your time on Earth as a celestial symbiote."

"Yes," she responds, "And as long as we're keeping score, I'm also in Paris, I'm in Bejing, and I'm helping to settle a dispute on a little planet in the Zarva system."

"There's a Zarva system?" Shamar asks, shaking his head.

"We've been through this, Shamar. Most life, including all shadows and most celestials, are uni-present. Their consciousness can only be in one place at a time. The Ancient is omnipresent, everywhere at all times. We Thrones are multi-present, able to be several places across time and space at once while never leaving our place by the Ancient's throne."

"So, when we go back, you're going to be witnessing you and Amesemi as you struggle to complete your joining. How is that going to feel?"

"Great, exciting, and if I'm honest, more than a little strange," she answers, smiling. "It will be good to experience it standing next to a friend."

"Fair enough. So, when do we lea ...?"

Before he can finish his question, he sees white light and feels himself turned inside out. It takes him a second to recalibrate, and when he does, he is hovering next to Adira in the Gray Zone. He sees David as he was, seconds after Shamar left three days ago, and he sees his past self in the distance, streaking across the sky as he hurried to reunite with his legion, to prepare them for the upcoming battle. Yes, this is a very different experience through time than sliding. Sliding is slower but gentler, and in all his other travels, he has never encountered a past version of himself. It is more than a little unsettling.

Adira cloaks them so that they are invisible to all beings here, not only the humans but the shadows and celestials as well. Shamar begins to ask a question, but David has arrived at where Amesemi is resting, and the commander wants to hear their interaction.

Seeing that Amesemi is stirring, David nudges her gently, asking, "Semi, are you awake?"

"Not Semi, Sothis," she answers, weakly, "Semi needs to sleep for a few more hours before our union can be completed and she can fully assume control. I took the liberty of waking up this body because it is unsafe to remain here much longer. It is difficult. I can only afford to use a small amount of energy because most of my strength is being used to facilitate our transition. Please, young David, help me to my feet."

She leans on David heavily and stands, and as she does, she stares straight at Shamar and Adira and cracks a knowing smile. *How strange.* Adira smiles back and the two lock eyes for a moment. Shamar will never get used to this.

Noticing Sothis staring off, David asks, with more than a hint of concern, "What is it? Is something there?"

"Nothing that you need to concern yourself with," she replies coyly.

"We need to get you out of that hospital gown. Here, I've got something for you." He picks up his backpack and reaches into it. "I got this from Amon Ra's safe house. He had a number of them, but something told me the velecor armor with the gold star was one he had specially made for his daughter."

He hands Sothis the velecor suit and immediately turns his back so that she can change.

"Thank you," she replies.

"When you're feeling stronger, I have a lorenth for you as well."

Sothis quickly puts on the armor, sends a spark through her beautiful, full hair and instantly changes her gorgeous, straight hairstyle into stunning, long, elegant braids.

"Is this better?" she asks, posing in her form-fitting body armor and her new hairdo. "The braids were Semi's idea."

She looks identical to her avatar in David's dreams, absolutely spellbinding, literally taking the young majestic's breath away. Shamar grins. He can both see and experience the thoughts and feelings of all the non-celestials in his presence. This is precious. David's so young, so hopeful, and so in love.

"Uh ... y ... yeah, it's great," he stutters, trying unsuccessfully not to gawk and stare. David composes himself and searches for words, trying desperately to be cool and say the right thing. "If she can't hear me, tell Semi she looks stunning. I always knew she was a princess."

"No need. She can hear you just fine."

David is blushing and he quickly changes the subject. "I know we need to get moving and get out of here. If you don't mind, I can pick you up and fly us somewhere, but I'm not sure where we are or where we need to go. Man, I can't believe I just said that sentence...fly somewhere. I said it as if it's normal." He chuckles. "I wish Eddie and B.J. could see me fly. That would be something."

"Oh, we saw you fly," says Brantley James as he, Daniel Vision, and Eden, descend in a golden sphere, landing a few feet from them. "How do you think we found you? We saw you fly. We saw you crash. We saw you come tumbling down. You put on quite a show."

"Guys, you're OK!" David exclaims as he races over and hugs both Eden and Brantley. "I was so worried about the two of you."

"Worried about us?" Eden replies. "You were the one 'consumed' by a purple fireball. It took us a few seconds to figure out that Semi saved you. That was very cool."

"It was cool," replies David, defensively, "but I mean, technically, we kind of saved each other."

"Uh oh, fragile male ego alert," answers Eden sarcastically.

Young David looks over at Brantley for support, but he shakes his head. "I can't help you with this one, bud. Super Saiyan Semi definitely gets credit for the save." He waves at Sothis and changes his voice. He lifts his eyebrows and does his best impression of a character out of an old American TV show. "Hey, Semi, how you doin'?"

"I'm fine, thank you, but I'm Sothis, not Semi," she replies. "Semi is getting some much-needed rest. Oh, and my eyes are up here, young Brantley. So, if you are done admiring the gold star on my chest, you would do well to remember that. Semi will be assuming control soon, and she wants me to inform you that she will not be as patient with your wanton lasciviousness as I am, and my patience for such behavior is not great. You wouldn't want us to sneeze and mistakenly go 'Super Saiyan' on you, would you?"

"N... no ... ma'am," He stammers, with a voice laced with embarrassment and more than a hint of fear. "I'm sorry."

Sothis nods her head, graciously accepting the young man's apology while Eden fakes a cough to suppress her laughter. Daniel bows his head toward Sothis deferentially, and she acknowledges this act with a knowing nod of her own. Typically, David comes to his humiliated friend's aide by changing the subject. He is loyal, perhaps, loyal to a fault.

"I'm just glad that everyone's OK." Turning to Daniel, David extends his hand. "You must be Danny Vision. Thanks for your help. It's good to finally meet you face to face."

Daniel shakes his hand and replies, "It's a pleasure to meet you, David, and not just talk to you through mind-speak. When I saw you open a door to the Gray Zone, we were fortunate to leap in behind you, close enough that we were eventually able to track you here. We were not followed, so we should be safe for now."

"I'm glad you guys found us. Why didn't you just reach out to my mind through telepathy, like before? Wouldn't that have been quicker?"

"We were split up from my team and the telepath that linked us earlier. I am Earthbound, and we Amar are empaths, not telepaths. On our own, we can only partake in mind-speak with those with whom we share a soul link."

"What's a soul link?" Brantley interrupts, "and what is this place? Are we on another planet or in another dimension, like the quantum realm from the movies?"

Ignoring Brantley, Daniel steps toward David and whispers, with more than a trace of exasperation. "Your friend asks a lot of questions, and he never stops talking."

David smiles. "You have no idea."

"Hey," says Brantley. "You know I can hear you as if you're shouting. I've got super hearing now."

"We know," David answers.

Eden grabs Brantley by the arm and leads him away, her eyes fixed on Daniel, saying, "C'mon, B.J., let the grown-ups talk."

She smiles at Daniel and bats her eyelashes as she moves Brantley, not even attempting to hide her infatuation with her new, Earthbound ally. Shamar wonders if it would be rude for someone to inform her that Daniel's good looks are an illusion, and he is over seven hundred years old. She'll learn soon enough that in this strange world, things are rarely what they seem.

"So, what's our next move?" David asks.

Daniel replies, "From what the queen has informed me…"

"Queen?" asks David.

"Queen Sothis," Daniel replies, somewhat surprised. "Sothis is a queen, queen of the Earthbound and the Amar, our descendants, and her host, young Iset, will assume that role after some seasoning, when she is ready. As Sothis' host, she is capable of mind-speaking with any willing Earthbound and some Amar across short distances. Sothis has informed me that she and Semi need six to ten hours of uninterrupted sleep before their union can be completed. We can't remain here for too long. The enemy has a small army looking for her, and it's dangerous to try to transport her to Avalon or a known safe house while she is so vulnerable because the paths to such places are being closely watched. You need to pick someplace safe, and we can bring her there."

"Me? Why me?"

"Semi trusts you, and the enemy does not yet know you or your world. Hide her among people you trust, somewhere far from here, and they won't have any hope of finding her until she is whole. Do you know of a place?"

"Yeah, I think so," David answers. "We can go to my aunt's house in the Bronx. My mom thinks I'm there anyway. We can crash there until Semi's at full strength. It's like one thousand miles from Atlanta, two hours and change by plane. How long will it take through the Gray Zone?"

"Including the time it'll take to round up your friends and ignore some more of B.J.'s questions, about twenty minutes by foot, five minutes flying. I wouldn't fly, though. It's too easy to be tracked." Seeing David's confusion, he explains further. "Focus on where you want to go. Picture it, and the Gray Zone will create a path for you."

David focuses and sees a path being illuminated before him, his eyes lighting up as if he just opened a new toy at Christmas.

"Yeah, that's it," Daniel encourages. "You're a natural."

They hear Sothis sigh, and they glance over at her as she grimaces, her eyes close, and she shakily drops to one knee. She is helped up by Eden and leans heavily on her.

"Whatever we're going to do, we need to do it quickly," Daniel continues. "The young Iset won't make it much further without getting some rest. I'm pretty confident that we weren't followed, so as soon as you round up your people, we can ... ahh ..."

Mid-sentence, a fiery red blade bursts through Daniel's torso. Eden gasps, Brantley screams, and David leaps back, telekinetically summoning his lorenth into his hand, a trick he was unaware he could do until now. Young David has Shamar's full attention. His amazing ability to compartmentalize and simply act in perilous situations, responding to need over fear, is a trait shared by every version of David that Shamar has encountered. Yet, it is still surprising to see it here and now when he is so new to this world. He masters his emotions and does what needs to be done. This is his gift and his bane depending on what version of his destiny he embraces. What happens next will do much to determine that course.

The attacker grabs Daniel's hair with his free hand, pulling back his head. He mocks his victim, revealing himself to be none other than Black Shuck, charred, not fully healed, but very much alive.

"Oh, you're wrong about that Ol' Danny Boy," he hisses. "You weren't the only one to follow the boy through the breach. Tracking you dolts was easy enough from there. That skin-walker pup over there is putting out an odor that's hard to miss."

"I...I saw you d ... die," grunts Daniel.

"Oh," he answers. "You should know by now, Black Shuck's not so easy to kill, a little crispy, but I'm still here. I'm always here. Out of respect, Danny Boy, I'll make it quick. You won't suffer much longer. Unfortunately for those pups you're protecting, I can't make any such promises. I'm going to have some fun with them."

"Get away from him!" shouts David, as the lorenth in his hand becomes living fire, this time pure, golden flame. "C'mon tough guy. Let's see how tough you are with someone you're not sneaking up on. I'm ready for round two."

Shuck grins, baring his fangs maliciously. "Sorry, Danny, you're going to have to suffer a wee bit longer. Seems like the kid has a death wish." He thrusts Daniel aside. "And I'm happy to oblige."

He pulls out his blade and rushes toward David, confident that the young warrior will fare no better than he did during their last encounter, but this time, there will be no one to save him. Shuck's attack is violent and powerful as he seeks to end his opponent's life quickly. He drives his young adversary back, gaining the advantage, but David's movements are quicker, more confident than before. He is not overthinking; he's letting his natural ability and the majestic's guidance move through him instinctively. It makes him far more formidable as he parries Shuck's advances and switches from defense to offense. After several intense exchanges, he kicks Shuck's knee. The ravager is taken by surprise and stumbles slightly, losing his balance. Stone seizes the opportunity and cuts off three fingers from Shuck's sword hand, disarming him, then, without hesitation, David turns and decapitates Black Shuck, sending his screaming skull flying through the air.

Eden and Brantley recoil, horrified by their friend's actions and the brutality of the battle, but David, unfazed by their reaction, gestures toward the still blinking head and causes both it and the body to burst into flame He then watches it burn to ashes.

"A little overkill isn't it, bud?" says B.J. as he fights to avoid vomiting and leans on his default mechanism of using humor to cope with trauma.

David's face is expressionless. "With the older ravagers, it's the only way to be sure. How's Danny?" he asks, not missing a beat, calm and focused as if this were simply part of his daily routine.

But that is a façade, of course, merely his game face. Inside, he is in turmoil. It is not an easy thing to kill someone. Human, fae, even a soulless ravager, it does not matter; a part of you dies in the process. The first kill is never easy. You see the light extinguish in their eyes, feel their presence leave, and you know that it was because of you. With this act, he lost his innocence today, and if he is not careful, he will lose part of his humanity. This will test his spirit and either drive him to his knees or lead him to ruin. Will he become a hero, a guardian, or a coldhearted killer? Will his life be defined by whom he slays or whom he saves? Both paths are open to him. He's hurting at the moment, but the key is to let it hurt. Taking a life should hurt. The way of the light is to care and yet still be steady in one's purpose. If he hardens himself, the darkness will have its beachhead in his heart, and it will not easily let him go. That is the crossroads before him, and how he responds to this moment will set him on his path. Only one thing is certain. He cannot go back to who he was before. That door is closed to him now.

Unseen by his friends, David closes his eyes briefly to quiet the dueling voices in his heart. And then, when he is steadied, he turns to see what else must be done.

Iset is kneeling over Daniel and has her hand on his forehead, while a kneeling Eden is clutching Daniel's right hand with both of hers. With his free hand, he covers his wound, seeking to heal it before it claims his life.

"He's alive, barely," Iset says solemnly. "He is trying to use his ability to manipulate matter to heal the wound, but he does not have the strength, and in my current state, I cannot be of assistance. He does not have much time."

"Can you show me how to heal him?" David asks hopefully.

"No, it is not possible," she answers. "You have the power, but it will be years before you will be able to master the healing arts. Destroying is easy, but healing is a gift that must be nurtured over time, and time is something that Daniel does not have."

"No, I can't accept that!" Eden cries out, passionately. "There has to be something that we can do."

She holds his hand within hers even tighter and blue light begins to emanate from her hands. A lone crystal-blue teardrop falls from her right eye, rolls down her cheek, and lands on Daniel's chest. It seems to explode with power, bathing him in it and causing his body to have an azure glimmer. Eyes closed in prayer, Eden is unaware of what is transpiring, and Brantley believes that Daniel is creating the glow, but Iset and David see it clearly and feel the surge of energy that is being produced.

David looks at Iset. "Is ... is she?"

"Yes," Iset answers, nodding.

Clueless, Brantley asks. "Is who what?"

Suddenly, Daniel takes a deep breath, and his eyes open wide.

"It's working," he gasps. "I'm healing."

"I knew it," Eden replies excitedly. "I knew you could do it."

"It's not me," he whispers, "Not m ..."

Before he can finish, Iset cuts him off, saying, "Shh, more are coming near."

"Three, make that four," Brantley adds as he sniffs the air. "Two of them are like Shuck."

David reaches out to his friends in mind-speak, creating a link among them and then speaks to them with his thoughts.

"Danny, are you strong enough to do what you did before, to hide us and our stuff?"

"I ... I don't know ..."

"Yes, Daniel, you can," Iset interjects, *"With Eden's help."*

"My help?" Eden exclaims. *"How can I help?"*

Iset replies reassuringly. *"Just keep clutching his hand, Eden Grace, keep believing in him. It will be enough."*

They scurry to grab their belongings and then join hands, forming a circle. A blue aura surrounds them, and they are transformed into rays of light, blending in perfectly to their surroundings. After several minutes, a hunting party of four arrives. Two ravagers, a male and a female, sniff the sector while the other two intruders look on. They spend exactly six minutes combing the area, but for the young heroes in hiding, it feels like hours. Finally, the female, the more experienced of the ravagers, addresses the others.

"They were here," she grunts. "That's a fact. That newborn skinwalker's scent is strong, and the new Iset was here too."

"So, where are they?" asks a grim, dark-haired man, evidently their leader.

"They killed someone here," the woman replies, pointing to the spot where Shuck's head was incinerated. "From the odor, they burned up that idiot, Black Shuck, but they've moved on. From what I can tell, they've moved as a group, but I'm not picking up a trail," she replies. "They've masked their scents as they left. Whatever they're using will wear off. We'll find them."

"You better," he answers. "Let's move out."

They depart, and after some time passes, Daniel transforms his allies once again into flesh and blood. He is still lying down and holding tightly to Eden's hand, but although his eyes are heavy from the exertion of hiding so many for so long, the color has returned to his face, his heartbeat is steady, and his aura is clear and bright, much stronger and healthier than before.

"I can't hear or smell them." Brantley whispers. "Thanks, Danny. They're long gone. That's a cool trick you've got there, dude. Pretty gutsy how you managed that from death's door."

"I didn't," he answers. "I mean, it was my know-how, but it was Edie, her power running through me, healing me, giving me the strength to do what I did."

"Me? How could it be me?" she asks, dumbfounded. "I don't have that kind of power."

"Y ... yes, child, you do," Iset says weakly as she is forced to sit down to conserve energy.

Adira is wincing along with Iset as if she is reliving each and every painful moment. Shamar can only imagine what she is experiencing, but it's obvious that watching helplessly is not easy for either of them.

Iset continues. "Just as the fallen's touch enabled your friend to absorb a ravager's DNA, it empowered you to clone the abilities of Daniel Vision, a qareen, and in your case, I suspect the duplicate is stronger than the original."

"I can feel it," David interjects. "Same energy, same flow, your touch was like a jump start, where a running car charges up a drained battery. Very cool, Edie, and you had no idea you were doing it."

"So, wait," Brantley interrupts. "You mean to tell me that the two of us can absorb someone's powers whenever we feel like it?"

"No," David replies. "Correct me if I'm wrong, Sothis, but I'm pretty sure it was a one-time thing. The blood of angels within Edie had been super active since we found Semi, but it seems depleted now, and the little that's left is dormant. Same with you, B.J., once your body stopped changing, most of Nameless's 'gift' was pretty much used up."

"You are correct, David," Iset answers.

"Are the changes permanent?" Eden asks.

"Yes, child," replies Iset softly. "What is done cannot ..."

"... Cannot be undone," Eden says, dropping her head and completing the quote. "Wow."

"Edie, man, this is great. Now, all three of us have powers," says Brantley gleefully.

"Yeah," she answers wistfully, fighting back tears. "It's wonderful."

But Eden knows the truth, knows that this is anything but wonderful. Throughout all of this, she was hoping that somehow the four of them could make it out in one piece, and the three of them, when the smoke cleared, could go back to their normal lives. As farfetched as that began to seem as their lives became increasingly bizarre, there was a part of her that held to the belief that once they got back home, everything would be OK. She looks down and stares at the blue flame as it flows from her hands into Daniel's and feels it surge within her; she looks up at her friend Brantley's new face and body, and David's flaming blade, and she finally allows herself to realize how ludicrous that notion had been.

Now, she sees clearly as the truth crashes in, impacting her with a gut punch. There is no going home. Eden reasons that they've lived through the equivalent of being struck by lightning, swallowing the super-soldier serum whole, and being bitten by radioactive spiders, so even if they survive all this unscathed, they will still lose their lives. Everything has changed. It was a fantasy to think that they could just hop in the family minivan, go back to high school, and finish senior year. If she is honest, part of her is excited by all of this. But part of her mourns the life that she has lost and is terrified by one absolute truth. It is the mantra of her favorite comic book character, Peter Parker. "With great power comes great responsibility." There is a burden with these gifts, an obligation that she never wanted but now cannot avoid. Like every protagonist in every story she has ever seen or read, she knows that her life and many others will be forever changed by what she does next.

Amid all this raw emotion, Eden cannot help but think about a book she once read, *Heroes Unleashed*. A young author wrote it, and in it she states that all of us have to decide who we are going to be in our own story. Are we going to be the hero, the villain, or a bystander? Don't allow life or circumstance to choose for you; the author implores; you have to choose for yourself. Edie thought the book was a good read at the time, but now—she's living it. This is her moment. Hero or villain—what will be her story? One thing is clear; whatever happens next, her days as a bystander are behind her.

Shamar nods approvingly. Eden Grace is wise beyond her years.

"You OK?" asks Daniel. "Sothis filled me in a little through mind-speak when I first got here. Touched by an angel, huh. That's unprecedented even in our circles. All this must be a lot for you to digest."

"I'm getting there," Eden answers. "The real question is, how are you?"

"Better," he replies with a sigh of relief. "You're packing a lot of juice, more than I do on my best day. It's sped up the process. I have some mojo back, so I should be able to take over from here. The wound has closed. It's going to take a few more hours of concentrated healing before everything is the way it needs to be internally, but I should be able to stand up and at least hobble down the road in a few minutes".

"Take as much time as you need. We should be safe here for the time being, right?"

"No," he answers grimly. "We definitely are not safe, far from it. Your friend's scent is like a beacon, broadcasting to every ravager and greasy skin-walker merc in the Gray Zone, and trust me, the good ones aren't going to be fooled by my mindbender tricks for long."

David, who's been eavesdropping, interrupts. "I've been thinking about that." He pauses and then raises his voice slightly. "Hey, everyone listen up. I was talking to Sothis, and I think we have a plan. Those purple flowers on that hill, if we rub some on us, it will dull our scent. That will help some. Edie, B.J., do you still have your old clothes in your backpacks?" They nod affirmatively. "Good. Take out anything valuable in your pockets and give the clothes to me."

As they rub the flowers on their skin and body armor, David takes Eden, Brantley, and his old clothes, combines it with Amesemi's hospital gown, tears the garments into pieces, and puts all of it into a backpack. When he finishes, he points to Brantley.

"B.J., come with me. Guys, we'll be back in a few minutes."

"I hope this is a great plan," says Brantley as he hustles to catch up. "The flowers stink, and those are my favorite pair of jeans."

David answers, "Well if it keeps the bad guys off of our trail, it should be worth it." They walk a little further, and then David continues, saying, "OK, this should be far enough. Look, B.J., you've got an important job in all this. I need you to use your heightened senses to play sentry. Block out everything and focus on what's going on around us. Try to spot anything or anyone coming this way while they're still a long way off."

"Sure," Brantley replies, hesitantly, "But if I pick up something, what's the plan?"

"Call out to me with your mind," David responds.

"Huh? How do I do that?"

"Just think my name real loud," David answers.

"Think loudly?"

"You'll figure it out. See you in a few minutes," David replies as he flies off with his backpack full of shredded clothes.

With his heightened vision, Brantley watches as his friend flies around, distributing torn sections of apparel to various locations, staying low to the ground as he darts around to avoid being spotted. As Brantley watches, he realizes that David is scattering garments carrying their scents in a variety of directions, hoping to throw the enemy off of their trail.

"Good plan," Brantley mumbles to himself. "This just might work."

"It probably will work, young Brantley," says a large, gruesome-looking shadow who has not even bothered to disguise his true form. "David will once again play the hero and save the day while you have a front-row seat to cheer him on. At least you're good for something."

Before he has time to react to the dark heart and his words, Brantley is surrounded by the shadow's friends. The whispers barrage him with lies, lies mixed with truth, laced with a double helping of hurt, and magnified by an abundance of unspoken fears. Their words come at him from all sides and drive him trembling to his knees. This is Brantley's moment, his test, his opportunity.

"Such a coward, a waste of space," one says. "New body, new powers, and still, all you're good for is screaming and telling weak jokes to hide your fear, the cowardly comic relief in your own pitiful story."

"Your father was right about you," another adds. "You are weak, a joke, so pathetic. He tried to beat it out of you. He truly tried, but there is no fixing what is wrong with you, Brantley James. Fancy school, new face, different beat, same old song."

"Never even helped your mother. Couldn't even save your sister," says still another. "You stood there and did nothing. You know what he did. You know what the other one is doing, and you did nothing. You do nothing. Loser, just like your father."

"Loser," another agrees.

It becomes a deafening chorus as they all chime in together, saying, "Loser, loser," over and over again.

Suddenly, David returns with an empty backpack slung over his shoulder. He wades through the crowd of shadows and grabs his friend by the arm, helping him up.

"Get away from him. Leave him alone," David commands.

The gruesome ringleader simply chuckles as he responds, saying, "That's not the way it works, little human. You cannot drive away another man's whispers. Don't worry, child. If you're lonely, yours will return soon enough."

David grabs his friend and pulls him close.

"Tell them to go, B.J. It's OK, just tell them to go."

"The aliens?" he answers, wiping his eyes, desperately trying to pull off a composed façade. "They're nothing. They took me by surprise is all, startled me. I just lost my balance."

"And their words?" David asks.

"I don't need your help, David. It's nothing. I've got it under control. They're just stupid aliens. Who cares what they say, anyway? See, they're gone already."

To Brantley's eyes, his "aliens" have conveniently disappeared as mysteriously as they arrived, but David sees the truth. They haven't left. The shadows have simply transformed into dark billows of smoke and entered into his friend. They are very present and still whispering their "truth" into Brantley's heart.

"B.J., listen to me. You need to tell them to go," David pleads. "They're not aliens, and they're definitely not gone."

"What? Is this more of your spiritual mumbo jumbo? C'mon D-Stone. Much as I love a good debate, we don't have time for that. Everything's fine. We've got to hurry back to the others and get going. We both know that your trick won't work for long, and those nasty flowers are already starting to wear off."

Shamar hangs his head. This is disappointing. He glances over at Adira, but she is staring off into the middle distance.

"It's not over," she whispers.

Obviously, she knows something that he does not.

Shamar fixes his eyes again on David, who sighs as he gives B.J. a frustrated stare. Finally, resolved that he's unable to convince his friend of the seriousness of the threat, he shakes his head disgustedly and reluctantly leads them back. Initially, they jog and then sprint as they embrace the urgency of their situation. Once they arrive, David quickly gathers the group together and brings them up to speed. The five of them have a window to escape, but they need to leave now. As they scramble to gather their belongings, David hurries over to Iset and bends down to pick her up. She is slumped over and fighting to keep her eyes open.

"Go ahead and get some rest," he says. "I've got you."

"No, David," Sothis whispers. "You need to lead the way and keep your sword hand free and ready in case there is trouble. Brantley is more than capable of carrying me. Let him do it."

"OK."

Knowing that B.J. and his magic ears heard their conversation, David summons his friend over and gently places Iset in Brantley's arms, and then David goes to help Eden with Daniel.

"Danny, let me help you to your feet," says Eden as she reaches down to help him up.

"Thank you."

"You can lean on me if you need help walking," she replies.

"No, no, I can't," he responds. "I'm not going with you."

"What?"

"I'll only slow you down," he answers. "Iset and I discussed it. It's for the best. I'm well enough to make my way to a safe place where I can continue to heal. Besides, I've got a few tricks up my sleeve that may give additional help throwing the bad guys off your trail. If for no other reason, I need to stay behind for that."

Eden is tempted to protest but quickly realizes the futility of it. Daniel turns and addresses David.

"You need to move out quickly. Don't use any of your powers unless you have to. You don't want anything to draw attention to you. When you get to where you're going, let young Iset have uninterrupted sleep until she's whole."

"How will we know when she's whole?" David asks.

"You'll know," he responds. "Semi will be in full control and strong. When she is ready, she'll lead you to Avalon. I'll meet you guys there."

"Sounds like a plan."

With haste, they say their goodbyes and head out, David leading the way, followed by Eden, with Brantley and Iset trailing. After a few minutes have passed, Iset, who had been pretending to be asleep, speaks up.

"They don't stop, do they?" she says.

"Who?" Brantley asks.

"The shadows," she answers. "They haven't stopped chirping at you since you encountered them face to face. If anything, they've gotten louder."

"You can see them?"

"No," she answers, "not in their current form, but I can hear them loud and clear as can you."

"I don't hear anything, and as you know, I have amazing ears."

"They are not speaking to your ears, young Brantley. They are whispering to your heart, and we both know that you hear every word even if you do not recognize the source. It is that voice of doubt and fear hanging over you like a dark cloud, weighing down your spirit and fueling the insecurity and anger that gives you no peace."

He neither confirms nor denies her statement but replies with a question of his own. "Really? Why would aliens do that? Forget about how. Why would they... oh, I get it. You're not saying that they're aliens. You're an 'angel,' right, so according to you, these 'shadows' are demons. What, they're whispering to me, trying to turn me to the dark side? Is that it?"

"What do you think?"

"You don't want to know what I think," says Brantley, his face reddening. "I think, despite all your help, you're either a liar or you're delusional. There's no such thing as angels and demons, lady. The world is full of wonders, full of mysteries, but the one thing I'm sure of is that they are not among them."

"Why is that Brantley?"

"Because I believe in science. I believe that there is a logical reason, a scientific reason for everything. Faith in a higher being is just a crutch for those who are too primitive, too stupid, or too scared to keep searching for real answers."

"Well, on this much we agree, young one," she says, with motherly patience. "I, too, am a firm believer in science. Everything has an explanation, a method, and a reason. The problem is that the science that I know is too big for your kind. You are inquisitive ants trying to grasp the secrets of the universe. It is admirable that you have ascertained as much as you have, but it is arrogant folly not to know in your spirit that there are questions and answers that are bigger than you and one who is bigger than it all."

"God," he seethes. "Wow, I knew *He* would come up eventually, the big, wonderful, year-round Santa Claus in the sky. There definitely isn't a God."

"The thought of him makes you angry. Why is that? Is it science that has led you there or something more? What did the Ancient do that you hate him so?"

"There is no God," he hisses. "I know ... I know. I tested the hypothesis and saw the experiment go terribly wrong. When I was young, I cried out to him, begged him to help me, to help us ... I ... I... I've been through some stuff. The things I've seen, a loving God wouldn't let happen to a child. I know from personal experience that the dude that Edie and David pray to doesn't exist. If he did... if he did...well, he doesn't, so I guess the point is moot."

"Child, the wonders of the universe are all around, and they speak to you. Listen. I suspect that you have let your hurt and anger and the lies of whispers blind you to the divine truths hidden in plain sight, right before your eyes. I could debate with you, talk to you about the consequence of humanity's free will, and explain to you why evil is allowed to exist in this world. I could explain so much, but there is no time for that.

"This is Semi's body, and when the new Iset is whole, Semi will be fully in control, and I will be the silent partner. So, listen to me carefully, child. Because after I fall asleep, we will never have the opportunity to speak again, and there is something that you desperately need to hear. Despite what you believe, you are not an accident, not a random result of chance and evolution. You were made with purpose and love, unique from all who have been made before. And you were placed, with some trepidation, into this great world, with all of its incredible light and its unfathomable darkness. I am sorry for the pain in your journey, young Brantley, sorry that the decisions of others have caused so much hurt for you and yours. It is not your fault. You had no control over that, but you do control what happens next. That is your gift, your true super-power. You decide whether you will transcend your past and use it to fuel your potential or whether you will let scars and dark memories rob you of your future. Whatever you believe about me, about the Ancient, or about the nature of the eternal war, you must embrace this one simple truth. Choice is the only thing in this world that is truly yours. Do not squander it, deny it, or give it away. No matter the source, there are voices speaking to your heart, child, always speaking. Constantly spurring you on, pulling you down, pushing you, chaining you, lifting you, calling you, there are so many voices. Your gift, your burden is that you get to decide which voices to believe. But be warned, son of Adam. What you believe is who you will become. Choose well."

With the last word spoken, Sothis' voice trails off, and she enters a deep sleep, leaving Brantley without the chance of rebuttal. He is simply left to ponder her words as he continues to walk, adding them to the multitude of words waging war within him.

Shamar glances over at Adira. Her eyes are fixed on young Brantley. Sadness wells up in them, and golden tears trickle down her cheeks. Why? What does she know? Are her tears for Brantley or for them all? He could ask her, but he is concerned that she might just share what she knows. He is not allowed to help them through these challenges or the difficult road he suspects they will face in the Bronx. Whatever is about to happen, it is enough to make Adira cry. Being so helpless, it is hard to see how knowing more would be of benefit.

"Are you OK?" Shamar asks.

"I will be old friend. I did not realize how difficult this would be for me. David, Eden, and Brantley James are in turmoil, and Semi and I are in great pain. We almost did not make it. I had forgotten how difficult this transition was."

"But that's not all of it, is it, Adira? You know what lies ahead for them in New York, don't you?"

"I do," she answers. "They face challenges greater than they can imagine."

"Thank you for coming with me," Shamar says as they watch the four of them begin to exit the Gray Zone and return to Earth Prime. "This was the place where their childhoods ended. It was painful for them and painful to watch. I am grateful that I was here to bear witness, but I am also grateful that I did not do it alone. I do not know all of what you know, Adira, but I know that war waits for them when they return to Perinesa. They are so unprepared."

"They are," she agrees, with a tinge of regret.

He knows the answer, but he feels compelled to ask. "Is there nothing we can do to assist them?"

"Come, follow me."

He follows her and they watch as a small pocket of air buckles then morphs into a swirling spherical portal of blue and gold energy, and the children step through, emerging behind a Bodega in the Kingsbridge area of the Bronx. David touches Iset's arm and Eden's shoulder, allowing Eden to dream up a casual outfit, befitting a teen, to serve as the visual avatar for Iset's armor. He then takes Iset from Brantley and carries her as he leads the way to his aunt's house on the edge of Kingsbridge, right before it becomes Riverdale. He uses his mind tricks on his aunt and cousins to make them believe that he and his friends were expected, and after some pleasantries, they settle in to get some rest. It is only 8:30 a.m., but they have been up through the night and are all exhausted physically and emotionally.

"I don't understand, Adira. Why are we still watching?"

"Be patient, old friend. All will be clear."

David's cousin Kenya is graciously sharing her bedroom with Eden. Brantley is knocked out in the room of cousins Sean and Andrew Jr., and Iset has been given the bedroom of David's cousin Karen who is away at college. David carries Iset upstairs and lays her on Karen's bed, tucking her in. As he does, Iset wakes up briefly, grabbing his hand.

"Thanks, Charming," she says, speaking in Amesemi's voice. Sothis has permanently assumed her supporting role. "How are you?"

"I'm fine, Semi," he answers softly. "Go back to sleep. You need your rest."

"N ... no ... really. How are you? It's not an easy thing to take a life. Believe me, I know."

David sighs, shaking his head. "I don't know. Shuck would have taken you and killed all of us. I had to do it. Chances are I'll have to take more lives before this is over. I'll do what I need to, Semi, but if I'm honest, it hurts. It hurts deep, and I don't know if that makes me weak or soft or..."

"Or human," she interjects. "David, it makes you human. Saving lives is what we do, and sometimes, we have to take lives to save them. But God help you if it ever becomes easy, if it ever stops hurting." Her voice starts to fade, she is obviously exhausted and in a great deal of pain, but she pushes through, finishing her thought. "It's OK that you're hurting, Charming, but you don't have to carry it alone. You don't ... you ..."

"Thanks, Semi," he replies, holding her hand tenderly. "Go ahead and get some rest. I'll watch over you. I'm not going to let anything happen to you."

She smiles weakly and responds in barely a whisper, "I keep telling you ... I ... I'm not that kind of p ... princess."

With that, she falls back into a deep sleep. David stands over her, love and concern in his eyes. After a few seconds, he sits down in a chair overlooking the bed, with his lorenth in his hand. The quiet moments are always the hardest. He feels the whispers stirring inside of him, whispers of insecurity, guilt, doubt, and fear, but he recognizes them and does something extraordinary. David scoots out of the chair and falls on his knees. He prays, and as he does, the shadows in the room dissipate, replaced by an incandescent glow as messengers, Shamar's brothers appear, surrounding the two of them and filling the room. David continues emptying his heart, tears in his eyes. His pleas cause the bedroom to shake and the whole house, now filled with messengers, to shine like a beacon. Eventually, he wears himself out and falls asleep on the floor at the foot of Semi's bed. His Aunt Liz checks in on him, covers him with a blanket, and props a pillow under his head, but seeing him at peace, allows him to stay where he is.

With a twinkle in her eyes, Adira asks, "Do you see?"

"I do," Shamar answers as he gazes in wonder. "I am at peace and truly ready to return now."

"As am I." She takes some time to bask in the power of the moment before she continues. "It is true that dark forces are coming, and that these brave souls are unprepared for what's going to happen next. And it is also true that there can be no help given by the two of us. But there is a greater truth that is comforting to remember. We are not the only ones watching or listening, old friend. Help is on the way."

SON OF WAR —DAVID

He is like seaweed on a wave, a leaf in a storm, tossed about by cyclonic winds, unable to control its destiny, landing only when forces beyond its control are through with it. That is David's journey right now, during his waking hours and even more when he closes his eyes. There is nothing peaceful about his sleep. There is no rest even when young Mr. Stone is resting. David feels it in his slumber, a pressure and a pull as Amon Ra invades his mind—not his mind, his very core, pushing and pulling David to see with his heart, with his soul. Why can't he just let him sleep?

Once again, he enters the hybrid palace fortress of Iken in the center of the war, and he is overwhelmed by the cacophony of troops on the move. Over the clanging of metal, the soldiers shout commands and encouragement in that strange singsong tongue known as Kolu, the most basic and humanoid-friendly of the angelic languages. There are so many voices. It's hard to make out specific conversations.

Suddenly, there is silence. Like the other visions, she appears, resplendent in a sparkling headdress and a magnificent golden gown. She is a goddess, and her entrance and regal gait temporarily quiet the throng as they pay her respect. But this is a historically accurate version of the dream, peeled from the mind of Amon Ra, so she is the same but different. She is not Semi but her aunt and mentor, Queen Iset, the previous host of Sothis. Slightly taller than Semi but with ornate braided hair and glistening chocolate skin, their physical similarities are striking. But she is not Semi. She is not a teen, not a newborn, not a princess attempting to find her way. Iset is a queen, a great queen and warrior at the height of her power, the closest thing to a goddess that this world has ever known. She stops and pivots gracefully as her dress transforms into glistening armor, equipped with a blazing saffron spear. Then she motions slightly, and an army of Earthbound, nasnas, kutchis, and fae file in behind her in response to her unspoken command. David believes in Semi. From the first time he gazed into her eyes, he knew she was capable of anything. He believes in her, but he doesn't envy her. Following in her aunt's footsteps is not an enviable job. The supernatural Wiki in his head is full of stories of Iset's legend, and it's clear from seeing her, Queen Iset is as advertised. She is not only a legend and a hero; she is the prototype for every hero who has ever succeeded her. Those footsteps are a tall order for anyone, even Semi.

Queen Iset's gaze is fixed on the center of the room, obviously drawn to something. David follows her eyes, trying to discover the source of her concern, and he's drawn in, getting a close-up of a particular interaction. Amidst the frenzy, in the center of the main room, stands a man and woman engaged in a heated, passionate conversation. The man is a regal figure, imposing in stature with dark brown skin and long braided hair. He is wearing minimal body armor, but his chiseled physique is more intimidating than any armor he could wear. This is Amon Ra, the legend of legends, in the flesh. Although he has no crown, he has the bearing of a king and is obviously these people's commander, radiating the kind charisma that can inspire courage in even the most cowardly. OK, David takes it back. Semi doesn't have the toughest job. That task belongs to the poor soul who will one day succeed Amon Ra. They keep saying that it's going to be David. He hopes not because seeing Ra in action, that just seems beyond impossible. Amon Ra is a force of nature, compelling loyalty by his sheer force of will. David can't wait to meet him in person, and he definitely pities the poor shmuck unlucky enough to attempt to fill his shoes, especially if that poor schmuck is him. Hopefully, Ra lives forever cause three years, even three hundred years, will never be enough time to grow into this role.

Yet, for all Ra's magnetism, his powers of persuasion seem to be lost on his female companion. She is beautiful, adorned in silk robes, rare jewels, and a glorious headdress. In addition, she has gorgeous, Egyptian style, straightened hair, striking features, and flawless golden-brown skin that seems to have a special glow about it. She's pregnant, very, very pregnant, with a little girl—Amesemi. This is Hathor, Amesemi's mom and Ra's wife, hours before Semi's birth. Hathor is majestic in her own rite, with a smoldering intensity that would make lesser beings wither before her. She is an icon, a queen, splendidly regal in all her ways, and as the two argue, she appears to be more than a match for Ra. At the moment, neither one of them is backing down. Something about the passion of their argument calls to him. David thinks it's part of the reason why he's seeing this. There is a revelation in this moment that David's meant to uncover. But as he strains to listen, a force blocks him, and as he tries to push through, it pulls him away.

David feels as if he's disintegrating. It's not painful exactly, but it's uncomfortable and incredibly disorienting, like he's being pulled in every direction and then broken into a thousand separate, sentient pieces that dissipate, reappear, and then reconnect. When he reassembles, his brain is scrambled. As he comes to his senses, he's realizes he's nowhere near the palace. He's in a different place and time, observing in detail another incident from Ra's past. It is a battle he took part in early in the war, nearly a thousand years earlier, on the day that Babel fell. After some time passes, he's pulled away again and again, bearing witness to various pivotal moments from Ra's six-thousand-year history. Some date back to the beginning of The Great War, while others are as recent as several weeks ago. Ra wears many different faces, but his eyes remain the same, smoldering with an intensity that could only belong to the son of War.

David witnesses excerpts of Amon Ra's life—the births and deaths of many of his children, the various times he has found love and lost it, his joy, his pain, his triumphs, and his failures. David's walking through Ra's memories, experiencing his feelings as if they're his own. It's quite a ride, but through all his trials and adventures, at his core, Ra remains the same. He is a man driven by passion, honor, love, and duty. Time and time again, he overcomes more powerful opponents with his superior skills, his preternatural gift for strategy, his obsessive attention to detail, and something else—a quality impossible to measure. He truly does not fear death. That is his secret weapon. David is inside his mind, surfing his emotions, and when it comes to Ra's mission, David can't find a trace of fear or uncertainty. Ra is not like the rest of them, definitely not like David. Every second of every day, David doubts himself, wonders about his place, and worries about his future, but Ra does not, not even a little. He truly doesn't fear death, and he doesn't waste one second of one day doubting his purpose, cowering from his destiny, or questioning what waits for him beyond the grave. It gives him a fearlessness and determination that few have ever possessed. It's terrifying to face and inspiring to follow. That singular focus is his true superpower. It's what makes him Amon Ra, the unbreakable prophet-warrior, leader of the Nistarim, and protector of the world of men. But the longer David surfs his soul, the more he senses there is more. There is something else that fuels him, something darker bubbling beneath the surface, simultaneously stoking his fire and breaking his heart. David's not sure exactly what it is, but his gut tells him that it has everything to do with Amon Ra's argument with Hathor in that palace. He thinks it's what Ra brought him here to see. Unfortunately, it's also what a part of Ra is trying to avoid. David has to find a way to get back to the palace so he can finally see all he was brought here to see.

He's evaporating again, but he's not reemerging back at the palace. David's being transported someplace else, to a time he's yet to visit. As he draws near, his stomach churns, and his heart is filled with dread. He appears before a scantily clad, towering figure standing over nine feet tall, more than two feet taller than Shaq, but this guy's no basketball player. He has a muscle-bound body that looks like it was borrowed from the Incredible Hulk, and his dark skin is thick, like that of an elephant. The giant's locked hair covers his tree trunk of a neck and falls on his mountainous shoulders, like a lion's mane. His hair compliments his square jaw and rugged looks and works as an effective backdrop for his intimidating grimace and menacing dark eyes. They're dead inside, filled with only fury and loathing. Who is this guy?

"This is Ra," answers a hooded man, draped in tattered robes, in a voice that is deep and majestic.

David's mouth is agape as he tries to make sense of what just happened. He takes a good look at the angular man in worn garments before him. A good portion of his face is obscured by his hood, but he has a thick salt and pepper beard, bronze leathery hands and feet, a long staff that seems like a prop from *The Ten Commandments*, and the most ancient, dilapidated sandals David's ever seen.

"You can hear my thoughts? Who are you? Are you real?" David asks, stopping himself before he rattles off the other hundred burning questions he suddenly has.

"This is a dream, child. Everything is thought. Am I real? Again, I remind you that this is a dream—so. I am your guide, created by Ra's memories and your gifts to help you navigate the maze in which you find yourself, ensuring that you do not get lost in it or miss what you are meant to see."

"What is your name?"

"Interesting question. For you, for now, call me Number Ten, Ten for short. No more questions about me, son of Adam. You have much to see and much to learn and very little time to do so. Please, turn your attention to the images around us. That brute before you is Ra but not a version of him that you would ever hope to see."

"How can it be?" he asks incredulously. "This guy is a monster."

Ten replies with a wry smile. "Most of us were monsters before we became men. Who you see before you, posing victoriously, carrying an oversized, curved blade in one hand and a severed head in the other, is Ra, the oldest child of the fallen they called War and heir to the strongest of the antediluvian bloodlines. The head he's grasping by its long dark hair belonged to Amon, another male giant, a vain peacock of a man, with his flowing locks, straight off the cover of a romance novel. But now, his hair is being used as a handle, and his head is being toted around like an oversized purse. His face is frozen in place with the horrified expression of a man who was killed mid-scream—killed by Ra.

"This is Ra as a young adult Nephilim, not quite six-teen years old. In their mammoth, original bodies, Nephilim aged faster than humans, reaching maturity by age twelve and only having a lifespan of forty to fifty years. Yes, the age of giants was short-lived but impactful, and even though their actions have been omitted from the history books and regulated to mythology, these terrifying brutes left a deep imprint on humanity's psyche—fee-fi-fo-fum and all that. They're in your myths. They're in your children's stories. They're in your nightmares. Humanity could erase them, but they couldn't forget them. So now, seeing one up close, young David, I'm sure you understand why."

David silently nods his head in agreement.

With the vision of the young Ra, David is barraged by a variety of images of Amon Ra in his past life, before he was a hero, when he was a rapist, a murderer, and a heartless conqueror driven by rage. David tries to cover his eyes, but how does that work in a dream, really? It's horrifying to watch, as horrifying as the earlier memories were heroic.

Once again Ten interjects. "His anger burned every day. That was the source of his barbaric behavior. I don't share it as an excuse, for there is none, but merely as fact. He hated his father and his father's people for being foolish enough to give up paradise and doom them all, and he hated his mother and her ilk for being too stupid to see the unlimited potential that humans possessed. But most of all, Ra hated the Ancient. How could the universe give birth to Ra and his kind, dooming them to a life without hope, a life without purpose? Ra decided that fear would be his legacy. The world would remember him when he was gone. It would remember his name and tremble. He developed a system of fighting known as shadow dancing, created a warrior caste, consolidated the Nephilim houses, and rained terror upon the earth. And then fixed his sights on a bigger goal. Amon Ra set out to conquer the world. And he succeeded."

When David's head stops spinning from the onslaught of information, he finds himself standing in a palace in Shinar. King Amon Ra is seated on a golden throne, wearing the face of a handsome, young Babylonian soldier, dressed in a regal tunic and an ornate, ceremonial scarf. He has won and is now the god of gods, conqueror of all the known world. He's stroking his thick black beard in the middle of a discussion with his brother, Osiris, and some of his advisors, but he looks positively bored, much more comfortable on a battlefield than in a throne room.

When a servant enters and interrupts them, Ra is more relieved than disturbed.

"Pay close attention to what happens next," says Ten, briefly interrupting the vision. "I believe you will find this very interesting."

"Excuse me, Your Excellency," says the servant as he falls to one knee and bows his head respectfully. "You told me to let you know when Hemen returned from his mission. He has returned and brought the captured rebel leader. Do you want us to q ...?"

"No, I'll come out to him," Ra replies eagerly. "I'd like to meet this 'threat' before we execute him." He turns to his brother. "Osiris, preside over this meeting in my absence. I will return after I have properly assessed these rebels."

"As you wish," Osiris replies, bowing his head deferentially.

With regal arrogance, Ra struts over to the holding area and sees Hemen and several of his finest soldiers surrounding half a dozen scrawny, ragged shepherds, who are in chains and on their knees.

Perplexed and more than a little annoyed, Ra barks at Hemen. "Hemen, is this a joke? Where is my adversary? Where is the terrifying nefarious Siru Khan, who challenges my throne and my authority?"

"I am Siru Khan," says the closest of the prisoners, confidently. He's a weathered man with liberal streaks of gray in his tousled, shoulder-length hair and long, thick beard.

Despite his rags and his chains, there is something majestic about him. Framed by the backdrop of his leathery, bronze skin, his eyes burn with conviction and a fearlessness that gets Ra's full attention. This is no ordinary shepherd. His eyes are the eyes of a warrior, even if nothing else about him resembles one.

Still perplexed, Ra asks. "What are you? Four of you are Nephilim. Why would you choose such common, feeble bodies? What kind of warriors are you?"

"We are not concerned with the outward appearance, noble Ra," Khan replies. "Beauty and power come from within."

"Really?" Ra responds, obviously both amused and curious.

Ra tells Hemen and the guards to stand their ground and then motions to Khan. "Rise before your god, Siru Khan. I wish to speak with you in private. I desire to learn more about you and your 'rebellion'. Perhaps you can persuade me to let you and your associates live."

"As you command, great king," he answers.

And with a casual gesture from Ra, Siru Khan's shackles fall off and he rises to his feet.

When they are a sufficient distance from the others, Ra speaks. "Tell me, Siru Khan. You do not strike me as a warrior. Tell me what kind of rebellion you are leading against me."

"I am not a rebel or a soldier, your majesty. My followers and I are simply truth-tellers, devoted to sharing truth to all who will listen."

"Is that so?" answers Ra skeptically. "So, what manner of truths are you sharing with the masses?"

"We proclaim the teachings of the divine light and the power of his deliverance. We teach them to resist the darkness and aspire to be better. The darkness never tires, great king; it never wavers; it never sleeps, but hope is a shield that will not fail."

Ra chuckles. "A truly beautiful speech. Yet, I sincerely doubt that your shield of hope can save you from my sword, truth-teller. Surely, you must understand that I am the only god who can save you now. So, tell me the truth, all of it, and you may yet live to see another day."

"As you wish," Khan answers, bowing slightly and staring fearlessly into Ra's eyes. "What is it you wish to know?"

"You and your followers are Noahites, are you not?" Ra asks pointedly.

"We are."

"And you are their prophet?"

"I am the Majestic, the tenth in the order of the heralds of the nine," Khan answers proudly.

"I love the way you say that. You say that as if it is important, as if it has real meaning and power. Yet, you know nothing of those things." Ra pauses and massages his beard before continuing. "I believe that it was Amon who killed your predecessor and put his head and the head of twenty of your brothers on stakes. Was it not?"

"It was."

Ra smiles. "Yet, that did not dissuade you and your brothers. It did not silence your voices. Amon was an insecure idiot. You zealots are an interesting breed. You are annoying irritants but relatively harmless. Traditionally, I have chosen to ignore you and yours. You are so far beneath us, and your rambling about the goodness of the Ancient is so misinformed that I find it mildly entertaining. Besides, persecution simply seems to cause your breed to multiply like roaches. My men know this, so you must have said something fairly extreme for them to classify you as a dangerous rebel. What has the Ancient instructed you to proclaim that has caused such a fuss?"

"You will not like it."

"Speak now," Ra commands. "I will not ask again."

Khan once more bows his head. "As you wish." Then he lifts his head and glares into Ra's eyes. "I have been given a prophecy about you, great king, and have been charged with sharing it with all who will listen. It states that deliverance from you and your demonic kingdom is almost here. A great warrior and herald is coming who will rescue mankind from your hand and the hand of all false gods. He will be a champion of the light who will keep the shadow's emissaries from the world of men. He will smash your throne, conquer your armies, and ignite the Age of Man. You and yours will never rule again. Babel's fall will be a sign. It will never see completion but instead will be destroyed even as the great herald rises."

Ra replies with a sinister calm. "That type of rhetoric will get you killed. So, who is he? Are you this prophet?"

"No, we both know that I am no warrior, mighty Ra."

"So, who is he?" Ra commands Khan to speak. "Where is he? Tell me, and you may yet live."

"He will be my successor, the eleventh majestic of the nine, and this herald will be the greatest warrior who has ever lived. Only Orion will ever surpass him. I did not know his identity until it was my privilege to have it revealed to me this day."

"Who is he?" Ra demands, furiously.

Siru Khan pierces into Ra's eyes and answers solemnly. "I am gazing upon his face, mighty Ra. You...you are the one."

Ra looks stunned, perhaps even moved, but then he leans back and begins to chuckle.

"Is this a joke? No, I can see it in your eyes. You are serious." With some effort, he stifles his laugh. "You really believe that I am destined to join you, that I would give up all of this and become a mindless syco-phant, proclaiming the 'virtues' and the empty promises of a heartless God?"

"The light does not lie," Khan replies. "Yes, I believe that you are the one."

"So, this is the great prophecy? You are mad, Siru Khan, brave and entertaining but quite insane. Yet, you are harmless, harmless to anyone but yourself. You do not deserve to die, and contrary to what is said, I am not a mindless butcher. I have no problem with killing, but killing serves a purpose. I take life to protect what I have and to gain what I want. You and your zealots are no threat to me, and you possess nothing that I desire. There is no reason for you to die this day."

"As you wish."

"There is one thing that you must do for me, Siru Khan. You have been a symbol of defiance. I need a different kind of symbolic act from you in return. Your head on a stick would accomplish this, but there is an alternative. If you and your band of dirt merchants kneel before me as your god, you will be free to leave."

"I cannot," replies Khan solemnly. "That would be a lie. We both know that you are no god."

"What is truth, prophet? It is what we make it. I am god because I choose to be; because I have made the whole world tremble before me. But believing or not believing, that is not your concern or mine. Unlike the jealous Ancient, I do not demand belief or devotion, only compli-ance. I simply require that you and yours bend a knee. That is a small price to pay in return for your life and your freedom. It is not important to me that you mean what you say, only that you say it. After you leave this place, I do not care what you do or say as long as it is far from me."

Khan replies, "There is only one who is worthy of praise. I bow before none but the Ancient himself."

"And you would stubbornly die for that conviction?"

"Gladly."

Mystified, Ra shakes his head and asks, "What has the Ancient ever done for you to earn such loyalty?"

"More than I could ever say."

"So be it," Ra answers, grimly unsheathing his blade and turning it into crimson fire. "Your life is forfeit."

"I only have one small request before I die," says Khan. "I have one last message to share with you. It is my dying wish."

"You may speak."

"The divine light wants you to know that you are wrong. You have believed a lie," Khan says passionately. "You are not a cosmic mistake but were created with purpose and love. The divine says, 'Just as light casts away the darkness, and the patience of water defeats the strongest wall, love breaks every curse and sets every captive free.' So, shall it be with you, Amon Ra. When you come to the light, remember these words, especially during your darkest times, and do not judge yourself too harshly for what you are about to do. All is forgiven."

"Is that it?" Ra asks.

"It is."

"Good," Ra responds without emotion. "Farewell prophet."

"Talioth Algo Daymon, Amon Ra."

"What?" Ra is puzzled by Khan's choice of final words. "Is that angelic? What did you say?"

Khan smiles, closes his eyes, interlocks his thumbs, crosses his arms across his chest, and replies, gently. "I will see you again."

With those words, there is a flash, and the majestic's head falls to the palace floor. Expressionless, Ra walks back to the others and instructs his men.

"Spare one and kill the rest and put their heads on spikes as a warning to the others," Ra commands. "Put Siru Khan's head up as well. He was brave and deserved better, but if he could not serve me in life, he will serve me in death."

"Do you have a preference who we spare?" asks Hemen.

Noticing a look in his eye, Ra points to the youngest looking of the Nephilim and asks, "Will you bow and worship me?"

"N...Never," he replies.

"You have heart, like your master. What is your name, Noahite?" Ra asks.

"T. ... T ... Tiron Nakar."

"From now on, they will call you Gilgamesh, for you have faced the great beast, the terrible anger of the mighty god, Amon Ra, and survived," says Ra. "Do you understand?"

"Yes," Gilgamesh replies.

"Hemen, after he has watched his brothers die, brand Gilgamesh with my mark and then release him. He can tell his fellow Noahites what has happened here today. He will be a witness to my greatness and the folly of all resistance."

David's heart falls, and he feels nauseous. Ra didn't do this. He couldn't have done this. But he did. He killed Siru Khan and ...

"What a second. That's you isn't it? Siru Khan, Number Ten, the tenth majestic of the nine?" says David as he stares at his guide in amazement. "How can you just stand there stoically, showing no emotion?"

Ten clasps his hands together, resting his chin on his index fingers, thoughtfully. "Child, do not mourn the living. Siru Khan has been in the glory lands rejoicing for quite some time. He has no regrets. I am just a memory, and this is not my story. Focus on what is important, young one, and do not allow yourself to be distracted or this journey will be for naught."

Focus? Focus on what, exactly? Why am I here? Why should I be subjected to seeing more brutality from this version of Ra and his cronies?

David gets it. Ra was a monster, a cross between Darth Vader and Negan from *The Walking Dead*, with an ample sprinkling of Thanos thrown in but worse, much worse. David is ready to turn the channel and go back to viewing Ra's heroic exploits or better yet, viewing nothing and just getting some real sleep. Unfortunately, he doesn't have the remote control. But of course, just when he thinks he's in a loop, and it can't get any worse, he is pulled away, once more going through the disorienting process of disintegration. As he tries to get his wits together, he sees the most amazing sight, a game changer.

David sees a procession of Ra and twelve of his chief advisors traveling along a road near Shinar when something unexpected happens. There is a flash of blinding, golden light in front of them, staggering the procession, and out of that event emerges a man made of living, aureate flame. And the burning man's voice is so thunderous that it shakes the earth and somehow, even as a dream, shakes David as well. As he marvels at this, David hears Ten's voice.

"You've been pulled two weeks forward. The moment when Siru Khan's prophecy came to pass. Two weeks is all it took for the world to turn upside down." He pauses a beat and continues on, his voice laced with reverence and wonder. "The Burning Man... not since its beginning has a power so great walked the earth, and even this collection of villains has enough sense to fall prostrate before him. This is Ra's personal crossroads, and everything changed for him that day. He was proclaimed the eleventh majestic, and he and his men were called to leave their old lives behind and embrace a higher purpose. From this point on, they were called to be watchers, serving and protecting the world of men. The emancipation of the Earthbound, the birth of the Nistarim, and the origin of the council of thirty-six, were born out of the tears shed here and the decisions they inspired.

"The twelve were honor bound to bear witness to Ra's new message and its origin, but in the moment of truth, five betrayed him. Led by Osiris, Ra's heart and soul, they championed a more pleasing message, one that kept the Nephilim in power and led many astray. There was fierce debate, but words were never going to settle what divided them, and those who worshipped power were never willingly going to relinquish it. Though it broke his heart, Ra knew what he must do.

"So, during the last days of Peleg, son of Eber, civil war broke out. Seemingly, the whole world fought on the plains of Shinar. Nimrod led the humans who fought by Ra's side, and Ra led them all, championing a coalition of Barac Navaar and men as they fought for freedom. Babel fell. Its tower was reduced to rubble, and furious, desperate battles followed. Uruk, Lemuria, Argos, Damascus, Xi'an, Ra and his son, Horus, led forces that repeatedly prevailed against incredible odds. They were a good team, the best, inseparable, unbeatable.

"Their enemies were routed; the newly freed human race scattered across the four corners of Earth. In defeat, Ra's opposition became splintered into factions, warlords fleeing in various directions seeking to set up strongholds. Although most humans were freed in the early phase of the war, it took another 1,000 years before Abydos, the last of the strongholds, fell during the battle of Taliath Garr."

As the high-speed images begin to slow down, at long last, David finds himself reappearing back in the palace-fortress of Iken during the moments before the great battle. This time, he's standing next to Hathor and Amon Ra during their heated exchange. He can hear every word now, though he is unable to understand most of it. Wanting to shield their words from prying ears, the two are speaking a much more obscure angelic tongue than Kolu, and they're speaking at a fast, animated clip. David turns to Ten for some help, maybe an assist with translation, or some of that running commentary he's been giving incessantly, but he's faded into the background, appearing as a silent specter in the distance. David's on his own. *OK, I can do this. It's like a puzzle, just put the pieces together.*

Hathor is irate, poking her finger into her husband's massive chest and raising her voice to levels that make even David uncomfortable as she crowds his personal space to emphasize her point. David knows that Osiris and Thoth lead the opposition forces. He's made that much out, and it's something about Kala Sarr. They invoked the right to Kala Sarr. *What's that?* Whatever it is, she's not happy about it. But Ra is unmoved, arms crossed, stone faced, forcefully, commandingly making his points. His steely gaze is intimidating, but not to her. She matches it and raises him with a fiery intensity that would make most bend to her will and break the rest. This is a lot of heat, all over this Kala Sarr thing. Kala Sarr...Kala Sarr...he's got it. It's a challenge to single combat. Ra's agreed to face their champion before the beginning of the battle, and Hathor is attempting to talk him out of it. But David still does not know why.

Anger gives way to desperate tears as she holds him close. She places his hand on her stomach so he can feel Amesemi and pleads with whispers where shouting has failed. Still, Ra is unmoved. Finally, he raises his hand, signifying that he has had enough. He leans forward to kiss her goodbye, but she turns her head in disgust. Angrily, Ra pivots and marches off. When he is out of sight, Hathor buries her face in her hands and sobs bitterly. David doesn't understand any of this. He wonders who Amon Ra is facing, and why it's making Hathor so afraid. Why is she sobbing as if Ra has already lost? Something about Hathor seems so familiar, but at the moment, David is unable to make a connection.

Everything is a blur. The dream skips forward without the disintegration stuff, but he's feeling dizzy. When it settles, David is in the valley of Taliath Garr and is witnessing the no holds barred clash between Ra and Osiris's helmeted champion. They are evenly matched—superb sword play, fluid, flawless fighting skills, each giving no quarter. The struggle is epic, both combatants a perfect blend of grace, power, and skill. David imagines that this event must have inspired songs and legends that echo through time to this very day. At long last, Ra is victorious, and the cheers from Ra's troops are deafening. They descend on the enemy in a ferocious wave, emboldened by the amazing victory of Amon Ra, their herald.

But the majestic is not cheering. He's clutching the corpse of his vanquished foe, cradling him like a newborn babe, seemingly oblivious to the onslaught around him. He is distraught over the death of his enemy. Tears stream down Amon Ra's face. Ra removes the fallen warrior's helmet and gently kisses his face. David realizes that Ra's foe was his son, Horus, and David's heart aches; his soul cries as Ra's immeasurable sorrow becomes his own.

Suddenly, Ten reappears, standing next to him, resuming his narration. "After a millennium of fighting by his father's side, Horus recently defected and pledged his allegiance to the house of his uncle, Osiris. No doubt, Osiris had Kala Saar in mind from the moment he began to recruit his nephew, turning Ra's heir, the commander of the Rephaim, against him. But Ra is not seeing a soldier at this moment. He sees only his baby, his firstborn son of choice. He sees him as he was when Ra cradled him in his arms, and Horus stared into his father's eyes as Hathor gingerly kissed his cheek. He was their baby, their first child together. Now, he is no more, killed by Ra's own hand, and no amount of tears can wash away the stain of his blood.

"The Battle of Taliath Garr rages on. Humans, ravagers, Earthbound, Nephilim, awwim, skinwalkers, and more clash and bleed. Mounds of bodies stacking up with each passing hour. Silver arrows turn into flaming lorenths and flash through the sky like lightning. Powerful marids, arwaah, and sila send bodies flying in their wake, the marids by bending the elements to their will and the arwaah and sila by creating rifts to the Gray Zone and unleashing unparalleled waves of force onto their foes. Troops ride horses and camels, some fly through the sky on crafts, or beasts, or by their own power. None of your movies, no director could create or imagine the spectacle before you. Pieces of this hidden history are sprinkled across the great stories found in your world mythologies, from Homer's version of the Trojan War, to the story of Zeus's triumph over the titans, to the Norse tales of Ragnarok, but no one knows the truth. Humans do not realize that the sources for these myths are anchored in reality, and they are all around you.

"Eventually, Ra joins the fray as a man possessed. As he seeks to fight his way to Osiris, he slays one foe after another, letting his grief fuel his fury. The bodies pile around him, and even his allies wisely give him a wide berth, afraid of being a victim of his wrath.

"We're skimming forward; hours have passed. It's almost nightfall, and the battle has been decided. Thoth and Osiris are nowhere to be found, having fled long ago. Abydos has fallen. Iset, Gilgamesh, and their troops are subduing the few remaining soldiers too stubborn to realize that their cause is lost. As Ra staggers through the battlefield, surveying the carnage, the blood of angels flows like rivers covering the ground. The blood of Adam as well, but the blood of angels... well, Ra can feel it in his bones. He can see the spirits rise or fall as the Barac Navaar leave this world. A third of the Nephilim on the face of Earth died during the One Thousand Year War, and half of those who perished were lost in this one battle. This is Liberation Day. Ra knows that he will be hailed as a hero for what has taken place, but for him, nothing feels heroic about this day, not one thing.

"Do you understand what you have seen, son of Adam?"

"I do," David answers.

"This concludes my portion of your journey, young one. Pay close attention to what comes next. Lives may depend on it."

"Huh, what ..."

But before David can finish his question, Ten vanishes, dissipating into vapor, and as much as he'd like to look for the old man, the scene before him has David's full attention. He and Ra are connected, and somehow, he's experiencing this moment with Ra in a visceral way. Ra's broken heart is David's narrator for this portion of this odyssey.

With trembling hands, Amon Ra gently bends down and picks up the body of Horus. No longer having the luxury of being distracted by his rage, he is left to wrestle with his grief, his guilt, and his anguish with each unbearable step. As he travels through the Gray Zone to bring his son home, he closes his eyes, vainly trying to steady his emotions, but all he sees are the eyes of his son, empty and lost, staring back at him. He knows that Hathor will never understand, but Ra did what he had to do. For reasons that Ra cannot share, no one could have faced Horus but him. He had turned his son into the perfect killing machine, taught him terrible secrets. A corrupted Horus was too formidable. Ra had to be the one. He had to be the one to stop him, and now...now, he has to find a way to live with that.

He arrives at Iken within minutes. His eyes linger on his son's face as he somberly leaves him with attendants, and he says a silent prayer as he makes his way to their chamber to face his wife and give her the news. She knew if Ra faced Horus in battle that she would lose one or the other. Ra wonders if she would have preferred to lose her husband rather than her son, and if, perhaps, he has lost his wife. How can she ever forgive him? What will she see when she looks at him? What will he see when he looks at himself? Ra did what he had to do. He did what was right, but at what cost? He braces himself, but not even he can anticipate what waits for him on the other side of the doorway.

As Amon Ra reaches the chamber, he sees Hathor sprawled on the floor, having already given birth to their daughter, Amesemi. But Hathor's not breathing, and their child is nowhere to be found. *No, not this, anything but this!* Ra rushes to her side, falling on his knees as he channels all the power within him and places his hand on her chest, sending healing life force from his body to hers. If there is a spark of life, he can reach her. He must. She does not stir. He places both hands on her and redoubles his efforts. He will empty himself if he needs to, exchange his life for hers. She cannot be dead, not Hathor.

As Ra desperately tries to save his wife, he can't see it, but there's something strange about the look of this. There's no sign of violence or forced entry, and no sense that anything happened here against her will. In addition, there's no evidence of Amesemi's birth. Obviously, it happened earlier in the day, and it seems unconnected to Hathor's present condition, but there's nothing. More importantly, there's a purple haze in the room, a fading violet residue on Hathor's hands, and magenta ashes from what seems to be a burned scroll on the chamber floor. David is only an observer, surfing Ra's memories, so it's easy for David to see. In fact, he's being guided to see it. He thinks there's a part of Amon Ra, the part that brought David here, finally putting pieces together, but pieces to what? He still can't see the bigger picture.

Young Mr. Stone watches as Ra continues his frantic attempt to revive his wife, even though he has completely drained himself and logic says that she is beyond his reach. But there's nothing logical about what he's feeling. He cries out physically and telepathically, giving voice to his pain, sounding the alarm, commanding a search for his missing daughter, and summoning every mystic and healer within miles to his side. Yet, despite all of his efforts, Hathor cannot be brought back, and Semi is nowhere to be found. Eventually, he sends everyone away, all the guards, doctors, mystics, advisors, and family and simply sits on the floor, sobbing in the dark, cradling his wife. When his sister, Iset, returns from securing Abydos, she does not speak a word. She merely joins him and holds them both, holds them until the sun rises and the shadows give way.

So, this is the life of Amon Ra, son of War. This is the distance that he's traveled and the burden he's had to carry. David is in awe, and his respect for Ra has grown.

And that's the end of the dream. David wakes up but keeps his eyes closed, meditating on everything he's experienced, making sure he doesn't forget one detail. There's a lot to absorb, but there's one thing, one really big thing that he's figured out. He realizes why Hathor seemed familiar. It wasn't her appearance. It was a look in her eyes, specifically the way she looked when she was angry with Ra. It reminded David of the way Tricia looked when she defended Semi at the camp. Eyes are the windows to the soul, and they had the same eyes, not similar, exactly the same. And that purple mist... David saw something like it when Serafina cast her spell but also when Tricia killed Semi's murderers. Purple is the color of eldritch energy, and its residue is a sign of either cosmic beings or dark magic. And there's something else. In Penfield, Tricia fought for Semi like...like a mother, a mother defending her child. *Wow, oh, man.* He thinks he's figured it out, but he really prays that he's wrong.

Semi, Ra, everyone thinks that Hathor is dead, that she died a hero, but she's not dead, and maybe she's not a hero. Hathor is Tricia, she's a dark witch, and she's very much alive. David doesn't know how, and he doesn't know what all of that means, but it can't be good. What he knows is that on top of everything else, he just found a new, immediate problem. How does he tell the woman he loves that her long-lost mom is alive, but there's a catch; her mom's probably a supervillain? He's drawing a blank. David needs to talk to Edie and get some help finding the words. This is big, and Semi needs to know. There's a lot going on in her world, but even so, this jumps to the front of the line. David doesn't understand much, but he knows that Hathor is alive, and somehow, she's at the center of all of it. This latest sleep time movie has made his complicated life even more complicated. This one caused all this new drama, and he didn't even get to kiss the girl. Man, this was the worst dream ever.

The Makeover —
Amesemi

After a while, Amesemi just couldn't stay in bed anymore. The memories woke her from her sleep, fragments desperately trying to knit themselves together. She vividly remembered the claws, the burning pain as she bled out, and David's face, his words as he held her close while she choked on her last breath. At that moment, darkness began to envelop her, and even though her body was as good as gone, she felt chills and pressure on her chest as dread seized her. But then there was blinding luminescence, unexplainable calm, and arms that lifted her high and lovingly wrapped themselves around her. And then...Did she die? How long has she been back, and how? Other than her last seconds with David, she doesn't have a clear recollection of anything, not really, not from the moment the Dark Star arrived until she saw David at Stone Mountain Park. For the four weeks in-between, there are lots of images racing nonstop through her mind. The battle, Tricia, dying, coming back, the hospital, it's all a blur, each memory like passengers on a bullet train speeding through her brain. And a little while ago, lying there with her head about to explode, she couldn't take it anymore.

So, despite the fact that Sothis was telling her that she needed more sleep, Semi got up a little before three in the afternoon, saw David asleep at the foot of her bed—he's sooooo cute— and that's when she noticed the mirror across the room. She's been standing here ever since trying to get acquainted with her new self, Amesemi 2.0.

She's frozen in place. It's partly because she is fascinated by her new appearance, and partly something else. She's desperately seeking a distraction from her thoughts, the growing boulder in her gut, and the overwhelming sorrow threatening to overtake her if she connects the dots and confronts the unbearable truth embodied by her new face. Either way, she is riveted by her reflection, barely able to recognize the image peering back at her. She's been staring in this full-length mirror for the last fifteen minutes. OK, maybe it's been more.

When she woke up a little while ago, she was wearing black velecor armor, with a gold star on her chest. Oh, and the armor is covering her sparkling, brand new body. She was so in and out before; she never got a chance to wrap her head around the whole change- into- a- butterfly thing. Now, she's getting her chance. And even for someone raised around the Nistarim, it's freaky, very freaky.

It started with the way she smells—flowers, intoxicating flowers, like a living breathing botanical garden. The aroma is incredible. First thing getting up, before her shower, before brushing her teeth—just Bam, she's little miss fragrance. And then there's the hair, her long, glamorous hair, and all she has to do is run her hands through it, and she can change it into another perfect, fabulous hairstyle. She simply can't cut it. Sothis is Semi's other, and she and the others for all sila are phobic about short hair. Semi's not sure why. In her case, Sothis has this affinity for long flowing, diva-style hair. She loves it. Now Semi, well, she likes braids, beautiful, Afro-centric, and practical, but every time she zaps her do into braids, Sothis changes it into straight, flowing hair down Amesemi's back. It's growing on Semi, but they are going to have to work out a compromise, maybe braids on weekends or something. She just can't imagine being glammed up 24/7. Looking like this, Semi feels like she should go into battle with a wind machine and her own theme song.

She's also taller, at least four inches taller, somewhere around five feet nine inches or so. And Semi's face, well, she recognizes parts of it. She still has dark skin, full lips, brown eyes..., but it's all so perfect now, and dainty. Her skin is soft and unblemished It looks like she has flawless makeup on, but she doesn't have on makeup. It's just her-—black, beautiful, Warrior Princess Barbie.

Oh, that's new. Semi's staring into her own eyes, watching them change color. *Is that happening because...* She realizes they change with her mood. *Good to know next time I'm playing poker.* She snickers at her own levity. Oh well, she won't be beating anyone at cards any time soon. She'll adjust; this stuff isn't even the hard part. The most dramatic changes are below her neck.

Amesemi's sister Bia always teases Semi and even gave her the nickname Uno because she says Semi's figure resembles the number one. Well, wait 'til she sees Semi now. She's got curves, serious curves, legs for days, and a perfectly blessed caboose. And those two melons where her twin girls used to be!

"These girls are huge! I really don't get this whole azaira thing," she vents. "I mean, I'm not aerodynamic at all. How am I supposed to fight like this? And where does someone even *find* bras this size? Bia and Thena are well endowed, and they don't seem to have any problem. I'm sure they..."

Oh no, did I just say all that out loud? Crap, I did. I did!

Dear God, please let David still be asleep. If he heard me, I'm going to melt into a big pile of teenage hormones and shame. Is it possible to be embarrassed to death?

She glances back at him. His eyes are closed. She thinks she's in the clear. Her little Charming still looks like he's lost in dreamland. Semi thinks he's hers. She wonders if he's her boyfriend—if you can have a boyfriend after one date. She did die for him, and he came looking for her. They are definitely a thing. So, does punching him through a wall qualify as their first argument? Semi can't believe she slugged his gorgeous face. She probably should apologize for that when he wakes up.

OK, enough of this. They need to get up and get moving, see if she's strong enough to head back to Avalon. First, Semi gets to have some quick fun and play dress up. She can't walk around like this, and what's Black Barbie without a wardrobe change? Besides, today, while they're running for their lives, it'll be kind of like her second date with David—soooo, no pressure.

As she goes through about fifteen different outfit combinations, everything from urban to elegant, she hears David stirring. He's watching her.

OK, play it cool... stay cool, Semi.

She quickly settles on a classy black dress and heels and turns to him.

"Hey, you're up," she says in her most chipper, casual voice. "How do I look?

"Oh, you look absolutely stunning—amazing," David replies, and for some reason, unknown to Semi, as he responds, he quickly wraps his blanket around his waist as if he's hiding something.

"Thanks," Semi replies, with a big ole goofy grin plastered on her face.

Not the look she was going for, but that spasm of goofiness just took over her face all on its own. It's strange; she knows she looks fabulous, but there's a charm in the way David says it that makes her feel good all over. It's embarrassing, and it doesn't make much sense. Well, if she's going to smile goofily around him, at least Semi has perfect teeth. That's something.

"Hey, Semi," says David, standing with the blanket still wrapped around his waist, even though he has pants on. "I need to run to the bathroom and brush my teeth and take a quick cold... I mean a quick shower. Don't go anywhere. I'll be right back."

"Sure thing."

Ok, that was a little strange. Oh well, guys are weird—cute, but weird. At least he has good hygiene. She knows that's not universally the case.

Well, at any rate, she has a few more minutes to get her look perfect before he comes back out. This velecor psychic wardrobe is harder than it seems. It's quick and easy, but there are too many choices. Part of Semi's obsession with her fake wardrobe is that her head's exploding, and she needs a distraction. All of her life, she's been a telepath. Semi could read thoughts, mind-speak, that kind of thing. Two of the first things she learned as a small child were how to shield her thoughts and how to screen out the thoughts of others. Now, that's all changed.

As a sila, Semi's an empath, not a telepath, a related skill but very different. She can't read minds anymore, and it feels crippling, like she's lost one of her senses, but she's picked up a brand new one, one Semi definitely does not know how to control. She feels everyone's emotions, everyone in the house. Heck, she's sensing half the neighborhood. Amesemi knows exactly what people are feeling, and although she used to debate her on the matter, Semi's aunt was right. Empathy gives you a much clearer picture of who people are than telepathy. Thoughts tell you a lot, but feelings get to the core of who someone is, and they're much harder for people to shield or manipulate.

For example, surfing through Eden's feelings, Semi loves her more. Amesemi's so impressed with Edie's courage and her loyalty. She's willing to die for David, who has essentially been her brother, but she has that same heart toward Semi, someone she barely knows. Semi's speechless and humbled. She just knows that the two of them are going to be close for as long as they're breathing.

B.J.'s emotions are all over the place. You'd never know it, but the kid has been through a lot. He's made out of tougher stuff than people think, much stronger than even he knows. His challenge is that he has so much fear in him, love too, but if he's not careful, that fear and anger are going to drown out the good in him, and there's a great deal of good there if he'll fight for it.

All sorts of other people's emotions are bouncing around in her head, adding to the rather overstuffed closet containing Semi's own. The only person's she can't sense are David's. Semi couldn't read his mind even before his powers, and now, she can't access his feelings. What's the deal? He's the one person in the world whose feelings she really wants to know.

God, this is a cruel joke, and I really wish you'd stop playing with me. Please, give me a peek into that man's heart, just a little peek.

Nothing. She guesses the big man's going to make her have to do this the hard way, hard and very scary. If she truly wants to know how David feels about her, at some point, Semi's going to have to ask him.

In the middle of stressing, and right when she's completed a few finishing touches to her outfit, David comes back. He's wearing a velecor suit but has his actual jeans on over the armor's pants. It's not very practical or fashion-forward, but who needs fashion sense when you have a smile like his? He keeps flashing that smile, and he can walk around in a pink plaid leisure suit, and she'd be fine. Besides, she figures she can help him with his much-needed makeover. She's learned a few things from her sisters over the years.

"Wow, did I tell you how great you look?" he asks, once again flashing that toothy superpower of his, which makes Semi feel all fuzzy inside.

But crazy as it sounds, there's a part of her that doesn't know quite how to take it. Semi's a sila now. Objectively, she's probably a fifteen on a scale of one to ten. Is David just enamored by her new Amesemi 2.0 body, with its bells and whistles, or is it still her that he sees? Is she crazy to ask herself that?

"Pretty impressive, huh," says Semi during a momentary lapse of her filter, a common problem for her. "So, are you as blown away by my perfect, new body as our friend B.J. seems to be?"

David looks straight at her as he slowly walks toward Semi. "I'm probably the wrong person to ask."

"Why's that?"

He moves uncomfortably close to her, staring into her eyes, and takes Semi's right hand. "Because I thought you were perfect before—nothing's changed."

Oh, he *is* a charmer. That was precisely the correct answer. He's either the one or he's doing a really great impersonation. Either way, all the awkwardness Semi was feeling is swept away, and they jump in right where they left off at the diner, talking like they've known each other forever. Actually, it's even better because now, she doesn't have to be secretive about who she is and what she does. Yeah, they're definitely a thing, and she likes it.

And then Semi has a scary thought. What if he kisses her? It's embarrassing, but she's never been kissed—kissed in that way. How does this work? David definitely has a very kissable face. Semi hopes he kisses her. Should she kiss him first? Is that too forward? No, she's certainly not doing that. Well, she promises herself if he tries to kiss her again, this time she will not punch him, but she can't make any promises about her father. This is going to be hard on him, but frankly, she doesn't care. Semi has someone, someone who sees her, who cares about her, and she thinks that's pretty cool.

They're lost in each other and have lost track of time; she knows she has. Leave it to David to try to steer them back on course. He's so mature. Amesemi likes that about him.

"I've really missed talking to you," he says, his voice cracking slightly. "For a while, it looked... Well, I didn't know what to think. Four weeks, a bloody handprint, I feared the worst. I wish we could stay here and talk all day, but if we're going to go, we're going to need to get ready. It'll be dark in a couple of hours. We should check on the others."

"They're fine," Semi replies, "And they're waiting."

"How do you know that?" he asks. "Danny Vison told me that the Amar can't read minds"

"I can't, but I can sense feelings. They're impatient, getting antsy, waiting on us."

"Speaking of feelings, how are you doing? Are you up to this? We can stay here longer, stay the night if you need to."

"I don't know. I feel way better than before, and I'm strong, crazy strong. I just...something doesn't feel quite right. I think after I eat, I'll have a better idea. I'm starving."

"OK," he answers, and then he pauses and peers at Semi as if he's reading her mind, but she knows he's not. Her other makes that impossible. "There's more, isn't there?" he continues. "Something else is bothering you. Is it something I said?"

"No, it's not you, definitely not you. It's just that staring in that mirror, seeing my new face, it makes it real. It finally happened. When I first learned that Sothis had chosen me to be my aunt's successor, I was eight, and I was so excited. There was nothing I wanted more than to be exactly like her. She was everything, my hero, my role model, the mother I never had...everything. She was perfect. It wasn't until I was older that I found out that Iset was going to have to die for me to inherit her power and carry on her legacy. I tried to act like I was OK, that I was a good little soldier and understood the whole next man up mentality, but I didn't. I cried myself to sleep for a week and prayed every day that this day would never come. She'd been Queen Iset for six thousand years. Why couldn't she be here for at least six thousand more? In my wildest dreams, I never imagined that it would come so soon and come like this."

Her voice cracks. Semi closes her eyes and steadies her emotions. Tremors of guilt and sorrow move through her body, welling up. Her eyes burn as she holds back tears, but she refuses to cry in front of David again. Besides, if she starts now, it may be a tsunami. There's so much she's feeling.

"Everything was going so fast before," Semi continues. "I was so in and out. It was like Penfield was a dream, but it wasn't. It's just...she's gone, David. She's gone, and I'm here. She's gone, and it was all my fault. I'm the last person who should be trying to carry on her legacy."

"That's not true. You don't need to carry that. You can't blame yourself."

"It's true," Semi answers in barely a whisper. "It's true. Iset died protecting Tricia, but Tricia shouldn't have been there. She was supposed to be in Avalon, and I was supposed to be watching her. There's so much security there. I didn't think it would matter if I sneaked out and watched the Dark Star. What could go wrong? I ..."

Amesemi's feeling pretty overwhelmed by the overflow of emotion, but she stops in midsentence. Something about the way David's staring at her. He has the oddest look on his face. It's like he's hurt or horrified. She shared too much; he must think Semi's terrible, some kind of monster.

"Why are you looking at me that way?" she asks. You must think I'm awful."

"No, nothing like that," he says.

But something's off. He still has that twisted, disgusted expression on his face, like he's just caught a whiff of a bad smell.

As Semi opens her mouth, her grief and guilt over her aunt turn into frustration towards David. "There's something you're not telling me. I couldn't read your mind, and for some reason, I can't sense your feelings either, but I can see it in your eyes. What is it?"

He's hesitant, but seeing that Semi's not going to let the matter go, he answers her. "It's just...well, you're going to find this hard to believe, Semi, but I understand exactly what you're feeling."

"Don't patronize me, David," Semi replies, her frustration starting to boil into anger. "You have no idea how I'm feeling. How could you kn ...?"

He grabs her right hand and places it on his heart. And with his other hand, gently caresses Semi's cheek.

"It's OK, Semi, you can trust me. You don't have to read my mind to know what's in it," he says gently, his brown eyes penetrating her defenses and touching her soul.

And then she feels his mind pulling Semi in telepathically, psychically knocking on the door of her mental defenses, asking her to let him in. It's scary, but she does, and she feels him pulling her mind into his.

"Princess, my heart is in your hands. With you, I'm an open book," he says to Semi through mind-speak. *"There's something you need to see."*

And just like that, he's giving her a tour through his memories. She only wanted a peek. This is definitely much more than she wished for, but it's amazing. She's never been in someone's mind quite like this. Obviously, as a telepath, she's mind-toured before, but it's never been so free, so unguarded. He's not holding back. It's heartwarming but challenging because Semi can't help but wonder if she'd be willing to do the same.

They go back almost to the beginning. Semi sees David as a small child, sees his parents, Anthony and Patricia, sees David and Edie in kindergarten, and witnesses the birth of the Stone twins, at least as much of it as David was allowed to see. She sees Edie on the day she and her brother Justin moved into the Stone's home. The Stones took the kids in and cared for them for almost two years. It was during a time when Edie's parents were going through some kind of crisis. Semi didn't know that. No wonder they're so close.

As she fast forwards through his memories, Semi's struck by how much love there was in his household and how happy he was growing up, traumatic move down south notwithstanding. These were happy times, but there's darkness up ahead. She can sense it. Something tells her that the good times didn't last.

The mind surf speeds through David's superstar football years and his increasingly big head as he soaked up all the praise and adoration from all sorts of people, including a whole lot of skanky girls. All of this for throwing some funny shaped ball around; Semi doesn't get it. Anyway, it led to increasing tension between David and his dad, who's concerned about how his son is changing. Semi witnesses several heated discussions, and then it skips ahead to David's birthday a year ago.

That afternoon, David and his father got into a terrible argument about some drugs Pastor Stone found in David's truck, and David angrily drove off. Later on, David skips the birthday party that his family is throwing for him and goes and hangs out at some wild teenage party instead. It's the first time he's done something like this. He gets drunk and doesn't show up at home until well past one in the morning. He's sobered up by butterflies and dread as he opens the door to his house, expecting to be in all kinds of trouble, but instead, he's greeted by his mom and the Garcia's. They tell him...they tell him. Oh no, this is it; this is the night his father died. He died while he was out looking for David.

As David hears the news, his emotions are raging. Pain, grief, shock horror, disbelief, shame, all kinds of shame; he feels it all. After the initial news, he doesn't hear another word that's spoken. He only hears one sentence over and over again, "It's all your fault." For months, he can't look his mom in her eyes or his brother and sister in theirs. He can't even face the members of his church without the chorus screaming in his heart. "It's all your fault," it says, and "You're the reason he's not here." Now, his mom has no husband, and his siblings have no dad, and David believes it's all because of him. And he believes something else, something darker. His dad's gone, and David's still here. He just cost the best man he ever knew his life. It should have been him.

Oh man, Semi's felt some of that too with Iset. Even standing in front of the mirror a few minutes ago, she felt the shame and the guilt, and though she didn't want to admit it, part of her wished that it had been her instead of her aunt. Wow, he wasn't exaggerating. He's lived it. He knows exactly how Semi feels. At this point, he knows her feelings better than she does.

But the memory tour isn't over. There's more that David wants her to see. He shows Semi the fallout, his actions over the following months, and the dark places he went to in his mind. After months of self-destructive behavior, he finds himself parked out in the woods with his father's gun in his lap, a clip in his hand, and drowning in hopeless darkness. After several hours, he loads the gun and starts to cock it, with a chorus of whispers telling him to end it and another chorus saying that the world will be better off without him. But there's another voice with him, calling to him gently. At first, he can't hear it, but as he goes to cock the gun, he senses love's kiss and notices as the voice speaks hope into his heart, just a little hope, just enough for him to lower the gun and drive to the home of Pastor Joe.

Now, Semi's balling. She's not sure if it's her physical body or her psychic avatar. Her guess is that it's both. Either way, she can't stop the tears; they're for his pain and hers. There's a lot in there, a lot she hasn't dealt with. His story has helped her to connect with her own.

"It's OK," he says as his avatar hugs hers. *"It's going to be OK."* After her sobbing slows down to a trickle, he asks, *"Are you ready to go back now?"*

Semi say yes, but as she does, she catches sight of another cluster of memories, a place with rainbows, hearts, and flowers. She thinks that's where David keeps his feelings for her. She's changed her mind. She wants to visit there before she goes back. Ignoring her protests, David's avatar simply laughs and pulls her away. Next thing Semi knows, her consciousness is out of his mind and back in hers. Oh well, she'll have to sneak a peek at Flower-land next time.

Semi opens her eyes. She and David are standing awesomely, uncomfortably close. Evidently, while his avatar was hugging her in there, their bodies were doing the same. One of them should probably take a step back, but she kind of wants to move a little closer. They just end up holding hands and staying where they are, which is wonderfully awkward.

"Thanks for showing me that, for trusting me," she says, breaking the ice. "I didn't know that you had been through that. I'm sorry."

"It's OK. It's just I thought it was easier to show you than to tell you. Guilt and shame is a dark road, Semi. You don't want to go down there."

"So, how do you deal with it?"

"It's still a work in progress. For one thing, I had to get honest with myself and with the people who love me, but for me, there's something else too." David sighs thoughtfully and then continues. "When I got to Pastor Joe's, we had a good talk. It was the first time that I'd opened up with anyone about how I was feeling, and it went differently than I had expected, different in a good way. Everyone was always trying to tell me that it wasn't my fault, and maybe it wasn't, but no one was ever able to convince me of that. Even now, right or wrong, there's still a part of me that feels responsible. Pastor Joe didn't bother with that.

"After he heard me out, he asked me something unexpected. He looked me straight in my eyes and asked, 'David, do you believe the stuff you've heard at church your whole life, even the simple stuff? Like, is there a God, and do you believe that your dad is with him in a better place? I want you to answer honestly, son, don't give me the preacher's kid answer.' It took me by surprise, and on top of that, he asked me to go into the garage and take as much time as I needed to think about it before I came back in and gave him an answer.

"All my life, I had been going through the motions. I grew up around people of faith; I just never stopped to ask if I had any of my own or if what they were saying was worth having faith in. I just straddled the fence. Now, I was being asked to make a choice. When I was honest with myself, I realized that, on some level, I believed, but I lacked the courage to have true faith. I told that to Pastor Joe, and it led to more conversation that evening. At the end of it, he told me that if I wanted to make a change, to begin by accepting two simple challenges, two challenges that still drive me."

"What were they?" Amesemi asks.

"The first one is that if I believed that my dad was up there watching, to live in a way that makes him proud," David answers, choking up as he does. "And the second challenge he gave was to live my life with the goal of seeing my dad again. Those words sparked something in me. When I left Pastor Joe that morning, I went to my dad's gravesite with a coffee and a box of Krispy Kremes, and we had the first of many graveside heart-to-hearts. I shed my first tears right then and there, and when I was done, I drove by Edie's house and gave the Glock to her dad, went home, and wept some more in my mother's arms. Those two basic challenges helped me start the journey out of the chasm I was in, and they still help me to keep things simple when my mind gets cluttered."

He pauses, clears his throat and chokes back some tears, but before she can thank him for what he's shared, he shares something else.

He squeezes her hand tightly and smiles at Semi, saying, "She's watching you, Semi, you know that don't you? And I know Iset's proud of you."

Now, she's the one choking back tears, trying hard not to start crying again.

"Thanks for that," she replies.

"So, have you decided what you're going to call yourself?" he asks, changing the subject to something lighter.

"Isis, I think I'm going to call myself Isis. I think it honors Iset's legacy, but it kind of gives it an individual twist as well."

"I like it," he says, softly edging even closer, "But, I'm never going to call you that."

"Really?" she asks playfully.

"No, Princess, you're always going to be Semi to me, the perfect princess I met at the diner."

He leans forward until their lips are almost touching and gently brushes a strand of hair from her face.

"I want to do something," he says with a mischievous grin, "But you've got to promise not to punch me through another wall."

Semi flashes a smile and brushes her cheek against his as she whispers, "I promise to punch you through the wall if you don't."

With a twinkle in his eye, he leans forward to kiss her. This is it. Semi would check her breath, but these days, that's not a problem. This is so amazing. S...

Just as their lips brush, David's twelve-year-old cousin, Sean, barges into the room, saying, "Hey guys, my mom and your friends are waiting for you downstairs. They wanted me to come and get y... Oh, snap, I didn't mean to interrupt you, cuz. OK, how much time do you need?"

"Nothing's going on here, Sean," David responds angrily. "We'll be right down...and Sean don't go running your mouth about what you think you saw."

"Yo, snitches get stitches, son. I gotcha," Sean responds as he heads back downstairs, laughing to himself.

"If he opens his mouth, I'm going to strangle him," David mumbles and then sighs. "Who am I fooling? In about twenty seconds, the whole block is going to know, and B.J.'s going to bounce up the steps giggling like he's ten."

"OK, Charming, we probably should head on down," she replies, "but only if you promise that we're going to finish our 'conversation' later."

"Princess, that's a date."

Semi collects her lorenth, and while David packs up his backpack, he asks, "So, about your hunger problem, what do you think about pizza?"

"New York pizza!" she answers excitedly. "It's my favorite."

"Is there any other kind?" he replies, with the smugness of a true New Yorker. "Once you get south of Jersey, buying pizza is just a waste of time. There's a place not far from here across from Van Courtland Park. Let me treat you to a slice."

"Or two."

He grins. "Or two, Princess. As much as you want."

"Oh, before we go down, do you mind if I help you with something?" Semi asks before her brain can stop her mouth.

"Uh, sure."

OK, her big mouth has put her out there now. There's no turning back. Here it goes.

"I wanted to help you with your velecor," she replies. "Take off your pants."

"Excuse me," he stutters.

"No, silly, not like that. It's just that your armor has pants. It's redundant. If you want to wear jeans, you can create that image."

"Yeah, but I need pockets. There are no pockets with the velecor."

"That's part of what I wanted to show you. The nanites create pockets and pouches as needed and can flatten stuff out in a way that's fairly sleek. Let me show you. Take all the important stuff out of your wallet. Now, take the individual credit cards, and so on. and put them in imaginary pockets on your armor's pants."

"OK," he says, "But I ... wow, pockets just magically appear."

"You can put your cell phone in there too, and it will create a scabbard on your back for your lorenth. Oh, and the armor remembers where things are, so you don't have to recall which item is in which pocket."

"That's very, very cool."

OK, so here comes the touchy part. She wants to tell David that he needs a makeover, but even Semi knows that's not the best way to approach the male ego. Her personality is somewhat a cross between Bast and Thena. Bast is tough but diplomatic, while Thena is much more of a blunt instrument. She needs to channel more Bast for this one and less Athena.

"So, what are you planning to wear?" she asks.

"I don't know, maybe jeans, a hoodie, and some coat. It's gotten a little cooler out there, so visually I gotta blend in."

"Do you mind if I try something?" Semi asks as she puts her right hand on his chest, his very large, very firm chest. *Focus Semi, focus.*

She adjusts his outfit, putting him in some sleek, fashionable, black, skinny jeans, a cream turtleneck, a black mid-long, trench coat jacket, and black, leather sneakers.

"What do you think?" She asks as he steps away so David can see the mirror.

"Do you like it?" he asks.

"Yes."

"Then, I love it," he replies.

That's a great answer, almost as great as his next move, as he leans in for first kiss attempt number three. Of course, at this exact moment, B.J. barges in. *Doesn't anybody knock around here?*

"Oh, I'm sorry," he says unconvincingly. They both know he's just being nosey. "I was just making sure everything's OK. Everyone's downstairs is waiting on you guys."

David doesn't say anything. He gives B.J. a death stare, and Semi swears she sees Brantley physically shrink as he backs out of the room.

"OK," B.J. stammers. "I'll tell them that you're fine and on your way."

"C'mon, Charming," Semi says, pulling on David's arm as he grabs his backpack. "Our fan club awaits."

"OK, but if you're up to it, maybe we can take a walk through the park after we eat and finally get a chance to finish this 'conversation'."

"I can't wait," Semi answers, doing her best to stop herself from giggling uncontrollably.

So far, Amesemi 2.0 is working out just fine. She loves her new life. Maybe she can forget about Avalon for a couple of days. The danger's behind them for now. They should be safe here, hidden away in the Bronx, so what's the rush? She has pizza, her health, and a young man who seems crazy about her. Why not enjoy it? What could possibly go wrong?

KINGSBRIDGE — AMESEMI

As she gets to the bottom of the staircase, Amesemi is met by six pairs of eyes fixed on her, glued to her, chronicling her every move. Who said the danger was behind her? She's welcome here, but she gets the distinct impression that just one misstep and things could change quickly.

Once downstairs, she's greeted by David's aunt, Liz, his mom's older sister, David's seventeen-year-old cousin Kenya, the annoying, twelve-year-old Sean, thirteen-year-old cousin Andrew Jr., and of course, B.J, and Edie. David's Uncle Drew, Andrew Sr., is at work, and the oldest one of his cousins, Karen, is away at college. She's a freshman at Syracuse, and winter break doesn't start for her for a couple of days.

Despite, her momentary misgivings, Semi finds the family warm and fun-loving, and as crazy as it sounds, she thinks his relatives might have been OK with the four of them showing up on their doorstep unannounced this morning, even without the mind voodoo David put on the household—with the possible exception of David and Semi sleeping in the same room. Semi doesn't have to read minds to know that his aunt would never have gone along with *that* without a telepathic push.

After a few minutes of chitchat, Sean and Andrew head to the back to play video games, and David and Edie step outside to talk about something important. Kenya escapes to her bedroom to get some privacy as she takes a call from her boyfriend, some young guy her mom despises. Semi thinks his name is Tyrone, but her mom and brothers sarcastically call him "Mr. Wonderful." That leaves B.J. and Amesemi talking in the kitchen with Aunt Liz, and she's got a million questions. Semi hopes Edie and David don't take too long.

While mingling with the family, Semi faintly hears David's voice. She whips her head around thinking that he's come back inside, but no, he's still out there. Closed door and all, even without trying, she can hear Edie and David's conversation. She just now realizes that the hearing and eyesight of this new body are extraordinary—not as sensitive as a ravager or feral, but they're pretty amazing. They're talking about her. David's getting Edie's advice concerning Semi, either about telling her something or maybe buying her something. Semi wonders if he's going to get a present for her. It's hard to make it out with all the other talking and background noise. This is so wrong, but she bets if she focuses harder, she can hear every detail. Should she do it? Probably not, but it's oh-so so tempting ...

"Are you OK, sweetie?" Aunt Liz asks, noticing that Semi's staring off into the middle distance, obviously distracted.

"I'm sorry, Mrs. Lipton," Semi answers. "I was just ..."

"Oh, sweetie, please call me Liz or Auntie," she replies. "Anyone who's a friend of my favorite nephew is family."

"Thank you, M...I mean Auntie. I really appreciate it."

As she overwhelms Semi with frenetic, aggressive, inquisitive, West Indian hospitality, Amesemi's mesmerized by her smile. She's shorter and stockier than her younger, slimmer sister, Patricia, David's mom, but she's super cute with her momma jeans and braided hair, pulled back in a bun. But what makes her stunning is her spirit. She has the kindest face and the warmest smile. When Semi closes her eyes and tries to imagine her own mother's face, it's how Amesemi dreams she must have looked, not the details but the spirit, the love, and the warmth. Semi likes to believe that a smile like that is what greeted her into the world. Much to her regret, she'll never know.

"So, sweetie, how long have you and my nephew been a couple?" she asks, continuing her barrage of questions and insights. Having finished catching up with B.J. and getting reports about him, his grades, his family, and his fictitious love life, she's switched to Semi.

As Amesemi prepares to answer this and the many other questions that she's sure are going to follow, Semi notices for the first time that B.J. has wisely been using his velecor suit and psychic mask to mimic his old appearance. She's assuming that everyone simply writes off the change in his voice as him maturing. From what she gathers, they haven't seen him since last November when they came down to Alabama to bury David's dad, so it's definitely believable.

Amesemi steadies herself and flashes her own mega kilowatt grin. "Oh, I feel like I've known him all my life. I actually just met him about a month ago on the way to Christian camp, but we really got close at the camp. It was a life-changing time."

"That's an understatement," B.J. mumbles sarcastically.

"Did you say something, B.J.?" Liz asks.

"Not really. I'm just so amazed at how everyone seems to be getting older while you get younger, Auntie," he replies, cleverly. "Whatever you're doing, you should bottle it."

She blushes momentarily and then returns her attention back to Semi. "So do you live near Alex in Alabama?"

It takes Amesemi a second to adjust to her calling David by the shortened version of his middle name, but when she does, she replies, "No, ma'am. I live in D.C., well near D.C. in the suburbs."

"My brother lives in Silver Spring, Maryland," Auntie continues. "That's a wonderful area with great schools. I'm so happy to see Alex's schooling back on track. I, for one, was glad that he put that football stuff behind him. You know, our family is very, very big on education. Youth and beauty fade, sweetie, but a great education can take you a long way. Where do you attend school?"

"Uh, well," she stammers. She's stuck. She hadn't thought about how to answer that one.

Semi's homeschooled for five days a week, twelve hours a day, on a slow day: five hours of academic study, two hours of conditioning, two hours of combat theory and three hours of sparring and simulations. It's school, but not anything that's going to make any sense to Auntie. How does Semi answer this without sounding totally crazy?

"She's modest, Auntie," B.J. chimes in. "She a senior at a really exclusive, private school, Avalon Academy, top of her class."

"Top of your class," Auntie responds, her grin getting even wider. "That's impressive."

"Yeah, and she's traveled everywhere," BJ. continues. "I think her dad's an ambassador or something cause she speaks several different languages. Isn't that right, Semi?"

"Yeah, yes...sure," she answers as she tries to figure out where this is going next.

"I imagine your mom and dad are very proud," says Auntie.

"No mom," Semi replies, with big, puppy dog eyes, angling for the sympathy vote. Maybe Auntie will feel sorry for her, and the questions will stop. "It's just me, my dad, and my sisters. My mom passed away during childbirth."

"I'm so sorry to hear that, Sweetie," Auntie replies as she gently grabs Semi's hand.

She's taking a breath. This is it. With any luck, Aunt Liz is going to stop or take the topic off of Amesemi.

"Well, I'm sure your family's very proud," she continues. "You've got to tell me all about them. What exactly did you say your father does?"

At that moment, David walks back in with Edie, just in time to come to the rescue.

My hero.

Wow, Semi really didn't see that interrogation coming. Auntie drew her in with that incredible smile and then stalked Amesemi with the ruthless efficiency of a great white, drilling Semi to make sure that she's good enough for her nephew. Semi can't say that she blames her. David is pretty wonderful, and from what Amesemi's seen from his memories, he hasn't had the best taste in women. She's sure Aunt Liz will be on the phone with her sister later to give her a full report. At least she would if she weren't getting mind-wiped. Semi's guess is that telepathic manipulation is going to be the plan once they're rescued. It's pretty much standard protocol to wipe or at least edit memories when there's an unusual incident involving civilians. In some ways, it sucks, but the good news is that she'll probably get a chance to make a better first impression the next time they meet.

"Hey, Auntie, you're not grilling Semi, are you?" David asks, in a manner that is somehow simultaneously pointed and disarming. "You know that thing that you do when one of us brings someone new over, and you do your best Johnny Cochran impersonation. Please, tell me that's not happening."

"No, dear," she answers. "You know me. We're simply having some friendly chitchat."

He walks over and gives his auntie a big hug and kiss as he says with a grin. "I do know you. I know your sister too. That's why I asked."

The two share a laugh, and then David changes the topic. "Hey, Auntie, we're going to step out for a little while and go to that pizza joint across from the park. We shouldn't be too long."

"No, Alex," she responds. "I was just starting to make some dinner, oxtail, peas and rice, one of your favorites. I was even going to have Kenya and Juni run to the corner and bring back some coco bread and some Jamaican patties to add to the meal. I don't want you ruining your appetite."

"Who's Juni?" Semi whispers in Edie's ear.

"That's what they call Andrew Jr.," Edie whispers back.

"We're teenagers, Auntie," David replies. "It's impossible for us to ruin our appetites. We're just going to grab a snack. Trust me, by the time you're done, we'll have plenty of room left. Besides, believe it or not, B.J.'s never had real pizza before. It would be a travesty to let another day go by without rectifying that."

"Hey, I've had pizza before," B.J. blurts out defensively. "I have it all the time."

"Kid, you've never had pizza north of Tennessee," David replies dismissively. "That stuff they call pizza down south doesn't count."

"Oh, I had pizza in North Carolina once," says Aunt Liz. "It was the absolute worst. I said, never again. Please, please educate dear B.J., but leave room. Drew gets home at six. We'll have dinner then."

"OK," David answers.

"Do you want to take the car?"

"No ma'am, I think we'll walk. It's not that far," he replies as he kisses his aunt goodbye. "Besides, it'll be good to stretch our legs."

As everyone is saying their goodbyes, Auntie turns to Semi, saying, "You're not going like this, are you? Honey, you look absolutely beautiful, but it's gotten chilly. You can't go out in that dress without a decent coat. Did you bring one with you?"

Semi looks around and realizes that David has on the fake coat she dressed him in, and Edie and B.J., who are "dressed" more casually than the two of them, have on seasonally appropriate, psychic jackets. The velecor does such a good job of regulating temperature, Semi forgot all about creating one for herself. Seeing Semi hesitate, auntie starts calling for Juni. Amesemi could have pretended to go upstairs to get her coat and simply used her velecor to generate one, but she froze. *Now what?*

"You know what," says Aunt Liz. "I've got just the thing for you." She turns to Juni as he enters the room. "Juni, get that coat that Alex left here. Semi needs to wear it."

"But ma, David gave it to me," he protests.

"Boy, was I asking your opinion?" she asks sternly.

"No, ma'am," he mumbles.

"Anyway, you don't even wear that jacket," she lectures. "You've got nothing but coats and jackets, and that one is too big for you. Now, run and get it."

Juni doesn't feel good about this at all. His feelings are full of all sorts of protests and rebellion, but he doesn't let on or say another word. Evidently, he'd learned a long time again that he has an old school, West Indian mom, so rebellion is not a good survival skill, and democracy is something that you get when you start paying some bills. He simply turns and sprints to his bedroom closet and emerges a minute later with the jacket.

"David, is that your letterman jacket from your junior year?" asks Edie.

He nods his head affirmatively, and although Semi has no idea what a lettermen jacket is or why it's a thing, she can tell it *is* one by the way everyone's feelings get engaged when they see it. Evidently, it's a big deal in teenage, high school culture for a jock to let a lady wear his jacket, but

David didn't ask her to wear it. His aunt did. Amesemi doesn't know how to feel about that.

"Man, I forgot I left it here," David says wistfully. "I packed up a box of my football stuff after everything happened and left it here with you guys when we visited last Christmas. The boys were always asking about my trophies, articles, and stuff, and I didn't have any more use for them. I haven't thought about it since."

Amesemi can't read David's feelings, but she doesn't have to. She was inside his mind. Football, his dad, that night... it's all so interconnected. So, David buried the game when he buried his father. It's not difficult to imagine the inner turmoil being caused by seeing his coat and everything it represents. He probably doesn't even want to see it, let alone give it to someone to wear. He walks over slowly toward his cousin, and when he gets there, he traces his finger over the large letter on the coat and some of the pins and then takes it from his cousin, lifting it in the air.

"Honestly, I never had any use for this," he says as he walks toward Amesemi. "Until now. Semi, would you do me the honor of wearing my jacket?"

She still has no idea what a letterman jacket is, but for some reason, she feels warm and tingly inside.

"Yes," she answers as he slides it on. "Definitely, yes."

Semi's not sure exactly what's happening now. She feels as though she's floating out the door. When her head stops spinning, she finds herself holding hands with David as they walk down the street.

"So, now you're the one mixing real clothes with velecor," says David, grinning. "I just need to let you know that a fashionista I know told me that doing that is a major fashion faux pas."

"She sounds very wise and very beautiful," Semi answers.

"She is."

"Well, just let her know that there's an exception to every rule," she replies, "And this is a pretty cool exception. Don't you think?"

"I couldn't agree more, Princess. It looks good on you."

The walk is longer than David remembered, but they don't care. Somewhere along the way, Semi realizes that she can mind-speak with Edie. Even though Edie's not technically an Earthbound, something about the way she got her powers allows her to function like one. She gets how big a deal this is, the whole jacket thing. The two of them are having their own private girl-chat giggling back and forth, much to the chagrin of David and B.J. Edie and Semi are going to be dangerous together.

When they get to the pizza place, they jump right in ordering slices, chips, and sodas and munching, crazy munching as they talk about a little bit of everything. There's been so much drama; none of them had realized quite how hungry they were.

"This is so good," shares, B.J., excitedly. "OK, I admit it. This is the best pizza I've ever had."

"I told you, kid," says David. "New York has the best pizza in the world, and this is not even the best spot in town."

"I don't know if it's the best in the world," responds B.J., at his instigating best. "I hear Chicago pizza is actually better."

"Someone, please, hold me back," shouts Edie, playfully, her Bronx accent kicking in. "I'm going to have to smack this guy. I cannot believe you just said Chicago has better pizza."

"Well, I'm not holding you back," Semi says, giggling as she chomps on her fourth slice. "Anyone who questions the supremacy of New York pizza deserves what he gets."

This is great. They laugh and joke and carry on like this for a while. Semi feels a little light in the head. Is she buzzed? Can you get drunk on pizza and soda? This is so much fun. She hasn't had fun like this since ... since ... since ever. She loves these guys.

"So, help me to understand—just for the record," Semi says, changing the subject to something more serious and inadvertently killing the vibe. "How exactly did you guys get your powers? I mean... I know that B.J. sucked the life out of a ravager, and I was there when Edie cloned Daniel's powers, but you used abilities you got from the camp to do those things. What happened at the camp? Sothis has only given me bits and pieces, and what I have doesn't make much sense."

"What part?" Edie asks.

"Well, David was touched by one of the fallen. Only someone with incredible power could survive that. But David, I met you before you went to the camp and you were a normal human, not an asura. All of you were. Normal humans don't have that kind of power."

"Explain this asura thing for me, Semi," says B.J. "Why does that make a difference?"

"Well, asura are humans that have DNA from the fallen in their bloodline. If it's strong enough, it can lead to them having powers and extremely long life."

"The fallen's DNA causes all that?" he asks.

"Indirectly. You know where they say that humans use ten percent of their brains? Well, all humans have the potential for incredible power. The blood of angels unlocks that ability, allowing an asura to use fifty to sixty-five percent of their full potential."

"So, were you an asura, before you became a sila?" asks Edie.

"No, not exactly. I was an exception to the rule. Sothis designated me as her next host when I was a toddler. She opened up my brain's pathways and gave me asura-like abilities, so I could develop powers and train even though my bloodline was fully human. That was unprecedented, but she simply opened up my pathways. She didn't radiate my body with an incredible amount of angelic essence. I couldn't have survived that. I don't think even a mighty and trained asura could actually survive it, but David, you easily absorbed it and created a filter for B.J. and Edie. I mean, your body is still supercharged with the blood of angels, like a battery, at levels I've never seen or heard of. With all this new knowledge you've gotten, do you have any idea how it happened?"

"No, not really," he answers. "Nameless told me that I had great power before he grabbed me, but I still have no idea what he meant. I had Sothis in my head and the other guy, but they haven't shed any light, not yet anyway."

"What other guy?" Semi asks.

"You know, the other guy," he mumbles. "Didn't Sothis tell you about him?"

"No," she answers in her suspicious voice. "Who or what is he?"

"Amon Ra," he answers, sheepishly. "He's been in my head, helping me."

"Amon who? You mean my dad? My dad's been in your head? Is he there now? When were you going to tell me?'

"I thought you knew."

Semi's hot and about to pour a gallon of gasoline on a difficult conversation when Edie starts talking to her through mind-speak. David's still talking, trying to mansplain, but Edie's the one who clams her down and helps her make sense of all this. Thank God for Edie. She helps Amesemi understand that David wasn't trying to hide anything. He was just being a guy. David and Semi talk some more, and it goes much better now that she understands, but the guys think that their mansplaining abilities are what turned it around. Semi's going to leave well enough alone and let them have the "win."

"I'm sorry, guys, sorry you've had to deal with all this," Semi shares, after things calm down. "And I want to thank you for everything all three of you risked to find me. I was raised around the Nistarim, raised around half-castes, meta-humans, hybrids, beasties, and more. Unusual and impossible is just another day in Avalon, but this stuff that we're dealing with is freaky, even for me. I know it has to be challenging for you three."

"Yeah, when David told me he had someone else inside him, I had visions of *Aliens*, *Invasion of the Body Snatchers*, and a list of other old sci-fi movies. I even thought about *Freaky Friday* for a moment," says B.J.

"What is that?" Semi asks.

"What is what? *Freaky Friday*?" he responds.

"All of it," she answers. "I've never heard of that stuff."

"Uh, OK," he continues. "What about *Star Wars*, *Lord of the Rings*, *Harry Potter*, *The Infinity War*, *Captain America the Winter Soldier*?" Seeing her blank expression, he just doubles down, adding, "*Despicable Me*, *Frozen*, *The Notebook*, *Crazy Rich Asians*..."

"None of it is ringing a bell," she replies.

"They're movies, Semi, really popular movies," says Edie. "What kind of movies do you watch?"

"Honestly, I haven't seen many movies, and I really don't watch TV outside of the news. I just study and train for the most part."

"Well, it's official," B.J. quips. "You and David need to break up. If you haven't seen any movies, what are you guys possibly going to talk about?"

"We do OK," says David jumping in.

"I know you're joking, B.J.," Semi replies, feeling the need to explain herself. "But I haven't experienced a whole lot of things that you guys would consider normal. I really haven't had much 'normal' interaction with people my age until I met you guys. I...Oh, this is my jam."

"You know this song?" asks B.J.

"Of course. It's Lizzo," she answers.

"So, explain this to me," he asks. "How is it you know Lizzo, but you've never heard of *Star Wars*?"

"I love music, all kinds of music. In fact, my first memory is a lullaby that my dad or someone used to sing to me when I was a baby. Besides, from an early age, dance was part of my training. I've studied all styles of dance, including social media videos, and if I say so myself, I'm very good. I got used to moving with music, so I play music every time I work out or train or spar, to wind down, basically all day every day."

"David and I are music fiends too," says Edie. "What's your favorite?"

"I love classical, country, pop, rock, singer-songwriter, R&B, gospel, contemporary Christian, pretty much all the popular artists. Name somebody, contemporary, almost any style, and I've got something of his on my playlist. I love old school stuff too, old school rock, R&B, and soul, you know, The Beatles, Aerosmith, Queen, Stevie Wonder, Lauryn Hill, Aretha. But when I'm training or stressed, my favorite is Hip Hop, everything from the Sugar Hill Gang to Nas, Biggie, Tupac, and Eminem, to Jay-Z, Drake, Kendrick, Cardi B, Lecrae, J. Cole, The Migos, you name it. Oh, and I go to musicals. I'm addicted to them. Broadway, Paris, Shanghai, Jinnestan City, I see them everywhere, whenever I have free time. I think I've seen *Hamilton* twenty-two times."

David shoots B.J. a look and smiles, and B.J. laughs and throws his hands up in surrender. "OK, you guys win. You two were destined to be together. The only other Hamilton lover I know with such crazy, passionate, eclectic taste in music is my man, David. What are the odds?"

"You didn't mention jazz," says David.

"I know," Semi answers. "My dad and my sister Thena have tried to get me into it, but it hasn't clicked."

David laughs, knowingly. "I've got just the thing for you. I was the same way, but a teacher shared a few key tracks with me, and it finally resonated."

And just like that, David and Amesemi are off again in their own world talking about Hamilton, jazz, hip-hop, playing the guitar, dancing styles, songwriting, and a million other topics. It's like B.J. and Edie have disappeared, along with everyone else in the pizza place, and it's just the two of them. It's paradise.

After a while, he asks, "So, Semi, now that you've eaten, how're you feeling?"

"Better," she answers, stifling a yawn. "A little tired, but I think I'm good."

"I think we should probably spend the night at my aunt's and leave in the morning. We're safe here, and a night of rest and more good food should do everyone good. What do you think?"

She stifles a yawn. "Sounds good to me. I could probably use a little more sleep, and this new body has an endless appetite. By the time dinner rolls around, I'll be starving again."

"Sounds like a plan," he answers, and then he pauses pensively before he continues. "Hey, Semi, before we take that walk, I promised you, there's something important I need to talk to you ab...OW."

What was that? Semi thinks Edie just kicked David from under the table, and pretty hard from the sound of things. Why would she do that? She'd ask her, but for some reason, her lips aren't moving. Suddenly, she's so tired, can't keep her eyes open. Oh, did she just face plant onto the table? She can't lift her head, can't open her eyes. She's so, so, tired.

"Semi, are you OK?" David asks.

She'd answer if she could move, but that's not going to happen at this moment.

"She's OK," Edie says to the gang, having checked on Semi through mind-speak. "She's exhausted. Good thing too, Mr. Stone," she continues angrily, her usually absent Bronx accent turned up to eleven. "What was that, David? I thought we agreed that you were going to wait on telling her."

Tell her what? What's the big secret? Semi wishes she could talk. She has so many questions.

"I know, I know," David replies, "But I hate keeping secrets from her. I'm looking into her eyes, and I just felt the need to tell her. Anyway, to quote the great man, 'Women always figure out the truth. Always.' So, I figured I should tell her before..."

"Shut up, just shut up and just listen," says Edie emphatically. "Lil' bro, you don't get to drag the great Han Solo into this one. What you and your evil twin, B.J., know about women could fit on a pinhead, so for once, you need to listen, unless you want a repeat of your 'Sleeping Beauty' incident from the hospital."

"OK, I'm all ears," he answers.

Edie continues, a little calmer, "David, this isn't about keeping secrets. It's about being sensitive. Look at her. The poor girl can't even lift her head. She's so worn out. She's just returned from being quasi dead, she's trying to adjust to a radically different body, equipped with new powers and another being living in her head, and she's trying to wrap her brain around the fact that every fiend in the shadow-verse has her on their most wanted list. Oh, and let's not forget, in the middle of all of this, she's struggling to get a handle on a whole bunch of brand-new feelings she's experiencing for some stupid but good-hearted guy she met in a diner. Do you really think that you need to dump more on her now?"

There's a silence that Semi's guessing involves David nonverbally agreeing with her. Amesemi wishes she could see what's happening.

Eventually, David speaks up. "OK, but why'd you have to call me stupid?" he asks in his hurt puppy dog voice—so, so cute.

"That's not going to work on me, mano," Edie replies coolly. "Say it." There's silence, and then she says it again. "Say it."

"You are right," David says, reluctantly.

"And?" she asks sternly.

"And I'm wrong," he continues.

"Now, doesn't that feel better?" she says in a southern sweet manner.

"I hate you," David mumbles, playfully.

"You're welcome," Edie counters.

"Not a word, Brantley," David barks.

"Now, scoop up your girl," says Edie, "and B.J. grab the leftovers. We've got to get Semi to bed."

"Wow, when did she get so bossy," B.J. complains.

"She came out that way," David quips. "Legend is she came out head first shouting orders to the doctor and nurses."

"In two languages," she replies, "not that I want to brag or anything."

Hey, I speak twenty-seven languages. At least I do when I can actually talk.

Something's happening. She feels like she's floating. *Oh, that feels so nice.* She feels drunk or high, not that she's ever been drunk or high, but she guesses it feels a lot like this, or maybe, just maybe, David is carrying her. Yeah, that might be it.

"Are you sure she's OK?" B.J. asks. "Man, she's out, really out."

"She's breathing OK," David answers. "Her aura's strong. I think Edie's right, she's fine."

She's fine, but something's very wrong. She has to tell them.

"And we're going to be OK carrying her like this in broad daylight?" B.J. asks. "Won't somebody call the cops? Do you need to do your mind thing to disguise us or something?"

Edie and David both laugh.

"Kid, you've got a lot to learn about New York," says David. "It takes a whole lot more than me carrying Semi down the street to get a second look around here. This doesn't even register on the weird meter."

No, they're not going to be OK. Semi's got to find a way to open her eyes, to let them know. She feels them; feels them all around her and her friends, the darkness is closing in. And Thoth's right hand is in the middle of it; she's here to claim Semi in person.

"Now, I might need to put the whammy on my aunt," David continues. "Walking in like this will cause way too many questions."

Semi can't speak, can barely even concentrate, but her fingers are moving. She digs her nails into David's chest to get his attention.

"OW!" he blurts out. "Semi, are you ..."

"We're not safe," she whispers in his ear, using all of her strength merely to get it out.

"What?" he asks, obviously startled.

"They're here. T ... They've found us," she mumbles, pushing herself beyond limits.

Semi's eyes are closed again; can't move. She hears the gang scrambling. They're under attack, and the guys are way out of their depth. Semi has heard so much about her, none of it good, but she's here, here for Semi. It's fight or flight. She's got to get up. S ... she's got to help ... before it's too late.

THE CHASE —EDIE

Frak, mega-frak, frak times a million.

This can't be happening again. Inside that pizza place, even though they talked about some of the crazy swirling around, it felt normal. It seemed like they were safe, and the worst was behind them. For a minute, Edie even considered swinging by her grandma's and sweet-talking her into making her famous empanadas. But Semi just destroyed all that with two simple words—they're here—and now they're back in the middle of it. Edie's beginning to believe that crazy is stalking them. She thinks of *The Godfather Part III*, and mumbles, "Every time we try to get out, it pulls us back in."

Surprisingly, right now, she's more frustrated than scared. Maybe she's in denial. She's sure scared is coming, but it just hasn't hit her yet.

"Edie, did Semi just say what I think she said?" asks B.J., obviously dreading the answer.

"Yeah."

"I don't know how they found us, but I can feel it now, too," states David. "Something dark is very close. Edie, B.J., do you guys see or hear anything?"

"Not yet," Edie answers, trembling. "But, to quote the great man, 'I've got a bad feeling about this.'"

"Yeah, you and me both," he replies.

"Hey, I love him as much as the next guy, but shouldn't we be running, instead of standing here in the middle of the sidewalk quoting Han Solo?" says B.J.

"Not yet," orders David. "We need to be ready. They could be coming from any direction or even multiple directions. Get your weapons out and be pr ..."

Frag, what's happening? Edie can't tell if she's moving faster or everything else is traveling slower. She sees the bullets first; sees them even before they hear a sound and watches as two pass right through her. How'd she do that? While other bullets wiz by, two strike B.J. in the chest before they see the gunmen appear out of the air, coming from the Gray Zone. David sends a bolt of blue force at the assailant, knocking the man off his feet.

"You OK, B.J.?" David asks.

"Yeah, I'm fine," he answers. "The bullets bounced off my armor. This velecor is legit. I bet it could stop just about anything."

Two more appear, near where the other one fell, both carrying flaming swords.

"I think this is a good time to run," says David. "Head for the park, and when you get there, cut across the fields and into the woods. If we have to make a stand, let's get away from bystanders."

Palms are sweating, lips trembling, muscles quivering, her heart doing double time. OK, yeah, there it is. Fear's back, better than ever. She's gone from zero to eleven in an instant. Hopefully, she can channel it into jet fuel for her legs.

And just like that, they've become a horrible horror movie cliché, teens running into the woods for safety. What's next? Is someone going to suggest that it's safer to split up? Edie and her friends are off to the races, and even in the middle of a life and death drama, she can't help but notice how quickly their dynamic changes when there's trouble. It's funny, but it's always been that way. Typically, she's the big sister of the group. But in tense situations, David has naturally taken charge, on the field or in life, and everyone's always followed, including them, no questions asked. It's like he was made for this. Funny, Edie's never once complained about David's firefighter eyes when she's been the one trapped in the fire, and this is a raging inferno.

This is frelling insane. They're moving fast, using all of their super-human speed. Despite carrying Semi, David is a little ahead of B.J., and initially, Edie's trailing both them, but suddenly she finds herself speeding ahead, kicking it into high gear. She's moving so fast she can't even feel her legs. in fact, she doesn't have any legs. She's become half mist and half woman, literally gliding on the air. Edie goes with it. She can't think too hard about any of this. Right now, she needs to focus on staying alive.

When they get to the woods, David stops. She's a little ahead, so Edie circles back to join him, and her body reforms to flesh and blood as she does.

"Edie, did you?" gasps B.J.

"Yeah, crazy, huh," she answers. "Why'd we stop here? Shouldn't we keep running?"

"We're not outrunning them," says David. "They're following along using the Gray Zone. Two goons are waiting for us just past the clearing, and the rest are just waiting."

"Waiting for what?" Edie asks.

"Their boss, I think," he responds. "We're going to need to fight our way out."

"No, no way. Edie can't you do that disappearing thing that you and Daniel did for us so we can hide?" asks B.J.

"I don't know how," she answers, "Not without him."

"It wouldn't help anyway," says David. "They're watching us. Get ready to fight."

"Let me try something," Edie replies. "I turned to air, touching air so ..."

She picks up a stone and focuses, feeling its energy merge with her own and experiences its strength radiating through her body. Edie looks down at her hands, and she literally is a woman of stone.

"G ... good job, Edie. Y ... you're like Daniel, like the qareen. If you focus, you can temporarily mimic almost anything," Semi mumbles. "Put me down, David. I ... I'm ready to fight."

Edie can tell that everything in him wants to say no, but against his better judgment, David places Semi down, and though she's wobbly, she manages to stand up and get into a defensive stance. There's a deadly silence, tense to the point that Edie not only feels her heart beating, she feels all of theirs as well. Suddenly, Semi starts softly singing *Hurricane* from *Hamilton*. Being *Hamilton* stans themselves, David and Edie grin and join in while B.J. stares on in disbelief. Hey, gallows humor, now that she's been in a few life-or-death situations, Edie's beginning to see the benefits. At least for her, singing *Hamilton* cuts the tension. She can actually breathe a little. Besides, if you're going to go, you might as well go doing what you love.

After a minute or so, David shushes them through mind-speak; it's about to begin. As they brace themselves, Edie can't help but notice that B.J. has his gun drawn, but he's pale as death, and his gun hand is shaking uncontrollably. Before she can give B.J. a pep talk, David breaks the silence, speaking to their invisible enemies by quoting a perfect line from Edie's favorite scene in *The Winter Soldier*.

"Before we get started," David says confidently, "Does anyone want to get out?"

Edie wishes she'd thought to say that. As last words go, they're not too shabby. But she still doesn't see any bad guys. Maybe, they lost them after all. Frak, just like that, there's a crimson, swirling energy signature above them. A redhead with short hair and a big, rough dude leap out of a hole in the air waving fire blades. And two guys, the ugly one who fired at them earlier, and a Zac Efron wannabe with electric hands, jump out of the woods behind them and lunge toward Semi.

David simply closes his eyes and lifts his right hand, and a protective sphere of swirling gold and blue energy appears around them. The two swordsmen are repelled by it, crashing to the ground after they face plant into it. The two charging from behind are forced back by the field as well; at least most of them. Edie gasps as she hears a thud and sees the gunman's right arm fall inches from her feet, and a few feet over, she sees both of two-dollar Efron's legs. Evidently, the sphere dissects anyone who partially falls within its boundaries.

She tastes bile in her mouth and barely stops herself from puking up all the pizza she just ate. This is too much, the danger, the horror of what just happened, the sounds of the screams and moans of the two injured men. Every part of her is shaking.

While the two men behind her writhe in pain, the red-haired lady and her partner get up and fire blasters repeatedly at the sphere, and though it frustrates them, Edie's grateful that their best efforts aren't making a dent. But what happens if they get through? They can't stay in here forever.

And as much as she wants to, Semi's not going to be able to help. She's valiantly fighting it, but she's perspiring profusely and she's out on her feet. Edie grabs her and Semi leans on Edie's shoulder, so she won't fall over. Eden Grace is just about to ask David what the plan is. but before she speaks, everything outside the sphere darkens, covered by a gloomy mist that would do Dagobah proud. Her stomach feels queasy, and her skin feels like a thousand spiders are crawling all over her.

"She's here," Semi whispers.

And before Edie can ask who, everything goes *Thor Ragnarok* and there are several strikes of red lightning outside the sphere, powerful enough that the ground shakes violently. And as much as Edie is propping up Semi, she's drawing strength from her as well. Weak as she is, the girl seems unflappable, and through their soul-link she's been pushing through her pain and giving Edie ongoing encouragement. It's helping. Edie holds on tight hoping that some of Amesemi's courage rubs off on her. After the fifth strike, the sky clears once more, the mist begins to fade, and the boss woman appears as a silhouette, standing in front of the red-haired woman and her companion. Those two have stopped firing and are waiting for instructions.

As the mist clears, Edie gets a good look at her, and she is both breathtaking and horrifying. Like Semi, this woman is supernaturally stunning, with an insane figure, dark bronze skin, long, dark hair, and cruel, piercing eyes that have turned from brown to hazel, to fiery red in the few seconds that she's been standing in front of them. Unlike their friend, their new problem takes great joy in flaunting it, with every calculated movement designed to both titillate and terrify. She's wearing the mess out of a black velecor catsuit and heels, filling it out in ways that should be illegal. Edie sneaks a peek over at B.J. to make sure that his eyes haven't popped out of his head from ogling. Yeah, death by ogling, with all the real danger surrounding them, that would be a strange and embarrassing way to go, but if anyone could pull it off, it would be B.J.

Ignoring her wounded men's cries, Madame Catsuit poses provocatively, slowly traces the symbol of a red rose that is on her chest, and then saunters closer to the sphere, moving her right index finger forward until she is skimming it across the barrier. And then closing her eyes, she smiles mischievously as if she just heard a funny joke.

"I like that movie," she says to no one in particular. "I think I saw it more than once. I have a fondness for the genre, despite its fatal flaw."

She pauses, licks her lips, and then turns to David.

"So, you like to quote movies, do you? I suppose you four young ones fancy yourselves, superheroes. Look at you. You are talented novices clothed in velecor and wearing psychic masks, but your masks can't hide your youth or your fear. So, young man, you made the protective shield, so I guess that makes you the captain. We'll call you, Captain Suburbia. And we have your teammates— Rock Girl, Shaky Hands Man, and the sickly and pitiful Princess Iset."

"It's Isis, my name is Isis, and I know who you are," says Semi defiantly. "You're Ishtar of the sila and Thoth's lap dog, a heartless murderer, an abomination, who has brought nothing but shame to our order. You're the one who killed my friends, Renenet and Adad, when I was a girl."

"Isis ... that's interesting. I see what you did there," she replies. "Yes, I killed them, little princess. In fact, I've killed more than my share, and I looked forward to killing you, killing you slowly, painfully. I thought that killing Iset's heir might be a small measure of revenge for the humbling encounters I had with your predecessor. She was formidable, a terror in her own right. Now that she's gone, I can admit that she is the only person that I have ever feared. But you...you are pathetic, hardly worth slaying. Besides, my paramour insists on bringing you back alive." Her voice is almost casual, as though she's reading from a list of wallpaper designs, none of which interest her. She yawns in mock boredom. "Gifting him your ashes and your talisman is not enough for him. He has special plans for you, little Isis, daughter of Amon Ra. As for me, seeing you suffer will have to suffice."

"It's not going to happen," Isis hisses, mustering what little strength she has. "I'm going to end you."

"Really?" Ishtar chuckles. "Oh, my poor, pitiful, perspiring princess, I think you're going to need to be able to stand before you can hand out threats. Why don't you rest up and let me talk to your friends? I have a proposition for them, but before I give it, allow me to introduce myself. See, you have to know me, really know me to understand the importance of what I am about to say."

Ishtar turns and motions to some unseen person.

"Serafina," she commands. "Bring our friend out."

Out of a circular portal of black fire steps the gothic, witch-woman from Stone Mountain Park, leading out a prisoner in high tech shackles and forcing him down to his knees beside Ishtar. *No, oh no, it's Danny.* He's been beaten badly, shoulders slumped, eyes swollen almost shut. Edie's senses are flooded by his physical and emotional pain. She can't breathe, and terror is rising from her gut. She wants to call out to him or beg Ishtar for his life, but Semi's in Edie's head, encouraging her to stay strong, strong for Danny. Them showing fear, falling apart is precisely what Ishtar wants. Edie knows what may be coming, and she can tell from Danny's expression that he has made his peace with it, but she hasn't. She can't. Tears stream down her cheeks, and every muscle is rigid as a silent scream rings throughout her body. There is so much courage in Danny's eyes. Edie is scared, more than she's ever been, but she needs to find a way to face whatever's coming with courage of her own.

"I ... I'm sorry," Danny stutters, barely able to speak.

His eyes make her heart break. She can't look at them, not anymore.

"It was a brilliant plan coming here, children," Ishtar states. "We never would have found you, not without some help from our mutual friend. Qareens, like Danny, cannot read minds, but they make a copy, a temporary map of memories. That is how they are able to use their devious talent to impersonate individuals." Now she's imitating Heath Ledger's version of the Joker, speaking in a sardonic, singsong manner, emphasizing every word. "He mapped your memories of this place, Captain Suburbia. My guess is that he did it as a backup, so he could reach you, you know, in case you needed his assistance. Unfortunately for him, my team found him first. Despite his training, the talented Serafina was able to read his map and bring us here."

"Will and training have their value, but the blood always wins," adds Serafina, grinning wickedly as she scratches Danny's face and licks his blood off her finger for emphasis.

"So, this is what you need to know about me, children," Ishtar proclaims. "I am fully and proudly the avatar of my paramour's will. He revels in collecting things that are useful to him and leaves it to me to dispose of things that are not, and I am very, very good at my job. Danny Vision was valuable, but his newly mapped memories were the easiest to access. Accessing his other secrets, claiming his talisman, breaking him, well, it is doable, and it could be useful, but it's hard work. And I think I've found a simpler, easier role for Mr. Vision."

"Do your worst," Danny grunts defiantly.

"I will, dear. I always do," Ishtar replies with a sinister smile.

Then, she places her hand on his forehead, and it bursts into incandescent flame. Danny screams as his life force is sucked out of his body. It is a sound like none that Edie has ever heard, every ounce of him crying out, from his core, from his heart, on and on until there's nothing left. Semi puts her hand over Edie's mouth to stop her from wailing or letting out the sobs that she can no longer control. She can barely see through her tears. This can't be happening; it can't, and there's nothing they can do. His body shrivels until he is simply a collection of bones, then Edie watches with both anguish and wonder as his soul moves on toward glory. His talisman hovers over his corpse for a moment, and Ishtar snatches it before it can move on, absorbing the talisman into her.

Her deed done, she turns to David and stares into his eyes menacingly.

"Do you know who I am, now, Captain?" She stresses the title.

"Yes," David answers, making no attempt to hide his disgust.

"Good, very good. This should make this next part easy. Serafina, be a dear and check with Mr. Copeland and the others and make sure our perimeter is secure while I finish my chat with these... 'heroes.'"

"As you wish," she answers as she disappears morphing into a sentient stygian mist that quickly snakes away from them.

As Serafina leaves, Ishtar continues. "As I said, I love the superhero genre, but the movies share a common flaw. In the end, the good guys always win. More than flying men and glowing hammers, that is the part I find improbable. As you can see, your journey certainly is not that kind of story. This is real life, children. You lost the minute I arrived. Your sphere is impressive, but there are levels to this, young Captain. I am Ishtar of the sila. This shield means nothing to me. I could have killed the three of you the moment I appeared and seized your precious friend. But you three are young, with unique, tantalizing powers, unspoiled by the Nistarim's stench. My lover, Thoth, would consider you a great additional prize if I could bring you to him healthy and whole, but I need your help. Lower the shield, Captain, and come with me freely, and the four of you will travel with me to meet Thoth. No harm will come to the three of you."

"And Isis?" asks David.

"Well, reconditioning will be a challenge, but after she submits, she will find great joy with us," she responds. Seeing the steely resolve in David's eyes, she adds. "If you resist, then you have no use, and, well, you know me, now. You know what that will mean."

She extends her right arm and makes a finger gun with her hand, pointing it at them.

"If you like, I can play the role of movie bad guy. What would one say? I've got it. If your shield is not lowered by the count of three," she says in her worst Hans Gruber from *Die Hard* accent. "I'll start picking you off one at a time until the shield is down or there's no one left but me and your wobbly princess."

She moves her hand back and forth, placing a different one of them in her sites as if she's having trouble making up her mind.

"Here we go," she says. "One ... Tw ... Oh, never mind."

A bolt of golden flame shoots from her finger, power like Edie's never felt. It easily punches a hole through David's sphere and strikes B.J. in the gut, disintegrating his armor and blasting a hole through him the size of a large fist. He falls immediately, eyes wide open—dead.

Edie screams hysterically, but her cry is drowned out by the sound of David's voice.

He roars B.J.'s name, and as he roars, he does something startling.

In a blur, he lowers the shield and unleashes a saffron fireball of amazing force. It burns away the red-haired woman's left side and strikes Ishtar, knocking her off her feet, throwing her at least fifty yards.

Edie can see by his face that David's as shocked by his incredible power surge as the rest of them, but he doesn't waste any time marveling at his handiwork or grieving for that matter.

He rips the air behind them and opens a golden portal, saying, "Edie, grab Semi and take her through. We've got to go."

"What about B.J.?" Edie replies, knowing the answer.

"We can't help him now. Go!" he commands. "I'm right behind you."

B.J.'s dead. He can't be, but he is; Edie saw it. She fights back her tears as she carries Semi and starts running through the Gray Zone. Edie can't process this now. None of them can, not if they're going to stay alive. She senses another flash of power from David before he leaps in and closes the opening behind him.

When he catches up to them, Edie pants, "No one's behind us. Do you think you were able to kill her?"

"Ishtar, no way, but I think I managed to tick her off. For some reason, her kind isn't fond of fighting in the Gray Zone. She's going to send someone else after us. We just have to get out of here before they find us."

After they run a little further, he makes a sign for them to halt. He stops and scans the surrounding area. Edie's not sure what he's looking for at first, but she quickly realizes that he's focused on the floating windows to the outside world that open and close at various places in the Gray Zone, trying to get his bearing.

"Run toward that window there," he says. "I think if we open a portal in that area, we'll end up in Pelham Park, on the other side of the Bronx. Maybe we can lose them there. Edie, are you OK carrying Semi?"

She's not OK. She's never going to be OK. Everything inside her is quivering with terror and heartbreak.

"I'm literally strong as a rock. We're fine," she answers as if saying it is suddenly going to make it true.

Edie's trying hard to imitate David's focus on the here and now. She knows if she thinks about B.J. or Danny she... Forget it. she just can't. She can't, for now. They have to keep moving.

"OK, you guys run ahead. I'll guard our rear," David says with increased urgency. "I'm right behind y ..."

He senses it before she does. An incredible power has arrived behind them, maybe more than one. Edie turns and looks, and it's that rough-looking, flaming sword thug who attacked them earlier, but he seems far more powerful now than he did then.

"Nice trick back there, kid. You've done quite a bit of damage to my team," he sneers, "But I'm Tobias Grimm." He cocks his head and smiles dangerously. "And I've got a couple of tricks of my own."

Before their eyes, he grows into a towering eight-foot humanoid, crackling with scarlet flame. He then spreads his hands about two feet apart and creates a giant qi energy ball, the kind you see in anime, and Edie can only assume it is meant for them. This can't be good. Somehow, she thinks that David's nifty force field isn't going to be of much use here.

As Grimm is about to unleash his qi sphere on them, David steps in front of them and does his best Goku impersonation, transforming into a seven-foot powerhouse covered in yellow and blue fire. How? What? As Grimm sends his power ball their way, David counters with one of his own. The two forces collide and compete for dominance until, after several long minutes, both orbs dissipate, leaving both combatants exhausted.

"This is impossible," grunts Grimm.

"As usual, you overestimate yourself, Tobias," says a well-dressed, flying man, who has just streaked into view.

As he lands next to Tobias, he continues, "You are little more than a novice yourself. Why should it surprise you that this child is your equal?"

Grimm eyes this new arrival with a combination of disdain and fear. Edie doesn't know if that means that the enemy of my enemy is my friend or merely a bigger, badder problem. This newcomer is a hand-some, dark-skinned man of average height, who looks like he just stepped off the cover of GQ, and Mr. GQ seems unimpressed with his giant, glowing companion. He eyes him the way an adult might eye an overconfident child. GQ Man's demeanor is relaxed and professional. It's clear that this is simply a business trip for him.

"I don't need your help, Gunab," grunts Tobias. "I've got this."

"Go home, Tobias," says Gunab dismissively, "or stay and learn. Either way, stand aside. You are a mere man. We elders are gods. It is time that you learned the difference."

With that said, Gunab transforms, creating an explosive wave of force as he does. The wave knocks Grimm down and nearly does the same to Edie and David though they are a considerable distance away. Now, two feet taller than Grimm, Gunab is a towering figure of golden fire. Wisely, David does not sit back and wait for Gunab to attack. He uses all of his newfound strength to unleash a qi attack toward him, one that feels considerably more powerful than what he used on Grimm.

As he attacks, he shouts to Edie. "Run, Edie! Don't look back, just run. Run to that window. Try to open a portal out. I'll follow when I can."

She hates leaving him, but she can't do anything for him right now, so she runs, runs as fast as she can. Edie even finds herself turning Semi and herself to mist form to speed them along. But the noise carries. She hears Gunab taunt David, totally unimpressed by his attack, and then every part of her starts to tingle, and she hears the sound of rushing wind. Edie knows she shouldn't, but she slows down and looks back and witnesses Gunab unleash a massive power burst at David. It consumes David's shields, lifts him off his feet, and sends him flying through the air. After traveling some distance, he hits the ground and rolls helplessly and painfully until he eventually stops, not far from Edie. Ishtar was right. This is not the kind of movie where the heroes win. They never stood a chance.

"David, are you OK?" Edie squeals.

"I'm s ... sorry guys," he mumbles. "I c ... can't. He's too strong."

It's over; Gunab is hovering, moving toward them. Edie's eyes tear up. She's fighting it, but she can't help it. She wants to be strong, but it's truly over. Her shoulders shake, her lips tremble, and she tastes salt from the river streaming down her cheeks as fear gives way to sorrow and dark acceptance. They're all going to die, right here, right now, just like B.J. and Danny. Edie, in human form, sits down on the ground and seats Semi beside her, letting her head rest on Edie's shoulder. David, a warrior to the end, is fighting to get up. But he's too weak to stand.

"It's going to be OK," Semi whispers, breathlessly.

"Surrender, children," Gunab calls out. "You are not going to be able to outrun me, not here, and obviously fighting me is not an option. Surrender, or I promise you that for my next attack, I will not be holding back."

"Oh, shut up already, Gu-nap," says a resplendent flying woman as she attacks Gunab with golden lighting. "If you fought as well as you talk, I wouldn't constantly be kicking your tail."

"They're here," mumbles Semi, right before she seems to completely pass out for the umpteenth time.

And just like that, several individuals pop up around them. Edie thinks this is the same group they saw fighting the bad guys in Stone Mountain. A stunning Asian woman helps David to his feet and gives out orders to her crew.

She turns to a massive blonde man, shouting, "More shadow dancers are popping in, reinforcing Gunab. Help Caprice. I need you two to hold them off until we get the kids out, and then I need you both to follow. Listen to me, Sigurd, no hero ball, follow right behind. They're coming in fast. The numbers aren't kind to us here."

While he turns into a golden fire giant and leaps into battle, the boss lady turns her attention to a striking redhead and a blonde, Ryan Gosling-looking soldier, carrying a massive gun, saying, "Cole, Tefnut, you take point. Get us a portal out of here and blow up anything that stands in the way. I've got the kids. We're not chasing bad guys today. The kids are our only priority. Let's move."

"What about me?" asks the bookish, young man flanking her.

"Same as usual, Tanen," she answers. "Stay close to me until we get out and then disappear, find a safe spot and work your mind magic." She turns to David, who has made it to his feet. "Can you walk?"

"I can. I can fight, too," David says, taking out his lorenth.

"I love your spirit, little lion," she says, smiling. "Stay close to Semi and watch her back."

She scoops up Semi with one arm as if she weighs five pounds and then cradles her in her arms, stroking her hair and whispering in her ear. "It's OK, Peaches, we're here. We're going to get you home."

"You're one of her sisters, aren't you?" Edie asks as she struggles to her feet.

Yes, I'm Bast," she answers with a playful grin, "the first and the best."

"I heard that," barks Tefnut.

"Stay focused, Red," Bast shoots back. "We can debate my obvious awesomeness later, assuming that we make it out of here in one piece." Turning to Edie, she says, "Bronx girl, I need you to turn back into stone and take care of my sister. Can you do that?"

"Yes, ma'am," she replies.

As she gently places Semi into Edie's arms, she whips out a golden lorenth and transforms into a human-leopard hybrid. At this point, Edie's far too emotionally exhausted to be surprised.

"Let's roll ladies," she growls. "It's time to make the doughnuts."

Cole opens a portal near the spot that David was aiming for, and it opens up into a park. Except that it's Central Park, not Pelham. Even with superpowers, David still has an awful sense of direction. At least some things are constant. Edie would tease him, but this really isn't a good time.

As they leap through, an army of enemy soldiers appears around them, some with guns, some with high tech plasma weapons, and a few with fire swords. The redhead, Tefnut, unleashes an earthquake attack, followed by a nasty, localized tornado and clears a path for them. And now they're off. Tefnut's elemental powers and Cole's big gun take out any and everything ahead of them. Caprice, Sigurd, and Bast mow down the rest. Whatever Edie and her friends were dealing with before, these three warriors' skills are on a different level. They whirl their blazing lorenth's as if they are an extension of their bodies, use telekinetic attacks to send bad guys flying, and strike opponents via elite meta-enhanced martial arts skills that break bones and crush wills. All three are exceptional, but Bast is clearly the best of the best. She's stronger, faster, and more fluid, anticipating each new threat before it appears.

But this is like the Wakanda battle in *Infinity War* because, for all the heroics, they're still screwed. They're winning, but they're not. It's like trying to squash roaches at Edie's cousin Benny's nasty apartment. For every one you kill, ten more appear. They're coming in waves, and as good as the heroes are, Edie doesn't know how much longer Bast and her crew can hold up. And that monster that killed B.J. is still out there somewhere. Edie may not know much, but she knows that Ishtar's a Thanos-level difference-maker. They positively need to get out of here before the Catsuit Queen shows up to rejoin the party.

The enemy is swarming. Cole has put away the big gun and is now using two plasma pistols and twin glowing blades that pop out of his gloves, showing his own impressive skills. Tefnut has switched to fire and ice, those seemingly being her close-quarters weapons of choice. Their five defenders have formed a circle around the three of them, with David hovering over Semi and Edie, taking out the few bad guys that limp through and deflecting any stray bullets or energy blasts that come their way.

"I think Thoth shops at Costco," Tefnut quips as she takes out two thugs. "He bought low rent mercs in bulk. I've never seen so many."

"Yeah, these are mainly scrubs, young ravagers, and asura novices, but he has some skilled shadow dancers mixed in," adds Caprice while she executes a killer spin move and takes out three bad guys. "He's hoping that they can catch us off guard while we're distracted by the fodder."

"That's his goal," adds Sigurd in mid-thrust. "And he might have heavy hitters waiting in the wings if we live through all of this."

"So, what's the plan, boss lady?" asks Cole. "Shouldn't our backup be here by now?"

"They should," Bast grunts as she disarms and dispatches a shadow dancer. "But you know what Iset always said about battle..."

"Yeah," Cole interjects. "These things never go the way you expect."

"So, to answer your question, Cole," says Bast. "The plan is to stay alive."

Cole ducks a swinging light blade, takes out the assailant, and grins. "Sounds like a plan."

Not to be negative Nancy but this is a bad plan, a real Kobayashi Maru of a plan! Where's Captain Kirk when you need him?

They need a cheat code because, short of that, she's not sure how they're going to make it out of here despite everyone's best efforts. And it's getting worse. It's like they're being sent through levels of a video game, and they've just made it to the next one, the tougher one, as more skilled, fire bladed warriors arrive.

At its worst, Semi taps Edie, motioning for Edie to set her down. David dispatches a straggler, but seeing Semi seated on the grass, he leans in to check on her.

"It's going to be OK, Semi," says David, taking her hand. "I'm not going to let anything happen to you."

Semi looks at him and smiles, eyes wide open, saying, "I told you, Charming, I'm not that kind of princess."

With that said, Sleeping Beauty takes off David's jacket and springs to her feet. She stands arms outstretched, eyes blazing like twin stars and her dress and hair blowing, like a Beyonce video, as celestial winds circle her. Semi then transforms into fire, like a golden phoenix, and there is a collective gasp as the throng of enemies senses her awakening, but they sense it too late.

Smurfing crazy as it is, Edie can swear she hears Semi beatbox for an instant, or was that mind-speak, just between those two? Either way, Semi cracks a smile at David and Edie and gives homage to Jay-Z as she raps, softly, "Allow me to re-introduce myself..."

And then there's an incandescent explosion as a tsunami of pure, living fire emanates from her and radiates in every direction, weaving around her allies and striking her enemies with unparalleled destructive force. Most of her attackers, even those with energy shields, are instantly incinerated, becoming golden embers. Their force fields save a few, but they limp away, badly injured. Within seconds, the heroes go from being overwhelmed by a horde to the eight of them being the only ones left standing. It turns out there really is a cheat code for the Kobayashi Maru. Her name is Isis.

She's stopped glowing, at least outwardly. While all of them are too stunned and relieved to say anything, Semi simply stands there like a Nubian goddess, surveying her land. After a few seconds, she picks up David's jacket and proudly puts it back on and is greeted by a big hug from her prince. Edie's still frozen, her mouth agape. What just happened? This is great, amazing, a wonder to behold, but it's a game-changer. She'll never see her friend, Semi, in the same way, but Edie gets it now. She understands why everyone wants a piece of Amesemi and why they fought so hard to get to her while she was down. She's a living, breathing weapon of mass destruction. No, she's more than that. Semi's Superman, the baddest person on the planet, and Edie is very, very glad that she's on their side. She just needs to remember to never tick Semi off. Yeah, if they play spades, the two of them will be partners, and if they play dominoes, Edie's definitely letting Semi win. To quote the great man, "It's not wise to upset a Wookie."

JACE RIDER —B.J

I'm dead.

That's the thought reverberating through B.J.'s mind.

This can't be right. I don't think you can feel pain if you're dead. Or even think for that matter. That means there's an afterlife. Wait, what? What am I saying? I know for a fact there's no such thing. And if I died before ever using this new, sexy body to get hotties, that would be one of the universe's great tragedies. There's no way I'm going to drift into the void as some nerd who only has Wanda Kravitz on his resume—no offense Wanda. Well, maybe a little offense.

He can still feel her braces pinching his lips. This has to be a dream, a horrible nightmare, or some kind of hallucination. This can't be his end, can it? But it is. He died. At least he did for a moment, but if the fire shooting through him is an indication, he didn't, not really. He literally had his guts blown out, had a hole made through him almost big enough to stick his arm through. Yet, somehow, he's still here, in excruciating pain, but he's still breathing. He's Brantley James Scott, The Human Cockroach, and he's hard to kill.

It happened so fast. When everything was going on, he stood there shaking, all the jabbering going on from that Ishtar lady was only white noise. All he could hear was his internal voice screaming, "I don't want to die." All these new powers and he was useless, terrified, just like he's always been. He hid behind David's shield just like he hid in the closet or under the bed from his old man when he was little, praying to a God who didn't exist. They say that what doesn't kill you makes you stronger. Well, he's living proof that those words are a lie. It didn't make him stronger. It didn't make him anything.

With each piercing stab of agony and every muscle convulsion, it's coming back to him. When B.J. was struck, he's pretty sure David saved his life. The instant B.J. was hit, David figured out that Brantley wasn't dead, and somehow David knew that B.J. would heal because of his vampire powers. David used his telepathy and stopped B.J. from screaming or moving. *He told me to play dead and said that was my only chance.* He did play dead initially, but a few seconds later, it didn't matter. His body went into some kind of healing sleep. He doesn't know for how long. A few minutes ago, he woke up lying on his back, on the grass, exactly where they'd left him, just lying there confused until the pain kicked back in—burning, searing, excruciating pain.

He's wiggled his fingers and toes, but he hasn't tried to get up. B.J.'s weak, and his midsection is on fire as his body works on knitting itself back together, Wolverine style. Nah, he's more of a *Deadpool* or *Deathstroke* guy. Anyway, everyone's gone. B.J. doesn't hear or smell his friends or the goons who were after them, other than that one guy, the guy they left behind. He's the one who lost his legs. Whatever his powers, he's not a healer. His life force has been bleeding out. At first, he was wailing. Now, he's just whimpering, waiting for the end, poor guy. Even if he did try to hurt them, B.J. wouldn't wish this kind of death on anyone.

B.J. can feel the man's pain, his hurt, and his fear; B.J. can even taste it. That's strange. And he can smell the man's blood, even from over here and taste it too, but somehow it doesn't seem like blood. It's sweet, like syrup or honey. Now, that's new–and weird and creepy—but that's not the creepiest part. Maybe B.J.'s losing it, but he feels a presence, cold and icy, a shadow in a woman's form, hovering over the injured guy. Death, something inside, maybe a residual memory from the boy band-looking vampire guy, tells B.J. that its Mistress Death come to claim her prize. That's crazy. He's probably imagining things, probably just hit his head on the way down, but it seems true, feels genuine, and if it is, B.J.'s just glad that she's hovering over the other guy and not him.

There's a part of B.J. telling him that he needs to get up and find and help his friends. He hopes they're OK. He has no idea what happened after he passed out. He should get up. With his hyper senses, he can probably track them, see if he can help. But that's the joke, isn't it? When has B.J. ever been a help? David's a hero and not because of his powers either. He's always been that dude. It's in his DNA. And Edie might be the most fearless person B.J.'s ever met. Semi, when she's not falling asleep, well, she's a freaking warrior princess, a freaking, crazy-sexy warrior princess. OK, that wasn't cool. She's David's girl, but still, truth is truth. At the end of the day, why wouldn't she want to be with David? Who wouldn't? Why would a girl like that take a look at B.J.? All three of them are amazing, natural heroes. Then there's him, a reject from the loser's table. What did that alien call him? The cowardly comic relief in his own pitiful story. Yes, that's him. Why should he rush to get up? Whatever is happening with them, they're probably better off without him.

"You can't honestly believe that, can you?" asks a voice, a ridiculously melodic, tenor voice.

B.J.'s eyes pop open. Startled, he looks up and sees a tall, impossibly handsome man standing over him, with awesome, perfectly coifed, blonde hair, sky blue eyes, and a magnetic smile. He is formally dressed, like wedding formal, in a suit and tie, wearing white from head to toe. From what B.J.'s seen, finding a stranger to smile at you in New York would be unusual enough, but to top it off, this man has wings, huge white wings, like an eagle or an ang...Nah, eagle-man makes more sense. He thinks he's probably seeing things. Death can do that to you, right? *Is this guy real? But I'm not dead!* His brain is screaming at him like he's watching a movie, everything in slow motion and hyper motion at the same time.

The winged man reaches out his hand to help B.J. sit up, but B.J, stares at him warily, hesitating. Assuming he's not a mirage, Bird Guy read his mind. How does B.J. know he can trust him? But there is something about his gaze that wins B.J. over. He grabs hold of Bird Guy's hand and slowly labors to move to a sitting position. Initially, the attempt is agonizing, but Bird Dude's touch is soothing, giving B.J. peace and works as an anesthetic for his pain.

"Who are you?" B.J. asks.

"My name is Mr. Morningstar, but that is not the question of the day, dear Brantley. The real questions are, who are you, and more importantly, who do you wish to be?"

"What do you mean?"

"You are both right and very wrong, young man. Brantley James Scott has been a loser, a waste of space, controlled by fear and constrained by rules and man-made morality that do not serve you or the greater good. You were made for more than that, far more, but fear has you and will not let you go, and that beast is a monster that cannot be overcome by will or happy thoughts, no matter what they say. And we both know that praying to a deaf and mute god will never quiet your fears. No, it must be devoured, and it can only be conquered by a bigger, stronger beast, one that you have in abundant supply."

He's selling something, but he has B.J. curious.

"What is that?" he asks.

"Anger, young man. Rage is the most potent power in the universe, and when it is justified, well, righteous indignation is the ultimate force for good. It can fuel transformation. It can fuel revolution. It can change the world. You have been hurt, abused, picked on, cast aside, and overlooked. You squander your days incessantly frustrated as you constantly attempt to make your astounding gifts visible to people who frankly are beneath you. All this hurt, all these insults, have built a fire inside you, but you have wrongly been taught to suppress those feelings and hide behind your southern-sweet, plastic smile and silly jokes. No, young man, if you want a new life, you need to fuel your fire. Let it burn, and when it is needed, let it out."

"I'm not that guy," B.J. stammers. "How could I possibly do that?"

Gone is Morningstar's toothy grin. He pierces into his eyes and utters the words, "You can't. You simply can't. You have to die, bury your old life, here and now, and someone new needs to be born. For Jace Rider to live, Brantley James Scott needs to die."

He pauses, letting his words rattle around in B.J.'s brain.

After a few beats, he continues. "There's a need for Jace Rider. Not only can Jace Rider do things that Brantley cannot, he can do things that none of your well-intentioned friends or all the shiny heroes in Avalon can accomplish. They are constrained by a code that simply does not consistently work in the modern world. Jace Rider will transcend their morality. Your only code will be achieving the greater good by any means necessary. What is that quote from that movie you love so much? Oh yes, 'Because he's the hero Gotham deserves, but not the one it needs right now. So, we'll hunt him. Because he can take it. Because he's not our hero. He's a silent guardian, a watchful protector, a dark knight.' The writer of that script did not know it, but he was not describing some fictional character. He was writing about you, about Jace Rider. Do you see it? Do you see?"

That quote is from the *Dark Knight*, B.J.'s favorite movie. B.J. followed along with Morningstar, mouthing that quote as he said it. B.J. can probably recite virtually every line from that movie, but that line in particular he can recite in his sleep while in the middle of a nightmare. He knows it that well. He just never imagined that it could be about him, though he often fantasized about being the Dark Knight. But it does feel right. It feels like his destiny.

"I do," B.J. answers as he feels the passion, the fire build in his heart.

"Listen well then, and you will be reborn. There are three keys. Number one: The antiquated code of shiny 'heroes' teaches the lie of self-restraint. That is not for you. Feed your hunger, indulge in your passions, and unapologetically enjoy the spoils of your new status. If your passions cross the line, move the line. As long as no one of value is harmed, why should you deny yourself any pleasure? Denying makes you weak. Be strong. Number two: Understand that right and wrong are defined by the end result, not by the process. If doing the 'right thing' will result in failure, how can it be the right thing? Always do what is necessary. Number three: Remember, to fight the darkness, you must have a little darkness in you. Pure do-gooders will never get the gritty jobs, the dirty jobs done, and they must be done. At times, your allies may condemn your actions. Just ignore those people. Whether they desire to admit it or not, they need Jace Rider. They need him desperately. Ultimately, you will be the greatest of them all. Always feed your fury, wear kindness and humor as a mask and a gift to your friends and loved ones. Unleash the full measure of your inner demons on your enemies, and no one will be able to stand against you. Do you understand?"

"Yes, yes, sir."

"Are you ready to let go of who you've been and become the hero that this world needs?"

"I am."

"Good," Morningstar replies. "So, Jace Rider, what is your next move?"

"Well, I'm going to get up and find my friends. They need me. I'm still so weak, though. I need to find a way to strengthen myself and speed up my healing process."

"Of course, you do. But you know the solution to that dilemma, don't you, Jace?"

His heart skips a beat as he embraces the unfathomable. B.J. does know. Truthfully, he's known since he first woke up. His fear and his sense of morality wouldn't allow him to consider the option before, but now he sees clearly. What was it the witch said? She said, "The blood always wins." B.J.'s like her; he didn't just steal that vampire guy's powers and face, he inherited his thirst as well. He's not only hurting from the injury, he's hungry, and now that he's finally able to see beyond the box of traditional morality, the solution is obvious. That guy over there with no legs is dying anyway. B.J.'s not killing him. For all intents and purposes, David already did that. The man's death might as well serve the greater good.

"Mr. Morningstar," B.J. says as he slowly labors to get to his feet. "I know what I need to do."

"Good, then my work here is done," he says as he flaps his wings and is suddenly hovering over B.J.'s head before B.J. can shake his hand, say thanks, or anything.

Morningstar—there's something familiar about that name.

"Mr. Morningstar, before you leave, tell me, are you related to Tricia Morningstar, that woman from the camp?"

He hoovers and gives a wry smile as he replies, "In a manner of speaking. We certainly have a connection."

"Thank you for everything. How do I get in touch with you?"

"I'm always close by. I'll be in touch. You and I are going to do great things together."

And just like that, he disappears in a flash, streaking across the sky. Cool, B.J. has a personal alien mentor, his version of a force ghost from *Star Wars*. And Morningstar chose him. He believes in him. Maybe it's time, way past time, that he believed in himself.

So now is the hard part, but B.J. knows what he needs to do. He sees death clearly now, hovering over the injured man as he fights to cling to life. B.J. has enough sense not to make eye contact with her as he approaches them, but he can feel her smiling at him, pleased with his intentions. Being in her presence makes him cold all over, frigid to his very bones. *Block her out. Keep moving forward. How do I go about doing this?*

And then B.J. feels them. Fangs pop out; claws do as well. The blood smells so good; being near it is like being near brownies cooking in the oven. B.J. falls on his knees near the man's throat, making sure to avoid his eyes, but Brantley can't help but notice that the guy's not a whole lot older than B.J. is. He whispers something. Someone normal wouldn't be able to make it out, but B.J., with his ears... he knows exactly what the man's saying. He's begging for his life. *Shut it out, Brantley, just shut it out. He's a dead man, anyway. Focus on the task at hand; it has to be done.*

I can't do it...I can't.

But Jace can. And just like that, B.J. grabs him by his hair, and his teeth sink into his neck. The blood is so good, so sweet, and there's a high, a rush that is so much better. And there's a barrage of memories, the dying man's memories coming in like a tsunami. He's an asura, and they call him Luis Shocker, but he was born Luis Rinaldi twenty-five years ago and was taken to be trained in the use of his powers at the age of one. He has, or rather, had the ability to generate and manipulate electricity, and he could send high voltage bolts, up to twenty-five feet during battle. Shocker had a pregnant girlfriend and a two-year-old daughter named Roxanne, and he became a mercenary to support them. And ... he's gone. Thankfully, no more memories are coming B.J.'s way.

B.J. stays there on his knees for a while. He can't believe that he did this, that he took a man's life for blood. How can this be right? How could he do this? What is he becoming? Ignore it. Shut it out. That's just weak Brantley talking. It had to be done. Shocker was going to die anyway, right? B.J. did what he had to do.

He remembers Morningstar's words: Always do what is necessary... to fight the darkness, you must have a little darkness in you...

There's no time for doubts, not now. His friends need him. B.J. focuses on his pain, the abuse, every slight, every hurt, and lets it fuel his rage, feeling the power surge within him as his fury and Shocker's blood work their way through his system. All healed up, he effortlessly springs to his feet and can't help but notice that he's so much stronger and so much more in control of his gifts than before.

Cavanaugh, that's the name of the ravager whose face and abilities B.J. stole. Genetic memory from him seems to have been activated by the blood. B.J. knows things now, like how to use his powers. In an instant, he's just become a very capable, very dangerous man, and it feels good. Bad guys beware.

B.J. reaches down and picks up a blaster from the ground, giving him two, and he finds an extra holster as well. He checks, and despite the giant hole in his armor, it's still able to generate illusions. So, he goes back to black, this time a long, black, leather trench and shades, with a monochromatic shirt, tie, and pants underneath, very cool. To paraphrase the great Deion Sanders, "You look good; you feel good. You feel good; you fight good." Sounds like a plan.

B.J. takes a deep breath, twirls his guns with startling speed and expertise, and cracks a mischievous smile as he slides them into their holsters. He has no more doubts, no room for regrets, and, most exhilarating of all, no fear. He's going to find his friends and mow down anyone who tries to stop him. Everything changed here today. For better or worse, he left a lot in that field. Brantley James Scott is dead. Long live Jace Rider.

Wait till they get a load of me.

FAMILY REUNION —
DAVID

G olden ashes fall on them like rain, shimmering in the sunlight. They fill the air, falling slowly, floating on the gentle breeze in the afternoon air. It would be a beautiful sight if one could forget what the ashes truly are, a testament to the fearsome battle they just survived and the danger that awaits them. And that danger should be his focus. But of course, it's not.

This feels good.

This is all he's thinking as he hugs his uber-super-powered girl-friend, cheek to cheek. If he closes his eyes, it feels like they're the only two people in the world. David and Semi, in their personal paradise. This is the perfect time for their first kiss. David leans back and gazes into her eyes, and then he edges forward and ...

"Enough of that, Romeo," says the mammoth, muscle-bound warrior, Sigurd, as he grabs David's shoulder and effortlessly pulls him aside. "Today's the birthday for Princess Isis. You can't hog the birthday girl for yourself."

Sigurd has a warm smile and has the military-style haircut, square jaw, leathered, wrinkled face, dye enhanced blonde hair, and the impossibly, He Man-ish physique of an HGH, steroid consuming, aging, action star.

"Welcome back, girlie," he says, giving Semi a bear hug that picks her up off her feet. "You've been dearly missed."

David gets pushed away, and her family and friends swarm her. Semi gives him a look signifying that she wants to talk, and David initiates a mind-link between the two of them.

"*Sorry, Charming,*" she says. "*It looks like I'm going to have to take another rain check on that kiss.*"

"*Hey, well, you're worth the wait.*"

Suddenly, David hears Edie's voice in his head, saying, "*You two still haven't kissed? What are you waiting for?*"

"*Edie, is that you?*" David asks. "*What are you doing in my head?*"

"*That's my fault,*" says Semi. "*I forgot that Edie and I are still linked through mind-speak from earlier.*"

"*Isn't that great, 'lil Bro?*" says Edie, knowing that, for him, this is beyond embarrassing. "*Now, we get to do a three-way call.*"

"*That's great,*" he answers, with mock enthusiasm.

One of the side effects of this is that they get to eavesdrop on Semi's interaction with her loved ones, and Semi gives them a running commentary, filling in details about everyone.

"Oh, Peaches," says Bast, the team leader, after she hugs Semi tightly and gives her a thousand kisses. "It's so good to see you alive and healthy. Girl, we were so worried about you."

"*Peaches? They call you Peaches?*" needles Edie.

"*Shut up.*" Semi laughs. "*I'm sure that your family has a few embarrassing nicknames for you.*"

"*Boy, do we,*" David cuts in. "*And I'm more than willing to share each and every one.*"

"*Shut up, David,*" Edie snaps back. "*Nobody asked you.*"

Their squabbling is interrupted by the redhead, who gives Semi a big wet kiss and hug and then stares at Semi's ... uh ... anatomy.

"What are those?" She pauses and adds, "By those, I was wittily referring to your twin girls, who have suddenly maximized their potential, and I was doing so by giving homage to a funny scene in yet another incredible movie that you have not seen."

"*Guys, what movie is she referencing?*" Semi asks.

"*The Black Panther,*" Edie and David answer in unison.

"I know the movie," Semi fibs. "It's the *Black Panther*."

"Oh, you saw *The Black Panther*?" the redhead asks, skeptically.

"Of course," answers Semi, less than convincingly.

"New body, new powers, but you are still such a bad liar," she laughs. "OK, what's it about?"

"Uh, uh," Semi stammers, "it's about a militant black power group in the sixties ..."

"Nice try, 'Lil Bit," she giggles as she waves at Edie and David. "If you're going to cheat on the test, you should have asked your friends for more info. It's good to have you back baby, low pop culture IQ and all," she says as she gives Semi another hug and kiss.

"*OK, that beautiful, Irish, redheaded goofball is the second youngest of my sisters, Tefnet,*" Semi shares, "*although we normally call her Tef or Red. She's a marid, a type of Earthbound, also known as an elemental. As you saw, like all her kind, she can control the elements, and she's a high-level fighter. At two hundred twenty years, she's relatively young for a marid, not even middle aged, so she's only going to get better.*

"*The Chinese bombshell, who tried to kiss me to death, that's my oldest sister, Bast. She's a powerful type of fae, called a nasnas, and is even more powerful and ridiculously tough in her leopard-woman form. She's the elite of the elite, on a shortlist of the very finest warriors in the nine worlds and might be the very best at hand-to-hand combat. I'd give you her age, but after six thousand years, everyone stops counting. I've got four other sisters who aren't here, Nephthys, Maat, Athena, and Bia. Hopefully, you guys will meet them soon.*"

"*Must have been fun fighting to use the bathroom in the mornings,*" quips Edie.

"*Oh, there's plenty of space in Avalon,*" answers Semi, "*but we definitely had our share of other issues.*"

Getting a rather strong hug from a team member, Semi flinches, and when she catches her breath, she continues her commentary.

"*OK, this petite South Indian cutie, who is trying to hug me to death, is called Caprice,*" says Semi. "*She's an asura. In fact, she is the youngest asura ever to become a shadow dancer, and some think that she's the most skilled asura ever. That big guy, the one who pushed David out of the way earlier, is Sigurd. He remains a great fighter, but he's one of the oldest asura still active in the field."*

The cool-looking guy with the guns and wrist blades goes up to Semi and shares a tender moment. He's blonde, with a fashionable haircut, perfect stubble, and a cool jacket, pants, and boots, which give him the look of a space cowboy. And like Bast, David recognizes him from his time walking through Ra's Avalon memories.

"This guy's name is Cole, technically Thomas Jefferson Cole, but everyone calls him Cole," shares Semi. *"He was a New York police detective, but he became a ravager five years ago. With help from my dad, he never completed the curse by taking a life for food, so he became a danag, basically a vampire with a soul. Cole, his wife Sarah, and their two kids are like a second family to me. I spend a lot of time at their place, either babysitting or tutoring his kids in school."*

After spending a few moments talking to Semi, Bast and Cole step to the side a little to have a private conversation. David's tempted to listen in, but he can't figure out how to do it.

"This is incredible, Semi," says Edie, through their link, with more than a hint of sadness. *"I just wish that B.J. was around to see it, to meet all these brave, wonderful people."*

"Yeah, well, he'll be here soon enough," answers Semi.

"Huh, what?" gasps Edie.

"B.J.'s not dead, Edie," Semi answers. *"Didn't David tell you?"*

"Tell me what?" Edie asks, not able to contain her outrage. *"What didn't you tell me, David?"*

"It's not like that, Edie," David responds. *"I knew that B.J. had some level of ravager healing ability, so I knew there was a good chance that he'd heal from his wound, but I didn't want to say anything until I was 100% sure. He got in touch with me while Semi was unleashing her power, and he should be here any second. Everything's happened so fast since. I let Bast know, so they'd be expecting B.J., and they wouldn't see him as a threat when he popped up, but ..."*

Edie steps toward David, blurting out, "David, I can't believe you ..."

"Don't be mad," says B.J. as he steps through a six-foot portal comprised of smoky mist, popping in between Edie and David right in the nick of time. "I asked him not to tell. I wanted it to be a surprise."

Edie leaps and gives B.J. a big hug, weeping tears of joy, and to the surprise of everyone, including her, plants a kiss on his lips.

They both step back, more than a little embarrassed, but B.J., as is his way, defuses the situation with a joke, saying, "If I knew all I had to do for that kind of reception was to die, I'd have done it more often."

David gives his guy a big bro hug, and Semi comes over and hugs him as well. The four of them catch up for a few seconds, and then Edie shares the idea for Semi to take B.J. around and have him meet the team that saved them, but before they can start, B.J. looks around quizzically and raises an eyebrow.

"So, why are you guys still here?" he asks. "Isn't the battle over? I smelled the ashes on the way here."

"Yeah, I was wondering the same thing," says Edie. "Shouldn't we be headed to Avalon?"

"It's not over," David answers reluctantly. "We're surrounded by a significant group of heavy hitters. We can't go anywhere yet."

"Are you sure?" B.J. asks. "I don't smell or hear anything."

"Yeah, I'm sure."

"What?" Edie asks. "How long have you known that? Is there a plan? We're just standing around chit-chatting like we don't have a care in the world. What's going on?"

"Look, we're in good hands," he replies. "I wasn't trying to keep any secrets. I just figured that it wasn't my place. The heroes are here. This is their show now. You know they have a plan. Bast will fill us in soon and let us know."

"Bast is the best," Semi agrees. "If she's not worried, we shouldn't be. Besides, I'm at full strength now, and I'm not going to let anything happen to you guys. My guess is that the bad guys probably haven't attacked because of what they saw me do. Trust me. They don't want these kinds of problems."

"You got that right," B.J. adds, twirling his guns impressively. "If they get past you, then they have to deal with me, and trust me, the new, improved, un-killable Jace Rider is their worst nightmare."

"So, you're still gonna go with the Jace Rider handle?" Edie quips.

"Oh, yeah," says B.J, flipping his weapons around like the Mandalorian.

They continue to chat among themselves, and David nods his head like he's listening, but his mind is elsewhere. Their situation is very serious, more dangerous than he let on, and he knows more than what he's shared, but he honestly doesn't feel like it's his place to say.

David reaches out psychically and knocks on the door to Bast's mental defenses, not knowing if she'll talk to him or not. Initially, there's no response, then to David's surprise, Cole connects the three of them to a mind-link.

"*So, the skin-walker, that's your friend B.J.?*" asks Cole.

"*Yeah, he's a cool guy,*" David answers, surprised that the subject of their talk is B.J. "*You should meet him.*"

"*I don't need to meet him,*" answers Cole, ominously. "*I can smell him from here. You'd be amazed at the story that a scent can tell.* Your friend's been busy."

Thankfully, Bast interrupts him, saying, "*C'mon, Cole, we can discuss his friend after this is over. There are bigger issues looming at the moment. David, you told your friends about the enemy surrounding us, didn't you?*"

"*Yes, ma'am,*" he answers. "*Did I do something wrong?*"

"*No, not at all,*" she chuckles, "*and don't call me ma'am. I'm old, but I'm not that kind of old. I look much too young to be a ma'am. Anyway, how long have you known about them?*"

"*I started sensing them from the time we portalled into Central Park. It took me until mid-battle to know exactly what I was sensing, but I felt them right away.*"

"*Impressive, very impressive,*" she responds. "*Those are high-level soldiers hiding, using advanced cloaking techniques. Not even Tefnet and the others sensed them until Cole and I alerted them.*"

"*You've got some skills, kid,*" Cole agrees, "*Crazy skills.*"

"*So, have you sensed the other thing as well?*" asks Bast.

"*Yes,*" David answers. "*That was the first vibe I got before I felt anything else. The moment we started leaving the Gray Zone, I felt a connection.*"

"*Have you been in contact?*" she asks.

"A little, not much."

"This is truly amazing, David," she answers. *"You have no idea how amazing this is."*

"Did you tell anyone, even Semi?" Cole asks.

"No," David answers. *"Something told me that I shouldn't, that it wasn't my secret to tell."*

"Good," he responds, *"You did good, kid."*

"Just sit on it for a little while longer," says Bast. *"Everything will come to light in a few minutes."*

"Yes, m...Yes, I'll do that." David replies.

"And one more thing, David. This is very important. Everyone who needs to know who you are already does. Tell no one your name, and do not take off your mask in front of anyone who does not already know your identity. I don't care if it's an ally or an enemy. This goes for your friends as well, but especially for you."

"OK," he answers. *"Will do."*

"David, did you hear that?" Edie says as she shakes his shoulder, jolting him out of his psychic conversation. "Can you believe B.J. said that to me?"

"Kid, you took it too far this time," David replies, totally clueless about what B.J. said.

Semi chimes in and Edie, hands on her hips, playfully tells B.J. off. Of course, he tries to defend himself, with some offbeat argument, like he always does, but somehow, he's different. David can't put his finger on it. Everything he's doing is exactly the same, just a little off, not the kind of thing that anyone would notice—no one but his best friend. It's probably nothing. Simply David's imagination. But even if it's not, who can blame him for being a little different. He just had a pretty insane near-death experience, and they're not exactly at a pizza place or in David's den talking nonsense. They're in the middle of a battlefield waiting for the fight of their lives—superhero style. Who's to say that normal would even be a good thing under these circumstances? If they were normal, they'd all be screaming and running for their lives. After what they've all been through, they're all different. There is no going back to old times. They just have to keep pressing forward and try to build something new, assuming that they survive today, that is. Surviving today, that would be a good place to start.

While his friends are still going back and forth, David feels it. He feels the darkness descending upon them. It's like a change in temperature, but it has nothing to do with weather or atmosphere; it's spiritual or metaphysical, depending on how you see the universe. People debate religion every day, and they debate good and evil, but if they're honest with themselves, what can't be debated is that darkness is real. Watch the news, stand in the playground of the local school, dig up the lies crumbling the perfect families in their nice suburban neighborhoods, and it's clear that this truth is irrefutable. Evil isn't a matter of perspective or a collection of ever-changing cultural norms. Evil is a living, breathing organism, ancient and ravenous. It is both predator and parasite, living off those who feed it and hunting those who are unprepared, stalking, always stalking, waiting for a moment when vigilance is lacking. Darkness calls to wounded souls and damaged hearts, giving comfort and solace, even as it consumes all hope. When it manifests in a concentrated way, its presence is undeniable. Skin crawls; stomachs get tight; bad stuff happens. Darkness is a real thing, and at this place, at this time, it is palpable. They are among us.

"OK, ladies and gentlemen," says Bast. "Recess is over. We've got visitors."

The enemy lifts the veil concealing their powers first, allowing the heroes to experience their might as it energizes the air around them. It is awe-inspiring, terror-inducing, cry for your momma level stuff. The group assembled against them could level this city if they saw fit. There's little doubt that despite the skill of their protectors and Semi's remarkable abilities, their opponents can make short work of them. It's hard to know, but it's easily more than fifty villains, all around them, coming from everywhere. Elementals, winged speedsters, wielders of dark light, you name it, they've got it, a gift waiting for them, all wrapped up with a bow.

The dark warriors remain unseen, letting the awesome level of their combined force radiate and marinate in the heroes' hearts. After a while, a thick fog rolls in, encircling them. It's impossible to see anything through it, but occasionally, they see flashes of glowing red or yellow eyes, and they hear a wicked cackle that seems to come from every direction.

Bast and her team step in front of the teens and brace for battle, and they show no signs of fear, not even a little nervousness. They look like this is Monday morning, and they're simply walking up the driveway to check the mail. David grabs Semi's hand and she grabs Edie's as they try to draw strength from each other. B.J. just stands near them, twirling his guns and whistling. OK, that's different.

"I think I want what he's having," mumbles David. "Maybe."

David wants to tell his friends what he knows, but he knows he shouldn't, and with so many powerful telepaths around, there's no way of knowing if he could tell them in a secure way, without being mind-hacked.

The shadows are here, pouring in, blackening out the sky, laughing, rejoicing at the good guys' imminent demise. They're hard to ignore as they call out to the heroes to join them, speak to their fears, and reach into their hearts siphoning off hope and replacing it with dread. They serve as a reminder of the true nature of this battle, of every battle. This is not a confrontation among powerful humanoids. He sees that now. This is a battle between light and darkness, and though the sky grows dim and the darkness seems insurmountable, David will still fight, against all odds, and cling to the hope that the light will find a way.

The shadows giggle in anticipation as the big event draws near, and their enemy finally shows his face. The first to step out of the fog is an angular, pale, goateed, hipster wizard, dressed in black. His physical stature is not intimidating, but the eldritch energy crackling from his fingertips radiates an energy signature revealing him to be a dark wizard of incredible power. But his eyes are what grab David's attention. They emote a regal arrogance, cunning, menace, and ruthless, coldhearted ambition devoid of morality. David locks eyes with him and sees the wizard's history flash before him. His name is Thoth. He's their leader. He is evil personified... and he doesn't even know it. Thoth's convinced that he is the hero of his own twisted story. As David witnesses the horrors that Thoth has inflicted on this world, it deepens David's conviction. Darkness is real, and it has found a willing avatar in Thoth. He knows this creature must be stopped no matter what it takes.

The supernatural Wiki in David's head is on overdrive as more figures emerge. Two appear, one on each side of Thoth. One is a big, hooded Nephilim, wearing shades, whose identity is impossible to determine. The other is Ishtar, the ridiculously powerful sila who cornered them earlier, brandishing a flaming red lorenth and emoting her signature sociopathic bloodlust. She's not the only sila in the group. A six feet four-inch, shirtless, dark-haired Adonis steps out and poses in tight, shiny, black, leather pants, looking like a very ripped hybrid of a male model, a bodybuilder, and the lead singer of a 1980's punk rock band. His name is Marduk, and, like all sila, he is one of the thirteen most powerful humanoids in the nine worlds.

Many others are coming out. Notable among them are three additional Earthbound heavy hitters—the deadly Ajuran sila, Serket, the petulant Sioux marid, Haokah, and the flashy, lightning-fast, winged, Icelandic arwaah, Remo Blaze. Aside from the Earthbound, there are older ravagers present as well, skilled in wielding dark-light blades called navatts, the eldritch equivalent of lorenths. Notorious dark-light wielders are everywhere, and names and resumes flitter through his mind, like random images from a bad dream.

Along with the ravagers, the skin-walker, Serafina, is present as are the two asura from earlier, Tobias Grimm and Gunab, joined by a mammoth, nine-foot, fire-breathing alitha. More and more are stepping forward. Most are either Nephilim or asura mercenaries whom David doesn't really care to know more about. At this point, what does it matter? No matter their background or physical stature, they are all giants compared to him, and he might as well be a gnat flying around trying to annoy them.

Focus, don't let fear out of the cellar—deep breaths, deep breaths. Keep your hands steady and your heart strong. Remember dad's words; stay calm and work the problem. Cool. So, how am I supposed to do that here?

His head hurts. He doesn't want to know any more names or backstories. The important thing is that there are a whole lot more of bad guys than good guys, and they are relishing the opportunity to slice up David and his friends and watch them die. That's a pretty serious problem to try and solve, way above his pay grade. Fortunately, he's not the only one working on it.

The air feels thicker, making it hard to breathe. It's the shadows. They swarm around them, weighing heavily on their hearts. Whatever they're doing, they're doing it well, and if his churning stomach and tight chest are any indication, it's affecting him, and he's probably not the only one.

In the middle of their onslaught, Edie, one of the bravest people David knows, whispers, "Be honest, guys. We can't beat them, can we? There are so many, so powerful."

Then something pops into David's head, a speech he heard Amon Ra give during David's time in Ra's memories. He spoke it to his weary, outnumbered soldiers before the legendary Battle of Uruk. For some reason, David feels compelled to recite it as a reply.

"They say their army is unbeatable, that we are few, and they are giants, that this is where our dream dies and our cause ends. Understand this. Giants fall. Everything that lives breathes, everything that breathes bleeds, and everything that bleeds will know defeat. Invulnerability is a myth. Unbeatable, unbreakable, too many, too strong... these are mere labels that can be stripped away. Battle is life, and life is a test. Your job is to find a way. Every warrior, every army, both great and small, has a weakness, so in the end, victory in battle is more about weakness than strength. You must exploit your opponent's weakness before he can exploit yours. These are the truths of war.

"Yet, there is a greater truth always at work, one that sways outcomes, abolishes strongholds, and defies all odds. Faith is that truth. Faith is one of the three supreme weapons granted by the universe, greater than all the powers of any adversary. In the end, on this day, only two things have meaning. What you believe, and how deeply you believe it. Let me tell you what I believe ..."

Recognizing the speech, midway through, Semi, with tears in her eyes, joins in. Now, Bast and the others, who have been listening, add their voices, finishing the quote along with them. Proudly, they speak the words together.

"I believe that this is not a contest between flesh and blood, but between darkness and light, and there is no night so dark that the light cannot prevail. The darkness never tires; it never wavers; it never sleeps, but hope is a shield that will not fail."

It is a powerful moment, each of them glowing as they join hands, and though faded and somewhat hard to see, an army of messengers encircle them as they speak. Even B.J., who is standing off to the side during it all, looks on in wonder. With each word, more shadows shriek and fall back from them. As they finish the last line, they lift their lorenths high and let them blaze in the sky, piercing the fog. Realizing what the heroes are doing, Thoth and his forces laugh scornfully at them. But in the middle of their laughter, they begin to gasp, and Thoth, whose face was full of arrogant confidence, now has a look of a vampire who has caught a whiff of garlic. David thinks Thoth just realized what David's known for some time.

There is a flash of golden light in front of them, and when it passes, there stands a figure dressed in black from head to toe, his long coat blowing as if by some supernatural wind. He steps forward clothed in unshakable resolve, brandishing a resplendent, aureate lorenth. There are seven other flashes, accompanied by seven more new arrivals, but all eyes are on the man in black. Amon Ra has revealed himself.

"What's going on?" asks Edie.

"Hope, Edie," David answers. "The light has just sent in the marines and turned hope up to eleven."

The shadows shriek in fear, engaging in full retreat as the army of messengers glisten and begin to sing loudly, voices filling the air until all other voices are quieted. They sing of bravery, hope, and glory, their song piercing his heart, and with each note, David's heart is filled with courage. And somehow, the giants don't seem so big anymore, not so big at all.

Invincible —Amesemi

This is amazing. Semi's dad's here, and what's crazy is that he's been hiding here the whole time. Wow, he's actually here, and he brought help. Semi guesses most daughters would be happy to see their dad arrive in the middle of a stressful situation, whether he could actually be of help or not. Well, Amesemi's stressful situation is a life and death battle, and she's fortunate that her dad isn't just offering help. He just happens to be the greatest warrior that has ever lived. As options go, he's not a bad person to come to the rescue at a time like this.

"My dad's here!" Semi shouts to David, Edie, and B.J. through mind-speak.

"That's great, Semi," answers Edie, a little confused about everything going on. *"Which one is he?"*

David chuckles, answering, *"He's the guy in black that has all the bad guys losing bladder control."*

Semi would yell at the top of her lungs and run around giving out hugs, but that's probably not proper etiquette on the battlefront, not that she's been on any battlefronts before this one. She's been in a few scraps before today, even before Penfield, but nothing like this. She's smack in the middle of the type of story that her sisters are always telling her. This is the kind of thing her family was always trying to keep Semi safe from—all-out war. So, she's going to keep her hugging to herself and pretend that she's done this before.

"*Wow, my dad brought some heavy hitters with him,*" Semi gushes. "*OK, that brown-haired Latina, to the left is my amazing sister Maat. She's a great warrior and our premier mind-witch. The glowing-haired, duo lorenth wielding beauty to my dad's right, wearing the mess out of her signature white catsuit, is my sister Athena, regarded as the most dangerous 'young' soldier in the Nistarim, but they haven't met me yet... so.*"

"*Who's the tall hottie in the white dress? If we survive, can you get me her phone number?*" jokes B.J. "*Seriously though, you two do favor each other. Semi is she your...*"

"*The woman in that tacky, way too tight, way too short dress is my sister Bia, but you can't call her that. These days she goes by the name Glamazon or Glam to her friends. Please, don't ask me why. We're sisters. I love her. She's great in a fight and as tough as they come, but believe me, we are nothing alike. She's a heartbreaker, B.J. Trust me. She's not your type.*"

"*Oh, I don't know about that,*" he replies. "*Jace Rider likes to live on the ...*"

"*That's enough out of you.*" interrupts Edie. "*We don't have time for your foolishness right now. Semi, who's the Joe Manganiello looking dude next to your sister, Maat, and also, who's that big, bronze guy with the perfect hair next to Glamazon?*"

"*I have no idea who Joe Magawhatever is,*" Semi answers. "*But I think you're talking about Mihos. He's a watcher, a heroic swashbuckler, and a playboy. Don't look him in his eyes, Edie. That's how he gets you. Anyway, he's good in battle, really good, and everyone else dad brought is equally impressive. We truly have an all-star team.*"

"*Oh, look at you, Semi, with a sports reference,*" says Edie. "*I'm proud of you.*"

"*All-star is a sports reference?*" Semi asks, shrugging.

"*Not to be negative, and I'm not afraid or anything,*" interjects B.J., "*but aren't we still pretty severely outnumbered. How are we going to win this?*"

"We win by staying alive," David answers. *"A while ago, the enemy built a blockade in the Gray Zone around the tristate area. That's why we couldn't flee earlier. Right now, the only help we have is help that's been hidden here the whole time, but Nistarim reinforcements are fighting to break through. We just have to hold on until they get here."*

Before Semi can reply or ask David how he seems to know everything before the rest of them do, her eyes open wide, and her jaw drops, and then a smile appears big enough to light up the park. Her dad is suddenly standing right in front of her. But how? This is his psychic ghost. He can't physically come over here now because he's busy staring down the opposing forces and giving telepathic commands to his troops, but he's created a telepathic hologram that, honestly, is difficult to tell from the real thing. He kisses Semi and hugs her so hard that she can't breathe, and Semi adores every second of it. After he's finished hugging her, he mutes Semi's mind-link with her friends. Leaning in close, he whispers sweet daddy things in her ear, words she will remember for the rest of her life.

As he turns to leave, he unmutes their mind-speak and says a few words to David.

"So, you're the young man who has been in my head," he says as he shakes David's hand. *"David Alexander Stone, it is an honor to finally meet you."*

"No, sir," David answers. *"The honor is all mine."*

"We were disconnected for a while after you left Danny Vision, but when the connection returned, it came violently, knocking me unconscious for hours. Once I regained consciousness, our connection was stronger. It brought me to you, and I was able to lay this trap for my old nemesis," Amon Ra replies. *"When I was down, I spent quite a bit of that time experiencing your life, and I can only assume that you were experiencing mine as well."*

"Yes, I did, sir," answers David, nervously. *"It was quite a ride."*

What? David literally was in her dad's head and walked through his memories? How? How's that even work?

"Yours wasn't boring either. For the record, you're much too hard on yourself, David. I have no doubt that your dad is very proud of you. I know I am," Ra says as he places his hand on David's shoulder.

David furrows his brow. *"Sir, I'm sorry for the timing, but I have something urgent to tell you."*

"It's going to need to wait until this is over, I'm afraid," Amon Ra answers, reassuringly. *"Oh, and by the way, I know you sensed my presence. Thank you for keeping my secret."*

"*You're welcome, sir*," says David, respectfully.

Secret? Oh, David knew that Semi's dad and his team were here the whole time. She didn't see that coming. *Man, remind me to never play poker with David.*

"*We have a lot to talk about when this is over, young man,*" says Ra.

"*I look forward to it, sir,*" David replies.

"*Semi,*" her dad says, with a playful wink. "*If it's not too much to ask, take care of this young man and keep him in one piece.*"

"*My pleasure."*

"*Children,*" he calls out, addressing all four of them. "*Brace yourselves. The battle is about to begin. Follow the instructions given to you without deviation, and I assure you that you will get through this safe and sound.*"

As dad's psychic ghost dissipates, three others appear. Semi's sisters Maat and Athena create their own, and because Bia is a fae and, like Semi, is an empath, not a telepath, Athena creates one for Bia so that she can tag along. Because of the imminent battle, it's a quick visit, and they just give her quick hugs and kisses.

As they get ready to leave, Bia looks over at David and asks, through a private mind-speak, *"Is Mr. tall, dark, and handsome as much of a snack under that mask as the rest of him?"*

"*More,*" Semi replies.

"*So, what's his name?*" she asks, eyeing David flirtatiously and striking a provocative pose, even more provocative than usual.

"*His name is Mr. Off Limits,*" Semi replies with a huge grin.

Bia giggles and asks, *"It's like that, sis?"*

"*Yep,*" she answers, with a confident wink as she snaps her fingers, with attitude. "*Get your mind out my snack drawer.*"

They both burst out laughing.

"*We don't have time now,*" Bia replies. "*but you have got to spill the tea on you and the masked 'Wonder Boy' when this is over. Stay safe—*

STARS IN THE DARKNESS

Ocho." As she says Ocho, she traces an eight in the air, exaggerating the curves. *"Yeah, you're Ocho, now. You've got waaaay too much going on to be Uno anymore."*

They get another quick laugh, and as the three of them disappear, Bia adds on, *"Love you, girl."*

"Love you too," Semi whispers back.

"Man, they're even hotter up close," B.J. gushes, in full pervert mode, *"But that Glamazon, wow, she must be, at least, six feet tall barefooted and fully loaded. What were you two talking about? Did I come up? I ..."*

"Shut up, B.J.," Edie and Semi say in unison.

"C'mon, guys," David interrupts. *"No more fooling around. It's show time. Time to focus."*

He's right; they can feel it in the air. The dam is going to break at any second. Both the shadows and messengers are waiting in expectation. Semi lets go of David's hand and takes off his jacket. She doesn't want to damage it in battle. She tries a trick that she's seen her aunt do many times, a few times with Semi inside it. She folds the jacket and encases it in a sphere comprised of pure chasmal and places the jacket under a tree. The sphere is pretty close to impregnable, and one this small should keep generating for about an hour or so. Semi then looks down at her pretty, black dress and ensemble, and she ends the illusion, except for the heels. She keeps them, of course. All that's left is Semi, her velecor armor, and her three and a half-inch stilettos. Word of advice— never get between a girl and her heels.

There are a whole bunch of warriors out there, and most of them are clothed in velecor; many are projecting some type of fake image, whatever puts them in the mood for battle. Some wear suits, some wear flowing gowns, some go shirtless with tight pants, some wear armor and spikes, one man has a kilt and blue face paint, and one poor woman is fighting in fake boobs and a chainmail bikini. Seeing her dear sister, Bia, preparing to fight in her trashy hooker outfit, showed Semi that the idea of going to war in a dress, even one as tasteful and elegant as hers, well, that just isn't her. Semi wants to feel like a warrior, and she can't do that in a black dress, but heels still work. They always work.

Seeing Semi, Edie and David imitate her and turn off their illusions while B.J. stays in his black trench coat look —hey, whatever works.

Semi draws close to David, gives him a peck on the cheek for good luck, and squeezes his hand, then they bow their heads and say a short prayer together. Now, there's nothing left but the waiting.

It's still, eerily still—no birds, no voices, no city sounds. Semi's never experienced anything quite like it, but that's not the only thing that's different. While she stands here waiting for World War III, her senses are awakening. For the first time, she starts to truly experience the world through the eyes of a sila.

Everything is connected. She sees that clearly now. All that has been made glows with divine light; its life-giving fire has kissed each molecule, endowing it with a unique energy signature, like a celestial fingerprint. Each has a purpose, and like snowflakes, no two are ever the same. Another truth she's discovered is that all of nature sings, every pebble, every raindrop, every particle of stardust, sings in its own voice, in its own language, but the song is always the same. It is the song of creation. The whisper that birthed a bang still echoes through all it has made, divine music for those who are willing to hear.

Semi sways instinctively to the celestial breeze that stirs all that is and all that will ever be, seeing, feeling, and tasting all the colors of its perfect movement. With each passing second, the magic of life becomes more abundantly apparent. Every person, every bird, every tree, every stone is sparkling, like Christmas lights, glistening with unique auras. Different colors and shades, strengths, depths, and densities, different vibrational frequencies. And every aura is lined with living fire, the creative and destructive flame of chasmal.

Chasmal—she feels a rush as her body absorbs it in ever-increasing measure. In the end, that is the secret behind the fantastic powers of the Earthbound, the reason why new bodies must be crafted for them at their rebirth. The Earthbound absorb and channel chasmal at levels that would be fatal for any other non-celestial, but among the Earthbound, only the sila and the arwaah channel its full spectrum and in its purest form. The arwaah can manipulate unimaginable levels of chasmal and, with their celestial wings, soar on cosmic winds across vast distances and through dimensional divides. But only the sila have the power not only to command the living fire but to store enormous amounts and store it indefinitely. This is why the raw power of the sila is unrivaled among those who walk the earth.

What concerns Semi now as she examines the auras of their opponents is a simple truth about Earthbound. The rule of thumb for Earthbound in general, but especially for sila, is that the ability to absorb and control chasmal grows with age. The older they are, the stronger they become. So, here's the problem, staring at Semi from across the field. She can read the auras of the three sila opposing them and tell their age, like reading rings to determine the age of a tree. Marduk over there, in the disco pants, is about nine hundred years old. Serket, a former citizen of the Ajuran Sultanate, a medieval Somali kingdom, is probably north of five hundred years old. The queen of mean herself, Ishtar, is from Palestine and has been at this for two thousand years. Semi, well, she's been a full-fledged sila for a little more than twenty minutes. So, there's that.

Amesemi feels it; their might is staggering. She should be afraid, right? Individually, they are unbelievably powerful, and they *should* be far more powerful than she, but it doesn't feel that way. Is she missing something? Is someone playing possum? Semi feels strong, impossibly strong, and that's only increasing with every breath she takes. Mighty as they are, Semi's stronger than any of those three. In fact, she feels stronger than the three of them put together. She knows this shouldn't be possible, so what is she missing? The other thing that Semi has going for her is that most new sila are peasant girls, students, grandmas—everyday ordinary people who are picked by the other and presented with the talisman after the old host has passed. They don't come into it with any previous knowledge, training, or fighting skills. Semi's been training from birth. She's no rookie; she knows how to fight. So, if you take her moves and you add her new strength, speed, and energy manipulation, that's pretty awesome. Semi shouldn't be afraid of them. They should be afraid of her.

Semi's jolted out of her reflection by the sound of her dad's voice as he calls out to Thoth, saying, "You don't look like yourself, Thoth. I hope I didn't ruin your party, showing up with a few friends unannounced."

"Well, you did catch me a little off guard," Thoth replies, smugly.

"But I'm glad you're here. You'll find that I have a few surprises of my own."

While those two exchange a few "pleasantries", Semi's super ears pick up Tef whispering to Bast, "So, when are we going to circle up? They're about to attack, and we're outnumbered and surrounded."

"We're not circling up," answers Bast, "Old man's orders." Bast smiles mischievously and adds, "We're charging."

"Huh?" Tef gulps.

Sounds good to Semi. She'd rather be the aggressor. She'll get a chance to flex her new muscles and finally see all that this body can do.

"Oh, by the way, Thoth," her father calls out. "Before we get started, I've got one more surprise of my own."

They appear hovering in the air above her father's head, six Earth-bound all-stars, having been expertly cloaked by Semi's sister Maat. They're a sight for sore eyes, but Amesemi's eyes are immediately drawn to the winged, Nubian goddess taking the lead, her sister Nephthys. She's the oldest and most powerful arwaah in the nine worlds, and since Iset's passing, many people consider Nephthys the baddest woman alive, a claim that Semi can neither confirm nor deny. This will be Amesemi's first time seeing her in action, and she's looking forward to it.

Joining Nephthys are two more Earthbound: The Korean heart-throb and arwaah, Mace Drifter and the powerful Samoan marid, Losi, with his trademark, rock star hair. Floating above them are three sila. There is the blonde, nineteenth century, Oklahoman cowgirl, Inanna, and the two most ancient and mighty of their order, excluding Semi of course: the dreadlocked, studly Cushite warrior, Apedemak, and the wise and immovable, stunner from ancient China, Qetesh. Wow, Semi knows they're still outnumbered nearly three to one, but it really feels like the Nistarim has the winning hand. No wonder dad's charging.

Right before her dad gives the order to attack, he disseminates some last-second orders. He pairs up the non-Earthbound warriors with the Earthbound, saying something about the non-Earthbound watching their partner's backs so that they can use their powers safely, blah, blah, blah, blah, and other stuff. Semi doesn't get it. She and the other Earth-bound are not the ones who need protection. Then he gives instructions to Semi and the other "children" to hang back and stay out of the fight as much as possible. Tef will stay back with them and protect them. *Really?* Amesemi's sister Tef is great, but when does a sila need anyone, even a marid, to babysit her?

Dad must have Semi confused with someone else. She's not little Semi anymore, and she's not the helpless newborn of a few hours ago who couldn't stand up straight. She's Isis, of the sila. In fact, she's the afreet, the princess of the Amar, soon to be queen, the most powerful person in the nine worlds. Asking her to run from this is like asking Eminem to run from an MC battle. Semi's not going to be able to do it. Sorry, she's not hiding from this fight. She was made for it.

It's started. Dad's given the signal to charge. More instructions are being spoken; even Semi's other is jumping in, saying something about hanging back, being cautious, and a bunch of other boring stuff. Semi starts to listen, but then she feels the rush, a power rage, as unparalleled amounts chasmal flow into her body. As energy crackles from her fingers, Sothis's voice and every other voice, for that matter, simply become white noise. Amesemi was strong five minutes ago, unrivaled two minutes ago; now, she is invincible. Now, not only are the words of her dad's famous speech from the Battle of Uruk memorized by every warrior and trainee, its principles are the basis of much of Nistarim combat theory. One of the pillars is her dad's belief that invincibility is a myth. Well, Semi hates to disagree with the great Amon Ra, but maybe, just maybe, she's the exception to the rule. She is Isis of the Amar, and Semi believes that she's invincible or at least the next best thing, and right here and now, she's going to prove it to the world.

Amidst ignoring Tef's cries of protest and Semi's other telling her to slow down, Semi speeds ahead, laughing as the celestial winds swirl around her. Hair on fire, eyes blazing as she rushes forward to the front of the battle line, knocking down everyone who gets in her path.

The first to confront her is a hideous looking ravager with flaming hands and a devilish smile. His name is Night Time or Dark Mist, or something. Semi thinks she read a file about this one, during a simulation, a simulation considered way above her level. That's funny. With an energy burst, she blasts off both of his arms and gives him a telekinetic shove that pushes him through a tree. Next she turns and incinerates a random ravager who jumps her way, and then ducks a punch from a giant alitha, named Basilisk, reciprocating by striking him so hard with her glowing fist that she sends him sliding two hundred yards. Cool, and she thinks she chipped one of his teeth. This is almost too easy. She needs to go big game hunting and hunt down Marduk, or that hooded guy or...no, Ishtar. Semi's going to hunt down Ishtar and make her pay, and...what was that?

There was a plasma blast coming toward her head, and someone blocked it. It's David.

She stops running for a second and turns to him. "Thanks for the thought, but I had that under control, Charming," she fibs as she pushes him out of the way and saves his life by incinerating a ravager that was surely going to slay him. "What are you doing here, anyway? You're supposed to be back there with Tef."

"So are you," he replies, lunging into a pretty intense sword fight with Tobias Grimm, one which Semi doesn't envision him winning. "Where you go, I go, Princess. It's in the contract."

"That's sweet...duck!" He ducks, and Semi cuts off Grimm's sword hand and right leg in two spectacular moves. "Well, it seems your schedule's just been freed up. You're too deep in this thing to go back now, so stay close to me, but not too close. I'm going after Ishtar."

"You're doing what?" he exclaims and probably says a bunch of other stuff in protest.

She can't really hear much at this point, other than David puffing, trying to keep up. Semi's in a dead sprint again. She's got Ishtar, the queen of mean, in her sites, and she's not going to let her get away. Ishtar's going to pay for what she did to Danny, to Adad, to Renenet, and all her other victims.

Ishtar sees Semi when she's still a ways off, and the evil sila stares at Amesemi dismissively as Ishtar sheaths her sword and places her hands behind her back. Semi doesn't know what that's about, and she doesn't care. If Thoth's lapdog wants to make this quick and easy for Semi, well, that's her loss. Semi's coming, and she plans to end that wretched woman. Maybe it's Ishtar's way of accepting the inevitable. At any rate, they'll know in a second.

As Semi draws close, she leaps forward, lorenth drawn, and shouts her enemy's name. "Ishtar, I've come to end you!"

Semi swings her lorenth, with skill, speed, and precision; Ishtar has no chance. Amesemi's lorenth is like lightning flashing through the sky. Her foe simply laughs and shifts to the side, slightly, and Amesemi misses her, Semi's momentum carrying her off balance. Ishtar makes no effort to attack but resumes her passive stance, arms behind her back. Semi turns and attacks again, this time under more control. She slashes and misses, swings and misses, kicks and misses, fakes a kick and jabs with the sword and still misses. And Ishtar never stops laughing at her.

"This is pitiful, baby princess, coming to me high, intoxicated by chasmal," she mocks. "My blade is reserved for professionals while you are barely a novice. Truly underwhelming, the power of the afreet is wasted on you."

"We'll see," Semi snarls.

Amesmei breathes in deeply, centering herself as she redoubles her efforts, attacking again. With the grace of a ballet dancer, Ishtar once more evades Semi, this time sticking her foot out as Semi passes, causing her to stumble. Semi spins out of it and surprises Ishtar with a counter, catching her off guard. Still, Amesemi's lorenth barely grazes her opponent, leaving a small burn on her face that heals almost instantly.

Startled and angered by the fact that the young sila was able to touch her, Ishtar has stopped laughing. Fun and games time is over. Her eyes narrow into slits as she calculates ways to do Semi harm. Well, the feeling's mutual. Semi can do this. She needs to focus, remember her training. She lunges again, perfect form, perfect technique. Ishtar dodges her blade, once again, but this time catches Amesemi's sword hand by the wrist, twisting it and then striking the young afreet's elbow with all her might. Fire, burning fire, Semi hears it snap and feels excruciating pain, but she doesn't scream. She will not give that witch the satisfaction.

Oh man, that hurts! How did Ishtar do that?

Semi's bones are as hard as steel rods and her tendons like metal cables. OK, she knows her sila opponent's are the same, but the old lady snapped Amesemi's arm effortlessly. *I can't think about that now. I've got to counter.* She tries to throw a kick, but Ishtar strikes the shin of the young princess's attacking leg with a powerful, flaming kick of her own, shattering Semi's tibia as well, causing an explosion of crippling agony. This is bad, but young Isis has hyper healing. The bones are already starting to mend, painfully but they're mending all the same. She needs to make a move, just buy a little time.

Rather than finishing her, the villainous sila has backed off admiring her work. That's her mistake. Semi's healing; she can feel it. She needs to do something, something to knock Ishtar off guard, give herself a chance to summon an energy strike. But before Amesemi can make her move, Ishtar strikes her in the face with her burning fist. It feels like someone just dropped a mountain on Semi's head. She tries to shake it off, to counter, but the old lady strikes her again. Young Isis is seeing double, swallowing blood, not sure if she can take another blow.

Suddenly, Semi hears the sound of a lorenth swinging in her direction. It's David. He finally caught up. Ishtar pulls her sword out with blinding speed and parries without looking. David counted on that, using the sword attack to disguise his actual move, an energy strike, but she's too fast.

"Clever boy, Captain Suburbia," she hisses as she turns to him and catches his hand just as he is about to release his attack, draining the energy before he can release it. "You almost had me again...almost. But this is a girls' only conversation. You're not invited."

David drops to his knees, weakened by the energy siphoning, then she backhands him and sends him flying a hundred yards. Amesemi can sense him. He's hurt, but OK. Good. He bought her time— the chance that she needs.

"You're going down," Semi yells as she summons a concentrated qi sphere with her left hand for a strike, but Ishtar's so fast as if she knows the young sila's moves before she does.

The elder sila knocks away Semi's hand, pulls her hair back, and strikes her windpipe.

I ... I can't breathe ... I can't ... I ...

While Semi fights not to blackout or succumb to the sheer panic caused by the lack of air, Ishtar picks Amesemi up by her throat, further crushing it and taunts her.

"You were saying, dear?" Ishtar chuckles. "Is there something in your throat? Lucky for your friend that I'm not allowed to kill him, or maybe it's lucky for me. Is he cute under that mask, princess? Maybe, there's a future for me and the good captain after this is over. What do you think, dear? What? Still speechless?"

She lifts the squirming Semi higher and causes the air above her to part, opening a fiery, crimson portal, handing her over to strong hands on the other side.

"Take her Gunab," she shouts to her accomplice. "Depower little Isis and contact Thoth to rendezvous with you. I'm going to grab the boy so that we can all get out of here before this battle completely turns."

"I've got this," he growls as he pulls Semi into the Gray Zone.

No, he doesn't have it. Short breath and another, Amesemi's throat is healing. She can breathe again. Her arm and her leg have mostly mended—well enough anyway. She's going to use her super strength and break Gunab's wrist, rip off his arm, and...she can't focus. What's wrong with her? It's like Gunab's in her head, stopping her from concentrating... but Semi's other, Sothis, doesn't she make her immune to someone messing with her head?

Woozy, everything is spinning. And as she fights to remain conscious, a load of information comes flooding into young Isis's mind from Sothis, stuff that she now realizes Sothis was trying to bring to her attention earlier. In the middle of her life and death struggle, on the verge of blacking out, Sothis decides to lecture her, giving her a lesson from Sila Powers 101.

"My love," she says in a tone that is simultaneously warm and slightly condescending. "the statement that sila are the most powerful humanoids in the nine worlds is not completely accurate. Actually, it's seven and a half of the nine realms. We are the strongest on Perinesa, Yaaru, and Akert and are even mightier on the four worlds, but Alchera is a different breed, and dream walkers are the apex predators there. In the Gray Zone, where we are now, it's more complicated. We are the most powerful here, but because of the Gray Zone's proximity to the spirit world, the Gray Zone plays havoc with any Earthbound's connection with his or her other. It makes it hard to utilize our powers and creates massive, cavern sized holes in our usually impregnable psychic defenses. So, in summary, we have astounding might here, but we can't use it. As you can now see, this makes us vulnerable in the Gray Zone, easy to defeat in battle, and even easier to mentally control.

"My dear, this is why the Amar try to avoid fighting in the Gray Zone, and, if cornered, we wisely choose flight over fight every time. On Perinesa, the greater the use of our ability, the more it creates portals around us, and a skilled shadow dancer can use these portals to pull us into the Neter-khertet and almost certain defeat. For this reason, your father gave the instructions he gave before commencing the battle. Please, take this information into consideration when making decisions for us in the future."

Is that all? Where's her plan? Where's Sothis's help? Future? What future? How can Sothis be so casual about this? OK, so Semi really should have read the instructions before playing with her new toys. *Thanks, Sothis. How's this massive 'I told you so' supposed to help me now?* Amesemi has no control over her body, and it feels like Gunab has reached into her head and severed her connection to her abilities. Even if she could somehow move, she's powerless. *Stay calm. There's got to be a solution, a way out of this—somehow.* Semi feels herself melting, as if her skin is actually dissolving, and there's nothing she can do. This is bad. It looks like her dad was right after all—major shocker. Invincibility is a myth, and...and giants fall.

TITANS —DAVID

Oh man, David hurts everywhere. He feels like he's been run over by a truck and then hit by a train, and all Ishtar did was swat him away with the back of her hand. Imagine if she really tried to hurt him. *OK, David, get up. I've got to get up. It's just pain.* He can worry about that later, but right now, he's got to get back to Semi. As amazing as she is, she can't do this on her own.

David looks up and sees Ishtar choking Semi, lifting her by her neck. No way, not on his watch. He scrambles to his feet and looks around for his lorenth when he senses someone behind him and ducks, barely avoiding a beheading by a no-good, Nephilim merc named Shed. David doesn't need this, especially now. He summons his lorenth, but Shed swats it out of the air. *Great, just great.*

Shed lifts his lorenth to take another crack at young Mr. Stone when suddenly the Nephilim's arms turn to mist, and his lorenth falls to the ground. Before he can react, he receives a plasma shot to the head and falls down, dead.

"Those are my Warrior, Alabama skills, son," says B.J. with his fake swag and dated *Matrix* get up. "We don't miss where I come from."

"Edie, B.J., thanks for your help. It's good to see you and all that but..." He picks up his lorenth and starts sprinting toward Semi. "Follow me! We need to save Semi."

True to form, Edie jumps right in, running right with him while B.J. shrugs and makes some kind of sarcastic comment that David completely ignores before B.J. takes off after them. As they get close, they see Semi getting pulled into a crimson circle of fire. OK, so they may need to jump in after her and...oh no. Ishtar has just turned their way, her red eyes staring daggers as she marches straight towards David, and as she approaches, she summons Serket and another high-level fighter to join her. *Great, just great. I'm really starting not to like that woman.*

At the last possible second, Athena arrives, blocking Ishtar's path, and before the three villains can engage her, there's a golden blur, and Nephthys appears as well. Ishtar's face falls. She doesn't seem particularly happy to see either of Semi's sisters, but that lack of enthusiasm seems to multiply at the prospect of fighting Nephthys, who's making a beeline straight for her. Athena's long hair seems to move as if it has a life of its own as its color changes from dark brown to auburn to smoky red as she attacks Serket and her partner with twin golden blades, elite skill, and the fury of a Tasmanian devil. Where Athena is the fiery aggressor, Nephthys's approach is the opposite. She's cool, relaxed, and lets Ishtar make the first move, drawing her in, but when she counters, it's with terrifying speed and precision. It's awe-inspiring, but as much as David would love to stay and watch Ishtar take a beating, he can't. He's got a princess to save.

After a dead sprint, they reach the spot where Semi disappeared. While they were running, he formulated a plan that he's communicated with Edie and B.J. through mind-speak. Now, they're implementing it. David opens a golden, circular door, sends Edie in as invisible mist, and quickly closes it behind her. They're not going to outfight whoever is on the other side. This operation is about stealth and surprise. If all goes well, Edie will signal them when it's time for them to jump in and follow.

"Are you sure about this, dude? We need to go in," says a fidgety B.J., twirling his guns, nervously.

"Hold on for a bit longer," he replies, pretending to be a whole lot calmer than he feels inside. "Edie can do this. She's the key. We'll move on her ... that's her now." And in true World of Warcraft style, he announces, "We're going in."

He re-opens the door, and they portal in and see a startled Gunab right as he's grabbing at some mist that used to be Semi. As Semi turns to smoke and disappears from his hands, David gives B.J. the signal for phase two. They need to move fast; he's not sure how long Edie can hold this, especially under these circumstances, and if the fiery tingling he's feeling down his spine is to be trusted, they have company—powerful company closing in fast.

B.J. fires his plasma pistols at Gunab, providing a distraction as David portals out the cloud that is Edie and Semi. B.J. jumps through right after them before Gunab can retaliate. Time for phase three. David hurls his most potent energy blast in an attempt to slow Gunab down and stop him from following right away. Gunab, not in the mood for the young warrior's foolishness, effortlessly slaps away his attack. That's not good. The teen was supposed to hit and run, but now, he doesn't believe he's going to get the opportunity to get out of here before Gunab attacks. Well, if this is it, there are worse ways to go. At least Semi and the guys are safe.

Unfortunately, it's worse than David thought. Thoth has arrived, hovering above Gunab. Stone tries to brace himself, creating his strongest shield, but he knows it's not going to be enough. He says a quick, silent prayer and hopes for the best. Then, it happens.

"How dare you put your hands on my daughter!" A booming voice bellows as a golden thunderbolt strikes Gunab, instantly turning him into embers and creating an explosion that sends shockwaves a mile in every direction.

Amon Ra is here, and he is not happy. Messengers cheer; shadows gnash their teeth, but Thoth has not moved. He doesn't even flinch, nor does he seem particularly impressed by Ra's explosive arrival.

In Central Park, Thoth seemed more mastermind than warrior. Despite his power, he was content to stand away from the fray, using his hooded bodyguard to shield him as he gave orders without actually getting his hands dirty. Here, in the Gray Zone or Neter-khertet as the old ones prefer to call it, he is completely transformed. His movements are regal, godlike even, and his demeanor is aggressively combative, more bloodthirsty warlord than aloof mastermind. Thoth is a great white shark, and the Gray Zone is his deep blue sea. This is his domain. Here he does not delegate; he destroys. Thoth smiles wickedly at his adversary, and in a flash, he transforms himself into a nine-foot, purple fire-demon and moves toward Amon Ra.

The paranormal flash drive in David's head tells him that asura, Nephilim, and even some skin-walkers are far more powerful here than they are on earth. Closeness to the barrier that leads to the spirit world allows them to manipulate energies at levels they would otherwise be unable to imagine, let alone achieve. Their increased might, coupled with the Earthbound's struggles on this plane, puts shadow dancers at the very top of the food chain here. But even among their kind, skills and physical abilities on Perinesa don't necessarily correlate to ability in the Neter-khertet. Some of the strongest warriors on earth can be among the weakest here and vice versa. No one knows what all the ingredients are that make for a formidable Gray Zone warrior. They know it takes practice, lots of practice. Humans actually have the most aptitude, but asura have hundreds of years to work on their craft, where Nephilim potentially have thousands. It's also known that a high level of telepathic or empathic aptitude is a must, and that the very best have discipline, incredible focus, drive, conviction, and just sheer strength of will. It's never been proven, but willpower may be the most crucial quality of all. That would make sense because the GOATs of Neter-khertet warfare, the absolutely greatest of all time, are Thoth and Amon Ra, and it's hard to imagine that two more stubborn, willful men have ever lived.

Ra comes streaking into view, a nine-foot, flaming, aureate avenger and stops, hovering a few hundred yards from Thoth.

"Where are all your doting sycophants?" Ra taunts. "This is your last chance to run back to Earth and hide behind them, Thoth. Not one of them is foolish enough to come to your aid and fight me here. You know that. No one is coming. In Neter-khertet, there are only messengers, shadows, you, and me, and your shadowy friends cannot give you aid. They only bear witness. There is no hiding here, Thoth. No lies. No tricks. This is a place of truth. If you remain, it is just you and me, to the end. Do you have the stomach for that?"

Thoth glares at him, and then replies menacingly, "I had such wonderful plans for you, Amon Ra, wonderful plans, but a showdown in Neter-khertet was not among them. In fact, for a man who prides himself on strategy, one could argue that this is not very strategic at all. But we both know this is bigger than all that isn't it? In the end, neither of us can thrive while the other breathes. I view you as the ultimate hindrance to my divine destiny, and you think me a monster. But everything I do, everything I have ever done, it is all business, a means to a justifiable end. It is always just business but not between you and me. We are way past that; this is personal. So, that brings us to where we are. You and I here, winner takes all." He strolls back and forth, first like a professor in a lecture hall, casual, informative, and impersonal, but as he continues, the menace and passion build with each spoken word.

"Maybe this is fated. We were born to be opposites, you and me. You were gifted with greatness from birth, the son of War, a head taller than the rest, but I built myself into a god, brick by brick. The land of Neter-khertet," he says, sweeping his hand in a semi-circle to indicate his territory, "this is the place where I discovered my godhood, my 'majestic'. It is only fitting that this will be the place where you finally bow down before it. So, let's finish this, Amon Ra. Let's finish this once and for all."

"Finally," Ra growls as he lunges forward, and David sees him as a whoosh of fire being sucked into a vacuum.

The titans clash. Each punch thrown sends shockwaves that have all indigenous life scurrying and sends tremors throughout the land. After several close-quarter exchanges, Thoth kicks Ra, creating some distance. Then, he unleashes an energy blast, an incredible wave of sheer force that engulfs Ra, sending him crashing through a mountain. He's buried under rubble. Thoth flies to the wreckage, hovering above it with a self-satisfied grin.

The rubble stirs, and a volcano of resplendent living fire erupts, striking Thoth and sending him more than a mile in the air. Ra bursts through, flying in Thoth's direction. His foe shakes off Ra's attack and streaks toward him. When they collide, it's as if an atom bomb has just been detonated.

David's more than a mile beneath them, but he's lifted off his feet by the waves of power emanating from their impact. This is insane, mind-blowing, even by his new standards. His granddad, dad, and uncles would always go on and on about how great the old school boxers were. They would gush about the classic fights, like Ali and Frazier and The Thrilla in Manila. Well, if you gave Frazier and Ali world breaking cosmic powers, increased the stakes to the fate of humankind, and increased the length of the feud by a few thousand years, you'd have Thoth versus Amon Ra, and David has the best seat in the house.

"David, where are you? Come back," he hears Edie calling him through mind-speak.

It all happened in a matter of seconds, and he totally forgot about his friends, who are in the middle of their own life and death struggle back on Earth. They may need his help. Fortunately, time moves faster in here than back in Perinesa. Hopefully, from their point of view, he hasn't been gone that long. Amon Ra is going to have to carry on without him. Right, like he could even make a difference.

He's getting better at this. With two effortless flicks of his wrist, David opens a door and rapidly jumps through and ends up a few feet from his crew. Fortunately, most of the enemy's heavy hitters are getting it handed to them by the good guys, and Tefnet has caught up to Semi and friends, offering protection even as she scolds them, especially Semi, for running off.

It's only been a couple of minutes since David sent them through. Edie and Semi are seated on the grass, exhausted, and the Cisco Kid, their very own B.J., paces back and forth like a caged animal, upset that Tef won't let him wander off and look for trouble.

There's not much trouble coming their way for the moment. The ones skilled enough to challenge Tefnet are occupied, and the ones that aren't want no part of her. While Tefnet stays vigilant for threats, the others watch the battle as spectators, astonished at the overwhelming ability and fury of the combatants. The Nistarim has had a few injuries, but no one from their side has been killed, yet. That's good news. Honestly, the best they could hope for.

While they watch the Battle of Central Park, David's eyes are up in the sky, watching the Rumble of Neter-khertet, the ongoing, no holds barred death match between Thoth and Ra. This is a new talent that Stone's just discovered—the ability to peer through the veil between Perinesa and the Gray Zone. He has to focus extremely hard, but he can see into the other world and follow those two fighting from here. They look different, sometimes appearing as living lightning, flashing across the sky, and at other times as voltaic, humanoid phantoms engaged in fierce, mortal combat. He doesn't know if anyone else can actually see them, but everyone can feel the combat taking place above them. Each punch, every attack, seems to shake the heavens, sending shivers through every meta-human within miles. While he watches, David also keeps up with his friends' conversation. It's his way of trying to multitask.

"So, I don't get it," says Edie. "This is all going on in the middle of New York, the most important city in the world. Where are the cops? The Marines? Where's CNN? Fox News? Where are all the civilians with their cell phone cameras?"

"Keeping our existence a secret is in the best interest of everybody, even our enemies," answers Semi.

"How?" asks Edie. "How do you keep all this a secret?"

"Remember that nerdy looking guy that came with Bast? His name is Tanen. And for every op, very powerful telepaths like him, known as storm watchers, provide convincing illusions for civilians, and we have people whose job it is to clear out bystanders, edit their memories, and do clean up after altercations. During this particular battle, they've used the illusion of a hurricane. On top of that, there are technopaths who manipulate digital signals and delete our digital footprint, and we have human allies in media and law enforcement who assist in keeping the concealed ones concealed."

"Like what happened with Penfield," Edie replies, "and the footage of the incident in the mall."

"I was right!" blurts out B.J. "I was right all along. It's men in black. They're everywhere." He's doing a little victory dance.

They keep going on, but David goes ahead and blocks them out. Multitasking's not working all that well. He needs his entire focus to keep up with the two gladiators in the Gray Zone. It's gotten even more intense. Those two have gone back and forth for a while. Finally, it looks like Ra has taken control of the fight. Good, for a moment he ...

"Hey, Troy Bolton," Tefnet says as she shakes his shoulder. "Keep your head in the game."

Tefnet just didn't make a *High School Musical* reference, did she? Really? She just lost all of her cool points from her *Black Panther* reference earlier.

"You're still in a battle zone, Hotshot," she continues. "Stop cloud gazing and keep your head on a swivel."

"Yes, ma ..." he starts to reply.

"No ma'am," she interrupts with a playful wink. "No ma'am, no Ms., no Mrs., on that Bast and I definitely agree. Call me Tef or Red. If you're really, really lucky, and you play your cards right, one day you'll get to call me sis. Call me any old lady names, and I'm going to freeze your lips, got it?"

"OK," he answers, nodding.

She's right. Not staying present in the middle of all this can be hazardous to his health and that of everyone else. Ra will be OK. David's got to keep his head in the game. Oh, no, now he's got that song stuck in his head. Great.

This is different. He hasn't been able to step back and be an observer here like he was in the Gray Zone. Most of the conflict is far enough away at this point that he finally gets to do just that. Flying, energy blasting, earthmoving, killer martial art moves, and elite swordplay... the power and skill of all these fighters is breathtaking, way beyond anything he could ever hope to pull off. It's amazing that the four of them survived in the middle of all this. No wonder Tef was so mad.

David can feel the blockade starting to crumble. Reinforcements will be here soon. At this point, a third of the enemy is more focused on escaping than fighting, and that percentage is growing as Nistarim forces get closer. He sees Ishtar running away, minus an arm, courtesy of her quality time with Nephthys. Unfortunately, she's a sila. Her arm will grow back. Hopefully, next time, Nephthys will get the rest of her too.

David sees a wounded winged soldier, an arwaah named Mace Drifter, one of theirs, fall down not far from them. Tef's eyes communicate that she's tempted to go help him, but David's guess is that she's afraid that the moment she leaves her post that the teens would be vulnerable, so she stays. Mace's right-wing is damaged, and there is a hole in his side from a lorenth. As he fights to get up, the hooded man with shades catches up to him to finish the job. David doesn't care about the risk. He's going in. He just can't stand there and watch that man die.

As if she read his mind, Tef grabs his arm in a vice-like grip and gives him the don't make me whip you in public look that David has seen so many times from his mom over the years. There's no way she's letting one of them run off again. Semi staggers to her feet, not completely healed from her fight with Ishtar and her ordeal in the Gray Zone. Still, he can tell she's about to break ranks and jump into the fray again. Hey, Tef only has two hands. She can't stop everybody.

Before Semi or The Hooded Man can move, Losi shows up, flowing locks and all, and uses his elemental ability to strike Hooded Guy with a gust of hurricane-level winds. Mr. Shades anticipates Losi's attack, deflecting it easily with some type of TK shield. With effortless speed and finesse, he cleverly closes the distance between him and Losi, forcing this to be a sword fight. Losi is the far more powerful of the two, but as someone who's walked through Ra's memories and has seen him fight countless times, David knows that being more powerful has very little to do with who actually wins. Skill, anticipation, cunning, and courage count for a lot, and when all else fails, lorenths are the great equalizer. They can literally slice through anything. In the hands of a master, there is nothing and no one that a lorenth can't cut down to size.

So, Hooded Guy is banking on his sword skills. He's in for a rude awakening. David saw Losi at work earlier. His swordplay is brill... what? It's over, over in three moves. Stone's not sure, but he thinks this guy has just killed Losi. In three moves, he kicked him, cut off his sword hand, and ran his lorenth through Losi's chest. David's never seen anyone move like that. That's not actually true. The only other person he's seen with those kinds of moves is fighting in the Neter-khertet. Who is this guy? Whoever he is, he's turned his attention to them and is walking their way.

Tefnet releases David's arm and pushes him behind her, saying, "Get behind me, kids. It's going to be OK. He has to get through me."

Stone pulls out his lorenth to give Tef backup, but Semi, being

Semi, does him one better. She takes out her lorenth and quickly steps out in front, ignoring Tef's protests, determined to be the one to take on their new guest.

Mr. Shades, takes off his hood, revealing his long blonde hair, tied in an unfortunate man bun. He cracks his massive neck and with catlike grace, proceeds to step closer and closer; until he unexpectedly stops in his tracks. It's hard to tell because of his sunglasses, but it looks like he's staring into Semi's eyes, and something about her mesmerizes him, making him freeze.

"Amesemi?" he mumbles as he takes a step backward.

Then he disappears, not entirely leaping into the Gray Zone, but skimming along its outer barrier instead, giving him the appearance of a ghost with the ability to fly away in phantom form. OK, that was new. David's heart can start beating now. That was too close, way too close. He walks over and grabs Semi's hand, and they stand together, perplexed but very much relieved.

"Not that I'm complaining," says Edie, "but what was that about? It's like he saw Semi and just freaked out."

"It's obvious," chirps B.J. "He got punked. He took one look at the mighty Isis, and he lost it."

"I wish," answers Semi, thoughtfully. "There's something else going on here. He acted like he knew me."

"You two are so cute," snickers Tef as she walks by the two of them, causing both Semi and David to blush. "Either way, it's over, guys. Let's be thankful for that. It could have been worse."

As she says that, she signals for them to follow and resolutely starts walking over to Mace and Losi. They split off, with B.J., Semi, and David checking on Mace while Tef and Edie see after Losi.

Mace is weak and in a great deal of pain, but he'll be fine. Arwaah don't heal as quickly as sila or ravagers, but they still heal ridiculously fast, even faster if they engage their wings to increase the level of chasmal in their system. According to Semi, at worst, he'll be as good as new in a couple of days.

"I'm fine," Mace grunts. "What about Losi?"

Tef nods solemnly as she replies, "Sorry, guys. Our friend is moving on." She kisses Losi on his forehead, closes his eyes, and whispers, "Salioth Algo Daymon, my friend."

Tef kneels over the body, secures his talisman, and looks up, so Semi and David look up too although he has no idea what Tef's watching. Then he sees it, Losi's soul shimmering as it rises from his body. And as it does, it shines with a blinding radiance that rivals the sun. David thought he caught a glimpse of something when Danny passed, but he sees it clearly now. Losi is going home.

Losi's met in the air by a company of messengers, who encircle him, singing a wonderful, soul-stirring song of victory. It sends chills, goose-bumps and chills in a good way. David fights to hold back his man tears, but he allows one Denzel Washington-style teardrop to trickle down the side of his cheek. In a day of incredible experiences, this, by far, tops his list.

"This is the most beautiful thing I've ever seen," gushes Semi.

David shakes his head in wonder. "It really is something else."

"What? I don't see anything," says a frustrated B.J.

It's strange, B.J. can see so much, but he can't see this. David totally doesn't understand how B.J.'s powers work and why they're so different than his. Who is he fooling? He doesn't understand how any of this works. The more he learns, the more questions arise. At least, no one's trying to kill them. That's something. And there's another bonus. He gets to stand here and experience this incredible moment with his girl.

He remains standing where he is, enthralled by the messengers, and he notices that all but a few enemy stragglers have fled the scene, and he glimpses something else as well. Losi's soul isn't the only one rising. There's a ghoulish woman, with pale, translucent skin, lips the color of blood, long hair mixed with billowing smoke and a gothic dress comprised of lifelike ebon mist, who is floating over a deceased body. That would be unsettling enough, but she's simultaneously hovering over multiple dead bodies, with a convoy of shadows accompanying her at each location. This is death or at least its avatar.

One by one, she reaches into the lifeless bodies and yanks out souls as they struggle to break free from her grip, but there is no escaping death once she has you in her grasp. Her resolve is unwavering, and her transactions final. There is no glimmer or gleam emanating from these spirits. They are the color of hopelessness and despair. She holds them in the air and breathes in sucking out something from them. David doesn't have near the wisdom to know exactly what, but eventually, when she has finished her part, and they have no resistance left in them, she releases them into the waiting arms of the shadows. As she does, the souls scream—a scream like he's never heard before and will never forget. They wail as the shadows ferry them to their ultimate destination.

Death has not come anywhere near Losi, not even looked in his direction, and she gives the messengers an extremely wide berth. The dichotomy is striking. While Losi's journey has the feel of a celebration, the ones presided over by her seem utterly tragic and final. It leaves David with so many questions, but one truth is, once again, crystal clear. All deaths are not created equal.

Something else is happening. The fight between Ra and Thoth is over. He sees Thoth skimming the barrier between worlds as he falls to Earth, badly hurt. Ra is on his heels, determined to finish this, but something is wrong, something is terribly wrong.

Seeing the look in David's eyes, Tef shouts, "No, don't you dare, not again. You're not going to go running off to the last danger zone left in this park."

Yes, he is. Actually, he already has. Tef has many skills, but she's nowhere near as fast as he is. He's figured out that he's pretty fast when he focuses on it even compared to other metas. Well, David's got the jets on, now. No one's catching h...

"Hey Charming, where're you going?" Semi asks.

Well, that's humbling. Even with a pretty good lead, she caught up to him, and she's barely trying.

"Toward your dad, I've got a bad feeling," he answers. "But, you don't need to come, Semi. I don't want you getting into any more trouble with your sister."

"Where you go, I go, Charming. It's in the contract," she replies with a playful wink. "Besides, I'm the impulsive one, remember. I'm not going to let you take that from me."

Just like that, they're here. Well, as close to the situation as it's safe to get. Thoth is on the ground, trying to drag himself away, but he's hurt so badly, he can't even manage a proper crawl. Amon Ra has ordered all of his forces to stay out of this. Ra's gait is deliberate and unhurried as he walks toward Thoth, with three of Thoth's best between Ra and their leader. Make that two...make that one. Ra's skill is breathtaking, nothing fancy, no wasted motion. When he's provoked, he has a ruthless efficiency, nearly unrivaled—nearly.

The sila, Marduk, is the last barrier standing between Ra and Thoth. He unwisely attempts to overpower Ra. He unleashes an energy burst strong enough to incinerate him, but the majestic easily dodges his attack. Ra quickly portals in and out of the Neter-khertet, maneuvering behind Marduk. His portals are so efficient that they barely cause a ripple. Then he grabs the sila by his arm, and effortlessly flips Marduk into the Gray Zone while never releasing him. Standing outside the zone, Ra turns his right arm into blazing golden fire, letting the flame travel down his limb until it engulfs Marduk, turning him into a chasmal bonfire. The majestic allows this status quo to continue for several seconds, with his eyes fixed on Thoth, until Ra finally takes his arm and Marduk out of the Gray Zone and throws the sila's charred, smoldering body to the ground. Marduk's alive, barely, but he's definitely out of this fight.

But Marduk did serve a purpose. He gave The Hooded Man time to portal in, leaping between Ra and Thoth. Also, the blockade finally collapses, and two of the enemies, instead of fleeing, have come here. One is crouched over Thoth, providing healing while the other, the winged Remo Blaze, grabs Marduk and quickly escapes back into the Neter-khertet.

The Hooded Man mirrors Ra, not letting him move toward Thoth. Finally, he attacks, and Ra parries. There is a brief, furious exchange, with neither one gaining an advantage. Then both step back as the two circle each other, studying for weaknesses.

"You are skilled," says Ra. "There's no denying that, but there is no winning this and no reason for you to die today. You are not leaving here with Thoth, but you do not need to die with him."

By this time, Tef, Maat, B.J., and Edie have shown up and are standing near the "runaways". In response to Ra's words, his opponent rises to his full height, takes off his hood, throws his shades to the ground, and glares into Ra's eyes.

"You killed me before, old man," he growls. "It didn't stick, but I found it liberating. I wasn't ready to end you then 'Herald', but I am now."

As he peers into his foe's eyes, the blood leaves Ra's face, and he has the look of a man who has just been confronted by the risen dead, and, if David's right, in a very real way, he has. The majestic staggers backward, lowering his lorenth. Ra's opponent begins to attack, but a glimmering purple and gold shield is placed between the two warriors by the woman nursing Thoth. She has Thoth and the hooded warrior with her in a sphere, one far more powerful than anything that David's been able to conjure.

"Belet-Seri, let me out," the warrior screams as he glares at Ra through the barrier. "Let me finish this, finish that old fool once and for all."

"Stand down. We've got to go now. My father is the priority," commands Belet-Seri as she cradles Thoth.

"No, this ends now!" the hooded man yells as he takes out his lorenth and starts to cut his way out of the sphere.

Ra stands on the other side of the shield, his lorenth lying on the ground. The barrier burns, but Amon Ra puts his hand on it anyway, ignoring the pain, and gazes at the face of his determined opponent. Ra no longer has the fearsome glare of the world's greatest warrior. Now, he looks like a father staring through the glass at his newborn child.

"Stand down," Belet-Seri orders even more forcefully. "You know that's what Thoth wants...what Osiris would want. You can kill your father another day. We've got to go while we can."

"Don't call him that," barks the warrior. "My father was a great king, and he died long ago. This old fool is nothing more than a twisted doppelganger whose time has come to an end." He sheaths his lorenth and backs away from the barrier, still seething. "Still, you're right. We need to go. Grab your father. I'll buy time and take out anything that gets in our way."

Nistarim forces from the Battle of Central Park and many of the reinforcements have now gathered around. Ra signals for them to stand down as they watch The Hooded Man take over the task of maintaining the sphere while Belet-Seri pulls out a flat silver disc from underneath her cloak and lays it on the ground. *How are they planning to escape? They are completely surrounded both here and in the Gray Zone.* As if she heard his unspoken question, the woman smiles slyly as she bends down and easily picks up her father, Thoth, and then steps on top of the disc. Golden light surrounds them, emanating from it, and they become resplendent particles before disappearing all together as if they'd been beamed up by a transporter straight out of *Star Trek*.

As he too steps on top of the small circular platform, the Hooded Man turns and yells at Ra, "We are not done, 'Herald'! There is a reckoning coming between you and me. It is destiny, and it will not be cheated."

And with a flash, The Hooded Man is gone. Even among the seasoned warriors who are gathered, jaws drop and there is a stunned silence. From what David could gather from stray thoughts, the escape was surprising, featuring tech they did not know Thoth had acquired, but the real dagger is the identity of The Hooded man. He showed his eyes, and everything changed.

David's focus, his only focus, is Ra. As Amon Ra picks up his weapon, he puts back on the stoic face of the warrior and gives orders to the newly arrived Gilgamesh concerning cleanup.

As David intently watches Ra, he hears Tef whisper to Maat.

"Was that?"

"Yes," Maat answers. "That's him. That very angry, very dangerous man is our brother, another gift from the Phoenix Curse."

Amon Ra locks eyes with David, appearing before him as a psychic ghost.

"That was Horus, my Horus. My son is back, but there's more, isn't there? It's time young man," he says. *"Tell me what you know, what you saw, all of it."*

"I'm sorry sir," David answers. *"I'm so sorry. It's Hathor, she's ..."*

Ra doesn't need the answer. The connection between David and Ra has grown, and Amon Ra's mind is flooded by images and information concerning Tricia and Hathor. The hurt from what Ra experiences causes David's body to clench up, resonating through him like a chilling psychic scream. The emotional trauma dissipates Ra's psychic ghost, but not their connection. The pain caused by what has been revealed leaves Ra stumbling away from the others and staring off into the middle distance. Ra is in turmoil and the young Mr. Stone feels it all.

David didn't want it to be true, but he sees it clearly, now. Somehow, Horus, child of Thunder, son of Ra, has returned and made himself known to the world. David knew there was something familiar about the way Hooded Man fought. He moved like Ra himself. Earlier, as Stone watched the messengers sing, his mind started to put it together, but he dreaded the conclusion and prayed he wasn't right. There were clues, so many clues. One look at her eyes, and their attacker knew that the new afreet was Amesemi. Who would recognize her? Who would it stun, and who would care so much that it would make him walk away from battle? Though David fought it, Semi's brother, Horus, was the obvious answer, her brother who would touch his mother's stomach and speak to his unborn sister, who loved her before she was even born. One look into Isis's eyes, and he knew that she was somehow Amesemi, now living in this time. In retrospect, all that should have been a dead giveaway.

Why would Horus wish harm to Amesemi? He didn't blame his sister or his mother for the plight of their people. He blamed Amon Ra, and those feelings have only seemed to intensify with the passage of time. Once David suspected who The Hooded Man was, Thoth falling to Earth raised red flags. He believed that if the mystery man were Horus, he would use this opportunity to confront his father. Either way, David knew he needed to be there. Why? What was he able to do to possibly help? Nothing, but there's a part of him that knew he needed to be by Ra's side anyway. They're connected somehow for better or worse. David knows that he needs Ra's help, but maybe there's something Ra needs from him as well.

The truth is, David understands the emotional tsunami raging through Ra, seeing his risen son face to face, in a way no one else can. He was there in Ra's mind, in his heart when David's soul walked through his life. He's felt the love Ra has for his son and felt Ra's heart break with every blow during the challenge of Kala Sarr. Stone has experienced Amon Ra's anguish as he carried the lifeless body of Horus back to Iken after the Battle of Taliath Gaar and watched Ra's life shatter after everything that transpired that evening. Through his faith and through the love of family, he put his life back together, piece-by-piece. That's a miracle, and David admires the majestic so much for how he has stood tall through every hardship he's endured. But how can even he survive living through it again?

People pray for second chances, knowing that it's not possible. David knows he does. The thinking is that if they had a second chance, somehow things would turn out better, and they could avoid the trauma in their past. No one ever considers the possibility that things might be worse.

So, Horus is back, and so is Hathor, the love of Ra's life. One is most likely a dark sorcerer who survived by committing some horrendous act. The other is possessed by the same myopic focus of killing his father and crushing the Nistarim that he had before. How is this better? This isn't a dream come true. This is Ra's worst nightmare come to life, and standing here, being linked with him, David feels Amon Ra's heart breaking all over again. Stone wishes there was something he could do.

Another death match with his son is the last thing that Ra could ever want, but it seems unavoidable. Horus was never an elite fighter within the Neter-khertet. Thoth was Ra's only real rival there. But on Perinesa, Horus is a legend among legends. He learned his father's moves, imitated his style perfectly, and had the will and intensity to match. Truth be told, on Earth, Horus is the only true rival Amon Ra has ever had. That is the reason Osiris recruited him in the first place. In all his individual battles, Horus has only lost one fight, and that was his final one, the one he lost to his father—the great Amon Ra. Horus is a giant among his peers. Who can stop him but another giant? This time around, who can stop Horus if it's not Ra? Is there anyone else? David doesn't know, but he knows that Horus craves a rematch, and as much as Stone thought that Thoth versus Ra was a clash of Titans, this promises to be on a whole different level.

His introspection is broken by a number of new arrivals. And as they file in, David walks over to Semi and takes a seat next to her on the lawn. The reinforcements are here, and the enemy has run away. For the first time in two days, David truly exhales, releasing the tension and the anxiety that has been his constant companion. And as he comes down off of his adrenaline high, he feels his aches and bruises, wincing and moaning like an old man after a workout as he tries to get comfortable. Every part of him seems black and blue, even his pinky toe is sore. At any rate, Horus and Hathor are tomorrow's problem, and honestly, like so many things, it is so far above his pay grade he can't even comprehend it. He just needs to stay in his lane, relax, and get some real sleep at last. This battle is over. Semi is safe, and so are David and his friends, so the good guys won this one, even if it doesn't totally feel that way.

The four of them are sitting on the grass, with Semi clutching David's jacket and leaning on him, her head on his shoulder. He doesn't know what Edie and B.J. are doing, but he and the princess are watching Ra as he stands alone in his thoughts, staring at the sky. David has a knot in his stomach, but he knows it doesn't compare to the boulder in Ra's. This definitely doesn't look or feel much like a win.

"So, that guy, he's really my brother Horus?" Semi asks for the tenth time, not because she doesn't know the answer but because she can't believe it. "My brother, the one Dad killed... I mean who died the day I was born, five thousand years ago?"

"Apparently," David answers again, trying to process all of it himself.

"This is too much," she sighs. "When we get back to Avalon, you're going to have to help me wash all this down with some chocolate and ice cream. I was born around crazy, and this just seems totally unreal. The one thing I've learned though, is that chocolate and ice cream make anything in life easier to process."

As she finishes her sentence, their special escort, wearing glistening, ornate, gold armor and carrying golden shields and spears, comes to take them to Avalon. For whatever reason, they are among the last group to go. The Nistarim's wounded have already been tended to and taken back, most of the warriors have departed, and Losi's body has been moved to Avalon as well. Flanked by their escort, the four of them wait in line and walk slowly across the lawn to a massive portal crackling with aureate energy, and as David looks around, he sees that some secretive government agency, wearing black with insignias that identify them as C.E.R.B.E.R.U.S., has shown up. B.J.'s real-life men in black have arrived. *Man, he's going to be insufferable.* According to the stray thoughts he's been able to pick up, C.E.R.B.E.R.U.S is supervising the cleanup of the park and the mind editing of stragglers who saw through the illusion provided by the storm watchers. David can only assume that some version of all this has already taken place in and around Van Cortland Park. Is his family included in this too? That's too weird to think about. But no amount of cleanup can remove the stain on this place or the dark cloud that weighs on them. He knows everyone is saying that the battle is over, but this battle doesn't have the vibe of a victory, and it certainly doesn't seem like the ending of anything. It feels like the preamble for something far, far worse. There's a storm cloud in the distance, and he prays they'll be ready when it comes.

David takes a quick look at the sky and scans the streets around the park, and it's impressive and unnerving. Broken trees, burned grass, huge trenches and impressions, cracked pavement, burning cars; this fight has left its mark, but it's more than that. Everything has changed for him, and this moment encapsulates it. He sees a lot more than the battle damage and the hustle and bustle of New York. The sky is full of shadows and messengers as they wage their eternal war, and the streets are full of them too. On the ground, the shadows take the form of whispers and sing their tantalizing songs. They are the Sirens from Homer, the Pied Piper from the children's tale, luring folks in, only to ruin them. He couldn't see any of this two days ago. Now, it's all he sees.

Just like that, everything has changed. There is no going home or going back, not really, because he can't turn off what's been sparked in him or force himself to go back to a simpler time when he didn't know what he knows now. Mom was wrong. There really are monsters under the bed, and the only thing that keeps them there are people like the brave souls who fought here. And now, the four of them are entangled in this as well. They're all part of that line, the line that cannot be crossed.

Yes, it's scary how much life can change in two days, terrifying even. He's entered a brand-new world, free-falling into an uncertain future. They've been on the run, going from frying pan to fire, so he hasn't had time to reflect, but now that he does, he really wishes he didn't. Now that all the excitement is over, his cellar door is wide open, and all the fears he ignored earlier have come marching in, comfortably taking up residence. It's a lot, and he's so far over his head that it's hard to breathe. What did Commander Shamar call him? The chosen one? Even after everything that's happened, that just seems like a cruel joke. *Trust in the one who chose you.* David keeps reminding himself, but he has to confess, some moments it's not so easy to do. Honestly, right now isn't a particularly good moment for him.

At the peak of his anxiety, he peeks over at Semi and remembers something. David reaches into a "magic", velecor pocket on his back and pulls out Semi's journal.

"I almost forgot. This is yours."

She beams at him and quietly takes the precious book, briefly riffling the pages.

"I can't believe you still have this!" She carefully places it in a "magic" pocket of her own and takes his hands in hers. "I've missed this. There's so much to write down. I'm sure you'll get a page somewhere, Charming." She needles, playfully.

"Only a page?"

She glances up with a twinkle in her eyes. "Well Charming, I might have a lot more to add if you keep your promise." she says, leaning in close. "Aren't you forgetting something?"

"You're right, Princess, and I always keep my promises."

David leans forward, caresses her cheek, and presses his lips against the softest lips ever. They actually kiss, and—it's magical, fireworks flashing, heart stopping magical, and he realizes that what his dad always said is true. It flashes in his mind now like a neon sign: "You've never been kissed until you kiss the right person for the right reason at the right time." Now, David finally understands. He's not sure how long it lasts, but it feels like a long, passionate, wonderful Hollywood version— like they're the only two people on the planet version, with uplifting orchestral music playing in the background and credits rolling. It's so amazing that when they're done, they... catch wicked side-eyes from both Athena and Tef. Where'd they come from? And David swears that Bast, who's a little ahead of them, looks back and growls at him. They both quickly take a step back, but David's way too giddy to be embarrassed, a little terrified maybe, but not embarrassed. Well, everyone's got to die from something, right? If he's going to get whacked for kissing Semi, he can think of worst ways to go. His face is frozen in a permanent smile, and so is Semi's.

As they walk hand and hand through the portal, he looks into her beautiful brown eyes, brown for the moment at least, and he can write a thousand songs based on how they make him feel. But, when he looks at them, he sees something he didn't see before. David sees his future. Where she goes, he goes. That's in his contract, and no matter what they're going to face going forward, there's something comforting in knowing that it's going to be together. He truly believes that together they can do anything. Something about Semi inspires him to be the best version of who he is.

David's sure that there will be days that the future will loom like a giant, waiting to crush them, but there's a truth that he's come to know. Giants fall. There is no foe so big or night so dark that the light cannot prevail. So, he's just going to march forward and knock down one giant at a time. With his friends by his side, he's ready to take on this grand adventure no matter where it leads. It should be fun, right? And if the storm comes, the earth shakes, and bad guys start raining from the sky, there's another truth that David knows. Hope is a shield that will not fail.

The End

The Story Continues...

A Prophecy of Shadows II

Whispers of Avalon

Coming Soon!

www.ingramcontent.com/pod-product-compliance
Lightning Source LLC
Chambersburg PA
CBHW070547260626
47161CB00002B/528